THE
Spanish
LOVE
DECEPTION

ELENA ARMAS

**SIMON &
SCHUSTER**

London · New York · Sydney · Toronto · New Delhi

First published in Great Britain by Simon & Schuster UK Ltd, 2021

This paperback edition published 2021

5 7 9 10 8 6 4

Simon & Schuster UK Ltd
1st Floor
222 Gray's Inn Road
London WC1X 8HB

Simon & Schuster Australia, Sydney
Simon & Schuster India, New Delhi

www.simonandschuster.co.uk
www.simonandschuster.com.au
www.simonandschuster.co.in

A CIP catalogue record for this book
is available from the British Library

Paperback ISBN: 978-1-3985-1562-8
eBook ISBN: 978-1-3985-1563-5

Typeset in Bembo by M Rules
Printed and bound by CPI Group (UK) Ltd, Croydon, CR0 4YY

To those chasing dreams, never give up on them.
We are not quitters, you hear me?

CHAPTER ONE

'I'll be your date to the wedding.'

Words I had never – not even in my wildest dreams, and trust me, I had a vivid imagination – conceived of hearing from that deep and rich tone reached my ears.

Looking down at my coffee, I squinted my eyes, trying to search for any signs of noxious substances floating around. That would at least explain what was happening. But nope.

Nothing. Just what was left of my Americano.

'I'll do it if you need someone that badly,' the deep voice came again.

Eyes growing wide, I lifted my head. I opened my mouth and then snapped it closed again.

'Rosie . . .' I trailed off, the word leaving me in a whisper. 'Is he really there? Can you see him? Or did someone spike my coffee without me noticing?'

Rosie – my best friend and colleague in InTech, the New York City-based engineering consulting company where we had met and worked – slowly nodded her head. I watched her dark curls bounce with the motion, an expression of disbelief marring her otherwise soft features. She lowered her voice. 'Nope. He's right there.' Her head peeked around me very quickly. 'Hi. Good morning!' she said brightly before her attention returned to my face. 'Right behind you.'

Lips parted, I stared at my friend for a long moment. We were standing at the far end of the hallway of the eleventh floor of the InTech headquarters. Both our offices were relatively close together, so the moment I had entered the building, located in the heart of Manhattan, in the vicinity of Central Park, I had gone straight to hers.

My plan had been to grab Rosie and plop down on the upholstered wooden armchairs that served as a waiting area for visiting clients, which were usually unoccupied this early in the morning. But we never made it. I somehow dropped the bomb before we ever sat down. That was how much my predicament needed Rosie's immediate attention. And then ... then he had materialized out of nowhere.

'Should I repeat that a third time?' His question sent a new wave of disbelief rushing through my body, freezing the blood in my veins.

He wouldn't. Not because he couldn't, but because what he was saying did not make any freaking sense. Not in our world. One where we—

'All right, fine,' he sighed. 'You can take me.' He paused, sending more of that ice-cold wariness through me. 'To your sister's wedding.'

My spine locked up. My shoulders stiffened.

I even felt the satin blouse I had tucked into my camel slacks stretch with the sudden motion.

I can take him.

To my sister's wedding. As my ... date?

I blinked, his words echoing inside my head.

Then, something unhitched inside of me. The absurdity of whatever this was – whatever perverse joke this man I knew not to trust was trying to pull off – made a snort bubble its way up my throat and reach my lips, leaving me quickly and loudly. As if it had been in a rush to get out.

A grunt came from behind me. 'What's so funny?' His voice dropped, turning colder. 'I'm completely serious.'

I bit back another burst of laughter. I didn't believe that. Not for a second. 'The chances of him,' I told Rosie, 'being actually serious are the same chances I have of having Chris Evans pop out of nowhere and confess his undying love for me.' I made a show of looking right and left. 'Nonexistent. So, Rosie, you were saying something about . . . Mr Frenkel, right?'

There was no Mr Frenkel.

'Lina,' Rosie said with that fake, toothy smile I knew she wore when she didn't want to be rude. 'He looks like he's serious,' she spoke through her freaky smile. Her gaze inspected the man standing behind me. 'Yep. I think he might be serious.'

'Nope. He can't be.' I shook my head, still refusing to turn around and acknowledge that there was a possibility my friend was right.

There couldn't be. There was no way Aaron Blackford, colleague and well-established affliction of mine, would even attempt to offer something like that. No. Way.

An impatient sigh came from behind me. 'This is getting repetitive, Catalina.' A long pause. Then, another noisy exhalation left his lips, this one much longer. But I did not turn around. I held my ground. 'Ignoring me won't make me disappear. You know that.'

I did. 'But that doesn't mean I won't keep trying,' I muttered under my breath.

Rosie levelled me with a look. Then, she peeked around me again, keeping that toothy grin in place. 'Sorry about that, Aaron. We are not ignoring you.' Her grin strained. 'We are . . . debating something.'

'We are ignoring him though. You don't need to spare his feelings. He doesn't have any.'

'Thanks, Rosie,' Aaron told my friend, some of the usual coldness leaving his voice. Not that he'd be nice to anybody. Nice wasn't something Aaron did. I didn't even think he was able to pull off friendly. But he had always been less . . . grim when it came to Rosie. A curtesy he had never extended to me. 'Do you think you can tell Catalina to turn around? I'd appreciate talking to her face and not to the back of her head.' His tone dropped back to minus zero degrees. 'That is, of course, if this is not one of her jokes that I never seem to understand, much less find funny.'

Heat rushed up my body, reaching my face.

'Sure,' Rosie complied. 'I think . . . I think I can do that.' Her gaze bounced from that point behind me to my face, her eyebrows raised. 'Lina, so, erm, Aaron would like you to turn around, if this is not one of those jokes that—'

'Thanks, Rosie. I got that,' I gritted out between my teeth. Feeling my cheeks burn, I refused to face him. That would mean letting him win whatever game he was playing. Plus, he had just called me unfunny. Him. 'If you could, tell Aaron that I don't think one can laugh at, or much less understand, jokes when one lacks a sense of humour, please. That would be great. Thanks.'

Rosie scratched the side of her head, looking pleadingly at me. Don't make me do this, she seemed to ask me with her eyes.

I widened mine at her, ignoring her plea and begging her to go along.

She released a breath and then looked around me one more time. 'Aaron,' she said, her fake grin getting bigger, 'Lina thinks that—'

'I heard her, Rosie. Thank you.'

I was so attuned to him – to this – that I noticed the slight change in his tone that signalled the switch to the voice he only used with me. The one that was just as dry and cold but that would now come with an extra layer of disdain and distance. The one that would soon lead to a scowl. I didn't even need to turn and take a look at him to know that. It was somehow always there when it came to me and to this . . . thing between us.

'I'm pretty sure my words are reaching Catalina down there just fine, but if you could tell her that I have work to do and I cannot entertain this much longer, I would appreciate it.'

Down there? Stupidly large man.

My size was average. Average for a Spaniard, sure. But average nonetheless. I was five foot three – almost four, thank you very much.

Rosie's green eyes were back on me. 'So, Aaron has work, and he would appreciate—'

'If—' I stopped myself when I heard the word sounding high-pitched and squeaky. I cleared my throat and tried again. 'If he is so busy, then please tell him to feel free to spare me. He can go back to his office and resume whatever workaholic activities he had shockingly paused to stick his nose in something that does not concern him.'

I watched my friend's mouth open, but the man behind me spoke before a sound could come out of her lips: 'So, you heard what I said. My offer. Good.' A pause. In which I cursed under my breath. 'Then, what's your answer?'

Rosie's face filled with shock one more time. My gaze remained on her, and I could picture how the dark brown in my eyes was turning to red with my growing exasperation.

My answer? What the hell was he even trying to accomplish? Was this a new, inventive way of playing with my head? My sanity?

'I have no idea what he's talking about. I heard nothing,' I lied. 'You can tell him that too.'

Rosie tucked a curl behind her ear, her eyes jumping very briefly to Aaron and then returning to me. 'I think he's referring to the moment he offered to be your date to your sister's wedding,' she explained in a soft voice. 'You know, right after you told me that things had changed and that you now needed to find someone – or anyone, I think you said – to go to Spain with you and attend that wedding because, otherwise, you'd die a slow, painful death and—'

'I think I got it,' I rushed out, feeling my face burn again from the realization that Aaron had heard all of that. 'Thanks, Rosie. You can stop with the recap.' Or I'd be dying that slow, painful death right about now.

'I think you used the word desperate,' Aaron chipped in.

My ears burned too at that, probably flashing about five shades of radioactive red. 'I did not,' I breathed out. 'I did not use that word.'

'You ... sort of did, sweetie,' my best friend – no, former best friend as of right now – confirmed.

Eyes narrowed, I mouthed, *What the hell, traitor?*

But both of them were right.

'Fine. So, I said that. Doesn't mean I'm that desperate.'

'That's what truly helpless people would say. But whatever makes you sleep better at night, Catalina.'

Cursing under my breath for the umpteenth time that morning, I closed my eyes briefly. 'This is none of your business, Blackford, but I'm not helpless, okay? And I sleep at night just fine. No, actually, I've never slept better.'

What was one more lie to the pile I was hoisting around, huh? Contrary to what I had just denied, I was truly, helplessly desperate to find someone to be my date to that wedding. But that didn't mean I'd—

'Sure.'

Ironically, out of all the damn words Aaron Blackford had said to the back of my head that morning, that one word was what made me break my stance of pretending I remained unaffected.

That *sure*, sounding all condescending and bored and dismissive and just so Aaron.

Sure.

My blood bubbled.

It was so impulsive, such a knee-jerk reaction to that four-letter word – which, uttered by anybody else, would have meant nothing – that I didn't even realize my body was turning until it was too late.

Because of his unearthly height, I was welcomed by a broad chest covered in a pressed white button-down that made me itch to fist the fabric and wrinkle it with my hands, because who pranced through life so sleek and spotless all the damn time? Aaron Blackford – that was who.

My gaze trailed up powerful shoulders and a strong neck, reaching the straight line of his jaw. His lips formed a flat line, just like I had known they would. My eyes travelled further up then, reaching his blue ones – blue that reminded me of the depths of the ocean, where everything was cold and deadly – and finding them on me.

One of his brows rose. '*Sure*?' I hissed.

'Yes.' That head, topped with raven hair, gave one single nod, his gaze not leaving mine. 'I don't want to waste more time arguing about something you are too stubborn to admit, so yes. *Sure*.'

This infuriating blue-eyed man who probably spent more time ironing his clothes than interacting with other human beings was not going to make me lose my temper this early in the morning.

Fighting to keep my body under control, I inhaled a long, deep breath. I tucked a lock of chestnut hair behind my ear. 'If this is such a waste of time, I genuinely don't know what you're still doing here. Please don't stay on my or Rosie's account.'

A noncommittal noise left *Miss Traitor*'s mouth.

'I wouldn't,' Aaron admitted in a level tone. 'But you still haven't answered my question.'

'That wasn't a question,' I said, the words tasting sour on my tongue. 'Whatever you said was not a question. But that's not important because I don't need you, thank you very much.'

'Sure,' he repeated, turning my exasperation one notch up. 'Although I think you do.'

'You think wrong.'

That brow rose higher. 'And yet it sounded like you really do need me.'

'Then, you must be experiencing serious hearing issues because, yet again, you heard wrong. I don't need you, Aaron Blackford.' I swallowed, willing some of the dryness away. 'I could write it down for you if you want. Send you an email, too, if that'd help at all.'

He seemed to think about it for a second, looking uninterested. But I knew better than to believe he'd let it go so easily. Which he proved as soon as he opened his mouth again. 'Didn't you say the wedding is in a month and you don't have a date?'

My lips pressed in a tight line. 'Maybe. I can't recall exactly.' I had said that. Word for word.

'Didn't Rosie suggest that if you perhaps sat in the back and tried not to draw any attention to yourself, nobody would notice you were attending on your own?'

My friend's head popped into my field of vision. 'I did. I also suggested to wear a dull colour and not the stunning red dress that—'

'Rosie,' I interrupted her. 'Not really helping here.'

Aaron's eyes didn't waver when he resumed his walk down memory lane. 'Didn't you follow that by reminding Rosie that you were the *motherfreaking* — your word — maid of honor and therefore *everybody and their mother* — your words again — would notice you anyway?'

'She did,' I heard Miss Traitor confirm. My head whirled in her direction. 'What?' She shrugged, signing her death sentence. 'You did, honey.'

I needed new friends. ASAP.

'She did,' Aaron corroborated, drawing my gaze and attention back to him. 'And did you not say that your ex-boyfriend is the best man and thinking of standing in the vicinity of him, *alone and lame and pathetically single* — those were your words again — made you want to tear off your own skin?'

I had. I had said that. But I hadn't thought Aaron was listening; otherwise, I would have never admitted it out loud.

But he had been right there, apparently. He knew now. He had heard me openly admit that and had just thrown it at my face. And as much as I told myself I didn't care – that I shouldn't care – the pang of hurt was there all the same. It made me feel all the more alone, lame, and pathetic.

Swallowing the lump in my throat, I averted my eyes, letting them rest somewhere close to his Adam's apple. I didn't want to see whatever was in his face. Mockery. Pity. I didn't care. I could spare the knowledge of one more person thinking of me that way.

His throat was the one that worked then. I knew because it was the only part of him I allowed myself to look at.

'You *are* desperate.'

I exhaled, the air leaving my lips forcefully. One nod – that was all I gave him. And I didn't even understand why I had done it. This wasn't me. I usually fought back until I was the one who drew blood first. Because that was what we did. We didn't spare each other's feelings. This wasn't new.

'Then, take me. I will be your date to the wedding, Catalina.'

My gaze drew up very slowly, a strange mix of wariness and embarrassment washing over me. Him witnessing all this was bad enough, but him somehow trying to use it to his advantage? To get the better of me?

Unless he wasn't. Unless perhaps there was an explanation, a reason, as to why he was doing this. Offering himself to be my date.

Studying his face, I pondered all these options and possible motivations, not coming to any kind of reasonable conclusion. Not finding any possible answer that would help me understand why or what he was trying to accomplish.

Only the truth. The reality. We weren't friends. We barely tolerated each other, Aaron Blackford and I. We were spiteful to each other, pointed out each other's mistakes, criticized how differently we worked, thought, and lived. We condemned our differences. At some point in the past, I would have thrown darts at a poster of his face. And I was pretty sure he would have done the same because I wasn't the only one driving along Hate Boulevard. It was a two-way road. Not only that, but he was the one who had caused our fallout in the first place. I hadn't started this feud between us. So, why? Why was he pretending to offer me help, and why would I humour him by even considering it?

'I might be desperate to find a date, but I'm not that desperate,' I repeated. 'Just like I said.'

His sigh was tired. Impatient. Infuriating. 'I'll let you think about it. You know you have no other options.'

'Nothing to think about.' I cut my hand through the air between us. Then, I smiled my version of Rosie's fake, toothy grin. 'I'd take a chimpanzee dressed in a tuxedo before taking you.'

His eyebrows rose, amusement barely entering his eyes. 'Now, come on; we both know you wouldn't. While there are chimpanzees that would rise up to the occasion, it will be your ex standing there. Your family. You said you need to make an impression, and I will accomplish exactly that.' He tilted his head. 'I'm your best option.'

I snorted, clapping my hands once. Smug blue-eyed pain in my ass. 'You are my best nothing, Blackford. And I have plenty of other options,' I countered, shrugging a shoulder. 'I'll find someone on Tinder. Maybe put out an ad in the *New York Times*. I can find someone.'

'In only a few weeks? Highly unlikely.'

'Rosie has friends. I'll take one of them.'

That had been my plan all along. It was the reason why I had grabbed Rosie so early in the day. Rookie mistake on my part, I realized. I should have waited to get off work and gotten Rosie to a safe, Aaron-free place to talk. But after yesterday's call with

Mamá ... yeah. Things had changed. My situation had definitely changed. I needed someone, and I couldn't stress enough that anyone would do. Anyone who wasn't Aaron, of course. Rosie had been born and raised in the city. There had to be someone she knew.

'Right, Rosie? One of your friends must be available.'

Her head popped in again. 'Maybe Marty? He loves weddings.'

I shot a quick glance at her. 'Wasn't Marty the one who got drunk at your cousin's wedding, stole the mic from the band, and sang 'My Heart Will Go On' until your brother had to drag him off the stage?'

'That would be him.' She winced.

'Yeah, no.' I couldn't have that at my sister's wedding. She'd rip his heart out of his chest and serve it as dessert. 'What about Ryan?'

'Happily engaged.'

A sigh left my lips. 'Not surprised. Ryan is a total catch.'

'I know. That's why I tried so many times to get you two together, but you—'

I cleared my throat loudly, interrupting her. 'We aren't discussing why I'm single.' I quickly glanced back at Aaron. His eyes were on me, narrowed. 'How about ... Terry?'

'Moved to Chicago.'

'Dammit.' I shook my head, closing my eyes for an instant.

This was useless. 'Then, I'll hire an actor. Pay him to act as my date.'

'That's probably expensive,' Aaron said flatly. 'And actors aren't exactly lying around, waiting for single people to hire and parade them as their plus-ones.'

I pinned him with an exasperated look. 'I'll get a professional escort.'

His lips pressed in that tight, almost-hermetic way they did when he was extremely irritated. 'You'd take a male prostitute to your sister's wedding before taking me?'

'I said, an escort, Blackford. *Por Dios*,' I muttered, watching his eyebrows bunch and turn into the scowl. 'I'm not looking for that kind of service. I just need a companion. That's all they do. They escort you to events.'

'That's not what they do, Catalina.' His voice was deep and icy. Covering me in his frosty judgment.

'Haven't you watched any romantic comedies ever?' I watched the scowl deepen. 'Not even *The Wedding Date*?'

No answer, just more of that arctic staring.

'Do you even watch movies? Or do you just . . . work?'

There was a possibility that he didn't even own a television.

His expression didn't change.

God, I don't have time for this. For him.

'You know what? Not important. I don't care.' I threw my hands up and then clasped them together. 'Thank you for . . . this. Whatever it was. Great input. But I don't need you.'

'I think you do.'

I blinked at him. 'I think you are annoying.'

'Catalina,' he started, making my irritation grow with the way he uttered my name. 'You are delusional if you think you can find someone in such a short amount of time.'

Once more, Aaron Blackford wasn't wrong.

I probably was a little delusional. And he didn't even know about the lie. My lie. Not that he'd ever do. But that didn't change the facts. I needed someone, anyone, but not him, not Aaron, to fly to Spain with me for Isabel's wedding. Because (A) I was the bride's sister and maid of honour. (B) My ex, Daniel, was the groom's brother and best man. And as of yesterday, I had learned that he was happily engaged. Something that my family had been hiding from me. (C) If you didn't count the few and pretty unsuccessful dates I had gone on, I had been technically single for roughly six years. Ever since I had left Spain and moved to the States, which had happened shortly after my one and only relationship exploded in my face. Something that every single attendee – because there were no secrets in families like mine and much less in small towns like the one I had come from – knew about and pitied me for. And (D) there was *my lie*.

The lie.

The one I had sort of fed my mother and consequently the whole Martín clan because privacy and boundaries did not exist when it came to us. Hell, by now, my lie was probably on the Announcements page of the local newspaper.

Catalina Martín, finally, not single. Her family is happy to announce that she will bring her American boyfriend to the wedding. Everyone is invited to come and witness the most magical event of the decade.

Because that was what I had done. Right after the news of Daniel's engagement had slipped past my mother's lips and reached my ears through the speaker of my phone, I had said that I'd be bringing someone too. No, not just someone. I'd said – lied, deceived, falsely announced – that I'd be bringing *my boyfriend*.

Who technically did not exist. Yet.

Okay, fine, or ever. Because Aaron was right. Finding a date in such a short amount of time was perhaps a little optimistic. Believing I'd find someone to pretend to be my made-up boyfriend was probably delusional. But accepting that Aaron was my only choice and taking him up on his offer? That was straight-up insanity.

'I see it's finally seeping in.' Aaron's words brought me back to the present, and I found his blue eyes aimed at me. 'I'll let you come to terms with it on your own. Just let me know when you do.'

My lips pursed. And when I felt my cheeks burn again – because how lame was I for him, Aaron Blackford, who had never even liked me a tiny little bit, to pity me enough to offer himself to be my date? – I crossed my arms over my chest and averted my eyes from those two icy and ruthless orbs.

'Oh, and, Catalina?'

'Yeah?' The word left my lips weakly. *Ugh, pathetic.*

'Try not to be late to our ten o'clock meeting. It's not cute anymore.'

My gaze shot to him, a huff stuck in my throat.

Jerk.

I swore right then and there that one day, I'd find a ladder high enough, climb it, and chuck something really hard at his infuriating face.

One year and eight months. That was how long I had endured him. I had been counting, biding my time.

Then, with nothing more than a nod, he turned around, and I watched him walk away. Dismissed until further notice.

'Okay, that was . . .' Rosie's voice trailed off, not ending the statement.

'Maddening? Insulting? Bizarre?' I offered, bringing my hands to my face.

'Unexpected,' she countered. 'And interesting.'

Looking at her between my fingers, I watched the corners of her lips tug up.

'Your friendship has been revoked, Rosalyn Graham.'

She chuckled. 'You know you don't mean that.'

I didn't; she'd never get rid of me.

'So . . .' Rosie linked her arm with mine and ushered me down the hallway. 'What are you going to do?'

A shaky breath left my mouth, taking all my energy with it. 'I . . . I don't have the slightest idea.'

But I knew something for sure: I was not taking Aaron Blackford up on his offer. He wasn't my only option, and he surely wasn't my best one either. Hell, he wasn't my *anything*. Especially not my date to my sister's wedding.

CHAPTER TWO

I wasn't late to our meeting.

Ever since that day a year and eight months ago, I was never late. Why?

Aaron Blackford.

One time. I had been late one single time in Aaron's presence, and yet he kept flaunting that fact every chance he got.

He never chalked it up to me being Spanish or a woman. Both unjustified stereotypes when it came to being notoriously unpunctual.

Aaron didn't do nonsense. He pointed out facts; he stated verifiable truths. He had been disciplined to do that, just like every other engineer in the consulting company where we worked, me included. And technically, I had been late. That one time all those months ago. It was true that I had missed the first fifteen minutes of an important presentation. It was also true that it had been Aaron leading it – during his first week in InTech – and it was again true that I had made a miserably loud entrance that might have involved accidentally knocking over a coffee pitcher.

On Aaron's stack of dossiers for the presentation. Fine, partly on his pants too.

Not the best way to make an impression on a new colleague, but tough shit. Things like that happened all the time. Tiny, unintentional, unexpected accidents like those were common. People got over them and went on with their lives.

But not Aaron.

Instead, week after week and month after month ever since that day, he had barked stuff like, 'Try not to be late to our ten o'clock meeting. It's not cute anymore,' at me.

Instead, every single time he entered a conference room and found me sitting there, painfully early, he checked the watch on his wrist and raised his eyebrows in surprise.

Instead, he moved coffee pitchers out of my reach with a warning tilt of his head in my direction.

That was what Aaron Blackford did instead of letting go of that incident.

'Good morning, Lina.' Héctor's kind voice reached me from the door.

I could tell he was smiling before I took in his face, just like he always did. '*Buenos días*, Héctor,' I told him in the mother tongue we shared.

The man that I considered like an uncle after he welcomed me into the close circle of his family placed a hand on my shoulder and squeezed lightly. 'Doing good, *mija*?'

'Can't complain.' I returned the smile.

'You coming over to the next barbecue? It's next month, and Lourdes keeps telling me to remind you. She's preparing ceviche this time, and you are the only one that will eat it.' He laughed.

It was true; no one in the Díaz family was a big fan of the fish-based Peruvian dish. Which, to this day, I still couldn't understand.

'Stop asking dumb questions, old man.' I waved my hand in the air with a chuckle. 'Of course I'll be there.'

Héctor was taking his usual place to my right when our three remaining colleagues in attendance poured into the room, mumbling their good mornings.

Lifting my gaze off Héctor's easy smile, my eyes tracked down the men walking around the table to assemble into our ten o'clock formation.

Across from me appeared Aaron, eyebrows raised and gaze quickly meeting mine. I watched his lips tip down as he pulled out a chair.

Rolling my eyes, I moved on to Gerald, whose bald head glinted under the fluorescent light as he folded his rather chubby frame into his seat. Last but not least, there was Kabir, who had been recently promoted to the position everyone in this room held – team leader of the Solutions Division of the company. Which pretty much encompassed all disciplines but civil engineering. Which was a beast on its own.

'Good morning, everyone,' Kabir started with the enthusiasm only someone who had been on the job for a month would display. 'This week, it's my turn to lead and protocol the meeting, so if you could, please say present when I call your name.'

An exasperated grunt with which I was familiar filled the room. Glancing at the blue-eyed man across the table, I found the irritated expression that went with the sound.

'Of course, Kabir,' I said with a smile even though I agreed with the scowling man. 'Please call away.'

Ocean eyes pinned me with an icy look.

Meeting his stare, I heard Kabir go through each of our names, obtaining confirmation from both Héctor and Gerald, an unnecessarily cheery *present* from me, and another grunt from Mr Grumps.

'All right, thanks,' Kabir said. 'Next point in the agenda is project status updates. Who would like to start?'

He was met with silence.

InTech provided engineering services for any entity that did not have the ability or manpower to design or engineer plans for their own projects. Sometimes, they outsourced a team of five or six people, and other times, only one person was needed. So, all five team leaders in our division were currently working and supervising several different projects for several different clients, and all projects never stopped moving forward. Eating away milestones and encountering all kinds of issues and drawbacks. We had conference calls with the clients and stakeholders on a daily basis. The status of each project changed so briskly and in such a complex manner that there was no way every other team leader could catch up in only a few minutes. That was why Kabir's question had been met with silence. And why this meeting wasn't completely necessary.

'Um ...' Kabir shifted in his seat uncomfortably. 'Okay, I can start. Yeah, I'll go first.' He shuffled through a folder he had brought with him. 'This week, we are presenting to Telekoor the new budget we've been developing for them. As you know, it's a start-up that's working on a cloud service to enhance mobile data on public transportation. Well, the resources available are rather limited and ...'

I absently listened to my colleague while my eyes roamed around the meeting room. Héctor nodded his head, although I suspected he was paying as much attention as I was. Gerald, on the other hand, was openly checking his phone. *Rude. So rude.* But I didn't expect anything else from him.

Then, there was *him*. Aaron Blackford, who I realized had been staring at me before my eyes met his.

His arm reached out in my direction, his gaze holding mine. I knew what he was about to do. *I knew.* The long fingers attached to that massive palm spread out as they met the object in front of me. The coffee pitcher. I narrowed my eyes, watching how his hand curled around the pitcher's handle.

He dragged it all the way across the surface of the oak desk.

Very slowly. Then, he nodded his head.

Infuriating blue-eyed grudge-holder.

I gave him a tight, closed-lipped smile – because the other option was launching myself across the room and pouring all the contents of the goddamn pitcher on him. Again. But this time, intentionally.

Trying to distract myself from that thought, I averted my eyes and furiously scribbled a to-do list on my planner.

Ask Isa if the bouquet she ordered for Mamá was peonies or lilies.

Order either a peony or lily bouquet for Tía Carmen.

If we didn't, she'd be giving me, Isa – my sister and bride – and Mamá the stink eye until the day she or any of us kicked the bucket.

Send Papá my flight details, so he knows when to pick me up from the airport.

Tell Isa to remind Papá that he has my flight details, so he picks me up from the airport.

I brought the pen to my lips, this awful feeling I was forgetting something important making me uneasy.

Chewing on my pen, I scrambled my mind for whatever it was I was missing. Then, a voice I was unfortunately doomed to never forget thundered in my head.

'You are delusional if you think you can find someone in such a short amount of time.'

My eyes bounced back to the man sitting across from me, meeting his gaze again. As if I had been caught doing something wrong – like thinking of him – I felt the heat in my cheeks and returned my attention to the list.

Find a boyfriend.

I scratched that.

Find a fake boyfriend. Doesn't need to be a real one.

'. . . and that's all I have to report.' Kabir's words registered somewhere in the back of my head.

I continued working on my list.

Find a fake boyfriend. Doesn't need to be a real one. And also, NOT HIM.

Surely, I had other options. Not the escort though. A quick Google search had confirmed that Aaron had been right. Again. Apparently, I had been lied to by Hollywood. New York seemed to be filled with men and women offering a wide range of varied and different kinds of services that were not limited to escorting.

I grimaced and then chewed harder on the pen. Not that I'd ever admit that to Aaron. I'd rather give up chocolate for a full year than admit to Aaron that he was right.

But I was desperate at this point. He had nailed that down too. I needed to find someone who would pretend to be in a serious, committed relationship with me in front of my whole family. And that didn't only include the wedding day, but also the two days of celebratory events that preceded that. Which meant, I was screwed. I was—

'. . . and that would be Lina.'

My name broke into my brain, making everything else vanish. I dropped my pen on the table and cleared my throat. 'Yes, here.' I tried to reinsert myself in the conversation. 'Listening. I'm listening.'

'Isn't that what someone who wasn't listening would say?'

My gaze shot across the room, meeting a pair of blue eyes on the verge of showing amusement if the man behind them was capable of human emotions.

I straightened my back and turned a page of my planner. 'I was writing down something for a call I have with a client later and lost track of the conversation,' I lied. 'Something important.'

Aaron hummed, nodding his head. Thankfully, he let it go.

'Let's recap a little bit. Just so we are all clear on where we stand,' Kabir offered in a gentle voice.

He'd be getting a muffin tomorrow.

'Thank you, Kabir.' I gave him a bright smile.

At which he blushed and reciprocated with a wobbly one.

I heard an impatient exhalation coming from across the room.

Now, he would not be getting a muffin tomorrow. Or ever.

'So,' Kabir finally said, 'Jeff wanted to attend today's meeting to tell you personally, but you know how busy the schedule of a head of division is. Lots of parallel appointments. He will forward you all the info you need anyway, but I thought it would be a good idea to give you a heads-up before.'

I blinked. What the hell are we talking about? 'Thank you again for that, Kabir.'

'You are welcome, Lina.' He nodded. 'I think that communication between all five of us is key to accomplish—'

'Kabir' – Aaron's voice filled the room – 'your point.'

Kabir's eyes jumped to him, and he appeared a little startled. 'Yes, thanks, Aaron.' Then, he had to clear his throat twice before he could continue, 'InTech will host an Open Day in a few weeks. A big group of people will attend, mostly potential clients who are curious about what we offer but also some of the biggest projects we are working on. Jeff mentioned that all attendees are pretty high in management, too, which makes sense because this is an initiative to expand and strengthen our network and to do it face-to-face. He wants InTech to show off. To look good. Modern. To demonstrate that we are up-to-date with the current markets. But at the same time, show all prospective and current clients that we are not all about working.' He chuckled nervously. 'That's why Open Day will last from eight a.m., when the attendees will be welcomed here at our headquarters, until midnight.'

'Midnight?' I murmured, barely able to conceal my surprise.

'Yes.' Kabir nodded enthusiastically. 'Isn't it refreshing? It will be a full-blown event. All kinds of workshops on new technologies, knowledge-exchange sessions, activities to get to know our clients and their needs. And of course, we'll have breakfast, lunch, and dinner catered. Oh, and after-work drinks too. You know, to lighten things up.'

My eyes had gradually widened as Kabir delivered his explanation.

'That . . .' Héctor started. 'That sounds different.'

It did. And it sounded like a complex event to plan in only a few weeks.

'Yes,' Gerald answered, sounding suspiciously smug. 'It will definitely put InTech ahead in the game.'

Kabir nodded as his gaze met mine. 'Absolutely. And Jeff wants you to be in charge of everything, Lina. How amazing is that?'

I blinked, resting my back against the seat. 'He wants me to organize it? All of it?'

'Yes.' My colleague smiled at me, like he was giving me good news. 'And host it too. Out of the five of us, you are our most attractive option.'

Blinking very slowly, I watched his lips turn down, probably because of the expression on my face.

Attractive. Taking a deep breath, I tried to steady myself. 'Well, I'm flattered to be considered the most attractive option,' I lied, willing myself not to focus on how my blood had started swirling. 'But I hardly have the time or the experience to organize something like this.'

'But Jeff insisted,' Kabir countered back. 'And it's important for InTech to have someone like you representing the company.'

I should ask what *someone like me* was supposed to mean, but I didn't think I wanted to hear the answer. My throat dried up, making it harder for me to swallow. 'Wouldn't any of us accomplish the same objective? Shouldn't someone with experience in what sounds like a public relations exercise throw together an event this important?'

Kabir deflected, not answering my question. 'Jeff said you would be fine with the organization. That we don't need to spend extra resources hiring someone. Plus, you are . . .' He trailed off, looking like he'd rather be anywhere else. 'Social. Perky.'

Clenching my fist under the table, I tried my best to hide my inner turmoil. 'Sure,' I gritted out. That was every person's dream, being referred to as *perky* by their boss. 'But I also have a job to do. I also have projects that I'm working on the clock for. How is this ... *event* more important than my own clients and current responsibilities?'

I remained silent for a long moment, waiting for my colleagues' support.

Any kind of support.

And ... nothing, just the usual loaded silence that followed these kinds of situations.

I shifted in my chair, feeling my cheeks heat up with frustration. 'Kabir,' I said as calmly as I could, 'I know Jeff might have suggested that I be in charge of this, but you guys understand that this doesn't even make sense, right? I ... wouldn't even know where to start.' This wasn't a thing I had been hired or was paid for.

But no one was going to admit that, even when their support would make a difference. That would lead to the real reason why I had been given this task.

'I'm already covering for two of my best team members, Linda and Patricia. I don't have hours in the week as it is.' I hated complaining and fishing for some – or at this point, any – kind of understanding, but what else could I do?

Gerald snorted, making my head swivel in his direction. 'Well, that's a drawback of hiring women in their thirties.'

I scoffed, not wanting to believe that he had just said that. But he had. I opened my mouth, but Héctor stopped me from saying anything.

'All right, how about we all help you?' Héctor suggested. I looked at him, finding him with a resigned expression. 'We could maybe all pitch in with something.'

I loved the man, but his soft heart and lack of confrontational spirit weren't helping all that much. He was only tiptoeing around the real issue.

'This is not high school, Héctor,' Gerald snapped back. 'We are professionals, and we won't be pitching in with anything.' Shaking his greasy, bald head, he followed that with another snort.

Héctor's mouth clamped shut.

Kabir spoke again, 'I'll forward you the list of people Jeff put together, Lina.'

I shook my head again, feeling my cheeks heat up further, biting my tongue so I wouldn't tell my colleague something I'd regret.

'Oh,' Kabir added, 'Jeff also had a few ideas for the catering. That's in a separate email that I will forward to you too. But he wants you to do a little research on that. Maybe even think of a theme. He said you'd know what to do.'

My lips parted with a silent curse word that would make my *abuela* take me to church by the ear. *I'd know what to do? How would I know?*

Reaching for my pen and holding it with both hands so I could squeeze some of the growing frustration away, I took a deep breath. 'I'm going to talk to Jeff myself,' I said through pressed teeth that formed a tight smile. 'I'd usually not bother him but—'

'Would you just stop wasting our time already?' Gerald said, making the blood in my face drop to my feet. 'You don't have to take this to our boss.' Gerald's chubby finger waved through the air. 'Stop making excuses and just do it. You can smile and be extra friendly for a whole day, can't you?'

The words *extra* and *friendly* echoed in my head as I stared at him with wide eyes.

This sweaty man, crammed into a dress shirt designed for someone who had a class he'd never achieve, would take any chance he could get to bring anyone down. Even more so if that happened to be a woman. *I knew.*

'Gerald' – I gentled my voice and increased the pressure on my pen, praying it wouldn't break and give away how outraged I really felt – 'the purpose of this meeting is to discuss issues like this one. So, I'm sorry, but you are going to have to listen to me do exactly—'

'*Sweetheart*,' Gerald interrupted me, a sneer breaking across his face, 'think of it as a party. Women know about those, don't they?

Just prepare some activities, get some food delivered here, put on nice clothes, and crack some jokes. You are young and cute; you won't even have to use your brain all that much. They'll be eating right out of your hand.' He chuckled. 'I'm sure you know how to do that, don't you?'

I choked on my own words. The air that was supposed to be getting in and out of my lungs was stuck somewhere in between.

Not able to control what my body was doing, I felt my legs straighten, bringing me upright. My chair screeched back, the noise loud and sudden. Smacking both hands on the surface of the desk, I felt my head blank for a second, and I saw red. Literally. In that precise moment, I understood where the expression had come from. I saw *fucking* red, as if I had slipped on a pair of glasses with crimson lenses.

Somewhere to my right, I heard Héctor exhaling heavily. Muttering under his breath.

Then, I heard nothing. Only my heart hammering in my chest.

There it was. The truth. The real reason why I, among the four other people sitting in this room, had been handpicked to do this damn thing. I was a woman – the only woman in the division, leading a team – and I had the *goods*, no matter how generous my curves were or not. Perky, cute, female. I was the attractive option, apparently. I was being showcased to our clients as the golden token that proved that InTech was not stuck in the past.

'Lina.' I willed my voice to remain firm and calm, hating that it hadn't. Hating that I wanted to turn around and let my legs carry me out of the room. 'Not *sweetheart*. My name is Lina.' I sat back on my chair very slowly, clearing my throat and taking one extra moment to rein it in. *I have this. I need to have this.* 'Next time, make sure to use my name, please. And address me with the decency and professionalism you do with everyone else.' My voice reached my ears in a way I didn't like one bit. Making me feel that weak version of myself that I didn't want to be. But at least I had managed to get it all out without flipping or running away. 'Thanks.'

Sensing how my eyes were starting to feel glassy out of pure outrage and frustration, I blinked a few times, willing that and everything else away from my face. Wishing that the lump in my throat had nothing to do with embarrassment, even when it did. Because how could I not feel embarrassed when I had snapped like that? When – even after what had happened all that time ago, even being that this wasn't the first time I'd had to deal with this kind of crap – I still didn't know how?

Gerald rolled his eyes. 'Don't take it so seriously, *Lina*.' He shot me a condescending look. 'I was just joking around. Right, guys?'

He looked over at our colleagues, searching the room for their support.

He didn't find any.

Out of the corner of my eye, I watched Héctor deflating in his chair. 'Gerald ...' he said, sounding tired and discouraged. 'Come on, man.'

Keeping my eyes on Gerald and trying to stop my chest from heaving with building helplessness, I refused to look at the other two men, Kabir and Aaron, who remained silent.

They probably thought they were not taking any side, but they were. Their silence was doing exactly that.

'Oh, come on what?' Gerald scoffed. 'It's not like I said anything that's not true. The girl doesn't even need to try—'

Before I could muster the courage to stop him, the last person in the room I had expected to speak beat me to it. 'We are done here.'

My head snapped in his direction then, finding him looking at Gerald with something so thick and chilling that I could almost feel the air in the room drop a couple of degrees.

Shaking my head, I snagged my gaze off Aaron. He could have

said anything in the last ten minutes, and he had chosen not to. He could remain silent for all I cared.

Gerald's chair scraped against the floor, allowing him to stand up. 'Yes, we are certainly done,' he said flatly, gathering his things. 'I don't have time for this either. She knows what to do anyway.'

And with that little pearl, Gerald walked to the door and left the room.

My heart was still hammering in my chest, pummelling in my temples.

Kabir followed suit, standing up and looking at me apologetically. 'I am not taking his side, okay?' His eyes moved in Aaron's direction quickly, returning to me just as fast. 'This whole thing came from Jeff; he wants you to do this. Don't think too much about it. Take it as a compliment.'

Not bothering to answer, I watched him leave the room.

The man who had almost taken me in and treated me as one more of the Díaz clan looked at me and shook his head. He mouthed, *Qué pendejo*, which plucked a weak smile out of me because even if that wasn't something we would ever say in Spain, I knew exactly what he meant.

And Héctor was right. What a total *asshat* Gerald was.

And then there was Aaron. Who hadn't even bothered to look at me yet. His long fingers methodically gathered his things, and his even longer legs pushed the chair back, making it possible for him to straighten to his full height.

While I glanced at him, still out of sorts from everything that had just gone down, I watched how his gaze shifted from his hands to me. His eyes, which I could tell had sobered up and returned to that semblance of aloofness, remained on me for a heartbeat and then dismissed me just as quickly.

Just like he always did.

I watched his tall and sturdy figure walk to the door and into the hallway, the hammering in my chest somehow speeding up and settling down, all at once.

'Let's go, *mija*,' Héctor said, now standing and looking down on me. 'I have a bag of *chicharrones* in my office. Ximena slipped it into my laptop bag the other day, and I've been saving it.' He followed that with a wink.

Standing up myself, I laughed lightly. Héctor's little girl was getting a bear hug from me the next time I saw her.

'You need to raise that girl's weekly allowance.' I followed him out, trying my best to return the smile.

Although I couldn't help but notice that after only a few steps, the corners of my lips wavered, breaking into something that didn't quite reach my eyes.

CHAPTER THREE

This wasn't how I had pictured my evening going.

It was late, InTech's headquarters had mostly emptied, I had at least four or five hours of work ahead of me, and my stomach was rumbling so loudly that I suspected it was about to start eating itself.

'*Estoy jodida,*' I said under my breath, realizing how screwed I really was.

One, because the last thing I had eaten was a sad green salad that clearly turned out to be a big mistake, even though it had seemed the most sensible idea, given that the wedding was a total of four weeks away. Two, I didn't have any snacks at hand and no change for the vending machine downstairs. And three, the PowerPoint slide on my laptop screen was still blinking at me, half-empty.

My hands fell on my keyboard, hesitating over the keys for a full minute.

A text pinged from my phone, drawing my attention. Rosie's name flashed on the screen. I unlocked it, and an image immediately popped open.

It was a photo of a luscious flat white, topped by a beautiful milk foam rosette. Beside it, there was a triple-chocolate brownie that shamelessly glinted under the light.

Rosie: You in?

She didn't need to specify the plan or send me the address. That feast could only belong to Around the Corner, our favourite coffee shop in the city. My mouth started immediately salivating at the thought of being in that caffeinated safe haven on Madison Avenue.

Muffling a groan, I wrote back.

> Lina: I'd love to, but I'm stuck at work.

Three dots jumped on the screen.

> Rosie: You sure? I saved you a seat.

Before I could type back a reply, another text came through.

> Rosie: I got the last brownie, but I'll share. Only if you get here quickly. I'm not made of steel.

I sighed. Definitely better than the reality of working extra time on a Wednesday evening but ...

> Lina: I can't. I'm working on the Open Day stuff I told you about. I'm deleting that photo, BTW. Too tempting.

> Rosie: Oh no. You didn't tell me more than the fact that you were stuck with it. When's it taking place?

> Lina: Right after I'm back from Spain. 🌀💀

> Rosie: I still don't get why you have to do it. Aren't you swamped with work?

Yep. That was exactly what I should have been doing, the job I was paid to do. Not organizing an open-doors day that served as an excuse to show around a bunch of suits that I'd have to feed, babysit, and be extra nice to. Whatever the hell that meant. But complaining wouldn't get me anywhere.

> Lina: 😖 It is what it is.
>
> Rosie: Yeah, well, I don't like Jeff all that much right now.
>
> Lina: I thought you said he was a silver fox. 😏
>
> Rosie: I said, objectively. And he can look good for a 50-year-old and still be a jerk. You know I seem to find those particularly attractive.
>
> Lina: You kinda do, Rosie. That Ted was a total assface. Happy you two are not a thing anymore.
>
> Rosie: 💩

The texts stopped coming long enough for me to think our conversation was done. Good. I needed to work on this crappy—
  My phone pinged again.

> Rosie: Sorry, the owner's husband just showed up, and I got distracted. #swoon
>
> Rosie: He is so handsome. He brings her flowers once a week. 🥺

Lina: Rosalyn, I'm trying to work here. Snap a photo
and show me tomorrow.

Rosie: Sorry, sorry. Did you talk to Aaron, BTW? 🤐
Is he still waiting?

I wasn't proud to admit that my stomach had dropped at the unexpected mention of something I hadn't let myself think about.

Liar. These past two days had felt like waiting for a bomb to drop when I least expected it.

No, ever since Monday, Aaron hadn't said anything about the whole I'll be your date to the wedding nonsense. Neither had Rosie because we had barely seen each other with how busy both our schedules were.

Lina: I have no idea what you mean. Is he waiting for
something?

Rosie: . . .

Lina: Something like a heart transplant? I heard he
doesn't have one.

Rosie: Ha, funny. You should keep the jokes for
when you two talk.

Lina: We won't.

Rosie: That's right. You two are too busy staring at
each other intently. 🔥

An unwanted blush rushed to my cheeks.

Lina: What's that supposed to mean?

Rosie: You know what it means.

Lina: That I want to light him up in a pyre like a witch? Then, okay.

Rosie: He's probably working late too.

Lina: So?

Rosie: So ... you could always go to his office and glare at him in that way I'm sure he loves.

Whoa. What the heck?

I moved uncomfortably in my chair as I stared at my phone screen in horror.

Lina: WTF are you talking about? Did you eat too much chocolate again? You know it makes you trippy. 😲

Rosie: Deflect all you want.

Lina: Not deflecting, just genuinely concerned about your health right now.

Rosie: 🙄

This was new. My friend had never directly addressed whatever nonsense she thought she *saw*. She still dropped a comment here and there every once in a while.

'Simmering tension,' she had said one time.

To which I had snorted so hard that a little bit of water came out my nose.

That was how ridiculous I thought her *observations* were.

In my humble opinion, all those soapy shows she watched were starting to mess up her perception of reality. Hell, and I was the Spanish one out of the two. I had grown up watching soap operas with my *abuela*. But I surely wasn't living in one. There was no simmering tension between Aaron Blackford and me. I did not glare at him in a way he loved. Aaron didn't love anything – he couldn't do that without a heart.

> Lina: All right, I have work to do, so I'll let you get
> back to your coffee, but stop raiding the pastry
> counter. I'm concerned.
>
> Rosie: Okay, okay. I'll stop – for now. 🖤 Good luck!
>
> Lina: 🖤 🔥

Locking my phone and placing it face down on the table, I took a deep, energizing breath.

Time to get this show going.

The image of the chocolate brownie popped into my head.

Assaulting me.

No, Lina.

Thinking of brownies – or any food – wasn't going to help. I needed to make myself believe that I wasn't hungry.

'I'm not hungry,' I said out loud, putting my chestnut hair in a bun. 'My stomach is full. Packed with all kinds of delicious food. Like tacos. Or pizza. Or brownies. Coffee and—'

My stomach grumbled, ignoring my visualization exercise and

invading my mind with memories of Around the Corner. The delicious scent of roasted coffee beans. The welcome sensory attack that involved taking a bite of a brownie that included three sorts of chocolate. The sound of the coffee machine steaming milk.

Another complaint rose from my noisy stomach.

Sighing, I reluctantly kicked all those images out of my mind and rolled up the sleeves of the thin cardigan I had to wear in the building, thanks to the AC being tuned up to the max in summer. 'Okay, stomach, work with me here,' I muttered to myself, as if the words would maybe make some kind of difference. 'I'll take us to Around the Corner tomorrow. Now, you need to stay quiet and let me work. Okay?'

'Okay.'

The word echoed in my office, as if it had been my stomach answering.

But I wasn't that lucky.

'That was odd.' The same deep voice came again. 'But I guess it goes with your personality.'

Not needing to lift my head to know who was behind that rich tone, I closed my eyes.

Damn you, Rosalyn Graham. You summoned this evil entity into my office, and you'll pay for this in chocolate.

Cursing under my breath – because, of course, it had to be him hearing me rally myself – I schooled my face into a neutral expression and looked up from my desk. 'Odd? I like to think of it as endearing.'

'No,' he answered quickly. Way too quickly. 'It's a little disturbing when you say more than a couple of words. And you were having a full conversation with yourself.'

I grabbed the first thing I found lying around in my desk – a highlighter. I breathed in and then out. 'I'm sorry, Blackford. But I don't have time to pick apart my quirks right now,' I said, holding my highlighter in the air. 'Do you need anything?'

I took him in as he stood under the threshold of my office door, his laptop under one of his arms, one of his dark eyebrows raised.

'What's Around the Corner?' he queried, starting in my direction.

Breathing out slowly, I ignored his question and watched his long legs closing the distance to my desk. Then, I had to watch him walk around it and stop somewhere to my left.

I swivelled my office chair, fully facing him. 'Sorry, but is there anything I can help you with?'

His gaze fell behind me, on my laptop screen, his big body bending down.

Realizing how very close his body was to my face and how much larger it seemed up close, I leaned back in my chair. 'Hello?' The word came out wobblier than I would have preferred. 'What are you doing?'

He placed his left hand on my desk and hummed, the soft noise sounding as close as he was. Right in my face.

'Blackford,' I said very slowly, watching how his eyes scanned the PowerPoint slide on my screen. It displayed a draft of the schedule I was assembling for InTech's Open Day.

I knew what he was doing. But I didn't know why. Or why he was ignoring me – beside the fact that he was trying to be the biggest pain in my ass.

'Blackford, I'm talking to you.'

Lost in thought, he hummed again, that damn noise sounding all hushed and masculine.

And annoying, I reminded myself.

I swallowed the lump that had just magically appeared in my throat.

Then, he finally spoke, 'Is that all you've got?'

He absently placed his laptop on my desk. Right beside mine.

My eyes narrowed.

'*Eight a.m. Meet and greet.*' One bulky arm flew in front of my face, pointing at my screen.

I plastered my body to the backrest of my chair, watching his biceps flex under the fabric of the plain button-down he wore.

Aaron continued reading out loud from my screen, pointing with his finger at every item, '*Nine a.m. An introduction to InTech's business strategies.*'

My eyes travelled all the way up to his shoulder.

'*Ten a.m. Coffee break* . . . until eleven a.m. That will require large amounts of coffee. *Eleven a.m. Pre-lunch activities.* Not specified.'

I surprised myself, noticing how his arm filled out the sleeve perfectly and completely, his muscles snuggled into the thin fabric and not leaving much space for imagination.

'*Noon. Lunch break* . . . until two p.m. Quite the banquet. Oh, and there's another coffee break at three p.m.' That arm I had been focused on halted in the air and then dropped.

Flushed, I reminded myself that I wasn't here to gawk at him. Or the muscles I noticed beneath his boring clothes.

'This is worse than I thought. Why didn't you say anything?'

I snapped out my trance, looking up at him. 'Excuse me, what?'

Aaron tilted his head, and then something seemed to catch his attention. My gaze followed his hand across my desk.

'An event like this one,' he said. Then, he picked up one of the pens I had scattered around. 'You have never planned one. And you don't seem to know how.' He dropped it in my cactus-shaped pencil cup.

'I have some experience with workshops,' I muttered as I followed his fingers repeating the action with a second pen. 'But just for colleagues, never for prospective clients.' Then a third one. 'Excuse me, what do you think you are doing?'

'Okay,' he answered simply, grabbing my favourite pencil, one that was pink, topped with a feather in the same bright colour. He looked at it strangely, his brows arching up. 'It's not ideal, but it's a start.' He pointed at me with the pencil. 'This? Seriously?'

I snagged it out of his hand. 'It cheers me up.' I dropped it in the cup. 'Does it offend your tastes, Mr Robot?'

Aaron didn't answer. Instead, his hands went for a couple of folders I had piled up – okay, fine, they had been rather dropped down somewhere – to my right. 'I know my way around events like this one,' he said, picking them up and squaring them on a corner of my desk. 'I organized a couple before coming to work for InTech.' He followed that up with going for my planner, which had been lying upside down somewhere in the mess that I was starting to realize was my working space. He held it in his paw-sized hands. 'We just need to work fast; there's not much time to put everything together.'

Whoa, whoa, whoa.

'We?' I ripped my planner out of his grip. 'There's no we here,' I scoffed. 'And would you *please* leave my stuff alone? What are you even trying to accomplish?'

His furtive hand moved again, going around the back of my chair. Aaron was almost sandwiching me between the desk and my chair as his head hovered above mine, his eyes roaming around my things.

I waited for my answer, watching his profile and trying really hard not to acknowledge the warmth I felt radiating off his body.

'There's no way you can focus; your desk is all cluttered,' he finally told me in a matter-of-fact tone. 'So, I'm fixing it.'

My mouth was hanging open. 'I could focus just fine until you got here.'

'Can I see the attendee list Jeff drafted?' His fingers flew over the keys of my laptop, opening a window.

All the while, I felt my body growing . . . warm. Uncomfortable. But at least he had stopped touching all my things.

'Oh, here it is.' He seemed to scan the document as I just stared at his profile, starting to feel overwhelmed by his proximity.

Jesus.

'All right,' he continued, 'that's not a lot of people, so at least the catering will be relatively easy to get sorted. As for the ... outline you prepared, that won't work.'

Dropping my hands on my lap, I felt dread spreading in my belly, making me wonder how in the world I was going to pull this off. 'I didn't ask for your opinion, but thanks for letting me know,' I said weakly, reaching for my laptop and bringing it closer. 'Now, if you don't mind, I'll get back to it.'

Aaron looked down just as I glanced up at him.

He searched my face for a brief moment that seemed to stretch into a full – and very uncomfortable – minute.

Stepping from behind me, he moved to my other side. He leaned on the table with strong forearms, which I might have looked at a second too long, and turned on his own laptop.

'Aaron,' I said for what I hoped was the last damn time tonight, 'you don't need to help me. If that's what you are trying to do here.' That last part I muttered.

I rolled my chair closer to my desk as I watched him punch in his password, trying hard not to focus on those infuriating broad shoulders that were right in my line of vision as he leaned on the wooden surface.

Por el amor de Dios. I needed to stop ... checking him out.

My starved brain was clearly struggling to behave normally. And it was his fault. I needed him gone. ASAP. At a normal distance, he was extremely annoying, and now, he was ... right freaking here. Being extra difficult.

'I have something we can use.' Aaron's fingers flew over the pad of his laptop as he looked for the document I guessed he was referring to. 'Before leaving my former employer, they had me put together a list. A manual of sorts. It should be somewhere here. Hold on.'

Aaron kept typing and clicking as I grew more and more irritated by the second. With myself, with him. With just ... everything.

'Aaron,' I said as a PDF document finally blinked open on his screen. I softened my voice, thinking maybe being as nice as I could ever be when it came to him was the way to go about this. 'It's late, and you don't have to do this. You have already pointed me in the right direction. Now, you can go.' I pointed at the door. 'Thank you.'

The fingers I was still watching gracefully tapped on the keys one more time. 'It includes a little bit of everything – workshop examples, key concepts for activities and group dynamics, and even objectives that should be kept in mind. We can go through it.'

We. That word again.

'I can do this on my own, Blackford.'

'I can help.'

'You might be able to, but you don't have to. I have no idea why you have this impulse to fly in with your red cape like a nerdy Clark Kent and save the day, but no, thanks. You might look a little like him, but I'm not a damsel in distress.'

The worst part was that I actually needed the help. What I had trouble accepting was that Aaron was the one willing to provide it.

He straightened to his full length. 'A nerdy Clark Kent?' His brows furrowed. 'Is that supposed to be a compliment?'

My mouth snapped closed.

'No.' I rolled my eyes even though he might have been a little right.

He sort of looked like the man behind Superman's secret identity. Not the one with the cape, the one who wore a suit, had a nine-to-five job, and was kind of . . . *hot* for a guy working in an office. Not that I'd ever admit that out loud. Not even to Rosie.

Aaron studied my face for a couple of seconds.

'I think I'm going to take it as a compliment,' he said as one of the corners of his lips bent up just the tiniest little bit.

Smug Clark Kent lookalike.

'Well, it's not.' I reached for my mouse, clicking to open a random folder. 'Thor or Captain America? That would have been a compliment. But you are not a Chris. Plus, no one cares about Superman anymore, Mr Kent.'

Aaron seemed to think about my statement for an instant. 'It sounds like you still care though.'

As I ignored that, he proceeded to walk behind me. Then, I watched him cross the office to the desk that belonged to one of the guys I shared the space with but who had obviously left hours ago. He grabbed his chair with one hand and rolled it in my direction.

My arms crossed in front of my chest as he placed that chair beside mine and let his large body fall on it, making it squeak and look rather frail.

'What are you doing?' I asked him.

'You asked me that question already.' He pinned me with a bored look. 'What does it look like I'm doing?'

'I don't need your help, Blackford.'

He sighed. 'I think I'm having another déjà vu.'

'You,' I stuttered. Then scoffed again. 'I ... ugh.'

'Catalina,' he said, and I hated how my name sounded on is lips in that precise moment. 'You need the help. So, I'm saving us both some time because we both know you'd never ask.'

He wasn't wrong. I would never ask Aaron for anything, not when I knew exactly what he thought about me. Personally, professionally, it didn't matter. I had been well aware of what he thought of me all this time. I had heard him myself all those months ago even if he didn't know that. So, no, I refused to accept anything from him. As much as that turned me into a grudge-holder too. Just like he was. I'd live with it.

Aaron leaned back and placed his hands on the chair's armrests. The shirt strained with the motion, the change in the tension of the fabric too flattering for my eyes not to unconsciously drift there.

Jesus. My eyes fluttered closed for a second. I was hungry, tired from dealing with all this, betrayed by my own two eyes, and honestly simply confused at this point.

'Stop being so stubborn,' he said.

Stubborn. Why? Because I hadn't asked for his help and I was supposed to take it when he decided to offer it?

Now, I was pissed. That was probably why I opened my mouth without thinking. 'That's why you didn't speak up during the meeting where all this was dumped on me and then some? Because I didn't ask for help? Because I am too stubborn to ever accept it?'

Aaron's head reared back just slightly; he was probably shocked by my admission.

I immediately regretted saying anything. I did. But it had somehow slipped out, as if the words had been squeezed out of me.

Something flashed through his otherwise serious expression. 'I didn't realize you wanted me to step in.'

Of course not. No one had. Not even Héctor, who I almost considered family. Didn't I know that by now? Yes, I was more than familiar with the fact that when it came to these situations, there were two groups of people. Those who believed that not saying anything made them stand in neutral ground and those who picked a side. And more often than not, it was the wrong one. Sure, it wasn't always as harmless as condescending and disrespectful comments like those Gerald had made. Sometimes, it was far, far worse. I knew that. I had experienced that firsthand a long time ago.

I shook my head, pushing the memories away. 'Would that have made a difference, Aaron? If I had asked you to intervene?' I asked him, as if he held the solution in his hands when he really didn't. I watched him, feeling my heart race with trepidation. 'Or if I told you I was exhausted from *having* to ask, would you step in then?'

Aaron studied me in silence, searching my face almost gingerly.

My cheeks heated up under his scrutiny, making me regret more and more that I had spoken.

'Forget I said anything, okay?' I averted my eyes, feeling disappointed and mad at myself for putting Aaron, out of all people, on the line when he didn't owe me anything. Not a single thing. 'I'm stuck with this anyway. It doesn't matter how or why.' Or that it wouldn't be the last time.

Aaron straightened, leaning his body toward me just the splinter of a hair. He took a deep breath as I seemed to hold mine, waiting for him to say whatever was brewing in his mind.

'You've never needed anyone to fight your battles, Catalina. That's one of the things I respect the most about you.'

His words did something to my chest. Something that created a kind of pressure I wasn't comfortable with.

Aaron never said stuff like that. Not to anyone and particularly not to me.

I opened my mouth to tell him that it didn't matter, that I didn't care, that we could just drop it, but he held up a hand, stopping me.

'On the other hand, I never pegged you for someone who would cower and not give their best when faced with a challenge. Whether it's unfairly imposed or not,' he said, turning away and facing his laptop. 'So, what's it going to be?'

My jaw clamped closed.

I . . . I wasn't cowering. I was not scared of this thing. I knew I could do it. I just . . . hell, I was just exhausted. It was hard, finding the motivation when something was this discouraging. 'I'm not—'

'What is it going to be, Catalina?' His fingers moved on the laptop pad with practice. 'Whining or working?'

'I'm not whining,' I huffed.

Clark Kent lookalike jerk.

'Then, we work,' he fired back.

I took a good look at him, taking in how his jaw bunched up with determination. Perhaps some irritation too.

'There's no *we* here,' I breathed out.

He shook his head, and I swore the ghost of a smile graced his lips for a fragment of a second.

'I swear to God . . .' He looked up, as if he were asking the heavens for patience. 'You are taking the help. That's it.' He peeked down at his watch, exhaling. 'I don't have the whole day to convince you.' Scowl back in place, he returned to the Aaron I knew. 'We've wasted enough time already.'

This scowling Aaron I felt more comfortable with. He didn't go around saying stupid stuff, like that he respected me.

Now, it was my turn to scowl, as I was painfully aware of how I wasn't kicking Aaron out of my office anymore.

'I'm as stubborn as you are,' he murmured, typing something on his laptop. 'You know I am.'

Returning my attention to my computer screen, I decided to allow this strange truce to settle between us. Just for the sake of InTech's reputation. For my own mental health, too, because he was driving me completely crazy.

We'd be two scowling idiots who would tolerate each other for an evening, I guessed.

'Fine. I'll let you help me if you are so set on it,' I told him, trying not to focus on that warm ball of emotion forming in my belly.

One that felt a lot like gratitude.

He glanced at me quickly, something unreadable in his eyes. 'We'll need to start from scratch. Open a blank template.'

Looking away, I tried to focus on my screen.

We had been in silence for a couple of minutes when out of the corner of my eye, I perceived movement. Quickly afterwards, he placed something on my desk. Right between us.

'Here,' I heard him say from beside me.

Looking down, my gaze found something wrapped in wax paper. It was a square, about three or four inches long.

'What's this?' I asked him, my eyes jumping to his profile.

'A granola bar,' he answered without looking at me, typing on his keyboard. 'You are hungry. Eat it.'

I watched my hands move to the snack of their own accord. Once unwrapped, I inspected it closely. Homemade. It had to be, judging by the way roasted oats, dried fruits, and nuts were assembled together.

I heard Aaron's long sigh. 'If you ask me if it's poisoned, I swear—'

'No,' I murmured.

Then, I shook my head, feeling that weird pressure in my chest again. So, I took the snack to my mouth, bit into it, and – *holy granola bars*. I moaned in delight.

'For Christ's sake,' the man to my right muttered under his breath.

Gobbling all the nutty and sugary amazingness down, I shrugged. 'Sorry, it was a moan-worthy bite.'

I watched his head shake as he was focused on the document on his screen. As I studied his profile, an odd and unfamiliar feeling settled in. And it had nothing to do with my appreciation for Aaron's unexpected baking skills. It was something else, something warm and fuzzy that I had gotten a whiff of a few minutes earlier, but now, I wanted to bend my lips into a smile.

I was grateful.

Aaron Blackford, scowling Clark Kent lookalike, was in my office. Helping me and feeding me homemade snacks, and I was glad. Thankful even.

'Thank you.' The fugitive words escaped my lips.

He turned to face me, and I saw him relax for an instant. Then, his eyes jumped to my screen. He scoffed, 'You still haven't opened a blank template?'

'*Oye.*' The Spanish word slipped out. 'You don't have to be so bossy. Not everyone has super speed like you, Mr Kent.'

His eyebrows rose, and he looked unimpressed. 'Quite the contrary. Some even have the opposite superpower.'

'Ha.' I rolled my eyes. 'Funny.'

His gaze shifted back to his screen. 'Blank template. And make it today, if that's not too much to ask.'

This was going to be a long night.

CHAPTER FOUR

'*Mamá*,' I said for the hundredth time. '*Mamá, escúchame, por favor.*'

It wouldn't really matter if I asked her to please listen to me a thousand more times. That wasn't something my mother excelled at, much less ever practised. Listening was reserved for those whose vocal cords took breaks.

A long and loud sigh left my lips as my mother's voice travelled from my phone to my ear in heavy spurts of Spanish.

'*Madre,*' I repeated.

'. . . so if you decide to go with that other dress – you know which one I'm talking about?' my mother asked in Spanish, not really giving me a window to answer. 'The one that is all flimsy and silky and falls to your ankles. Well, as your mother, I need to tell you that it's not flattering. I'm sorry, Lina, but you are short, and the cut of the dress makes you look even shorter. And green is not your colour either. I don't think that's a colour the *madrina* of the wedding should wear.'

'I know, Mamá. But I already told you—'

'You'll look like a . . . frog but in heels.'

Gee, thanks, Mother.

I chuckled and shook my head. 'It doesn't matter because I'm wearing the red dress.'

A gasp came through the line. '*Ay.* Why didn't you tell me this before? You let me talk for half an hour about all your other options.'

'I told you as soon as it came up. You just—'

'Well, I must have let myself get carried away, *cariño*.'

I opened my mouth to confirm that, but she didn't give me the chance.

'Perfect,' she cut in. 'That is such a beautiful dress, Lina. It's classy and flirty.'

Flirty? What was that supposed to mean?

'Your boobs will be entering the banquet before you.'

Oh . . . *oh*. So, that was what she meant.

'But the colour does really flatter your skin, body shape, and face. Not like the frog dress.'

'Thanks,' I muttered. 'I don't think I'll ever wear green again.'

'Good,' she said far too quickly for it to be taken as a good-hearted comment. 'So, what's this boyfriend of yours going to wear? Are you going to match? Papá got a tie in the same shade of baby blue I'll be wearing.'

A tiny groan slipped out of my mouth. 'Mamá, you know that Isa hates that. She specifically told us not to match.'

My sister had been very insistent – no matching couples. I even had to fight her over not adding that instruction on the invites. It'd cost me a lot of energy and patience to convince her that she didn't want to be that kind of bride.

'Well, given that I gave birth to the bride and that I already bought that tie for Papá, I think your sister is going to have to make an exception.'

Leave it to her to be stubborn. I certainly was, my sister probably even more so, but our mother? The woman had created the term bullheaded as she opened her eyes to the world the day she was born.

'I think she'll have to,' I admitted under my breath.

Reaching for my planner, I scribbled on my to-do list to call Isa to warn her.

'I have an online voucher you can use, I think,' Mamá commented while I unlocked my laptop and absently checked my inbox. 'Although maybe it does not work outside Spain. But it should, shouldn't it? You are my daughter, and you should be able to use my vouchers, no matter where you are in the world. Isn't that what the internet is supposed to be for?'

I clicked on an email notification for a new series meeting I had received. 'Yeah, sure.' A quick scan of the contents of the description told me I should have probably waited for my mother to hang up before opening it.

'Yeah, sure, the internet is for that? Or yeah, sure, you'll use my voucher?'

I leaned back on my seat, reading through the information attached.

'Lina?'

What are we even talking about? 'Yes, Mamá.'

'Well, you'll have to check the voucher yourself; you know I am not good with this internet thing.'

'Of course,' I said, still not knowing what I was agreeing to.

'Unless he has a tie already?'

He.

All my attention returned to the conversation.

'Does he?' she insisted when I didn't answer. 'Your new boyfriend.'

Small beads of sweat formed on my forehead at the prospect of discussing this.

Him.

The boyfriend I didn't have but my family believed I did. Because I had told them.

Lied to them.

All of a sudden, my lips were magically sewn together. I waited for my mother to conveniently change the topic in that chaotic

and speedy way she always did while my mind went into a panicky frenzy.

*What am I supposed to say anyway? No, Mamá. He can't have a tie,
because he doesn't even exist. I made him up, you see. All in an attempt to
look a little less pathetic and lonely.*

Perhaps I could hang up. Or pretend to be busy and terminate
the call. But that would fill me with remorse, and frankly, I didn't
think I was able to take on any more of that. Also, my mother
wasn't stupid.

She'd know something was up.

This was the woman whose womb I had come out of.

More seconds ticked away as nothing came out of my mouth, and
I couldn't believe that for the first time in probably ever, the Martín
matriarch was waiting for my answer in silence.

Shit.

A few more seconds ticked away.

Shit, shit, shit.

Confess, a little voice in my head said. But I shook my head,
focusing on one of the little droplets of sweat trailing down my
clammy back.

'Lina?' she finally said, her voice unsure. Worried. 'Did something happen?'

I was a horrible, lying human being who had unquestionably put
that concern I could hear into her voice.

'No . . .' Clearing my throat, I ignored the heaviness that felt a lot
like shame settling in my stomach. 'I'm okay.'

I heard her sigh. It was one of those sighs that smacked into you.
Making me feel bad about myself. As if I could see her looking at
me with eyes filled with defeat and a little sorrow, shaking her head.
I hated it.

'Lina, you know you can talk to me if something happened.'

My guilt deepened, souring my stomach. I felt awful.

Stupid too. But what could I even do, besides keep lying or coming clean?

'Did you guys break up? You know, it would make sense because you have never talked about him before. Not until the other day at least.' There was a pause, in which I could hear my heart drumming in my ears. 'Your cousin Charo said something yesterday, you know.'

Of course Charo knew. Anything Mamá knew, the rest of the family knew.

'So, she said,' she continued when I didn't say anything, 'that you don't have any photos of him on Facebook.'

I closed my eyes.

'Nobody posts anything on Facebook anymore, Mamá,' I told her in a weak voice while I kept battling with myself.

'And Prinstanam? Whatever it is that you young people use now. No photos there either.'

I could picture Charo scouting all my social profiles, searching for this imaginary man and rubbing her hands when she hadn't found any.

'Charo said that if it's not Prinstanam official, then it's not serious.'

My heartbeat hammered louder in my chest. 'It's called Instagram.'

'Fine.' She sighed again. 'But if you broke up with him or if he ended things – I don't care who did what – you can talk to us about it. To Papá and to me. I know how much you have struggled with this dating thing ever since . . . you know, since Daniel.'

That last comment was a knife to the chest. It turned that heavy sensation into something ugly and painful. Something that made me think of the reason why I'd lied, why I struggled – as my mother had put it – and why I was in this predicament in the first place.

'You have never brought anybody home in all these years you've been away. Never talked about a man you were seeing. And never talked about this one before you told us you were dating him and that you'd bring him to the wedding. So, if you are alone again . . .'

A very familiar and very sharp pang pierced my chest at her words. 'That's okay.'

Is it?

If it was really okay, I could tell my mother. I had the chance to end this lying circus, bury all that regret somewhere deep and dark, and breathe. I could tell her that, yes, I was no longer in a relationship, and consequently, I was no longer taking my – non-existent – boyfriend home. That I'd attend the wedding alone. And that it *was* okay.

She had said it herself. And maybe she was right. I just needed to believe she was.

Taking a deep breath, I felt a surge of courage and made up my mind.

I'll come clean.

Attending alone wouldn't be fun. The pity looks and whispers of a past I didn't want to think about would certainly suck. And that was putting it lightly. But I had no options.

Aaron's scowling face popped up in my mind. Unannounced.

Definitely unwelcome.

No. I kicked it out.

He hadn't even mentioned it again since Monday. It had been four days. Not that if he had, it would have changed anything. I was on my own. But I had no reason to believe he had been serious.

And it was okay; Mamá had said so.

I opened my mouth to follow up with my decision of growing the hell up and to stop acting like a compulsive liar for something I should have the maturity to face alone, but of course, luck wasn't on my side. Because my mother's next words immediately killed whatever I was about to say.

'You know' – the way her voice sounded should have tipped

me off on what was about to come – 'every person is different. We all have our own pace to put back together our lives after going through something like that. Some people need more time than others. And if you haven't managed to get there yet, then there's nothing to be ashamed of. Daniel is engaged while you are not. But that isn't important. You can come to the wedding alone, Lina.'

My stomach dropped to my feet at the thought.

'I'm not saying Daniel needed to put his life back together in the first place because, well, he jumped off that boat, unscathed.'

And wasn't that the damn truth? Something that, on top of everything, would make things even worse. He had merrily continued his life while I had . . . I had . . . gotten stuck. And everybody there would know. Every single person attending that wedding would know.

As if reading my mind, my mother uttered my thoughts: 'Everybody knows, *cariño*. And everybody understands. You went through a lot.'

Everybody understands?

No, she was wrong. Everybody thought they understood. Nobody did. They didn't realize that all those *pobrecita, poor little Lina*s, accompanied by all those pitiful looks and nods, as if they got why I had been scarred and not able to find somebody else, were the reasons why I had lied to my family. Why I wanted to crawl out of my skin at the prospect of showing up alone when Daniel – my first love, my ex, the groom's brother and best man – being there with his fiancée would only reinforce their assumptions about me.

Single and alone after fleeing the country, heartbroken.

Stuck.

I was over him; I truly was. But, man, all that had happened had . . . messed me up. I realized that now – not because it'd suddenly hit me that I had been single for years, but because I had lied – and what was worse was, I had just made up my mind not to go back on my lie.

'*Everybody understands. You went through a lot.*'

A lot was a very gentle way to put it.

Nope. I couldn't. I wouldn't do it. I wouldn't be that Lina in front of my whole family, the whole damn town. Daniel.

'Lina . . .' My mother said my name in that way only a mother could. 'Are you still there?'

'Of course.' My voice sounded wobbly and heavy with everything I was feeling, and I hated that it had. I straightened myself in my chair. 'Nothing happened with my boyfriend,' I lied. Lies, lies, and more lies. *Lina Martín, professional liar, deceiver.* 'And I am bringing him, just like I said I would.' I forced out a laugh, but it sounded all wrong. 'If you'd just let me talk before jumping to silly conclusions and sermonizing me, I could have told you.'

Nothing came through the speaker of the phone. Only silence.

My mother wasn't stupid. I didn't think any mother was. And if I believed for a second that I was out of the storm, I was probably wrong.

'Okay,' she said oddly softly. 'So, you are still together?'

'Yes,' I lied again.

'And he'll come to the wedding with you? To Spain?'

'Correct.'

A pause, making me realize my hands were sweating so much that the phone would have slipped if I hadn't been gripping it as tightly as I was.

'He's in New York too, you said?'

'Yep.'

She hummed and then added, 'American?'

'Raised and born.'

'What's his name again?'

My breath got stuck somewhere along my throat. *Shit*. I hadn't given him a name, had I? I didn't think I had, but . . .

My mind raced through my options very quickly. Desperately. I needed a name. What an easy, manageable thing. A name.

A simple name.

A name of a man who didn't exist or I still had to find.

'Lina . . . are you there?' my mother chimed. She laughed, somehow sounding nervous. 'Have you forgotten your boyfriend's name?'

'Don't be silly,' I told her, hearing my distress in my voice. 'I . . .'

A shadow caught my eye, distracting me. My gaze shot to my office door, and exactly as he had wedged himself into my life one year and eight months ago – with horrifyingly bad timing – Aaron Blackford stepped over the threshold and placed himself in the eye of the storm.

'Lina?' I thought I heard my mother say.

In two strides, he was in front of me, across my desk, letting a stack of papers drop onto its surface.

What was he doing?

We didn't visit each other's offices. We never needed, wanted, or bothered to.

That icy-blue gaze of his fell on me. It was followed by a frown, as if he were wondering why I looked like a woman currently dealing with a life-threatening crisis. Which was exactly what I was doing. Getting caught in a lie was far worse than lying. After only a couple of seconds, his expression morphed into an appalled one. I could see the judgment in his eyes.

Out of every single person who could have walked into my office right now, it'd had to be him.

Why, Lord? Why?

'Aaron,' I heard myself say in a pained voice.

I was vaguely aware when my mother somehow repeated his name, 'Aaron?'

'*Sí,*' I murmured, my gaze locked with his. What in the world does he want?

'Okay,' Mamá said.

Okay?

My eyes widened. '*¿Qué?*'

Aaron, who had caught the Spanish words, put two and two together with an ease that shouldn't have surprised me.

'Personal call at work?' he queried, shaking his head.

My mother, who was still on the line, asked in Spanish, 'Is that him, the voice I'm hearing? This Aaron you are dating?'

My whole body locked up. Eyes wide and mouth agape, I stared at him as my mother's words resonated inside my clearly empty skull because what in the world had I done?

'Lina?' she pressed on.

Aaron's frown deepened, and he sighed with resignation as he stood right there. Not leaving.

Why isn't he leaving?

'*Sí,*' I answered, not realizing she'd take that word as confirmation. But she would; I knew she would do exactly that, wouldn't she? 'No,' I added, trying to backpedal.

But then Aaron tsked and shook his head again, and whatever had been about to leave my lips scattered.

'I . . .' *Oh God, why is it so warm in my office?* '*No sé, Mamá.*'

Aaron mouthed, *Your mother?*

'*¿Cómo que no sabes?*' came at the same time.

'I . . . I . . .' I trailed off, not really knowing who I was talking to. The scowling man or my mother. I felt like I was flying on autopilot while my plane approached the ground at a breakneck speed, and I couldn't do anything to stop it from crashing. None of my controls were responding.

'*Ay, hija,*' my mother said with a laugh. 'What is it? Yes or no? Is that Aaron?'

I wanted to scream.

All of a sudden, I had this powerful urge to cry or open the window and shove the phone out and into New York's merciless traffic. I wanted to break something too. With my bare hands. While I stomped my feet with frustration. All at once. I wanted to do all those things.

Curiosity filled Aaron's blue eyes. He tilted his head, watching me as I struggled to even take a decent breath.

I covered my phone with my other hand and addressed the man in front of me in a broken, defeated voice, 'What do you want?'

He waved one hand airily. 'No, please, don't let me – or work – get in between you and your personal call.' He crossed his arms in front of his stupidly wide chest and brought a fist under his chin. 'I'll just wait here until you are done.'

If smoke could physically leave my ears, a black cloud would have been trailing up and circling over my head.

My mother, who was still on the line, spoke, 'You sound busy, so I'll let you go.' I kept my eyes on Aaron, and before I could even process her words, she added, 'Wait until *Abuela* hears about you dating someone from work. You know what she'll say?'

My dumb brain must have been still flying on autopilot because it didn't skip a beat. *'Uno no come donde caga.'*

Aaron's lips puckered lightly.

'Eso es.' I heard my mother chuckle. 'I'll let you get back to work. You'll tell us about this man you are dating when you two come for the wedding then, okay?'

No, I wanted to tell her. *What I'll do is die, choked in my own web of lies.*

'Of course, Mamá,' I said instead. 'I love you. Tell Papá I love him too.'

'Love you too, *cielo*,' my mother said right before hanging up. Filling my lungs with much-needed air, I glared at the man who had just complicated my life tenfold and dropped my phone on the desk as if it were burning my palm.

'So, your mother.'

I nodded my head, incapable of speaking. It was better that way. God knew what would come out of my treacherous mouth.

'All good at home?'

Sighing, I nodded again.

'What does it mean?' he asked me with what might be genuine curiosity. 'What you said in Spanish at the end.'

My head was still swirling with that horrible, catastrophic phone call. With what I had done and how much I had messed up. I didn't have time to play Google Translate with Aaron, who, on top of everything, was the last person I wanted to chat with at the moment.

Jesus, how did he manage to do that? He showed up, and in the span of a few minutes just—

I shook my head.

'Why do you even care?' I snapped.

I watched him flinch. Only slightly but I was almost sure he had.

Immediately feeling like a jerk, I brought my hands to my face as I tried to calm myself.

'Sorry,' I whispered. 'I'm a little . . . stressed. What do you want, Aaron?' I asked him, softening my voice and fixing my eyes somewhere on my desk. Anywhere but on him. I didn't want to face him and give him a chance to see me this . . . unsettled. I hated the idea of him seeing me at my lowest. If it wouldn't be completely inappropriate, I would drop to the floor, crawl under my desk, and hide from him.

Given that I refused to look at him, I could only notice the difference in his tone when he said, 'I printed out some more documents you can use for one of the workshops we outlined.' His voice was almost gentle. For someone like Aaron, that was. 'I left them on your desk.'

Oh.

My gaze tracked down the wooden surface, finding them, and I felt like an even bigger jerk.

That emotion churned in my gut, turning into something way too close to helplessness for me to feel any better.

'Thanks,' I muttered, massaging my temples with my fingers and closing my eyes. 'You could have just sent them by email.' Maybe that way, all this could have been avoided.

'You highlight everything by hand.'

I did. When something required my full focus, I needed to print it on paper and then review it with a highlighter in hand. But how ... *oh hell.* It didn't matter that Aaron had somehow noticed. He probably had because it was a waste of paper or bad for the environment anyway. And that didn't change that I was still a jerk for snapping at him like that.

'You're right, I do. That was ...' I trailed off, keeping my gaze on the desk. 'That was nice of you. I'll go through them over the weekend.'

Still not lifting my head to look at him, I reached for the thin stack and placed it in front of me.

A long moment passed where neither of us spoke.

I could tell he was still standing there, all statuesque, not moving and just looking down at me. But he didn't say anything, not giving me an excuse to look up. So, I kept my eyes trained on the papers he had so nicely printed out for me.

That long moment seemed to stretch into a painfully awkward amount of time, but right before I was about to lose the weird battle and look up, I sensed him leave. Then, I waited a full minute until I was sure he was long gone. And ... I let it all out.

My head fell on my desk with a muffled thud. No, not on the desk. My head had fallen on the stack of papers that Aaron had come to deliver – *very nicely* – right before I put my foot in my mouth and somehow told my mother that the name of my made-up boyfriend was Aaron.

A groan slipped out of me. It was ugly and miserable.

Just like I was.

I softly bumped my head against the surface of my desk. *'Estúpida.'* Bang. *'Idiota. Tonta. Boba. Y mentirosa.'* Bang, bang, bang.

That was the worst of all. Not only was I an idiot, but I was also a lying idiot.

The realization pushed another groan out of me.

'Whoa,' came from the door. It was Rosie's voice.

Good. I needed someone I trusted to retrieve me from this madness I had gotten myself into and register me into the closest mental facility. I couldn't be trusted to . . . adult properly.

'Is everything okay, Lina?'

Nope.

Nothing about what I had just done was okay.

~

'WAIT, WAIT, WAIT, WAIT.' Rosie shoved her hand between us, making the universal sign to hold your horses. 'You told your mom *what?*'

Gobbling down the rest of my pastrami panini, I shot her a look. 'You gnow whatf I saifd,' I told her, not caring that my mouth was still full.

'I just want to hear that last part again.' Rosie leaned back on her chair, her emerald eyes wide with shock. 'You know what? How about you start from the beginning again? I must be missing something because this whole thing sounds a little too much, even for you.'

Narrowing my eyes at her, I gave her a fake, toothy smile that I was sure showcased some of the contents of my panini.

I didn't care that anybody in the coworking space on the fifteenth floor, where we were having lunch, could see me. At this time, there weren't many people left on this floor anyway. Leave it to a company in New York City to dedicate this much space – and money, because the decor was right out of hipsterland – to a coworking and shared space for a bunch of workaholics who didn't make use of it outside of their lunch break. No more than a couple of tables to my right were occupied by now – the ones closest to the impressive floor-to-ceiling windows, of course.

'Don't look at me like that.' My friend pouted across from me. 'And please, I love you, but that's not a nice look. I can see some . . . lettuce hanging out of your mouth.'

I rolled my eyes, chewing and finally washing down my mouthful.

Contrary to what I had hoped, food had done nothing to appease my mood. This pounding ball of anxiety was still asking to be fed. 'I should have ordered a second panini.' On any other day, I would have. But the wedding would be in no time, and I was trying to watch what I ate.

'Yes, and something else you should have done? Told me about all of this before.' Her voice was gentle, just how all things Rosie were, but the weight behind those words prickled at my skin all the same. 'You know, like from the moment you decided to make up a boyfriend.'

I deserved it. I had known Rosie would – sweetly – kick my ass as soon as she found out that I had kept from her all of that *me lying to my family about being in a relationship* business.

'I'm sorry.' I reached my hand out across the table, taking hers. 'I'm so sorry, Rosalyn Graham. I should never have kept this from you.'

'No, you shouldn't have done that.' She pouted some more.

'In my defence, I was going to tell you on Monday, but we were interrupted by you know who.' I wouldn't say his name out loud, as he often appeared out of thin air when I did. I squeezed her hand.

'To make it up to you, I will ask my *abuela* to light a few candles to one of her saints, so you are rewarded with many children.'

Rosie sighed, pretending to think about it for a moment. 'Fine, I accept your apology.' She squeezed back. 'But instead of children, I'd much rather get introduced to one of your cousins maybe?'

I reared back, shock etched on my face. 'One of my *what*?'

As I watched the light blush rise in her cheeks, my surprise only grew when she said, 'The one who surfs and has a Belgian shepherd? He is kind of dreamy.'

'Dreamy?' None of my savage cousins could ever be considered *dreamy*.

Rosie's cheeks turned a darker shade of red.

How the hell is my friend acquainted with one of the members of the Martín clan? Unless . . .

'Lucas?' I sputtered, immediately remembering that I had shown her a few of his Instagram stories. But it had all been because of Taco, his dog. Not because of him. 'Lucas, the one with the buzzed head?'

My friend nodded casually, shrugging her shoulders.

'You are too good for Lucas,' I hissed. 'I'll let you take part in the kidnapping of his dog though. Taco is also too good for him.'

'Taco.' Rosie giggled. 'That's such an adorable name.'

'Rosie, no.' I retrieved my hand and reached for my bottle of water. 'No.'

'No, what?' Her smile was still there. Hanging on to her lips as she thought of my cousin, I supposed, in ways that—

'No. Ew. Yikes, woman. He is a barbarian, a brute. He has no manners. Stop daydreaming of my cousin.' I took a cleansing gulp of water. 'Stop, or I'll be forced to tell you some horror stories from our childhood, and in the process, I'll probably ruin the male specimen for you.'

My friend's shoulders fell. 'If you must . . . not that it would help my case anyway. I don't think I need extra assistance for that.' She paused, sighing sadly. Making me want to reach out again and tell her that her prince would eventually show up. She just needed to stop picking up only the assholes. My relatives included. 'But before that, we can actually talk about your horror story.'

Oh. That.

'I already told you everything about it.' My gaze fell to my hands as I played with the label on the bottle. 'I gave you a play-by-play recap. From the moment I blurted out to my parents that I was dating a man who doesn't exist to the moment I somehow made my mom believe his name was Aaron because of a certain blue-eyed jerk who had appeared out of nowhere.' I scratched harder, ripping the label completely off the plastic surface. 'What else do you want to know?'

'Okay, those are the facts. But what's on your mind?'

'Right now?' I asked, to which she nodded. 'That we should have picked up dessert.'

'Lina ...' Rosie placed both arms on the table and leaned on them. 'You know what I'm asking.' She glanced at me sharply, which, when it came to Rosie, meant patiently but without a smile. Or a smaller than usual one. 'What are you going to do about all of this?'

What the hell do I know?

Shrugging, I let my gaze roam around the coworking space, taking in the chipped, old barn tables and the hanging ferns adorning the red brick wall to my left. 'Ignore this until my plane touches Spanish ground and I have to explain why my boyfriend is not with me?'

'Sweetie, are you sure you want to do that?'

'No.' I shook my head. 'Yes.' Bringing both hands to my temples, I tried to massage away the start of a headache. 'I don't know.'

Rosie seemed to take that in for a long moment. 'What if you actually consider him for this?'

My hands dropped from my temples to the wooden surface, and my stomach plunged to my feet. 'Consider who?'

I knew exactly *who*. I just couldn't believe she was even suggesting it.

She humoured me by replying, 'Aaron.'

'Oh, Lucifer's favourite son? I don't see how I should consider him for anything.'

Watching how Rosie clasped her hands together on the table, as if she were readying herself for a business negotiation, I narrowed my eyes at her.

'I don't think Aaron is all that bad,' she had the nerve to say.

All I gave her was a very dramatic gasp.

My friend rolled her eyes, not buying my bullshit. 'Okay, so he's ... a little dry, and he takes things a little too seriously,' she pointed out, as if using the word little would make him any better. 'But he has his good traits.'

'Good traits?' I snorted. 'Like what? His stainless steel interior?'

The joke bounced right off. Ugh, that meant serious business.

'Would it be that bad to actually talk to him about what he offered you? Because he was the one who offered himself, by the way.'

Yes, it would. Because I still hadn't figured out why he had done that in the first place.

'You know what I think of him, Rosie,' I told her with a no-nonsense expression. 'You know what happened. What he said.'

My friend sighed. 'That was a long time ago, Lina.'

'It was,' I admitted, averting my gaze. 'But that doesn't mean I've forgotten. It doesn't mean that just because it happened a handful of months ago, it's now somehow been written off.'

'It happened over a year ago.'

'Twenty months,' I corrected her far too quickly to hide that I had somehow kept count. 'That's closer to two years,' I muttered, looking down at the crumpled paper sheet that had wrapped my lunch.

'That's my point, Lina,' Rosie remarked softly. 'I have seen you give second, third, and fourth chances to people who have messed up far more. Some even repeatedly.'

She was right, but I was my mother's daughter and therefore stubborn as a mule. 'It's not the same.'

'Why not?'

'Because.'

Her green eyes turned harder; she was not letting this go. So, she was going to make me say it. We were going to talk about it.

Fine.

'How about because he told our boss that he would rather work with anyone else in InTech? On his second day of work.' I felt my blood rushing to my face at the memory. 'Key on *anyone*. Even Gerald for crying out loud.' I hadn't overheard Aaron mention Gerald in particular, but I was sure I had heard everything else.

'Anyone but her, Jeff. Just not her. I don't think I could take it. Is she even capable of taking on this project? She looks young and inexperienced.'

Aaron had told that to our boss on the phone. I had happened to walk past his office. I had accidentally overheard, and I hadn't forgotten. It was all etched in my memory.

'He had known me for two days, Rosie. Two.' I gestured with my index and middle fingers. 'And he was new. He came here and discredited me to our boss, indirectly kicked me out of a project, and put in question my professionalism, and for what? Because he didn't like me after the two minutes we talked? Because I looked young? Because I smile and laugh and I'm not a cyborg? I've worked hard. I've worked my ass off, getting to where I am. You know what comments like that can do.' I felt my voice pitch high. Same went for the pressure of my blood now pumping into my temples.

Making an effort to calm myself, I released a shaky breath.

Rosie nodded, looking at me with the understanding only a good friend would. But there was something else there too. And I was under the impression I wouldn't like whatever she had to say next.

'I get it. I do, I swear.' She smiled.

Okay, that was good. I needed her to be on my side. And I knew she was.

I watched her walk around the table and take a seat beside me. Then, she turned and faced me.

Uh-oh. This wasn't all that good anymore.

Rosie placed a hand on my back and continued, 'I hate to remind you of this, but you didn't even want to be on the Green-Solar project. Remember how much you complained about that client?'

Of course I'd had to go and find a best friend who had a border-line photographic memory. Of course she remembered that I had been glad to be relocated to a different project.

'And,' she continued, 'as you very well said, Aaron didn't know you.'

Exactly. He hadn't bothered to do that before he decided to label me as a hindrance and talk shit about me to our boss.

I crossed my arms in front of my chest. 'What's your point, Rosalyn?'

'My point is that, sure, he judged you based on only a couple of days,' she patted my back. 'But you can come across a little … informal. Relaxed. Spontaneous. Sometimes loud.'

My protest was heard all the way in Spain. 'Excuse me?' I gasped loudly. *Dammit.*

'I love you, sweetie.' My friend smiled warmly. 'But it's true.' I opened my mouth, but she didn't give me the chance to speak. 'You are one of the hardest workers here, and you are amazing at your job, while you manage to create a light and fun working atmosphere. That's why you are a team leader.'

'Okay, I like this direction far better,' I muttered. 'Keep going.'

'But Aaron didn't have a way of knowing that.'

My eyes widened. 'Are you defending him? Shall I remind you that we – as friends – should hate each other's enemies and nemeses? Do you need me to print a copy of the best-friend code for you?'

'Lina' – she swivelled her head, looking frustrated – 'be serious for a minute.'

I sobered up immediately, deflating in my chair. 'Okay, fine. Sorry. Go ahead.'

'I just think you were hurt – understandably so – and that bothered you enough to write him off this long.'

Yes, I had been outraged and hurt too. Something I despised was people making judgements based on shallow impressions. And that was exactly what Aaron had done. Especially after I had gone out of my way and tried to welcome him to the division with the best and warmest intentions. I couldn't believe I had shown up in his office with a stupid welcome gift – a mug with a funny quote about being an engineer. To this day, I didn't know what had come over me. I hadn't done that for anyone else. And what had Aaron done? He had just looked at it in horror and gaped at me like I had grown a second head as I cracked jokes like a total awkward dumbass.

So, to overhear him say that kind of stuff about me not more than two days after that … it had just made me feel small and all the more pathetic. Like I was being shoved aside after not measuring up to the real adults.

'I'm going to take your silence as confirmation of what I said,' Rosie told me, squeezing my shoulder. 'You were hurt, and that's okay, sweetie. But is it reason enough to hate him forever?'

I wanted to say yes, but at this point, I didn't even know anymore. So, I resorted to something else. 'It's not like he has been trying to be my friend or anything. He's been a constant pain in my ass all this time.'

Except for that life-saving homemade granola bar, fine. And those papers he'd printed out for me when he didn't have to, sure.

And maybe for the fact that he'd stayed late, working with me on Open Day last Wednesday.

Fine, okay, except for those three occasions, he had been a constant pain in my ass.

'You have been too,' she countered. 'You two are equally bad. Actually, it's even cute how you've both been looking for excuses to trip each other and—'

'Oh, hell no,' I cut her off, turning in my seat to fully face her. 'Let me stop you right there before you launch yourself into this weird shit about looks and whatnot.'

My friend had the nerve to cackle.

I gaped at her. 'I don't know you anymore.'

She recovered, pinning me with a look. 'You are oblivious, sweetie.'

'Am not. And you seem to need a reminder, so here's how things are.' I pointed in the air with my index finger. 'Since I overheard him saying those ugly and prejudiced things about me, to our boss no less, his name has been on my blacklist. And you know how seriously I take that. That shit is carved on stone.' I punched my palm with my other hand to be clear. 'Have I forgiven Zayn Malik?'

Rosie shook her head, snickering. 'Oh, Lord knows you haven't.'

'Exactly. In the same way that I haven't forgotten what David Benioff and D.B. Weiss did to us on May 19, 2019.' I waved my index finger between us. 'Didn't Daenerys Stormborn of the House Targaryen, First of Her Name deserve better than that?' I paused, just to let it seep in. 'Didn't we, Rosie?'

'Okay, I'm going to take your side on that one,' she admitted. 'But—'

'No buts,' I stopped her, holding a hand in the air. 'Aaron Blackford is on my blacklist, and he will stay there. Full stop.'

I watched my friend consider my words, mulling over what I'd just said. Or more like passionately stated – whatever.

Rosie deflated with a sigh. 'I just want what's best for you.' She gave me one of those sad smiles that made me think she might be disappointed in me.

'I know.' Like the hugger I was, I launched myself at her, wrapping my arms around her and giving her a good squeeze. Frankly, it probably wasn't her who needed it the most. This whole thing was draining the life out of me. 'But that's not Aaron Blackford.' I let myself enjoy the embrace, my eyelids falling shut for a second or two.

Much to my dismay, when my eyes opened up again, they tracked a towering figure that could only be one man.

'Dammit, Rosie,' I whispered with my arms still around her, making eye contact with the approaching man. 'We've summoned him again.'

I watched Aaron Blackford close the distance with quick strides. His long legs stopped right in front of us. We were still hugging, so I peered at him over Rosie's shoulder.

Aaron took in our embrace, looking somewhere between appalled and engrossed. I couldn't be sure because he did a good job at hiding whatever he was thinking behind that infamous frown.

'What? Who have we summoned?' I heard Rosie say as we disentangled our arms from each other under Aaron's attentive gaze. 'Oh. Him,' she whispered back.

Aaron had definitely heard that, but he didn't react. He confined himself to standing in front of us.

'Hello, Blackford.' I forced a tight-lipped smile. 'Fancy seeing you here.'

'Catalina,' he answered. 'Rosie.' He looked at his watch and then back at us – or rather at me – with one of his eyebrows up. 'Still on lunch break, I see.'

'Break police have arrived,' I muttered under my breath. His other brow joined the one that was almost touching his hairline.

'If you are here to impart any of your lessons on how to become a working robot, I don't have the time.'

'Okay,' he replied simply. Then, he turned toward my friend. 'But it's Rosie whom I have a message for.'

Oh.

I frowned, feeling something tug in my stomach.

'Oh?' my friend echoed.

'Héctor is looking for you, Rosie. Something about a project falling through because someone he called Hand-breaker had a fit,' he explained. 'I've never seen Héctor so worked up.'

My friend sprang up. 'Oliver "Hand-breaker"? It's one of our clients. He . . . he shakes hands so hard, you can literally feel your bones grinding together.' She shook her head. 'That's not important now. Oh crap.' She picked up the few things she had – the corporate badge, office keys, and wallet. 'Oh no, no, no.' A panicky look took over her face. 'That means the conference call is over. I had meant to be downstairs by now, but with this whole mess with Lina and—'

I pinched her arm, stopping her before she said too much.

Aaron perked up – if his eyes narrowing slightly could count as perking up.

Rosie continued, 'About Lina's cat—'

Another pinch. I didn't have a cat, and she knew this. 'Neighbour's cat?' Rosie looked everywhere but at Aaron or me, her cheeks turning pink. 'Her neighbour Bryan, yeah. Yes, that's it. Bryan's cat. Mr . . . Cat.' She shook her head.

Aaron's eyes narrowed further and then jumped to me. He searched my face as my friend stuttered through her obvious lie.

'Lina is taking care of Mr Cat this week because Bryan's grandma is sick and he's out of town. You know how much Lina loves to help.'

I nodded my head slowly, as if Rosie's gibberish had made any sense.

'Aren't you allergic to cats?' Aaron asked, shocking the hell out of me.

'I am.' I blinked. 'How do you . . .' I cleared my throat. *I don't care.* I shook my head. 'It's a hairless cat.'

His hands slipped in his pants pockets, taking a moment to assess that. 'A hairless cat.'

'Like in *Friends*,' I said, trying to sound as casual as I could. 'Rachel's cat. A Sphynx.' I watched Aaron's face, not a sign showing that he knew what I was talking about. 'You live in New York, and you are American, yet you haven't watched *Friends*?' Nothing there. 'Ever? Oh, never mind.'

Aaron stayed silent, and I pretended he hadn't caught us in a blatant lie.

'Okay, phew,' said Rosie, gifting us with a wide and toothy grin. The fake one. 'I really need to go talk to Héctor.'

She looked at me apologetically. I stood up, too, scared of being left behind to explain more about Mr Cat.

'Thank you, Aaron, for coming to get me. That was very' – she glanced at me quickly – *'very* kind of you.'

I rolled my eyes.

Rosie elbowed me softly. 'Wasn't it, Lina?'

She probably thought she was being clever. She wasn't.

'The kindest,' I said with a clipped tone.

'Right. I'll talk to you later.' Rosie rushed toward the staircase, leaving us behind.

An awkward silence surrounded Aaron and me. He cleared his throat. 'Catalina—'

'What's that, Rosie?' I cut him off, pretending my friend was calling for me. *Coward*, I thought. But after everything that had gone down today and having to relive our rocky start during my conversation with Rosie, the last thing I wanted to do was talk to Aaron. 'Oh, you are holding the elevator door for me, you say?' I shot after my friend, not paying attention to how Aaron's lips had pressed in a flat line as I left him behind. 'I'll be right there!'

Then, I turned one last time, quickly glancing over my shoulder. 'Sorry, Blackford, I gotta go. You can send me an email maybe? Yes? Okay, bye.'

When I turned my back to him, Rosie came into view. She was repeatedly pressing on the call button for the elevator.

'Rosalyn Graham!' I called after her, willing my head not to turn and check on the pair of blue eyes I was sure was drilling holes in my back.

CHAPTER FIVE

You knew the universe didn't like you all that much when, after an exhausting week that had been crowned with a catastrophic Friday, it started pouring down the minute you stepped out of the office.

'*Me cago en la leche,*' I cursed under my breath, looking out through the glass of InTech's massive entrance door and taking in the dark clouds crowding the sky, rain falling from it almost violently.

Pulling up my phone, I checked the Weather app and discovered that the summer storm would probably hover over Manhattan for a couple more hours.

Perfect, just perfect.

It was already past eight in the evening, so staying in the office to wait out the rain wasn't an option. I needed my bed. No, what I really needed was a can of Pringles and a pint of Ben & Jerry's. But that wasn't a rendezvous I would be having today. Instead, I'd probably trick my stomach with whatever leftover veggies I had in the fridge.

Thunder rumbled somewhere nearby, returning me to the ugly present.

The rainfall increased, now with gusts of wind veering the falling water from one side to the other.

Still in the safety of InTech's entrance hall, I extracted from my bag the light cardigan I wore in the chilly building and covered my head with it in the hope that it would somehow act as a barrier between the rain and me. Thankfully, the bag I had grabbed that morning, even if not the prettiest, was waterproof.

Looking down at my beautiful and brand-new suede loafers – which, contrary to my bag, were gorgeous and unfortunately not resistant to water – I took in their pristine state one last time. 'Farewell three-hundred-dollar shoes,' I told them with a sigh.

And with that, I pushed the glass door and stepped out into the dark, wet evening as I held my cardigan over my head.

It took me about five seconds under the rain to know that by the time I got to the C Line, I'd be completely and absolutely drenched.

Fantastic, I thought as I speed-walked under the unforgiving downpour. *I only have a forty-five-minute commute to the part of Brooklyn I live in anyway.* Time I'd spend soaked to my bones.

As I turned the corner of the building, another clap of thunder roared somewhere above me, the rainfall increasing and turning my pace slower and clumsier, while more water fell heavily on top of my useless cardigan umbrella.

A gust of wind stuck half my hair to my cheek with a wet smack.

Trying to get the wet locks out of my face with my elbow, I kept hopping around, realizing quickly how bad an idea that was.

My right foot slipped on a puddle, sliding forward, as my other leg remained rooted to the sidewalk. My hands, still holding the cardigan, whirled in the air as I fought to keep my balance.

Please, please, please, please, universe. My eyes closed, not wanting to bear witness to my own fate. *Please, universe, don't let this horrible week end this way.*

My foot drifted one more inch as I held my breath before coming to a miraculous stop.

I opened my eyes. My legs were close to doing the splits, but I was still standing.

Before I could fully straighten and resume my way under the rain, I noticed a car pulling up a short distance in front of me.

I knew someone who owned a vehicle in that same midnight blue.

Keep walking, Catalina, I told myself as I restarted my graceless hopping.

Out of the corner of my eye, I watched the passenger window roll down.

Without moving any closer to the vehicle I strongly suspected belonged to someone I was in no mood to interact with, I turned my body and zeroed in on the driver's outline as I still held the stupid and dripping wet garment above me.

God-freaking-dammit.

Aaron was sitting inside. His body was leaning toward the passenger door, and while I could see his lips moving, I couldn't make out what he was saying, with the noise of the traffic, the wind and the rain hitting the pavement with the characteristic force of a storm.

'What?' I shouted in his direction, not moving an inch.

Aaron waved his hand, probably indicating that I come closer. I stood there, squinting my eyes at him, wet as a drowned rat. He aggressively waggled his pointer back and forth at me.

Oh, hell no.

I watched his expression change to his usual scowl as he mouthed a couple of words that looked a lot like impossible and stubborn.

'I can't hear you!' I howled over the rain, still rooted to the spot.

His lips moved around what I assumed was something like *for fuck's sake*. Unless he was telling me how much he wanted a *milkshake*. Which, judging by that scowl, I wouldn't put any money on.

Rolling my eyes, I stepped closer. Very slowly, so that I wouldn't slip and slide across the sidewalk again. Not in front of him, of all people in New York City.

'Get in the car, Catalina.' I heard Aaron's exasperation clinging to his voice, even over the furious and relentless rain.

Just like I had suspected, he hadn't wanted a milkshake.

'Catalina,' he said as that blue gaze fell back on me, 'get in.'

'It's Lina.' After close to two years of him exclusively using my full name, I knew correcting him was of no use. But I was frustrated. Irritated. Tired. Soaked too. And I hated my full name. Papá – being the history nerd he was – had named both his daughters after two distinguished Spanish monarchs, Isabel and Catalina. My name being the one that never came back in trend in my country. 'And what for?'

His lips parted in disbelief.

'*What for?*' he repeated my words. Then, he shook his head. 'For an improvised trip to Disneyland. What would it be otherwise?'

For a long moment, I looked inside Aaron Blackford's car with what I knew was an expression of genuine confusion.

'Catalina' – I watched his face go from irritation to something that bordered on resignation – 'I am driving you home.' He stretched his arm and opened the door closest to me, as if it were a done deal. 'Before you catch pneumonia or almost break your neck. Again.'

Again.

That last part he had added very slowly.

Blood rushed to my cheeks. 'Oh, thank you,' I gritted through my teeth. I tried to push down how embarrassed I was and plastered a fake smile on my face. 'But there's no need.' I stood in front of the open door, my wet hair sticking to my face once more. I finally dropped the stupid cardigan and started wringing the water out of it. 'I can manage myself. This is just rain. If I've survived this long without breaking my neck, I think I can get home on my own today too. Plus, I'm not in a rush.'

Also, I have been avoiding you since you walked out of my office earlier today.

As I uselessly twisted some more water from my cardigan, I watched his eyebrows knit, regaining his earlier expression as he processed my words.

'What about the cat?'

'What cat?'

His head tilted. 'Mr Cat.'

The water must have been seeping through my skull because it took me an extra second to pin down what he was talking about.

'Your neighbour's furless cat that you are not allergic to,' he said slowly as my eyes widened. 'Ryan's.'

I averted my eyes. 'Bryan. My neighbor's name is Bryan.'

'Not important.'

Ignoring that last remark, I couldn't help but notice a line of cars forming behind Aaron's.

'Get in the car. Come on.'

'No need, really.' One more car piled up. 'Mr Cat will survive a little longer without me.'

Aaron's mouth opened, but before he could say anything, the blaring sound of a horn startled me, making me give a little jump and almost collide against the car's open door.

'Por el amor de Dios!' I squealed.

Turning my head with my heart in my throat, I discovered it was one of New York City's infamous yellow taxis. After a few years of living and working in the metropolis, I had learned my lesson when it came to angry drivers. Or pissed New Yorkers in general. They'd let you know how they felt exactly when they felt it.

Proving my point, a trail of ugly-sounding words was thrown in our direction.

I turned back just in time to watch Aaron curse under his breath. He looked just as furious as the taxi driver.

Another nerve-racking honking noise – this time much, much, much longer – blared in my ears, making me jump again.

'Catalina, now.' Aaron's tone was severe.

I blinked at him for a second too long, a little dazed by everything going on around me.

'Please.'

And before I could even process that word that had slipped out of him, a yellow blur was driving past us, gifting us with a ragey, '*Assholes!*' and blaring his horn with something close to devotion.

Those two words – Aaron's *please* and that *assholes* – propelled my legs into the safety of Aaron's car. With impressive speed, I found myself letting my body fall onto the leather seat with a wet thud and smacking the door shut.

Silence instantly engulfed us, the only sounds the muffled rattle of the rain against the shell of Aaron's car and the dull roar of the engine moving us forward and into the chaos that was New York's traffic.

'Thank you,' I croaked, feeling extremely uncomfortable as I fastened my belt.

Aaron kept his eyes on the road. 'Thank *you*,' he answered, delivering that *you* with sarcasm, 'for not making me get out and carry you inside myself.'

The visual of what he had just said caught me completely off guard. My eyes widened then just as quickly narrowed at him. 'And how in the world did you think that would be a good idea?'

'I was wondering myself, believe me.'

That answer did not make any sense. And for some reason, it made my cheeks heat up. Again.

Turning my head away from him and focusing on the almost-lawless array of moving cars ahead of us, I shifted awkwardly in my seat. Then, I stopped abruptly, noticing how my wet clothes made weird squishy noises against the leather.

'So . . .' I started as I slid to the edge, stretching the seat belt along with me. More noises followed. 'This is a very nice car.' I cleared my throat. 'Is it an air freshener that makes it smell all new and leathery?' I knew it wasn't; the interior was in pristine condition.

'No.'

Moving my ass further up to the very end with yet another

squishy sound, I cleared my throat. Straightening my back, I opened my mouth, but nothing came out, not when my mind was stuck on the fact that my clothes were probably ruining the most-likely expensive fabric underneath them.

This was a bad idea. I should never have climbed in his car. I should have walked.

'Catalina,' I heard Aaron from my left side, 'have you ever been inside a moving vehicle before?'

My eyebrows wrinkled. 'What? Of course. Why do you ask?' I queried from my perch at the edge of the copilot's seat. My knees were touching the dashboard.

He slid me a glance, his eyes assessing my position.

Oh.

'Well, just so you know,' I added quickly, 'this is how I always sit. I love watching everything from up close.' I pretended to be engrossed by the traffic. 'I looooove rush-hour. It's so—'

We came to a sudden halt, and my head and whole body were pushed forward. So much that my eyes closed on instinct. I could already taste the flavour of the PVC that covered the refined lines of the dashboard. The elegant details in the wood too.

Although something stopped me midway.

'Jesus,' I heard being muttered.

One eye opened, taking in the delivery truck crossed in front of us. Then, my other eye popped open, too, and my gaze slid down, finding out why my face wasn't tattooed onto the polished surface of Aaron's dashboard.

A hand. A big one, all five fingers splayed across my collarbone and ... well, chest.

Before I could blink, I was being pushed back, an array of squeaks accompanying the motion. Right until my whole back was flush against the seat rest.

'Stay right there,' came the order from my left as his fingers heated my skin through my drenched blouse. 'If you are worried about the seat, it's just water. It will dry off.' Aaron's words weren't reassuring. They couldn't be when he sounded just as angry as a few minutes ago. If not a little more.

He retrieved his hand, the movement brisk and stiff.

I swallowed, grabbing on to the seat belt that now rested where his palm had been. 'I don't want to ruin it.'

'You won't.'

'Okay,' I said, stealing a quick glance at him.

His gaze was on the road, shooting daggers at whoever had been responsible for that little mishap.

'Thanks.'

Then, we were moving again. The car was filled with silence while Aaron's attention remained on his task and mine took the chance to scatter.

I surprised myself, thinking of Rosie's words.

'*I don't think Aaron is all that bad,*' she had said earlier today. But why had that thought waited until right now to seep in?

To sound so loud and clear in my head? It wasn't like Mr Sunshine here was being any nicer than he usually was.

Although he had sort of just saved me from the rain. And a good blow to the head.

Silently sighing, I cursed myself for what I was about to do. 'Thank you for printing out those papers for me, by the way,' I said quietly, fighting the impulse to take it back immediately. But I didn't. I could be diplomatic. At least, right now. 'It was very nice of you, Aaron.' That last part had me wincing, the admission feeling funny on my tongue.

I turned to look at him, taking in his hard profile. I watched the tight line of his jaw relax a little.

'You're welcome, Catalina.' He kept his gaze on the road.

Whoa. Look at us. That was . . . very civil.

Before I could delve any more into that, a shiver crawled all the way down my back, making me shudder. I hugged my middle in the hope of getting warmer inside the wet clusterfuck that was my clothing.

Aaron's hand shot to the console, changing the temperature setting and switching on the heating of my seat. I immediately felt the pleasant hot air brushing my ankles and arms, my legs growing gradually warmer.

'Better?'

'Much. Thank you.' I faced him with a small smile.

His head turned, and he searched my face with a sceptical expression.

It was almost as if he were waiting for me to add something.

I rolled my eyes. 'Don't let all these thank yous get to your head, Blackford.'

'I wouldn't dare.' He lifted one of his hands from the wheel. And I swore there was a hint of humour in his voice. 'Just wondering if I should enjoy it or if I should ask if you are okay.'

'That's a good question, but I don't think it's one I can answer.' I shrugged my shoulders, fighting the snappy comeback rising to my tongue. I sighed. 'Honestly? I'm soaked to my bones, and I'm hungry and tired. So, I'd enjoy it if I were you.'

'That bad of a day?' That tiny pinch of humour was gone.

Sensing the start of another shudder, I burrowed myself into the heated fabric of the seat. 'More like a bad week.'

Aaron hmmed in response. It was a deep sound, a little like a rumble.

'This might not surprise you, but I have been close to murdering a few people this week,' I confessed, taking the truce I had imposed as a green light for venting to him. 'And you are not even at the top of the list.'

A very light and very subdued snort came from him. Truce and

all, I guessed I was allowed to admit that I liked it. It made my lips
bend in a smile.

'I . . .' He trailed off, considering something. 'I don't know how
to take that either. Should I be offended or grateful?'

'You can be both, Blackford. Plus, there's time until the day is
over. You can still claim your rightful place as the number one
person who awakens my most murderous side.'

We stopped at a light. Aaron's head turned slowly, and I was
caught off guard by how light his expression was. His ocean eyes
were clear and his face more relaxed than I'd ever seen it. We stared
at each other for two or three long seconds. Another shiver curled
at the nape of my neck.

I blamed the wet clothes.

Without missing a beat and as if he had eyes on the side of his
head, he turned to the road as the light changed to green. 'I'll need
directions from this point on.'

Puzzled by the implications of his request, my head spun in the
other direction. I took in the layout of the wide avenue we were
driving through. 'Oh,' I murmured. 'We are in Brooklyn.'

I had been so . . . distracted that I had forgotten about telling
Aaron where I lived. Although he wasn't too off track. Or at all.

'You live in this part of the city, right? North Central Brooklyn?'

'Yeah,' I blurted. 'Bed-Stuy.' I confirmed with a nod of my head.
'I just . . . how did you know?'

'You complain.'

What? I blinked at his explanation.

He continued, 'This way okay, or should I turn?'

Clearing my throat, I stumbled over my words. 'Yes, stay on
Humboldt Street, and I'll let you know when to turn.'

'Okay.'

I gripped my seat belt, feeling a little too warm all of a sudden.
'So, I complain?' I mumbled.

'About the commute,' Aaron answered calmly. I opened my mouth, but he continued, 'You have mentioned that it takes you forty-five minutes to get to the part of Brooklyn you live in.' He paused thoughtfully. 'You rant about it almost every day.'

My lips clipped shut. I did complain but not to him. I pretty much vented to everybody else. Yeah, half the time, Aaron was somewhere around, but I never thought he was interested in what I had to say if it didn't concern work. Or if it concerned *me*.

He shocked me by asking, 'Who's made the top besides me then? The list with the people you might have wanted to murder this week.'

'Huh ...' I trailed off, surprised that he was interested enough to ask.

'I want to know my competition,' he said, sending my head swivelling in his direction. 'It's only fair.'

Was that a joke? Oh my God, it was, wasn't it?

Studying his profile, I felt myself smiling warily. 'Let me see.' I could play this game. 'All right, so Jeff' – I counted with my fingers – 'my cousin Charo' – a second finger – 'and Gerald. Yes, definitely him too.' I let my hands drop to my lap. 'Hey, look at that; you didn't even make the top three, Blackford. Congratulations.'

Frankly, I was genuinely surprised myself.

I watched how his brows furrowed.

'What's the problem with your cousin?'

'Oh, nothing.' I waved my hand in the air, thinking of what Mamá had said. What that Sherlock Holmes wannabe had said about not finding photographic evidence of my made-up boyfriend. 'Just some family drama.'

Aaron seemed to consider that for a long moment, in which we drove in silence. I used the time to look out the passenger window, watching the blurry streets of Brooklyn through the droplets running down the glass.

'Gerald is a prick,' came from the man in the driver's seat. Eyes wide, I looked over at him. His profile was hard, serious.

And I didn't think I'd ever heard Aaron curse.

'One day, he'll get what he deserves. I'm shocked that hasn't happened yet, if I'm being honest. If it were up to me ...' He shook his head.

'If it were up to you, what? What would you do?' I watched a muscle jump in his jaw. He didn't answer, so I averted my gaze, letting it fall back onto the passing traffic. This conversation was pointless. And I was too drained of energy to attempt to have it anyway. 'It's all right. It's not like it's my first rodeo with him.'

'What does that mean?' Aaron's voice had a strange edge.

Trying not to pay attention to that, I answered as honestly as I could without getting into too much detail. I didn't want Aaron's pity or compassion. 'He hasn't been exactly pleasant and agreeable ever since I got promoted to team leader.' I shrugged, clasping my hands in my lap. 'It's like he can't compute why someone like me has the same position he does.'

'Someone like you?'

'Yeah.' I exhaled heavily through my mouth, my breath fogging up the glass of the window for a couple of seconds. 'A woman. At first, I thought it was because I was the youngest team leader and he was sceptical about me. It would be fair. Then, it also crossed my mind that he might have an issue with me being a foreigner. I know a few of the guys used to make fun of my accent. I once overheard Tim call me Sofia Vergara in a mocking way. Which, honestly, I took as a compliment. Having half the curves or the wit that woman has wouldn't be the worst thing in the world. Not that I'm unhappy with my body. I'm okay with being ... the way I am.' Normal. Plain. And I was. Everything about me was pretty standard where I came from. Brown eyes and brown hair. On the shorter side. Not thin, but not fat. Wide hips but rather small bust. We were millions of women that fit that description. So, I was ... average. Not a big deal. 'It wouldn't hurt, losing a couple of pounds for the wedding, but I don't think whatever I'm doing is working.'

A sound came from my side, making me realize that I had not only overshared, but I had also rambled my way out of the topic at hand with Aaron, who didn't even compute small talk.

'Anyway' – I cleared my throat – 'Gerald doesn't like me being where I am, and it has nothing to do with me not being an American or me being younger than him. But that's how the world works, and it will work that way until it doesn't anymore.'

More silence followed my words.

I peeked at him, curious to know what it was that he was thinking that kept him from lecturing me or telling me that I was whining or if he did not care what I had to say. But he only looked mad. Again. His jaw was all bunched up, and his brows furrowed. Out of the corner of my eye, I saw the intersection that signalled my street. 'Oh, take the next right, please,' I instructed Aaron, taking my eyes off him. 'It's at the end of that street.'

Aaron followed my directions in silence, still looking like he was bothered by something I had said. Thankfully, my block came into view before I was tempted to ask.

'There.' I pointed with my finger. 'The building on the right. The one with the dark red front door.'

Aaron pulled up and stationed the car on a free spot that had somehow been magically waiting right in front of my apartment. My gaze followed his right hand as he killed the engine.

Silence engulfed the confined space of the vehicle.

Swallowing hard, I looked around. I tried to focus on the characteristics of the brownstones of this borough of Brooklyn, the few trees scattered along the street, the pizzeria on the corner – where I usually picked up dinner when I was feeling lazy. Or just hungry. I focused on everything, except the way in which the silence pressed on me, the more I waited inside the car.

Fumbling with my seat belt and feeling the tops of my ears heat for no reason, I opened my mouth. 'All right, I'm going to—'

'Have you thought about my offer?' Aaron said.

My fingers froze on my seat belt. My head lifted very slowly until I was facing him.

For the first time since I had placed my drenched ass inside, I let myself really look at Aaron. Study all of him. His profile was lit by the dim glow coming from the few lamps perched on my street. The storm had somehow died, but the sky was still dark and angry, as if this were just a short pause and the worst was yet to come.

We found ourselves pretty much in the dark, so I couldn't be sure if his eyes were the deep shade of blue that usually told me he was serious and all business – which I hoped wasn't the case – or that lighter blue that preceded a battle. The only thing I could notice was how his shoulders seemed tense. A little wider than usual. They almost dwarfed the otherwise spacious interior of the car. Hell, looking at him now, his whole body seemed to do exactly that. Even the distance between his seat and the steering wheel was overly wide to accommodate his long legs. So much that I bet a person could easily fit in there.

By the time I found myself wondering what he would say if I jumped on his lap to test my theory, Aaron cleared his throat. Probably twice.

'Catalina.' He drew my attention back to his face.

'Do you . . .' I trailed off, a little shaken by the fact that my mind had taken me to Aaron's lap. *I am ridiculous*. 'Do you want to pee or something?'

Aaron frowned and rearranged his body in his seat, angling it toward me. 'No.' He looked at me weirdly. 'I'll probably regret asking this, but why do you think I want to?'

'You are parked in my street. In front of my building. I thought maybe you needed to use the bathroom. And I hoped it wouldn't be number two, honestly.'

I watched his chest inflate with a deep breath and then release all the air out.

'No, I don't need to use the bathroom.'

His gaze studied me, as if he couldn't figure out why I was there, inside his car. And in the meantime, I wondered exactly the same thing.

My fingers finally made work of the seat belt, snapping it free as I felt his eyes boring holes into my side.

'So, what's your answer?'

My whole body froze. 'My answer?'

'To my offer. Have you thought about it? And please' – *dammit, that word again* – 'stop pretending you don't remember. I know you do.'

My heart tripped, tumbling down for a horrifying second. 'I'm not pretending,' I murmured, doing exactly what he had asked me not to.

But in my defence, I needed to win some time to figure this out. How to . . . deal with the situation. And more importantly, to figure out *why*.

Why was he offering? Why was he insisting? Why was he going through the hassle? Why did he think he could be the one to help me? Why did he sound like he meant it? Why . . .

Just *why*?

Expecting a sarcastic comment, or a roll of his blue eyes at my playing dumb, or even for him to retract his words because I was being difficult on purpose and he never had patience for that, I braced myself. But of all the things I expected him to go with, he went with the only one I wasn't ready for.

A defeated sigh left his lips.

I blinked.

'Your sister's wedding. I'll be your date,' Aaron said. As if he'd be willing to repeat himself as much as he possibly could as long as I gave him an answer.

Or as if he were offering something simple. Something that would obtain a straightforward answer that didn't require much consideration. Something like, *Would you like dessert, Lina? Why, yes, of course. I'll have the cheesecake, thank you.* But Aaron's offer was everything but simple and as far away from cheesecake as one could get.

'Aaron' – I shot him a look – 'you can't be serious.'

'What makes you think I'm not?'

How about everything? 'Well, for one, you are you. And I am me. This is us, Aaron. You just can't be,' I repeated. Because he couldn't be.

'I'm perfectly serious, Catalina.'

I blinked. Again. Then, I laughed bitterly. 'Is this a joke, Blackford? I know you struggle with that, and let me tell you, you shouldn't go around making jokes without a real feel of what's funny and what's not. So, I'm going to help you here,' I looked at him straight in the eye. 'This is not funny, Aaron.'

He frowned. 'Not joking.'

I kept staring at him for a long moment.

Nope. *No.* He couldn't not be joking. He couldn't be serious either.

Bringing my hands to my tangled and wet hair, I shoved it back a little too briskly. I was ready to get out of here. And yet, I remained rooted to the spot.

'Did you come up with any other options? A better option than me?'

Both his questions hit the mark I assumed he'd aimed at because I felt my shoulders fall in defeat.

'Do you even have any other options?'

No, I did not. And the fact that he was being so blunt about it didn't feel all that great either. My cheeks heated, and I remained silent.

'I'm going to take that as a no,' he said. 'You have no one.'

And that felt a little like a kick to the stomach.

I tried really hard to keep the hurt off my face – I did. Because I didn't want Aaron Blackford to get a glimpse of how pathetic and silly his words had made me feel.

How lonely I must be when my only option was a colleague who didn't even like me all that much in the first place.

But he wasn't wrong. And as much as it hurt to admit it, at the end of the day, I had no one else. Just Aaron. He – and only he – completed my list of options. In a world where I'd consider taking him to Spain as my made-up boyfriend, that was.

Unless—

Oh my God. Holy shit. Did he notice – understand – what happened back in my office? That I accidentally told my mother that my boyfriend's name was Aaron?

No. I shook my head. *No way. Impossible.*

'I don't understand why you're doing this,' I told him with what I was sure was the most sincerity I had ever spoken to him.

He sighed, the air leaving his body almost softly. 'And I don't understand why it's so hard to believe that I would.'

'Aaron' – a bitter chuckle left my lips – 'we don't like each other. And it's okay because we couldn't be any more ... different. Incompatible. And if we barely manage to share a space for more than a handful of minutes without bickering or wanting to bite each other's heads off, why in the world would you believe this was a good idea?'

'We can get along just fine.'

I bit back another laugh. 'Okay, that was actually funny. Good job, Blackford.'

'Not joking.' He scowled. 'And I am your only option,' he shot back.

Maldita sea. He was still right about that.

My back leaned against the closed passenger door as he continued delivering blows, 'Do you want to attend that wedding alone? Because I'm the one who can fix that.'

Ugh, he truly believed I was that desperate and resourceless.

Yes, a voice said in my head. *Because you are both those things.*

'Okay,' I said very slowly. 'Let's say I entertain this ridiculous idea. If I accept your offer and let you do this, what's in it for you?' I crossed my arms, noticing how my still-wet clothes were sticking to my skin. 'I know you, and I know you don't do stuff just for the sake of it. You must have motivation. A reason. A goal. You must want something in exchange; otherwise, you would never help me. You are not that kind of person. At least, not with me.'

Aaron's head reared back, almost unnoticeably, but I was sure I had seen it. He was quiet for a long moment, and I could almost hear the wheels in his head turning.

'You could do the same for me,' he finally said.

The same? 'You'll need to be more specific, Blackford. Is your sister getting married too?' I paused in thought. 'Do you even have siblings? I don't know, but, well, I guess it doesn't matter if you do or don't. Is there a wedding you want me to go to as your date?'

'No,' he answered. And I didn't know if he was talking about having siblings or not. But then he added, 'Not for a wedding, but you could be my date.'

Be his date?

Why did it sound so ... so ... different when it was him asking me? Why did it sound so freaking different when Aaron was the one needing someone and not me?

'I—' I stopped myself, feeling self-conscious for a reason I didn't understand. 'Do you need a date? Like' – I pointed a finger at him – 'you? A woman to be your date?'

'I don't intend to show up with a chimpanzee, like you suggested. So, yes, a woman.' He paused, that scowl taking shape slowly. 'You.'

My lips snapped closed and then opened back up, probably making me look like a fish. 'So, you want me' – I pointed at myself – 'to pretend to be your date?'

'I didn't say that—'

'Don't you have a girlfriend?' I interrupted him, the question bursting out of me.

'No, I don't.'

I watched his eyes close for a heartbeat, his head shaking once.

'Not even a casual someone you are seeing?'

He gave me another shake.

'A fling?'

He sighed. 'No.'

'Let me guess. No time for that?' I regretted it as soon as it had left my lips. But frankly, I was curious. So, perhaps, if he answered, I wouldn't regret the question completely.

His shoulders shrugged lightly, his back relaxing slightly. As if he had accepted that he'd have to give me an answer or I'd press for one. 'I have time, Catalina. Plenty of time in fact.' Even in the darkness of the car, I saw those ocean-blue eyes of his pin me down with an honesty I hadn't been prepared for. 'I'm simply saving it for someone who's worth it.'

Well, that was incredibly smug. Sort of conceited too. And shockingly, kind of . . . sexy.

Whoa. I shook my head. *Nope.* The only S-word Aaron Blackford could ever be thought of as was . . . sarcastic. Scornful. Secretive. Stoic. Maybe even sour. But not sexy. *Nope.*

'Is that why you don't have a date already?' I managed to ask him next, feeling the need to sound indifferent and cold. 'Because your standards are as high as the sky?'

Aaron didn't miss a beat. 'Is that why you have no one to take to that wedding?'

'I . . .' I wished that were the reason instead of plain stupidity and being a compulsive liar with no instinct of self-preservation. 'It's complicated. I have reasons.' I let my hands drop in my lap, keeping my eyes on the section of the console in front of me.

'Whoever claims to act without having a reason pushing them to do so is lying.'

'So, what's pushing you to do this?' I asked him with my eyes still on the dark and smooth material that adorned the interior of the car. 'What pushed you to ask me, out of all people, to pretend to be your date?'

'It's a long story.' Even if I wasn't looking at him, I heard him exhale. It sounded as tired as I felt. 'It's a social commitment. I can't promise you it will be fun, but it's for a good cause.' He paused for moment, in which I didn't speak and I limited myself to take in the scarce details he had given me. 'I'll tell you everything – if you accept, of course.'

My head shot in his direction, and I found Aaron's blue eyes already on me. They were filled with a little challenge. And a little expectation.

He was baiting me. Offering me an insight into Aaron Blackford's unknown – and presumed to be nonexistent – personal life. He knew I'd want to know.

Well played, Blackford.

'Why me?' I asked him, being drawn to the light like a stupid moth. 'Why not anyone else?'

His gaze didn't waver when he answered, 'Because if all these months we have worked together have taught me anything, it's that you are the only woman I know crazy enough to do something like this. You might be my only option too.'

I wouldn't take that as a compliment because it hadn't been one.

He had just called me *crazy*. But shit. Something about it – about the way he had said it, about this bizarre day and this unexpected turn of events in which I had found out he also needed someone, just like I did – seemed to wear me down.

'You do know that you'll have to fly to Spain with me for a whole weekend, right?'

A simple nod. 'Yes.'

'And in exchange, you want just one night? One single night of me pretending to be your date?'

He nodded again, and this time, something solidified in his stare. In the way his jaw was clamped and his lips formed a determined line. I knew that look. I had argued against that look on many occasions.

Then, he spoke, 'Do we have a deal?'

Have we really lost our minds?

We gazed at each other in silence as my lips played with the answer, moving wordlessly until they didn't. 'Okay.' There was a big chance we had really lost our minds, yes. 'Deal.'

Something flickered across Aaron's face. 'Deal,' he repeated.

Yep, we have definitely lost them.

This deal between us was uncharted territory. And the air was suddenly thick with something that made it hard for me to take in a full breath.

'All right. Okay. Good.' I brushed a finger over the surface of the impeccable dashboard. 'So, we have a deal.' I inspected an imaginary dust particle, feeling my anxiety rise with every extra second I spent inside. 'There's a mountain of details we need to discuss.' Namely the fact that he'd need to pretend to be the man I was supposedly dating and not just my wedding date. Or the fact that he'd have to pretend he was in *love* with me. 'But we can focus on you first. When is this social commitment I'm helping you with?'

'Tomorrow. I'll pick you up at seven p.m.'

My whole body came to a halt. 'Tomorrow?'

Aaron shifted in his seat, facing away from me. 'Yes. Be ready at seven. Sharp,' he remarked. I was so ... out of it that I didn't even roll my eyes at him when he continued shooting orders, 'Evening gown ideally.' His right hand went to the car's ignition. 'Now, go home and rest, Catalina. It's late, and you look like you could use some sleep.' His left hand fell heavily on the steering wheel. 'I'll tell you everything else tomorrow.'

Somehow, Aaron's words registered only after I closed the front door to my building behind me. And it was only a few seconds later, right after Aaron's car roared to life and faded away, that I allowed myself to really process what it meant.

I'd be going on a date tomorrow. A fake date. With Aaron Blackford. And I needed an evening gown.

CHAPTER SIX

I was not panicking. *Nope.*

My apartment was a war zone, but I was chill. The clothing explosion? Under control.

I looked at myself in the generous mirror placed against one of the walls in my studio apartment with what I promised would be the last outfit I tried on. It was not that I didn't have anything to wear; my problem was far simpler. The root of my predicament – and as of now, the biggest headache of the month, and all things considered, that was saying something – was that I didn't know what I was dressing for.

'Be ready at seven. Sharp. Evening gown ideally.'

Why I hadn't pressed for more details, I did not have the slightest idea.

Except for the fact that it was a mistake I was unfortunately familiar with. This was how I approached things. I rushed into them. The reason why I'd somehow managed to weave my existence into knots I didn't know how to untangle.

Evidence number one: *the lie.*

Evidence number two: what the lie had led to.

In other words, the deal I had struck with someone I would never, not even in my wildest dreams – no, nightmares – have imagined needing. Or being needed by. Aaron Blackford.

'Loca,' I muttered to myself as I unzipped another garment. Was

it even an evening gown? *'Me he vuelto loca. He perdido la maldita cabeza.'*

Slipping out of it and throwing it onto the bed with the rest of the discarded dresses, I reached for my robe. The fluffy pink one because I needed all the comfort I could get and I couldn't think of any other way to get it. It was either this or stuffing my mouth with cookies.

Taking in the state of my apartment, I massaged my temples. Not having walls separating the living room from the bedroom and kitchen areas was something I usually loved. Something I liked to see as an advantage of living in an open studio space – even if limitedly small, since this was still Brooklyn. But inspecting the mess I had made of the entire apartment, I sort of hated not living somewhere roomier. Somewhere with walls that would stop me from wrecking the *whole* place.

There were clothes, shoes, and bags scattered everywhere – on the bed, sofa, chairs, floor, coffee table. Nothing had been spared. The usually tidy apartment that I had so carefully decorated in whites and creams with some boho details here and there – like the beautiful woven rug that had cost me more than I'd ever admit – resembled a fashion battlefield more than a home.

I wanted to scream.

Tying the belt of my robe tighter, I grabbed my phone from the top of my dresser.

Two hours until seven *sharp*, and I was helpless. Outfit-less. Because I didn't have any dress that resembled a gown. Because I was dumb. Because I didn't know what I was dressing for and I hadn't asked.

I didn't even have Aaron's phone number to text him an SOS and a few hostile emojis to make myself clear. It wasn't like I had ever found pleasure in fraternizing with the enemy, so I had never needed his number.

Not until now, apparently.

Throwing my phone on top of a discarded pile of garments, I headed for the snug space that was my living room. Grabbing my laptop from the round ecru coffee table I had picked up from a flea market a few weeks ago, I placed the device on my lap and let my body fall onto the sofa.

Once settled in the padded cushions, I logged in to my corporate email account.

It was my last resort. With a little bit of luck, his workaholic ass would be sitting in front of his laptop on a Saturday. And wasn't this ... deal we had made a little like a business transaction? It had to be. We weren't friends – or even friendly – so that didn't leave room for more than a purely I scratch your back, you scratch mine kind of deal. A favour between colleagues.

With no more time to waste, I opened a new email and started typing.

From: cmartin@InTech.com
To: ablackford@InTech.com
Subject: Urgent Info Needed!

Mr Blackford,

I was irritated – at myself yes, but also at him – and I wasn't in a first name basis kind of mood.

As per our last conversation, I'm still waiting for you
to disclose the details of our upcoming meeting.
I find myself without all sources of information,
which will consequently lead to an unsuccessful
completion of the contract discussed.

I had watched all seasons of *Gossip Girl*, and I knew the terrible consequences of wearing the wrong thing to a 'social commitment' in New York freaking City.

> As no doubt you are aware of, it is of utmost
> importance that you share all info needed at your
> earliest convenience.
>> Please get back to me ASAP.
>> Warm regards,
>> Lina Martín

Smirking at myself, I hit Send and watched my email leave my outbox. Then, I stared at my screen for a long minute, waiting for his answer to pop up in my inbox. By the third time I unsuccessfully refreshed my email, the smirk was long gone. By the fifth, little drops of sweat – which were partly due to the fact that I was clad in a winter robe – started forming on the back of my neck.

What if he didn't answer?

Or even worse, what if all this wasn't more than a prank? A mean way to mess with my head and make me believe he'd help me. What if he'd *Carrie*'d me?

No, Aaron wouldn't do that, a voice in my head said.

But why wouldn't he though? I had more than enough evidence compiled to prove that Aaron was very much capable of something like that.

Did I even know him at all? He attended 'social commitments' that had to do with 'good causes', for crying out loud. I did not know him.

Fuck. I needed those cookies. I'd indulge.

When I returned to my laptop, cookie package in hand and mouth full of sugary and buttery comfort, Aaron's answer was waiting for me. A tiny sigh of relief left my lips.

Biting on a new cookie, I clicked on Aaron's email.

From: ablackford@InTech.com
To: cmartin@InTech.com
Subject: Re: Urgent Info Needed!

I'll be there in an hour.
    Best,
    Aaron

'What in the f—'

A fit of coughs prevented me from finishing that, the mouthful I had been chewing on getting stuck in my throat and not moving anywhere.

Aaron was coming. To my apartment. In one hour. Which was an hour before we had agreed he'd pick me up.

Grabbing some water from the kitchen, I looked around, taking in the chaos. *'Mierda.'*

I shouldn't care; I knew I shouldn't. But Aaron seeing this? Hell no. I'd rather choke on another cookie than give him ammunition against me. I wouldn't hear the end of it.

I placed the glass back on the counter, and without losing a second more, I put myself to work. One hour. I had sixty minutes – and knowing Aaron, it wouldn't be a second more or less – to fix this wardrobe mayhem.

And just like that, it took me the whole hour to leave the apartment presentable enough, so when the doorbell rang, not only had I not had any time to change into something that didn't make me look like a human-sized Furby, but my frustration had also only increased.

'Stupidly punctual man,' I muttered under my breath as I stomped toward my apartment door. 'Always on time.'

I buzzed him in.

Fixing the messy bun atop my head, I tried to cool off.

He's helping you. Be nice, I told myself. *You need him.*

A knock on the door.

I waited two seconds and took a deep breath, readying myself to be as nice as I could manage.

Grabbing on to the handle, I arranged my expression into a neutral one and threw the door open.

'Aaron,' I said in a clipped tone. 'I . . .' I was about to say . . . something else, but whatever that was vanished. Along with that neutral expression I had been going for. My lips parted, jaw hanging open. 'I–' I started again, not finding any words. I cleared my throat. 'I – hi. Hello. Whoa. Okay.'

Aaron stared back at me with a funny look while I simply blinked, hoping that my eyes hadn't grown too big in my face.

Although how could they not? How couldn't any pair of eyes not grow two sizes bigger at the sight of what was in front of me?

Because that wasn't Aaron. No. Nuh-uh. Here was a man I had never seen before. A version of Aaron that was different from the only one I knew.

This Aaron was . . . drop-dead gorgeous. And not in an easy-on-the-eyes way. This Aaron was elegant. Classy. Sleek. Attractive in an overwhelming *ladies and gents, grab your fans* kind of way.

Shit, why did he look like that? Where was the Aaron in dull slacks and a boring button-down that I had blacklisted and filed under do not touch? How in the world had it taken me nothing more than a single look at him to stutter like a schoolgirl?

Blinking, I found the answer right in front of me. That tall, lean body that I shouldn't have been noticing this much was clad in a black suit. No, it wasn't a suit. It was a tuxedo. A freaking tuxedo that belonged on a red carpet and not in the door to my apartment in Bed-Stuy, if you asked me.

Nothing about him belonged here with me. Not his midnight hair, not the crisp white shirt and bow tie, not that deep blue gaze that surveyed me and my reaction, not the freaking movie-star tux, and certainly not those dark brows that were drawing together on his forehead.

'What the hell are you wearing?' I asked in a breath. 'Is this a joke? What did I tell you about trying to be funny, Aaron?'

'What am *I* wearing?' I watched his eyes leave mine and travel down my neck, looking me up and down a couple of times. 'Me?'

Something changed in his expression, as if he couldn't understand what he was seeing.

'Yeah.' Feeling extremely exposed and uncomfortable, I waited for his gaze to return to my face, not knowing what else to say or do. 'What is *that*?' I whispered loudly for a reason I couldn't fathom.

'I feel the obligation to ask you the same question. Because I wasn't specific.' He pointed a long finger in my general direction. 'But I imagined you were smarter than to assume I'd take you to a slumber party.'

I swallowed, fully aware my ears were turning red. But I shook my head. This was actually good. This Aaron I could deal with. I knew how to do that. Unlike the other version that had punched the breath out of my lungs. That I had no idea what to do with.

I squared my shoulders. 'Oh, you think I should really change?' I grabbed the hem of my pink robe, trying not to think of how ridiculous I was actually feeling and hiding that emotion behind all my bravado instead. 'I wouldn't want to show up overdressed to the slumber party you mentioned. Do you think there will be any snacks?

He seemed to consider that for a long moment. 'How are you not boiling up inside there? That's a lot of velour for such a tiny person.'

Velour?

'And that's a deep knowledge of fabrics for someone whose wardrobe is made of two different pieces of clothing.'

An emotion flickered across his face, one I didn't catch in time. He closed his eyes very briefly.

He was irritated. His patience slipping away from him. I could tell. *We won't make it. We are doomed.*

'First,' he said, regaining his composure, 'you blatantly ogle me.' That sent a wave of heat straight to my cheeks. *Busted.*

'Then, you reprimand me for what I'm wearing. And now, you criticize my sense of style. Are you going to let me in, or do you always keep guests outside your door while you insult them?'

'Who said you were a guest?' Not hiding my irritation at him calling me out, I turned around and walked away, leaving him standing before the entrance to my apartment. 'You invited yourself over,' I said over my shoulder. 'I guess you don't mind letting yourself in either, huh, big boy?'

Big boy? I closed my eyes, extremely thankful to be facing the other way.

Still not able to believe I had really called Aaron Blackford *big boy*, I headed for the kitchen area of my studio and opened the fridge. The cool air graced my skin, making me feel only slightly better. I stared into it for a full minute, and when I finally turned, I did so with a fake smile.

Aaron Blackford – and his tuxedo – leaned against the narrow island that delimited my kitchen and living room spaces. His blue gaze was somewhere above my knees. Still studying my attire, which he seemed to find so outrageously intriguing.

It bothered me, I realized. The way he looked at it made me feel inadequate even though I was at home and he was the intruder who had shown up earlier than we had agreed. It was stupid, but it reminded me of how small he had made me feel all those months ago when I overheard him talking to Jeff. Or how he had almost thrown that mug I had gotten him as a welcome gift at my face. Or how all the remarks and jabs that came after that had never stopped bothering me.

Rosie had been right; I was incapable of letting it go. I was still holding my grudge like my life depended on it. Like my grudge was a door floating on the ocean and I was out of life jackets.

'It seems rather inappropriate for summer.' Aaron nodded at my robe.

He wasn't wrong. I was boiling up, but I had needed the comfort.

I imitated him and leaned on the kitchen counter behind me. 'Can I offer you something to drink, *Anna Wintour*? Or would you like to point out any other way in which my robe is outrageous instead?'

I watched his lips twitch, fighting a smile. Me, on the other hand, I found none of this remotely funny.

'How about water?' He did not move a single muscle besides the corners of his lips, which were still battling against that smile.

'You know' – I retrieved a water bottle and placed it beside him. Then, I grabbed another one for myself – 'you could have just emailed me back. You didn't need to show up here this early.'

'I know.' *Of course he did.* 'I did you a favour, coming here ahead of time.'

'*A favour?*' My eyes narrowed to thin slits. 'Doing me a favour would have included showing up with your pockets filled with churros.'

'I'll try my best to remember that,' he said, sounding like he meant it. And just as I was opening my mouth to ask him what that was supposed to mean, he continued, 'Why didn't you call me instead of sending that ... intricate email? It would have saved us both some time, *Miss Martín*.' That last part he added with a scowl.

Ha, I knew that Mr Blackford would strike a nerve.

'Okay, first of all, I didn't ask you to come here. So, that's on you.' I opened the lid of my bottle and took a gulp of water. 'And secondly, how would I have called you if I don't have your number, smart-ass?'

I looked at him over the bottle.

Aaron's dark brows knitted. 'You should have it. On our last division's team-building event, we passed along all our private phone numbers. I have yours. I have everyone's.'

I slowly lowered the bottle and screwed the lid on. 'Well, I don't have yours.' I had refused to save Aaron's number because, again, I was a grudge-holder. Something that didn't make me feel all that great right now, but that didn't change the truth. 'Why would I have needed it anyway?'

I watched him take in my words for a moment, and then he shook his head lightly. Straightening, he leaned away from the kitchen island.

'What was so important then?' He got us back on track. 'What details do you need *disclosed* with so much urgency?'

'I can't pick an outfit if I don't know where we are going, Blackford,' I pointed out with a shrug. 'It's like *Dressing Up for Dummies* 101.'

'But I told you.' One of his eyebrows rose. 'A social commitment.'

'That's what you said.' I placed the bottle on the counter and then brought my hands together. 'And it wasn't enough information. I need a few more details.'

'An evening gown,' the hardheaded, blue-eyed man answered. 'That should have been enough information to pick a dress.'

I brought a hand to my fluffy pink chest and clutched my metaphoric pearls. 'Enough information?' I repeated very slowly.

A nod. 'Yes.'

I sneered, not believing my ears. He genuinely thought he was right about this. 'One- and two-worded responses are not *enough information*, Aaron.'

Especially after seeing that he looked ready to jump into an Upper East Side gala where people air-kissed each other and talked about their vacations in the Hamptons. I certainly didn't have anything like that in my wardrobe.

'What's so hard to understand about the words evening and gown?' His hand absently went to the sleeve of his tux jacket. 'They are gowns for evening events. Dresses.'

I blinked.

'Are you really explaining that to me?' I started to feel a new wave of frustration rush to my head. 'You are just . . .' I continued, fisting my hands, edging very close to really throwing something at him. '*Ugh.*'

Aaron's hands went to his pants pockets as he eyed me, looking all . . . handsome and classy in that goddamn tux.

Something must have bubbled all the way to my face because the way he looked at me changed.

'It's a charity event. A fundraiser that takes place every year,' he explained.

My lips parted at that crucial piece of information. 'We will have to drive into Manhattan – Park Avenue.'

No, no, no, no. That sounded fancy.

'It's a black-tie thing, so you'll need to dress up. A formal evening gown.' His gaze went up and down my body with doubt, finally settling back on my face. 'Just like I said.'

'Aaron,' I gritted out through my teeth. '*Mierda. Joder.*' The Spanish bad words rolled off my tongue. 'A fundraiser? A charity event? That is so . . . upper classy.' I shook my head, my hair almost coming off my knot. 'No, it sounds upper *I wipe my ass with dollar bills* classy. And no, I don't mean to be judgy here, but, Jesus.' I found myself pacing the few feet that comprised my kitchen space. 'A little heads-up would have been nice. You could have told me yesterday, you know? I would have gone shopping this morning, Aaron. I would have prepared, I don't know, a few options for you to choose from. I have no idea what I'm going to do now. I have a couple of formal gowns, but they are not . . . right.'

It was past six in the evening and—

'You would have done all that for this?' His lips parted very briefly, giving him a bewildered air that I was not used to seeing in him. Then, his jaw returned to its former position. 'For *me*?'

I stopped pacing. 'Yes.' Why was he so shocked? 'Of course I would have.' Studying his face, I took in the weird way in which he was looking at me. 'First of all, I would hate to show up to your "charity event" — I air-quoted — 'looking like a clown. Believe it or not, I do have some sense of self-esteem and the ability to get embarrassed.'

Aaron's eyes kept shining with that quality that made me nervous.

'And second of all, I wouldn't want you to retaliate and wear God knows what to my sister's wedding, just to spite me. Or like, back out on me for some kind of etiquette infringement now that I'm counting on you coming to Spain with me. I . . .' I trailed off, losing my voice. 'I kind of need you, you know?'

That last part had somehow materialized on my tongue. I didn't realize it had left my mouth until it was too late and I wasn't able to take it back.

'I'd never do that,' he answered, catching me by surprise. 'I won't back out. We have a deal.'

Feeling exposed by my admission, I averted my eyes. I focused on his hands, which had fallen out of his pockets and rested by his sides.

'I won't do that, Catalina,' I heard him say. 'Not even if you really pushed me to, and I know that you can.'

I had the feeling that he had purposely said that with sarcasm. Just enough to bait me into snapping back. But for some reason, I didn't. His words felt sincere. But I just . . . couldn't know if he meant it. It was really hard for me to get past our history. All the jabs, nudges, and shoves. All the small ways we had made sure the other one didn't forget how much we disliked each other.

'Whatever you say, Blackford.' I didn't sound like I believed myself, but it'd have to do. 'I don't have time for this.' Whatever this was, I wasn't sure anymore. I brought my hand to the side of my neck and massaged that spot absently. 'Just ... make yourself at home. I'll see what I can find for this fundraiser we are attending.'

I walked to where he was standing, his large frame blocking the opening that gave way to my living area. Coming to a halt a step before him, I looked up and arched an eyebrow, asking him without words to please move. Aaron towered over my short stature, staring down at me, his eyes flying all over my face. Down my throat and around my neck. Right where my fingers had massaged my skin a moment ago.

His eyes returned to mine with something I didn't recognize in his blue gaze.

We stood close, my bare toes almost touching the point of his polished shoes. And I felt my breathing increase its pace at the realization. My chest moved up and down more quickly with every second I was under Aaron's scrutiny.

Refusing to look away, I held his stare.

Leaning my head back, I couldn't help but notice that he felt larger than ever. As if his frame had expanded a couple of sizes more. Seeming much taller and bigger than me, all clad in that tux that had the power to turn him into someone I was finding hard not to look at. Not to drink up every detail that sparked with this newness he seemed to be carrying around today.

Aaron's tongue peeked out and travelled along his bottom lip, driving my gaze to his mouth. His full lips shone under the light of my kitchen.

My skin started turning too warm beneath the fabric of my stupid robe. Standing this close, I was feeling too hot, seeing too much of him, noticing way too many things at once.

I willed my gaze up, back to his eyes. They were still studying me, that something still locked in. Hidden behind them. A heartbeat passed, and I could have sworn that his body inched in my direction, just the splinter of a hair. But maybe it was just my imagination.

It didn't really matter.

'I was serious.' His voice was low and hushed, the quality of it almost raspy, hearing it this closely.

Every rational thought was long-lost, but I knew what he was talking about. Of course I did.

He exhaled softly, and I smelled the mint on his breath. 'I wouldn't retaliate in any way. I know how important your sister's wedding is.'

The truth behind his words hit me harder than the lack of distance between our bodies. My lips parted, and my stomach dropped to my feet.

'I won't go back on my word. I never do.'

Was Aaron Blackford really reassuring me? Guaranteeing me that no matter what was or had been between us, this was safe ground? That he would keep his word, fair and square? That he wouldn't go back on it? Was he doing all that? It certainly sounded like it. Which told me that either he read minds – which I honestly hoped he didn't – or that perhaps Rosie hadn't been wrong about him.

Maybe Aaron wasn't all that bad.

Maybe I had been wrong about him. I . . . I didn't know what to say to him. What to do with any of this, frankly. And the longer I spent in silence, with him radiating this openness right on me, the more he made me warmer and dizzier, and the harder it was for me to think clearly.

'Do you understand me, Catalina?' he pressed, that warmth coating my whole body.

No, I wanted to say. *I don't understand a single thing that's going on here.*

My throat moved, my vocal cords somehow failing at voicing an answer. A strange sound left my lips, making me clear my throat right after. 'I should go,' I finally managed to get out. 'If you don't mind, I should change. We will be late otherwise.'

With a motion surprisingly smooth for someone his size, Aaron moved out of my way. He placed his body to one side, still too large and wide for my cramped apartment. Still taking up too much space and still making me feel itchy and tingly. Especially when I walked past him and my robe-clad shoulder brushed his chest.

His very hard chest.

All the heat I felt in my body rushed back to my face.

Stop. I moved on weak legs, my skin feeling clammy. *I just need to get out of this robe,* I assured myself, tugging at the neck. *That is the only reason why I am flushed and warm.*

I made myself think about something else.

Like ... Dresses. Not Aaron. Not him in a tux. Or his minty breath. Or his chest. Or any other body part. Not what he said either.

But my head started turning, wanting to look back. At him.

No.

Reaching my wardrobe, I threw the doors open. Rummaging around as I searched for whatever I owned that would rise to the occasion, I slowly regained my focus.

I fished the *one* piece of clothing with the potential to save my ass out of the depths of my wardrobe, grabbed the pair of heels I reserved for special events, a couple of accessories, and headed for the bathroom.

On my way, I gave Aaron a sideways glance. He was hovering somewhere close to the velvety blue sofa, dwarfing it, his gaze on the screen of his phone. He didn't even lift his head when I walked in front of him.

Good. Better than him snooping around or flaunting his apparently very distracting body around.

It had to be the tuxedo. This behavior of mine – this reaction he had caused in me – wasn't normal.

'I will ... get ready in there,' I said over my shoulder to the man who seemed to take all the space in my small apartment. 'Make yourself ... comfortable.'

Once inside the only walled room in my apartment – the bathroom – I felt somehow lighter. My skin cooler. It didn't have a lock, so I simply shut the door and hung the dress from the shower bar and started with my make-up and hair.

After what seemed like an eternity – and at the same time, not nearly enough time – I was finally content with how I looked. The woman who stared back at me from the full-length wall mirror I had cleverly installed in the bathroom was wearing a sleeveless floor-length dress. A colour somewhere between black onyx and midnight blue. The cut and the fabric were rather simple – and definitely not evening gown-ish enough – but the slit that travelled along the skirt all the way up, stopping above my right knee, gave it a graceful and classy touch. Although the real star of the show was the neckline, which – even if it didn't give an inch of cleavage away, closing around my neck like it did – was embedded with white beads that imitated pearls. It was absolutely beautiful. That was exactly why I had impulsively bought it months ago. And why I hadn't had the chance to wear it yet and had forgotten it was even there.

I inspected the waves of brown hair falling on my shoulders. Nowhere near perfect, but it would have to do. Next I considered putting on red lipstick. But I quickly discarded that idea, thinking it would be overdoing it. I'd rather reserve that for a real date.

Sighing softly, I felt an uncomfortable twinge in my chest.

I hadn't gone on a date in what felt like an eternity. Not that I considered myself unworthy or unattractive enough not to pique someone's interest. I had gone on a few dates here and there shortly after moving to New York. But at some point, I had stopped trying. What was the point when it was clear there was something wrong with me? I might have left Spain, but somehow, I had managed to leave my *trust* – my willingness to fall in love ever again – somewhere across the ocean.

Looking at myself in the mirror, I realized I hadn't put much effort into my make-up, hair, and clothes for just as long. And now, I wished I hadn't noticed that.

Because pitying myself was something I had long ago promised myself I wouldn't do. It was a route I swore I wouldn't take.

Then, why was I feeling this way? How had I let myself get here? To the point that for the first time in months, I was putting actual effort into my appearance and my clothes, and I was doing it for something that wasn't even real. A fake date. A deal. A sort of business agreement. Jesus, how had I gotten to the point where I needed to invent a relationship, so I didn't feel like a total failure?

My fears rang as true as ever. I was broken. I was—

A knock on the door returned me to the present, reminding me of who was waiting for me outside my bedroom. Impatiently, if the pounding on the door was any sign.

'How much longer is it going to take you, Catalina?' Aaron's notoriously deep voice carried through the bathroom door. 'You've been in there long enough.'

I looked at the little clock I had on one of the bathroom shelves – 6:45 p.m. Still fifteen minutes to spare if we went by the time he had initially agreed to pick me up. I shook my head.

Another knock. This one was harder. More impatient. 'Catalina?'

I decided to answer his lack of patience with silence. Someone had to show him that he couldn't always get his way. Plus, I had been promised fifteen – all right, fourteen – minutes more.

Still feeling the crack that had reopened in my chest, I slipped my right foot inside one of my heels and lifted it to the toilet seat. Meticulously, I worked on the strap.

Taking my time, I did the same with the left one. I still had a few minutes, and I planned on—

A third knock never came. My lockless door flew open, startling the crap out of me and revealing a very restless man.

Aaron's simmering blue eyes found mine.

'Catalina.' A speck of relief surfaced in those blue pools of impatience. 'Why didn't you answer when I called your name? You've been in here for a whole hour.'

I watched his eyes travel down the length of my dress, his expression hardening with every inch he navigated. I could see his jaw cramping down tightly by the time his gaze made its way back to mine.

Was he . . . was he mad?

A subdued voice in my head told me that he probably regretted ever asking me to come to this thing with him if he looked so displeased. I ignored the discomfort in the pit of my stomach and snatched the first emotion that I could get ahold of. One that was extremely easy to summon when it came to him.

'Aaron Blackford,' I hissed, finding my voice. 'What in the world is wrong with you?!' My chest heaved up and down. 'Don't you know how to knock?'

'I knocked.' His tone was hard, matching his expression. 'Twice.' That stupidly deep voice of his reverberated through my bathroom.

'I could have been naked, you know.'

Aaron shifted in front of me, not letting go of the doorknob. His large fingers gripped it so fiercely it made me wonder if it would give out under the pressure.

'But you aren't,' he said, voice still hard. 'You are definitely not naked.'

His expression clouded further as we looked at each other for a long moment.

My palms grew damp the longer neither of us said anything.

Jesus, what is even happening?

My heart raced faster, the more the air filled up with a tension I didn't understand.

It was almost suffocating. Much more than earlier in the kitchen. So much so that I felt how my guard came down, all kinds of thoughts assaulting my mind with nothing to stop the bruising.

'Is there . . .' I broke the silence, my voice coming out breathy. 'Is there anything wrong?'

He shook his head. Just once. His eyes ranged over my body again very quickly. 'You found a gown.'

'I did,' I admitted, looking down briefly. 'It's been such a long time since I last went on a date that I forgot it was even there.' I watched his expression take on a new edge, making me feel incredibly stupid for saying something like that. 'Well, that doesn't matter. Not that I'd wear this to any date anyway, I guess. It's the only one I have, so I hope it's okay.'

I passed my sweaty palms along my thighs, stopping myself at the prospect of messing with the fabric.

Aaron's throat worked. 'It'll do.'

It'll do?

I had no idea what I had been expecting him to say, but I'd be lying if I said that hadn't stung a tiny little bit.

'Good,' I answered, looking away, not letting my shoulders sink. 'Let's go then.'

He remained where he was, not uttering a single word.

'Come on,' I told him, instructing myself to smile. 'You don't want to be late, do you?'

A couple of seconds after, he moved out of the way. Without a stare-off, which I appreciated because I wasn't in the mood to look at him just yet.

I stepped out of the bathroom, and I made sure of two things. One, I didn't brush his chest with my shoulder. And two, I didn't have any reason to feel hurt by whatever Aaron Blackford said.

CHAPTER SEVEN

We had been driving in silence for the longest fifteen minutes of my life when I decided I could not take it any longer.

I wasn't in the mood for small talk, and I knew that waiting for Aaron to say something would be like waiting for a brick wall to crack open and reveal the entrance to a wizardly world. But if I didn't say anything to fill in this silence, I'd have to jump out of the moving car.

'So, a fundraiser.' My words fell into the reduced and quiet space, sounding too loud.

Aaron nodded, his gaze remaining on the road and both hands on the steering wheel.

'For a good cause, naturally.'

Another nod.

'And it takes place every year?'

An affirmative grunt.

If he didn't start talking, saying *anything*, I wouldn't jump out of the moving car; I'd be pushing him out.

'And . . .' I needed a question that wouldn't strictly require a yes or no answer. 'How are the funds going to be raised?'

He seemed to consider that for some time, almost making me believe I'd really have to shove him out.

'An auction.'

Finally. 'What's being auctioned?' I fidgeted with the simple gold cuff bracelet that circled my wrist, waiting for an answer that never came. 'Is it art?' I turned the smooth piece of jewelry around. 'Golf lessons?' Another turn. 'A yacht?' I looked at him. Nothing. No answer. 'Elvis's underwear?'

That got me a reaction. He sent me a puzzled look and then returned his attention to the road.

'What?' I shrugged one shoulder. 'I'll have you know that some-one auctioned a dirty pair of undies Elvis had worn to a concert in the seventies.'

I watched Aaron's head shake. Mr Proper was probably scan-dalized, but he was still not talking, so I kept filling in the silence.

'Chill. Nobody bought them.' I studied his profile for any reac-tion. Still nothing. 'Or bid for them,' I corrected myself. 'I don't know much, if anything, about auctions.' More silence. *Okay.* 'But the conclusion was that, apparently, no one wanted Elvis's used underwear.' I snickered. 'Which, frankly, it sort of strengthened my faith in society. Not all is lost yet, right?'

A muscle in his jaw jumped.

'Who would want to own something like that? And what's even more daunting, what for? To frame it?' A grimace bent my lips. 'Imagine being invited to a home and finding a dirty pair of under-pants framed, hanging above the sofa. Or the toilet.'

Aaron shot me a quick glance, something that looked a lot like wonder filling his eyes. Then, he finally spoke, 'I never know with you, you know?'

And that's what he decided to go with?

'You never know what?' Frowning, I watched his head give another light shake.

'I never know what's going to come out of your mouth.' His voice sounded almost thoughtful. 'You always find a way to catch me completely off guard. And that's not something many people can do.'

Uh . . .

What was I supposed to do with that? Was that . . . a compliment? I had been rambling about Elvis's used underwear hanging in some-body's living room, so I was going to go with no. Not a compliment. Plus, this was Aaron we were talking about, so double no.

'Well, I have more fun facts for you, if that's what you want,' I offered with a smile. 'Of all kinds, not only underwear-related.'

'Of course you do,' he muttered.

'Unless you want to use this precious time to, I don't know, give me some kind of context about tonight.' I waited one, two, three seconds. Once more, he seemed to fall silent when I asked. 'You could maybe explain to me why I'm here, pretending to be your date. That's a good start.'

His fingers gripped the steering wheel tighter; it was hard to miss because, well, I had been carefully watching him for the last couple of minutes.

And yet, he was still not talking.

I frowned, starting to feel frustrated in a way that wasn't very char-itable. 'You said you would tell me everything if I agreed to come.'

'I did say that, didn't I?'

'Yep,' I answered, not getting why he was being so . . . privy. Although that was just how Aaron was, wasn't it? It shouldn't have surprised me.

I watched his hands move up along the steering wheel, the action tensing the fabric of his tux jacket. As I was unable not to notice how his arms filled the sleeves, my mind wandered away for an instant, this weird sensation I had experienced back in the apartment returning.

I was being sidetracked by . . . *him*. His presence, his proximity, the way he looked. Again. Objectively speaking, it was hard to do much else besides stare at him, dwarfing the car's seat like he pretty much did with everything else – especially when he wasn't talking and giving me an excuse not to. But there was nothing objective about the way my eyes involuntarily trailed up his arms, his shoulders, all the way up to his profile. Stoic. So stoic and serious. He wasn't smiling – Aaron never did that – and I'd never been more aware of that fact.

It wasn't just the tux, I realized.

So far, I had somehow been able to overlook how attractive Aaron was. Not that I hadn't noticed he was good-looking – I had. Although I had only needed to remember his dry and sour personality to gloss over that rather quickly. But that did not change the truth. And that was that Aaron had all those things that made my head turn and take a second look. All those things I didn't look for but for some reason I felt compelled by. All those things I wasn't. Tall – he stood so tall and unmovable. All lean muscles and controlled movements. Every gesture so composed and disciplined. Or the way in which his pale skin and dark hair made his eyes stand out, a deep and intense shade of blue that I had never seen before I met him.

Ripping my gaze off him, I cursed myself for allowing my mind to go there. *What the hell am I even doing?* There were important things to discuss. I didn't have time to think about his stupidly big and apparently alluring tux-clad body. *Damn tuxedos.*

'You are playing hard to get, Blackford. But it's all right,' I said, realizing Aaron still hadn't given me that explanation he owed me. 'I can guess why I'm here.' *I'll do that if it helps me to stop thinking crazy, stupid stuff about you.* 'I'm game if you are.'

More silence.

'All right, I'll take that as a yes. Let's play.' I shifted in my seat, angling my body to my left side. 'Why am I here? Let's see . . . am I here to protect you from a crazy ex-girlfriend?' Basic, but I had to start somewhere. 'You look like a man who would attract crazy.'

He looked at me sideways, his forehead wrinkling. 'What's that supposed to mean?' He shook his head, returning his gaze to the road. 'You know what? I don't want to know.'

'Okay, fine. I guess that was a no. No crazy exes.' I brought my index finger to my chin. 'Hmm . . . if it's not protection you need' – I tapped my finger – 'am I here to make someone jealous?'

'No,' he answered quickly.

'Are you sure?' I wiggled my eyebrows. 'No former lover you want to get back at? Show the one who got away what she's missing? Rekindle your love story?'

'I said, no exes.' His shoulders rose with tension.

'Okay, okay, I got it. Calm down, Blackford. Don't get your panties in a bunch.'

I watched his lips twitch. In anger or humour, I didn't know.

'I don't know,' I continued, enjoying myself far too much. 'If it's not that, then – oh! Is it unrequited love? It is, isn't it?' I brought my hands together in front of my chest. 'It's gotta be someone unaware of your longing puppy eyes. No, wait. I don't think you are capable of pulling off puppy eyes.' I tilted my head, something occurring to me. 'You know that you can't go around giving women the cold eye if you are interested in them, right? I know puppy eyes was going a bit too far for you, but if there is someone out there who awakens that stone cold heart of yours—'

'No,' he fired back, cutting me off. 'You are not here for any of that.' He inhaled deeply, his chest rising. Then, he puffed out the air. 'I don't like to play games, Catalina.'

My hands dropped to my lap. 'This particular game or . . . games in general?' I paused, wondering where his reaction had come from. 'Or are we talking about sexy games? Like seduction games?'

My lips snapped shut as soon as I heard my own words. I couldn't believe I had said that. To Aaron.

Neither could he, apparently, because he let out a . . . noise that I had the impression was supposed to be a laugh. Although it couldn't have possibly been that, sounding closer to . . . something strangled.

'You . . .' His head swivelled with consternation. 'Jesus, Catalina.'

Forehead wrinkling, I opened my mouth to say something, but Aaron spoke first, 'If I end things with a woman, I end them.' His voice went at least an octave down, a rumble in the confined space between us. 'And if I am interested in someone, I make myself heard. I will find a way for her to know. Sooner or later, she'll know.' Aaron didn't look at me, not once. He just spoke with his gaze on the road ahead of us. 'I wouldn't use you, or anyone else, for something like that. As you said back in your apartment, I'm a big boy.'

I felt a wave of warmth climb all the way up to my face. Flushed. I was flushed, and my make-up was probably not doing anything to hide the dark shade of red spreading through my cheeks. I looked away. 'Oh, okay.' I fought the urge to touch my face, check if the blush was heating my skin too. 'I see.'

I wasn't *seeing* a single thing. And frankly, I didn't understand why his words were making me feel this way either. Or more importantly, why he had asked for my help if he *didn't play games* and was a *big boy*.

But where this man was concerned, I hadn't seemed to be understanding much lately. Especially when my body had decided to stop cooperating and was acting up in all these stupid ways that turned my skin warm and flushed.

I stared through the window, watching the city lights flick away as we drove. 'You said you would tell me everything if I agreed to do this.' I swallowed, not wanting to sound like I cared as much as I did. 'If we . . . did this thing for each other.'

'You are right,' he said, not adding anything else for a long moment, in which I didn't turn to look at him. 'I used to play football in college,' he admitted, catching me completely by surprise.

Very slowly, I gripped the strap of my seat belt while I tried to muffle down the *holy shit* that had travelled all the way to the tip of my tongue.

Okay, so that wasn't an explanation. It wasn't the answer I had expected. But it was the first thing I had ever heard from him that wasn't work-related. In almost two years. So, if my ears were not deceiving me, Aaron had just opened up – for the first time ever. Because I'd count it as that. Just a tiny little bit, fine, but it was a crack on that hard exterior all the same. And all of a sudden, I wanted to swing a hammer and pummel my way to the other side.

'Football? The one with the helmets and the melon-like ball?' I asked instead, keeping my voice as flat as possible.

I wasn't a sports doofus, but I was European. I needed to be sure we were talking about the same sport.

'Yes, not soccer. The one with the melon.' He nodded. 'I played back home in Seattle, where I went to college.'

'Seattle,' I repeated, chewing on this new piece of information he had given me. More. I wanted just a little more. 'That's Washington up north, right? I know because of *Twilight*. Forks is supposed to be a few hours away.' I kind of regretted mentioning *Twilight*, but beggars couldn't be choosers, and besides the few places I had visited, my knowledge of American geography was based on books and movies.

'That's the one,' he said, his shoulders relaxing downwards. Just an inch. Which in Aaron's language meant a green light for more questions.

'So, this thing we are going to tonight, does it have to do with your football days then?'

Aaron nodded. 'I'm still invited to some events. Because I played, but mostly because of my family's involvement in the NCAA,' he explained, driving us along one of the wide avenues in Manhattan. 'Once a year, a charity event for an association of animal welfare is hosted here in New York, and a number of personalities attend.'

'Are you one of those personalities?' I'd have to google what the NCAA was later, but I had a feeling there was something he wasn't telling me. 'Oh my God, Aaron Blackford, are you telling me you come from, like, a long line of football royals?'

Aaron's brows knitted. 'Catalina.'

In pure Aaron fashion, that was all the answer I got. 'Will your family be there tonight?'

'No,' he said, his profile hardening for a heartbeat and confirming my suspicions.

I guessed I'd have to google that too.

'Tonight's event is for raising money that will eventually go to shelter, rehabilitate, and find homes for rescued animals in New York. I attend whenever I'm able to. It's good to see a few people I've known for most of my life, and it's for a cause I care about.'

I immediately forgot about whatever it was that he wasn't telling me about his family. Aaron cared about the welfare of animals? About rescuing them and finding them new homes?

Right on cue, something fuzzy and warm tingled in my chest. And the feeling got only worse when I found myself picturing Aaron holding a bunch of cute puppies that he cared about and raised money for in his bulky arms. As he knelt on a field. In his football gear. Tight pants. Shoulders that went for miles. Dirt smudged on his cheeks.

That warmth turned a little thicker and harder to ignore. 'That's . . . great,' I said, trying to kick those images out of my head. 'Really nice of you.'

Aaron's gaze turned to me, and one of his eyebrows went up.

He was probably weirded out by how hard I was blushing.

Why can't I stop blushing?

'Do you always bring a fake date to this event?' I blurted out without thinking.

'No.' Aaron's lips pressed in that usual flat line. 'I've always attended alone. This is the first time I'm bringing a date.'

A date.

A date?

My eyebrows wrinkled. A *fake* date, not a real date.

I was about to correct him, but he spoke first, 'We are almost there.'

I sat in silence as I processed everything I had just learned. This new depth to Aaron I had discovered. A little peek through that crack he had revealed to me. And all those dangerous mental images I had acquired, which, much to my dismay, would stick with me for a long time. That was something that needed some processing too.

'Wait,' I let out as he made a turn to the right. 'You didn't tell me what's being auctioned. Or why I'm here.'

The vehicle came to a slow stop in front of one of the numerous skyscrapers on Park Avenue. Looking over, I spotted a parking valet waiting on the sidewalk.

Eyes wide, I turned to Aaron. *A freaking valet? Shit.*

His eyes settled on me one last time, and I swore there was something wolfish, something a little wild, about them.

'Me.' He tilted his head, holding my gaze. 'That's what's being auctioned.' His voice matched the quality of his eyes, making a shiver trail down my arms. 'And that's what you'll be bidding on tonight, Catalina. *Me.*'

Eyes even wider and jaw probably lying somewhere around my high heels, I blinked and watched Aaron throw the driver's door open. He walked around the car as I – unsuccessfully – tried to gather my wits. He gestured to the valet not to open my door.

Aaron opened it himself.

The humid summer breeze grazed my arms and legs as this blue-eyed man, about whom I was starting to understand I knew very little, offered his hand.

'Miss Martín, if you please.'

I blinked at him, my whole body numb with ... things I failed to pin down and identify.

One of the corners of his lips bent with the start of a smirk; he was clearly enjoying how discombobulated I was. How scattered I must appear. *God*, he looked as amused as I had ever seen him.

'Today better than tomorrow, Catalina.'

That comment was so Aaron, so like the Aaron I knew and was familiar and comfortable with – the one who was curt and demanding, not the one who was taking me to a fundraiser so I could bid on him in an auction – that my hand shot to his, being immediately engulfed in his much larger one.

He helped me out of the car, the long skirt of my gown that wasn't really a gown cascading down my legs. Aaron let my hand drop all too quickly, leaving my palm warm from his touch. Then, he held the massive and sumptuous door of the Park Avenue skyscraper open for me.

I took one step forward, trying to keep the hammering in my chest under control.

All right.

My other foot moved in front of me.

So, I'd be fake-bidding for my fake date tonight. For my soon-to-be fake boyfriend if our agreement was still up after tonight.

No big deal, right?

CHAPTER EIGHT

When Aaron had mentioned *fundraiser*, followed by *auction*, I had pictured a fancy but frilly room filled with wealthy and uptown old people. Don't ask me why. But I had not expected the spectacular rooftop where we had been welcomed with a flute glass of the tastiest sparkling wine I had ever had the pleasure to drink. And surely, not the trendy – and rather extravagant – array of people of all ages and backgrounds in attendance.

Who knew that the upper spheres of the Big Apple could be so . . . colourful?

Not that I had met everybody here. Actually, we had pretty much stuck to those somehow related to the football world. Which seemed natural after Aaron's revelation about his past and his family's involvement in it. For the last hour, I had been introduced to a couple of coaches and team coordinators, a sportscaster, and a number of influential people whose positions I wasn't familiar with but that I nodded to like I knew exactly what they did. The only people we had talked to outside the sports bubble were a few entrepreneurs whose corporations, enterprises, and whatnot I had never heard of either.

Every time we encountered a new group of people, Aaron introduced me as Catalina Martín, not adding any kind of label before or after my name. Which somehow helped me lose all that tension I had carried with me from the car drive and definitely aided my newfound intention of trying to enjoy myself.

This was my first time at an event like this one, and it would most likely be my last, so the least I could do was have fun.

'I already said so, but I'm so happy to see you, Aaron.' Angela, a lady in her fifties who was clad in a dress that was probably worth two or three times my month's rent, smiled. 'Especially with someone on your arm.'

I felt my cheeks grow hot, so I distracted myself by taking a sip from my fancy flute glass.

We had been chatting with her for a few minutes now. And the whole time, I had been silently watching the woman with fascination. Her elegance and poise had me in awe. And unlike more than a few people here, she had kind eyes. The fact that she was the mind behind tonight's event was only the cherry on top.

'So, tell me' – Angela's lips inched higher – 'you'll be taking part in this year's auction too, I presume? I still haven't gotten the chance to check the final list.'

'Yes, of course,' Aaron answered from his post at my side.

We hadn't had time to discuss what the deal with this whole *me bidding for him* was. By the time I had somehow pulled it together, we had been walking out of the elevator and into the party. We'd been quickly jumping from one small group of people to the next, so I hadn't had the chance to interrogate him about it.

'That's lovely to hear.' She took a sip of her drink. 'I had my doubts, if I may be completely honest.' Angela threw her head back and laughed. 'Last year's auction was … intense. Very entertaining, to say the least.'

Aaron shifted by my side. Glancing at him, I could tell by the way his shoulders tensed that he was slightly uncomfortable with where the conversation was going.

That piqued my curiosity.

Angela continued, 'Good thing you brought someone tonight. I'm sure it will keep the evening alive.' She turned to me. 'Catalina dear, I hope you are ready for some fierce competition.'

I sensed Aaron shifting some more. 'Fierce competition?' I repeated, thinking of Aaron's words – *'And that's what you'll be bidding on tonight, Catalina. Me.'* – and piecing together that perhaps that was exactly why I was here.

Aaron's grip on his glass grew a little tighter. 'Nothing you should worry about.'

I watched him for a few seconds, my curiosity doubling. Then, I turned to Angela, who was smiling with something that looked a lot like mischief.

'Oh, but I'm not worried.' A smile tugged at my lips, one I was going to bet was very similar to Angela's. 'I'm always here for a good, entertaining story.'

I heard Aaron's resigned sigh from my side.

Angela's grin widened. 'I think I'm going to leave the honours to Aaron to tell you that .' Then she leaned towards me and added in a hushed voice, 'I'm sure his side of the story is all the more captivating. Especially the part nobody got to see.'

Oh?

Before I could press for the details I was dying to hear, Angela's attention was caught by something – someone – behind us. 'Oh, there's Michael. If you'll please excuse me, I must go say hi.'

'Of course.' Aaron nodded, his body still stiff, although he was probably glad Angela was moving on to someone else. 'It was nice seeing you, Angela.'

'Yes,' I gave her a polite smile. 'It was a pleasure meeting you, Angela.'

'The pleasure was all mine, Catalina.' She leaned in again and air-kissed my cheek. 'Don't let him off the hook too easily.' She winked and then walked away towards the area of the rooftop where most people were gathered. A space filled with high tables that looked straight out of a design catalogue and lines of wicker floor lamps that served as the only source of illumination.

I turned to look at Aaron, finding that pair of blue eyes already on me.

Pushing down the slight blush climbing up my neck, I cleared my throat. 'I'm all ears, Blackford.' I brought my glass to my lips and finally finished the sparkling wine I had been nursing for the last hour. 'I think it's time you fill me in.'

Aaron seemed to think about his words for a moment. 'As I'm sure you have already deducted, tonight's main event is a bachelor auction.'

'A bachelor auction,' I repeated slowly. 'Just your run-of-the-mill Saturday night activity, I assume.'

Aaron sighed.

I rolled my index finger in the air. 'Keep going. I want to hear the rest.'

'I don't think there's much else to say.' He balanced his glass in his hand.

'Well, forgive me, Blackford, but I think there must be plenty. Plus, I want to make sure I understand the concept of tonight's main event correctly.'

He shot me a glance.

I suppressed my smile. 'Right. So, during this auction of yours then . . . bachelors are acquired, you say.'

'Correct.'

'By, I assume, single women and men?'

He nodded.

'For an amount of money,' I pointed out. 'All in the name of charity, of course.'

Another nod.

I tapped my finger on my chin. 'I just wonder . . . no, never mind. It's stupid.'

Aaron shot me a tired glance. 'Out with it, Catalina.'

'If people are bidding – buying – all these bachelors' – I watched his eyes narrow, exasperation written all over his face – 'what happens next? When the bachelor is acquired, what is he acquired for?'

Those flat, pressed lips again.

I continued, 'I mean, this is not like bidding for a boat or a Porsche. I guess you cannot take the bachelor for a ride.' Okay, that sounded . . . wrong. One could technically take someone for a ride. A certain sort of ride. 'Not that kind of ride,' I rushed out, watching Aaron's expression change. 'Not like a ride in a *yeehaw* kind of way. I said that because one takes cars for a ride. Like, for a spin. But not men, not in that way. At least, I have never taken a man for a spin.' I shook my head. I was making it worse, and the more I talked, the more Aaron's lips paled. 'You know what I mean.'

'No,' Aaron answered simply, bringing the glass to his mouth and taking a sip. 'More often than not, I don't know what you mean, Catalina.' He brought his hand to his right temple. 'Whoever offers the highest bid, which will be donated to the cause, gets to go on a date with the man in question. That's what the bachelor is *acquired* for.'

Hold up, what? 'A date?'

His brows knit. 'Yes, a date.'

'Like a date, *date*?'

'A date, date. Yes. You know, normally, two people who engage in a social appointment that often involves eating. Sometimes, other kinds of activities.' He levelled me with a look. 'Like going for rides and spins.'

My lips parted. No, my mouth hung open.

Was he . . . had he just . . .

'Ha, hilarious.' My cheeks heated. But I didn't have time to be embarrassed. Because that meant . . . 'So, do we have to . . . you know, do it?'

'What exactly?'

'The date thing,' I explained, lowering my voice so nobody could hear us. 'I know I'm only your fake bidder. So, do we have to do it anyway? Like, fake do it? Because you said I'm here to fake bid on you, so I just . . . you know.'

Judging by Aaron's expression, there was something from all the things I had just said that he found particularly unpleasant. His throat worked slowly, looking as if he were swallowing something sour.

'Never mind. We'll figure it out later. I guess it's not important.' What was important now was climbing out of this hole I had just dug for myself. 'So, do you take part in the auction every year?'

His eyes looked away for a heartbeat and then settled back on me. 'Ever since I moved to New York. This is my third time.'

'And you . . . take all these bidders on dates?' Okay, that wasn't exactly changing the topic of conversation, but a part of me wanted to know. Kind of.

'Of course. It's part of the deal.' His earlier words came to mind.

'And you don't go back on your word.'

'Exactly.'

That confirmation, that *part of the deal* bit, felt like a punch to the stomach. Back in my apartment, I had thought he'd sounded sincere when he told me that he wouldn't pull out of our deal. And I had felt . . . sceptical in a way, yes, but a part of me had also felt *special*. For lack of a better word. Like he was doing that for me and I could count on him. Perhaps because he knew how important it was for me, how much I needed him. But now, it seemed I had been wrong. This was the way Aaron was wired.

It didn't have anything to do with me.

And that made sense. The dumb thing to do had been thinking otherwise.

'And what do you do on these dates?' I asked without thinking much of it, just so he wouldn't get a chance to see anything on my face. 'Where do you take them?'

'Nothing special,' he admitted with a sigh. 'The bachelor usually picks the activity and puts everything together. So, the two times I have participated, I have organized something at one of the animal shelters in the city. Spending some time there, volunteering and helping out or even taking a few dogs for a walk.'

That was ... sweet. Generous and kind and way more than I would have ever expected from him, if my heart skipping a teeny-tiny beat was any indication.

I looked down, realizing my fingers were playing with the cuff around my wrist again. 'That's where you took last year's bidder then?'

'Yes.' I could feel him silently asking me not to go there. Not to ask what Angela had mentioned earlier.

'Oh,' I said distractedly. 'Speaking of last year' – I had to ask – 'what happened during the auction?'

Aaron's shoulders tensed, his face falling with resignation. 'Not much.'

'Oh yeah?' I feigned surprise. 'So, this fierce competition that Angela was talking about, the one I should not be scared of, doesn't ring any bell?'

I watched his lips twitch and then bend in a pout.

A pout. On Aaron's lips.

'Like no bells whatsoever?' I pressed, getting acquainted with that expression of his for the first time ever. 'Really none?'

Aaron Blackford kept pouting, which in turn made me want to smile as wide as I could go. Not that I would. I suppressed the urge.

'Oh, okay.' I shrugged. 'I'm sure getting mobbed by overexcited bidders is a common occurrence for you then, Blackford.' I teased him because how could I not when he looked all ... mortified and ready to come out of his skin? Plus, he had teased me first anyway. 'How did it happen exactly? Did they fling themselves at you? Or was it perhaps something subtler? Like hurling their money at your feet? Then their underwear?'

If this man had the ability to blush, I would have bet all my money on those cheeks turning red any moment.

'There's nothing to be embarrassed about. You are a big boy anyway.'

Aaron's eyebrows shot up his forehead. 'Yes, we have established that.' He moved one step closer. 'I can fend for myself.'

'It didn't sound like that.' My voice came out wobblier than I would have liked.

Then, he took one more step, and something fluttered in my belly.

'Luckily' – he leaned closer, fixing his blue eyes on me – 'you are here tonight.'

The flutter intensified. Which did not make any sense. I should have been . . . what? What should I have been feeling?

'And the highest bid will be yours. Not anyone else's.'

My heart raced as I looked up at him, feeling overwhelmed in a way that wasn't strictly negative given how close he was standing.

Aaron didn't step back; instead, he continued talking, his voice coming closer and closer, 'I will take care of the money. The donation will leave my pocket, not yours, so don't be shy with the bid as long as you beat everyone here. Hurl the money at my feet, if you will. Just make sure it's you' – he paused, and I felt my throat drying up – 'the one buying *me*. Understood?'

Those last few words seemed to echo in my mind, mingling with the fluttering sensation in my belly, making my skin tingle.

I had to literally step back to force myself to process what he had just told me. I didn't think I'd be able to donate more than a few hundred dollars on my own, so it was a good thing Aaron had concocted this plan with his chequebook and not mine.

Which led me to consider one of two possibilities: either Aaron Blackford truly cared about the cause, or he was wealthy enough not to care how much I donated in his name as long as I spared him a date.

A *date* we were supposed to go on after this, if we followed the rules. But one that wouldn't be real. Because this wasn't real. It was all an act.

'Well, a deal is a deal, Blackford,' I told him with an awkward shrug, shoving away the strange and hazy thought of going on a date with Aaron. To an animal shelter. And seeing him play with a bunch of cute pups. In his football gear, with—

Por el amor de Dios, I have to stop all these mental images.

Aaron's mouth opened, but before he could speak, a man approached us. He placed a hand on Aaron's shoulder. The latter turned at the contact and relaxed as soon as he took in the man by his side.

'I cannot believe my eyes.' He patted Aaron's back firmly. 'Is this Aaron Blackford, gracing us with his company tonight? It must be my lucky day.'

Aaron snorted; it was a short and light noise, but I had heard it. 'It certainly isn't mine now that you are here too,' he muttered, the right corner of his lips bent with the ghost of a lopsided smile.

The man – who I assumed was or had been close to Aaron at some point, if his reaction was any indication – shook his head. 'Oh hell, that hurt.' He brought a hand to his chest as the dark skin around his eyes wrinkled. 'How long has it been since I last saw your nasty face?'

'Not long enough, if you ask me.' Aaron's face, that usually remained so expressionless, opened up. His body seemed to loosen up as he faced the other man. 'How are you, TJ?' I could hear the warmth in his voice. The familiarity.

'I've never been better,' TJ – or so Aaron had called him – nodded. 'Happy to be back, believe it or not. Damn, I never thought I'd miss the city.'

A chuckle left me at this exchange, as I was engrossed by this wholly new and different Aaron in front of me. One who was relaxed – just enough to almost smile – and joked – barely – with someone who seemed to be an old friend.

'But – oh, I see your lonely ass has company tonight. Hi.' TJ straightened, a toothy grin taking over his face. He was probably around Aaron's age, give or take. His frame was just as wide and almost as tall. His brown eyes took me in with an interest that caught me by surprise. I didn't think it was interest in me, nope. He seemed to mirror my own fascination with Aaron having someone by his side. 'Aren't you going to introduce me, Big A? Where are your manners?' He elbowed Aaron in the ribs.

Aaron didn't even flinch at the friendly shove, remaining the immovable wall that he usually was; he was Big A after all, a nickname I'd make sure to query him about later. Those lips that I had seen pouting just a few minutes ago opened, but they did so too late. 'Fine. I can introduce myself to the lady,' Aaron's friend said, not giving him a chance to do so himself. He stretched out his hand. 'Tyrod James. A pleasure to make your acquaintance.'

I heard a noise coming from Aaron. Something very close to his earlier snort.

'TJ for those fortunate enough to call me a friend.' His grin widened.

Taking his hand, I shook it with a light laugh. 'It's very nice to meet you. I'm Catalina Martín, but please, call me Lina.'

TJ's warm palm held my hand, his head slanted in enquiry. 'And what brings you here, Lina?'

Smiling awkwardly and not having any idea what to say, I shot Aaron a sideways glance and opened my mouth. 'I . . . erm—'

Aaron intervened. 'TJ and I were teammates in Seattle.' He turned toward his friend. 'Catalina is here with me tonight.'

TJ's eyes stayed on me as he still waited in silence, clearly wanting me to elaborate on Aaron's introduction. All right, the whole Catalina is with me was vague and redundant, but I could definitely go with that.

I cleared my throat. 'Yes, we came here together, Aaron and I.' I waved my hand between us. 'He ... picked me up and then drove us here. In his car. Together.' I nodded my head, seeing TJ's eyes light up with amusement, which made me uncomfortable. Which, in turn, made me itch to fill in the silence. 'I have a driver's licence. But New York's traffic is scary. So, I have never dared to drive in the city myself.' *Unnecessary, Lina.* 'So ... it's a really good thing Aaron picked me up. He doesn't look like he's scared of the traffic. Actually, it's him who can be a little scary sometimes.' I chuckled, but it died away quickly. 'Not that I'm scared of him. Otherwise, I wouldn't have gotten in his car.' *Shut up, Lina. Shut. Up.* I felt Aaron's laser eyes boring holes into me. TJ's too, but in a much less hostile way and a much more absorbed one. 'So, yeah, long story short, we came here together.'

Cringing internally, I reminded myself that this was what I deserved for lying in the first place.

Aaron's friend chuckled, bringing both his hands to the pockets of his maroon tuxedo. TJ's eyes jumped between us, his gaze bouncing a couple of times from Aaron to me and then right back again. Whatever he found, it was enough for him to nod his head with something that looked a lot like trouble.

'Hmm,' he said, shrugging his shoulders. 'Well, Aaron can be a scary motherfucker.' He winked. 'Me, on the other hand? Nothing but charm.'

'I can tell.' I smiled, just glad TJ had taken over the conversation.

'As I'm sure you already know, there is a bachelor auction going on tonight, and not only am I a bachelor myself' – TJ held both hands up, mischief written all over his face. Then, he peered at Aaron, as did I, and found him shooting daggers at him – 'but I have also signed up for the auction. And while I'm sure I'll be expensive, I can promise you, I am worth your—'

'TJ,' Aaron cut him off. 'That won't be necessary.'

Aaron's body somehow shifted closer to me, my shoulder almost brushing his arm. That kernel that had been planted back in my apartment – that awareness of Aaron's body, the way his proximity was really hard to ignore all of a sudden – sprouted.

I looked up at Aaron, finding his eyes already on me as his head leaned down.

'You can stop pitching yourself,' he told his friend as his gaze snared mine. Then, I felt the ghost of a touch on the small of my back. Or so I thought because it was gone far too quickly to be sure it had been real. 'Catalina is bidding on me tonight.'

I blinked. Trapped by Aaron's eyes and how close his words had fallen, almost gracing the skin of my left temple.

'You seem very sure of that,' I heard TJ say, my eyes still locked with Aaron's. 'At least for someone who sounded more like her driver than her date.'

Aaron tore his gaze off me, landing on his friend. And I did the same.

Something passed between the two men, and for a heartbeat, I felt like I should intervene.

Then, TJ threw back his head and laughed, breaking whatever tension had seemed to take shape around us. 'I'm just joking, Big A.' Another cackle. 'You should see your face. For a second there, I thought you were actually going to tackle me to the floor or something. You know that's not my style. I'd never go after a friend's girl.'

'I'm not—' My mouth opened to correct TJ, telling him I wasn't Aaron's girl. But the lines delimiting our deal were blurry, and I had no idea if I'd be inserting my foot in my mouth. I was his fake date and fake bidder, but did that mean I was his fake girl too? Damn, we definitely needed to talk this out before Spain. This test run was proving to be far more challenging than I had expected. 'He wasn't going to tackle you, TJ.'

Aaron's body seemed to relax with a sigh, somehow shifting and angling toward me. His chest brushed my arm just lightly, making me feel his warmth. 'I see that's something that hasn't changed,' Aaron muttered. 'How hilarious you think you are.'

'Come on,' I intervened. 'He was just teasing you.' Just how I would have if I wasn't still feeling all tingly and weird and I could focus on something besides the point where my shoulder grazed Aaron's chest. 'It was harmless fun.'

'See? Listen to your girl. I was just pushing your buttons.' TJ's smile persisted, lighting up his whole face. 'Just like old times.'

A question popped up in my head then. Why had TJ felt the need to push Aaron like that? Was this how they were with each other? It must have been. Aaron had gotten territorial in a matter of seconds right out of nowhere.

'Oh, speaking of old times,' TJ said, his face somehow taking on a sombre quality. 'I heard about Coach, and I'm sorry, man. I know you guys don't talk, but he is still your—'

'It's okay,' Aaron cut his friend off. I could feel the tension emanating off his body. The shift. I could sense how uncomfortable and on guard he was all of a sudden. 'Thanks, but there's nothing you have to be sorry for.'

I looked up at him, finding him pinning his friend with a warning in his eyes.

'All right,' TJ complied. 'I'm sure I don't need to tell you because you have lived through it yourself, but time doesn't wait for you to make amends, man. Time waits for nobody.'

TJ stared back at his friend with something I failed to identify. An emotion that I wanted to understand where it was coming from. How and why did it affect Aaron, and what did it have to do with that man TJ had called Coach?

'I convinced my pops to come tonight. I signed him up for the auction.' That mischievous smile was back. 'It's time he gets out there and starts living his life again. He's very excited.' Before Aaron or I could say anything – Aaron because he still looked a little lost himself and me because I was trying to understand why – TJ turned to me. 'So, Lina, if you get tired of his boring face, just know there are not one, but two James men available on the stage.'

'I'll make sure to remember that.' I smiled at him, trying to lighten my tone. 'Although I think I have my hands full with this one.'

I felt Aaron's eyes on me, warming up my face.

Why did I say that?

'Which reminds me,' TJ said. 'The auction will be starting soon, and I was sent to steal this ugly bastard away. So, if you don't mind, Lina, we should get going.'

'Oh, of course.' I let my gaze roam around, realizing how most of the people had shifted closer to the stage, which was at the far end of the rooftop. A wave of nervousness washed over me. 'You guys should go.' My smile turned tight. 'I can spare the company for a little while.' I lowered my voice. 'I'm sure you know how chatty he can get.' I pointed at Aaron. 'So, my ears can use the break.'

TJ cackled again. 'Are you sure you want to spend your money on him, Lina? I'm telling you—'

Aaron glared at him. 'Quit it already, would you?'

'Okay, okay. I was just saying, man.' TJ's hands went up.

I chuckled, but it came out a little strangled because Aaron had eaten the distance that separated us, my arm now fully coming into contact with his chest, and all of a sudden, I didn't want him to go.

My eyes landed on Aaron, who was looking down at me with an apology shining in the blue of his eyes. I must have looked and sounded as nervous as I felt if Aaron was feeling bad for leaving me to myself for a little while. I shook my head, telling myself to stop being silly.

'Yes, I think I'm sure, TJ,' I answered TJ's initial question while I searched Aaron's face. 'Go. I'll be fine on my own.'

He seemed to hesitate, not moving from my side, and I felt bad for making him feel like he needed to babysit me.

'Don't be silly, *Big A*. I'm fine, and you have to go.' I absently patted Aaron's chest, my palm freezing on the spot.

Aaron looked down at my hand very slowly, just as electricity shot up my arm. I retrieved my hand immediately, not having the slightest idea why I had done that besides the fact that the touch had come naturally to me. Aaron had felt bad for leaving me alone – probably because I had looked like someone had kicked my puppy – and I had automatically tried to comfort him with physical contact. A friendly pat. But we weren't friends, and I shouldn't forget that.

I cleared my throat. 'Go, seriously.' I lifted my empty glass in the air, feeling my cheeks heat for the umpteenth time tonight. 'I'll busy myself with getting a refill.'

'I can stay a little longer, explain to you how the bidding works.' His voice was oddly gentle. It made me uncomfortable. 'Get you another drink too.'

The urge to touch him again – to reassure him I'd be fine – was back. I suppressed it. 'I think I can figure it out on my own,' I told him softly. It couldn't be all that complex.

'What if I still want to tell you about it?'

My urge to antagonize him – to attempt to get us back to how we were supposed to be – somehow pushed me to rise onto my tiptoes. I leaned in, so only he could hear me. 'I'll figure it out. And if I don't, I swear, I will try not to spend all your money on something stupid, like a yacht or Elvis's used underpants. But I make no promises, Blackford.'

I leaned back, expecting to find him rolling his eyes or scoffing. Anything that would indicate I had succeeded and this was still us – the Aaron and Lina I was comfortable with. Instead, I was welcomed by blue eyes that were full of . . . something that churned and made me uneasy.

He hid it with a blink. 'Okay.' That was the only answer he gave me.

No snarky comeback. No scolding comment about how unfunny and inappropriate it would be to spend his money on a boat. No appalled glance after mentioning Elvis's knickers.

Nothing, except okay.

Okay then.

'All right, let's go,' TJ said, encouraging Aaron to take a step away from me. 'I'll see you later, Lina.' He winked.

'Yeah,' I mumbled and then shook my head and tried to look like I wasn't as confused as I felt. 'Woo those flocks of bidders, guys!' I cheered with my fist in the air.

TJ laughed openly, and Aaron remained looking at me with something I hoped was not regret at asking me to do this whole fake date thing for him.

Both men turned then and walked away side by side, the sight too enticing for me not to watch them as they went. I saw how TJ leaned into my fake date's side and said something probably just for him. Aaron didn't even break step; his only reaction was a shake of his raven head. Then, he shoved TJ away with a force I was sure would have sent anybody else flying.

Another one of TJ's cackles resonated in the air.

And I found myself grinning as I watched them stride off. Thinking about how seeing Aaron around all these people who belonged to a life I hadn't had the slightest clue existed – one that he had kept well guarded, just like he did everything else – was as outlandish as it was fascinating.

~

My hand rose of its own accord, catching me by surprise. 'Fifteen hundred for the lady in the beautiful midnight-blue gown,' Angela – who had been in charge of conducting the auction for the last hour – called from behind the microphone stand with a rather shocked smile.

My throat dried up, making it impossible for me to swallow my own audacity.

I was a despicable human being because I had just bid a dizzying amount of money on someone. A man. A bachelor no less.

One that wasn't Aaron.

The seemingly sweet and older man I had just bid on gave an enthusiastic cheer from the centre of the stage, relief taking over his wrinkled face. He bowed in my direction.

As much as I felt horrible and guilty and honestly a little terrified, I couldn't help but smile at him in return.

Willing my eyes to stay put – and not to jump to Aaron, who was a few feet to the left of the stage, waiting for his turn to be auctioned – I tried to shake off the well-deserved sense of guilt that had settled between my shoulders.

Chill. I needed to chill. Someone else would bid higher. The old man just needed a little push to get this going.

And that was exactly what I had done. Or what I had found myself doing after the five minutes of awkward and heartbreaking silence following that sweet-looking man stepping on the stage. I had recognized that smile immediately. I had seen the same one playing on TJ's lips.

'Ladies and gentlemen, sixteen hundred for Patrick James.' Angela's voice came through the speakers.

No hands rose in the air. Not even one.

Dammit.

The man I had correctly assumed was TJ's pops, Patrick, stood on the stage with his gray hair and suspenders, his back a little curved with age, looking completely out of place when compared with every other man who had been up for grabs – or bids, whatever – that night. He smiled, satisfied enough with being there. With just having one bidder, which happened to be me. And that was bad, bad, bad. Because I was here to bid on Aaron. Not for a man who, according to Angela's introduction, was a widower who was looking for a second chance not in love, but in living life.

Jesus, I'd take him on a date if I had to. I hadn't been able to stand there and do nothing when a man who reminded me so much of my own passed *abuelo* for some damn reason, a man I knew was TJ's pops, was waiting for someone, for *anybody*, to bid on him. This was a fundraiser, for Christ's sake. Weren't people supposed to be donating their money?

That was what I had done. Only perhaps I had technically bid with money that wasn't mine.

I grimaced.

Don't look at Aaron, Lina. Don't.

I'd pay for the donation with my own funds. The most pressing issue was, could I bid for two bachelors?

Shit. I really hoped so.

Angela continued pitching the sweet man on the stage. 'Mr James has an affinity for candlelit dinners, and he is a believer in fulfilling his own destiny.'

Patrick's head nodded. No hands were visible.

Mierda, mierda, mierda.

I couldn't look at Aaron. I'd bet he was fuming. But I'd apologize later. I'd . . . explain.

'He is a sailing aficionado, an activity he picked up ever since his grandson bought him a beautiful sailboat. One that he intends on putting to good use on his date.'

Out of the corner of my eye, I tracked down around five women who were in the mood for a sailing date placing their bids.

Relief filled me so instantly that I felt about ten pounds lighter.

My gaze searched for Aaron then. And it didn't take me any time to find him. My eyes seemed to know exactly where he was standing.

My breath caught for a second. *Stupid, stupid tuxedo.*

I had been so wrapped up in what was happening that he, looking all imposing and striking on top of that stage, caught me completely off guard.

The auction for Patrick continued in the background, my eyes making their way to Aaron's. They were narrowed. Probably assessing what the hell that had been. Other than that, he looked . . . fine. Neutrally stoic. Just like he usually did. Except for the distracting tux that hung on his body like a glove.

Finding a little comfort in the fact that Aaron didn't seem to be completely furious, I shrugged my shoulders and mouthed, *I'm sorry, okay?*

Aaron's eyes narrowed further, and then his head shook lightly. *You're not*, I watched his lips enunciate.

I huffed. *I am*, I mouthed back. I was very, very sorry, and he—

He shook his head again, disbelief in his eyes. *You're not.*

Aggravated by the words Aaron had mouthed – twice – even though he had every right to and I had sort of anticipated it, I threw both my hands up with irritation.

Jesus, this man—

'Nineteen hundred for the lady in midnight blue.' Angela's voice reached my ears.

Wait, what? No.

I flinched, then dropped my hands to my sides, and stuck them there. Looking at Angela for confirmation of what I had done, even if this time accidentally, I found her pointing in my direction.

Shit.

Returning my gaze to Aaron, I watched him roll his eyes, lips pressed into that thin line I knew so well.

Grimacing, I sent him a tight smile that I hoped communicated how *really* sorry I was and hoped Patrick had another one of those boats. Because I needed somebody else to bid on the old widower man.

Angela announced the next sum, not obtaining an immediate answer.

The guilt returned, together with a pinch of embarrassment. Which pushed me to pin Aaron with a serious look as I mouthed again, *Sorry*, very slowly and methodically. Making sure he understood the sentiment behind it.

Aaron's eyes held mine, one of those deadpan expressions in place.

I swear. I made my lips form the silent words in the most exaggerated manner I could. Then, I curled my lips into a sad face, keeping the rest of my body still – just so I wouldn't accidentally bid on any more bachelors. *I am really sorry*, I mouthed like a total idiot.

And I was. Sorry, that was. Although a bit of an idiot too.

A few heads turned and sent me a fair share of weird glances, but I didn't let that deter me, and I kept my lips bent down. Telling Aaron with my eyes that I was sorry. Although, if you asked me, it was on him for bringing me of all people to do something that I was clearly not qualified for.

The sight must have been truly something because before I knew what was happening, Aaron's shoulders shook a couple of times, his stance broke, and one of his hands went to the back of his neck as his head dipped. I couldn't see his face, so I had no clue of what was going on. All money was on him bursting in frustration and anger and turning into the Hulk. And just when I was about to really start worrying, he lifted back that raven-haired head of his and revealed something I would never have bet on.

The biggest, widest, and handsomest smile was splitting his expression. Wrinkling the corners of his eyes. Transforming him into a man my own eyes couldn't take in fast enough. A man I had never seen before. One who was beginning to make it really, really hard for me to hate him.

My own face lit up at the sight. I felt my cheeks tense with my answering grin – one just as big, just as wide, just as unexpected.

And then Aaron started laughing. His head tilted back, and his shoulders shook with laughter. And he was doing it on a stage, in front of all these people and in front of me, as if he didn't have a care in the world.

Neither did I, apparently. Because in that moment, the only thing I could focus on, think of, care about was Aaron's unexpected and glorious smile and laughter. So much that my fingers itched to pull out my phone and snap a photo so I had proof that this had happened. So I could revisit the moment – in which Aaron Blackford, someone who had the power to irritate me with nothing but a word, had fucking lit up the place with a smile he had kept locked up from me ever since I met him – whenever I wanted.

And how messed up was that? Or furthermore, how messed up was it that I didn't even care about it being messed up in the first place?

Before I could recover from it – the effect of something as mundane as a smile, but which was so rare in the man I couldn't stop looking at – he was striding toward the centre of the stage.

Angela's voice came over the speakers. 'Lovely. I'm sure Patrick and his lucky bidder, the lady with the blue fan, will enjoy whatever he has prepared.'

Too caught up in my fake date who knew how to really smile, I hadn't noticed someone else bidding for Patrick.

'And last but not least, we have Aaron Blackford. Ladies, gentlemen, let's start at fifteen hundred and remember—' Angela's eyes widened, and then she chuckled. 'Oh, I guess I don't need to remind you to please place your bids on our last bachelor tonight if you want to contribute to the cause.'

Looking around, I discovered the reason why. More than ten different bidders had their arms already in the air.

'I love seeing your involvement,' Angela continued with a knowing smirk. 'Fifteen hundred for the lady in red.'

Turning, I located this involved–with–the–cause lady in red. She was in the first row, and looked about twenty years older than me, give or take. And while I didn't want to be judgemental or superficial, just by looking at her I could imagine how generous her donation would be.

My gaze shot back to the stage, clashing against Aaron's. That grin had been wiped off, his features now hard and empty. I felt a pang of disappointment I had no time to examine.

I had one job tonight, and I was failing at it. For the second time.

Readying myself, I released a breath. I couldn't let myself be distracted by something as wonderfully shocking yet pointless as Aaron's ability to smile or laugh.

'Seventeen hundred?' Angela announced, and I gestured with my hand to place my bid. Too late. 'For the lady in red.'

Lady in Red had beaten me – and around another five or six hands – to it again.

A quick look at Aaron's tense shoulders told me he felt as unhappy about it as I was.

I squared back my shoulders, focusing on Angela and her next words.

'Wonderful,' she said into the microphone. 'Let's raise this up, ladies and gentlemen. Mr Blackford is after all in high demand. How about nineteen hun—'

My hand shot up in the air, keeping an eye on Lady in Red, whose bid had been faster than mine. Again.

Angela chuckled and pointed at Lady in Red again, acknowledging her bid.

To my shock and surprise, Lady in Red turned in my direction with a smug smile on her face.

My eyes narrowed. *Oh, hell no.* This wasn't about charity. This had just gotten personal.

Angela announced the next amount, and I launched my hand in

the air with impressive speed, so much that I almost pulled a muscle, but Angela's next words made up for possible injuries.

'For the lovely lady in midnight blue.' Angela smiled from behind the stand.

I returned it, feeling a weird burn in the pit of my stomach, matching the one on my shoulder.

Next bid was called, and it was mine again.

Ha! Suck that, Lady in Red.

As if she had heard me, her head whirled around. Her eyes narrowed to very thin slits, and her lips pursed. The woman whipped her blonde hair back and dismissed me.

I knew in that moment that I had been right to assume this was personal. This lady was after Aaron. And I wasn't going to let her get my Aaron—

Not mine, I corrected myself. *Just Aaron*. I wasn't going to let her get Aaron.

The call for the next bid came, and before Angela's words were out, it was already mine. Lady in Red sent me a look that could have frozen the sun on a heated New York summer day, and I was tempted to stick my tongue out, but after reminding myself that would be about a hundred ways of inappropriate, I limited myself to smirking.

Lady in Red and I battled for about five or six more rounds. Each of them becoming brisker, our arms flashing up faster, the looks we sent each other growing icier. My breath quickened, and the skin on my face felt as if I'd just sprinted across Central Park like I was chasing the freaking ice cream truck. But so far, it was worth it because Aaron remained mine.

Not mine. Just . . . whatever.

I had been so absorbed by this duel we had going on that I had almost forgotten about the man on the stage. I had barely checked on him since the bidding bloodshed started.

Just as I was about to turn my attention to Aaron, my hand rose in the air one more time – as high as the ridiculous amount of money we had reached – and this time, it did so alone.

Angela waved in my direction. 'Going once for the lady in midnight blue,' she called.

My heart thumped against my chest harder. I caught a glimpse of a grey-haired man beside a tight-lipped Lady in Red, who stood with her arms crossed in front of her chest.

'Going twice,' Angela continued as I watched the man whisper something in Lady in Red's ear, to which she just sighed and nodded. Reluctantly.

Come on, come on, come on. Aaron is almost mine.

'And sold to the very lovely and very passionate lady in the midnight-blue gown.' Angela closed the bidding with a wink.

I felt the celebratory holler climbing to my throat as my head finally turned in Aaron's direction. I wanted to do a little victory dance. To throw my hands in the air too. I also felt the urge to shout a couple of inappropriate words, which, in hindsight, I would have realized was extremely stupid and I would have immediately regretted it.

But as Aaron came into view, that whirling emotion that had been too loud a moment ago, fell silent on its own. He wasn't even smiling. He simply . . . looked at me.

The disappointment at not finding that grin I had gotten a glimpse of earlier returned, and I wondered if it would be this way from today on. Me searching for Aaron's smile and him keeping it locked away again.

I swallowed that up, shoving those stupid thoughts out of my head.

My lips tugged up regardless of all that, and I gave a half-hearted cheer. To which Aaron simply nodded, looking like he did when he had something in his mind. Something that bothered him.

Frowning, I watched Aaron's long legs climb down the stage and walk to my side, all the while ignoring how the way he wasn't even celebrating with me made me feel. Instead, I focused on keeping what I hoped looked like a genuine smile in place.

The blue-eyed man I had just *bought* for a date that would never happen stopped in front of me. He dipped his head, his chin almost touching his collarbone. I waited, but he didn't say anything.

I reached for something to say and came up empty-handed, returning the silence.

That awareness I had been familiarizing myself with far too rapidly for my own good and comfort came rushing back, raising the short hairs on my arms. It hit me then how weird, how strange, and how shocking in many different ways it was that we'd found each other in this situation. How tonight didn't even seem real.

Shifting on my feet under the weight of Aaron's gaze, I swallowed. One more time, I wasn't capable of taking in this heavy silence that settled between us. 'I hope you come with a boat, Blackford,' I finally said, my voice sounding a little off. 'Otherwise, I might regret not sticking with Patrick.'

Aaron's eyes didn't waver. They held mine. And as they did so, I watched how they warmed up for just a heartbeat. The skin around them wrinkling only slightly with the smile I now knew he refused to give me.

I felt something shift in my chest. Something very subtle and small that I almost missed, but it didn't help my breathing – still all over the place from the auction – to return to normal.

He took one step closer. 'Sometimes, I'm convinced you enjoy making me suffer.' His usually deep voice sounded hushed. Giving his words an afterthought quality.

'Oh.' I frowned. My mouth opened, but I still struggled for a few more moments. 'Okay, you have every right to be pissed, but in all fairness, we are even because you should have warned me it would get that intense.' I laughed awkwardly. 'If I had known, I would have added a ninja star or two to my outfit. They would have definitely come in handy with Lady in Red.'

Aaron towered over me, quiet and still gazing at me in that way that made me shift on my feet again.

Silence settled between us once more, bringing to my attention that we were no longer surrounded by the crowd that had gathered in front of the stage. Instead, the murmur of voices accompanied by a mellow tune came all the way from the other side of the rooftop.

Aaron broke the silence, saying, 'Dance with me.'

CHAPTER NINE

He offered his hand, letting it hang in the small space between our bodies.

Gaping at it, I hesitated. Not really sure whether I had a reason to doubt his offer or if it was just the way I automatically reacted to Aaron.

'Is this part of the deal?' I heard myself ask.

Aaron frowned.

'Us dancing, I mean. Just for show, right?' I explained.

I wasn't blind – or stupid – and I was pretty sure that dancing wasn't something we needed to do. But a big part of me was effectively confused, and I was growing more so by the moment. So, by saying that out loud, I was simply throwing myself a lifeline I could grab on to until I could clear up the mess in my head.

'Right,' Aaron answered, that frown disappearing and his hand still waiting for my decision. 'Just for show.'

I accepted his offer, letting his large palm wrap around mine, unsure of how good an idea this was.

Aaron pulled me gently behind him, and my legs shook with a weird mix of anticipation and unease. His hand was warm and firm against mine, making me feel good and tingly even though at the same time it weighted down that lifeline I was trying to hold on to with teeth and nails.

I was still unsure of how good an idea it was when he

softly dragged me to where a small group of people had gathered to dance.

But it was when he stopped walking, turned, and stepped close – so very close – that my mind finally flagged this as a bad idea. So much that a part of me started debating whether I should run away or pretend I fainted right there and then so I didn't have to face what we were about to do.

Dancing.

Together.

As in Aaron Blackford – the man I had been antagonizing for so long – and me.

Oh sweet baby Jesus.

Aaron draped his arms around my waist, and I felt a shock of electricity spreading across my body from the points where his hands rested on my back. My breath caught, and something heavy and solid dropped to the bottom of my stomach.

Swallowing hard, I tilted my head back. I thought I saw dare and wariness in his gaze. All at once. And that sent an unsolicited spur of anticipation through me.

I placed my hands on Aaron's chest – noticing how hard and toned it felt under my fingers – but unlike earlier tonight, when I had accidentally touched him, this time, I let my hands rest there. Only then did he bring me to him. My small frame immediately cradled in his much larger one.

A heartbeat later, we were moving, almost every part of our bodies from our chests down pressed together. Aaron's motions were sure, directing, while mine were stiff and non-compliant.

Releasing a breath through my nose, I tried to relax my limbs. To focus on the mechanics of dancing. To calm that red-hot awareness raging inside of me. But the knowledge of how close our bodies were was setting off alarms inside my head and making it impossible for me to think about much else besides that.

Dancing. We were dancing. Bodies flushed. And that was something we weren't supposed to be doing. A situation in which *Aaron and Lina, who barely tolerated each other*, shouldn't be finding themselves because this wasn't something that people who couldn't stand each other did.

Aaron spun me in a circle with a swift motion and pressed me against him one more time, making my heart quicken in a way it had no business doing.

The music was slow, perfect for swaying and forgetting about everything outside the smooth rhythm. Ideal for getting lost in the peace that being in someone else's arms could bring. But the more we swayed, the further I was from feeling anything that resembled peace. Not when Aaron was so ... big and hard and warm against me.

That was probably why I tripped. Before I knew what was happening, my feet had messed up the beat and tangled together, and they would have probably sent me straight to the floor if not for the man who held me in place, the pair of strong arms wrapped solidly around me.

'Thank you,' I muttered, feeling my face heat up and my body tense up further. 'And sorry.'

God. I had never blushed so much in one single night. I didn't recognize myself.

Aaron's arms tightened around me. 'Just for precaution,' he said, bringing me even closer.

Each and every nerve ending I possessed turned into the end of a live wire. My skin tingled, my heart raced, and my mind whirled.

'Oh. Okay.' The words reached my ears, strangled, as if it had come out of me in a gurgle. 'Thanks.'

The skin on my face heated up even further.

Aaron hmmed, just as his thumb brushed my back very lightly, drawing one single circle that left a tiny trail of goosebumps behind it. Goosebumps that travelled to every nook and corner of my body.

As much as I told myself that this was a simple physical reaction to being held against a male body, being held by a man's arms, it was Aaron's male body and Aaron's arms after all. So, either I had been alone for too long or I was losing my mind. Because this felt . . . good. Really good.

Too damn much.

Those ocean-blue eyes shifted to my lips briefly. So quickly that I was convinced I had imagined it. It didn't matter though because then his face dipped, getting as close as it had ever been and making me forget all about that. Making me notice instead details that I had never paid attention to before. Like how full those lips were, which I had seen pressed into a line so often. Or how his eyelashes were long and dark and framed the blue in his eyes so perfectly. Or how I could see the lines of the soft creases adorning his forehead, right above the spot where that frown that was almost a fixed feature rested.

I was so lost in all that that I almost tripped again, but Aaron's arms tightened their grip around my waist as he bent his head down to one side of mine.

'Aren't you supposed to be good at this, Catalina?' he asked a few inches from my ear. I felt the air leaving his mouth on my temple.

Trying not to pay any extra attention to how close his lips were to my face, I focused on my feet and answered almost absently, 'What do you mean?'

Aaron's diligent and smooth motions spun us one more time to the soft tune.

'I thought you were supposed to carry the beat in your blood,' he explained in a low voice, his head not giving up an inch of space. 'Or was it the music in your veins?'

I hoped my ears were not red with mortification. 'This is not my style,' I lied. I'd never done a worse job at dancing, and it had nothing to do with the music and everything to do with the man I was currently flush against. 'Or maybe it's my partner that's not the best fit.'

Aaron chuckled. It was low and short-lived, but it reminded me of the way he had laughed earlier, leaving me a little out of breath.

And so, I inhaled deeply, trying to restore my breathing and immediately regretting it. Because what an awful idea that had been. *The worst idea.* All I had accomplished was filling my lungs with Aaron's scent.

Aaron's very nice and very heady and very, very masculine scent.

Could I unsmell it, please, universe? Please.

'Was that you admitting something you are not good at?' Aaron asked, pulling me out of my head. 'To me?'

'I never claimed to be a spectacular dancer.' Not when my partner was someone who certainly succeeded in distracting me so damn much. 'Plus, all that rhythm in your blood stuff is nothing more than a stereotype. There are more than a few hundred Spaniards who can't follow a beat to save their lives.'

'I bet there are. I'll keep leading then.' His voice was low, a little closer to my ear than before. 'But just in case you belong to those few hundreds.'

'If you must,' I muttered because what was the point of denying something that was so obvious? I was doing a poor job at it. 'I didn't know you danced.'

Just when I thought it was physically impossible for Aaron's body to fold around mine any more, for our bodies to come any closer, he dipped his head further. Impossibly low. His lips hovered directly above the shell of my ear. 'There are a few things you don't know about me, Catalina.'

My body went even more rigid in response. A flutter taking flight in my stomach.

I forced myself to remember that I was here to pretend I was his date – of sorts. That I had put on a little show at fighting that woman over him at the auction. So, fake or not, to everybody else, I was supposed to be someone who would welcome this kind of closeness and not someone who would jump back, startled.

So, I settled my hands on his hard chest with a little more decision. Unfortunately, the gesture only managed to turn that flutter in my stomach to a full-on flapping and waving and whirling riot.

'What's on your mind?' Aaron asked, sounding genuinely curious.

Being caught off guard by the question – and the interest – I blurted the first thing that came to mind, 'You said this had nothing to do with a woman.' I shifted my palms across his chest. 'But it looked to me like it had everything to do with one.'

'I've never seen Mrs Archibald so riled up,' he admitted.

I adjusted my hands on his chest again, trying not to get lost in how warm his skin felt, even beneath all the layers of fabric. 'So, you are familiar with this Mrs Archibald, huh?' I felt his head nod once, his jaw brushing my temple. 'Let me guess. Tonight was not her first time getting into a little charitable quarrel over you.'

'It wasn't.'

'Aaron Blackford, the cougar magnet.' I laughed lightly, the sound coming out a little shaky.

A soft puff of air hit my ear, rousing a wave of shivers. 'It wasn't only Mrs Archibald enthusiastically bidding, if memory serves me well.'

'Smug,' I muttered.

But Aaron was right. There had been many other people – younger, attractive – interested in him.

'Is this why you asked me to be here?' Aaron didn't immediately answer, so I continued, 'I guess it all makes sense. What Angela said earlier and TJ kind of confirmed.'

'And what's that?'

'That Aaron Blackford is scared of a bunch of overly motivated wealthy ladies who want to buy his company.'

His palms shifted on my back, spinning us into the changing rhythm of a new song. 'Are you teasing me?' he said right into my ear.

I was. But I would never admit to such a thing out loud. I felt myself relax just the splinter of a hair in his arms. 'Does it happen often?'

'What exactly, Catalina?' he asked very slowly. 'Almost being exchanged for a man with a boat or having a questionable dancing partner?'

'Neither.' Feeling the smile tugging at my lips, I went on, 'Women flaunting themselves at you. I saw how tense you were on the stage. You looked ready to jump out and get out of there.' I thought about that for a second. Him bringing me here ... it kind of made sense now. 'Does that kind of attention make you uncomfortable?'

'Not always.' I felt the brush of his jaw against my cheek, the simple and light gesture causing an electrifying wave of sensation to trail down my neck. 'I'm not scared of a woman's interest in me, if that's what you're asking. I don't send them all away.'

'Oh, okay.' My voice came out breathy and unsure.

Of course he didn't. I was sure he had *needs*. And those needs were something I wasn't willing to think about with his arms around me.

Aaron's right hand shifted on my back, trailing down an inch or two. Meanwhile, the skin of my face – no, my whole freaking body – burned.

His arms tightened around me one more time. 'Thank you,' he said.

And I felt those two words like a soft breath of air against my hair.

'What for?' My voice was barely a whisper.

'For not stepping on my foot.' I opened my mouth to apologize, but he continued, 'But also for not being deterred by Mrs Archibald. Last year, things got a little ... uncomfortable when she found out our date consisted of cleaning dog kennels and spending a couple of hours walking and playing with them.' I felt his sigh on the skin on the side of my neck. 'Not that it dissuaded her this year.'

Something that felt a lot like protectiveness flickered in my chest.

I shook my head lightly, trying to make sense of myself. All this dancing and spinning was clearly messing with me. 'Well, as much as I'm sorry for your wallet, considering the amount the donation reached, I'm happy I got to see that sulky face when I beat her,' I admitted, shocking myself at how pleased I had really been. 'I'm also sorry for those doggies and what they had to endure last year with that woman. What kind of hypocrite donates money for a charity that focuses on animal shelters and doesn't like dogs? Those poor guys. I'd adopt them all if I didn't live in a tiny studio apartment. Hell, I'd happily volunteer to spend some time with them any day.'

'I can take you, if that's what you want.' Aaron's words hung in the air. A part of me wanted to say yes. Yes to the chance of seeing a new side of him. Perhaps another smile too. 'You just bought a date anyway.'

'With your money.'

'Regardless,' he countered. 'It's part of the package deal.'

That pang of unprecedented hurt hit me again, reminding me of what this was. *Part of the deal.* That was Aaron, a man of his word.

Aaron's head reared back, revealing his face. His gaze was searching.

'I . . .' I hesitated, feeling stupid for considering for just an instant that maybe he'd offered because he genuinely wanted to take me there. 'I just . . .'

Shit.

Everything that had happened tonight was spinning in my head. Aaron in a tux. All these . . . new and different ways I was feeling around him. The auction. His smile. His laughter. Dancing. My body against his, flushed together. All of that and then the fact that we would be going to Spain in a matter of a few weeks.

Everything tangled together in knots that messed with my head.

Aaron kept looking at me, a strange emotion behind his blue eyes. He was probably waiting for me to say something that wasn't mumbled words.

'Would that . . .' I shook my head. 'I wouldn't want to get you in trouble,' I finally managed to say. 'I guess that someone could check if the auction contract was fulfilled?' I didn't know if this contract existed. Didn't even know if anybody would even check anything. 'The last thing I'd want is to hamper the good that the fundraiser has achieved tonight.' I kept going, Aaron's features unchanging, 'Nobody needs to know that the date is fake anyway. Right?'

He kept looking at me in that searching way I didn't understand. 'No. Nobody needs to know.'

'Or that we are going as friends, right?' That had not sounded right. Were we even friends?

'Is that what you want to be, Catalina?' Aaron shot back calmly. 'Friends?'

'Yes,' I answered. But did I? We had never been, and that had never had anything to do with me. That hadn't been on me. 'No,' I rectified, remembering that one big obstacle that had stood between us since the beginning. One that Aaron had put there, not me. It had been him, the one who never liked me, not the other way around. It wasn't fair of him to ask me now. 'I don't know, Aaron.' My palms felt clammy and my throat dry, and I was . . . confused. 'What kind of question is that?'

Aaron seemed to ponder my words. 'Yes or no?' he pressed.

My mouth opened and closed. We had stopped dancing at some point. My palms, which had been on Aaron's chest, dropped down. Aaron's gaze followed the motion. Something locked tightly behind that unreadable mask that was his expression.

'Forget I said anything,' he said, his arms, which had been still around me, falling down. 'This was a bad idea.'

That made me physically flinch, and I didn't really understand why I had done that or what he'd meant by this.

Both of us stood in front of each other, unmoving. And as much as Aaron had been distant and dismissive in the past, he had never looked this . . . aloof. Almost as if I had said something that hurt him.

The urge to reach out and place my hand on his chest resurfaced again. And I couldn't, for the life of me, begin to fathom why. Not when a small voice in my head – which I assumed was common sense – was telling me that I should be glad, that this was us getting back on track to where we should stand.

But I wasn't any good at listening to sense these days. So, when my arm lifted – because I was like that and I couldn't help but comfort those around me with hugs or touches or whatever they needed – and Aaron stepped back, away from me, it actually stung. So much that I had to scold myself for being that stupid.

'See?' I said under my breath. 'This is why I don't know if we can be friends. Why we have never been.'

Tonight had been a fluke, and this was the reason. Everything always escalated out of control when it came to us.

'You are right.' His voice was unspeakably flat. 'Being your friend has always been the last thing on my mind.'

His words, together with mine, felt like hail falling unrelentingly on me. On us, as we stood there in front of each other. Poking holes in the little bubble we had been in for the past few hours. The one we had been in while we danced. Right before the truce that had been silently established blew up in our faces.

Just like I should have expected.

I blinked at him, not knowing what to say.

'If you'll excuse me,' he said, 'I'll be back in a few minutes and take you home.'

He turned around and left me right where I was. Rooted to the spot.

Standing on legs that I didn't trust without the support of his arms. My heart beating ruthlessly against my chest. Feeling the cold seep through my blood in his sudden absence and my head questioning everything that had happened tonight, regardless of how much I reminded myself that it meant nothing.

Nothing at all.

We had never been friends.

We were back to being the same Aaron and Lina we had always been, and that was something that would never change.

CHAPTER TEN

When I entered InTech headquarters the following Monday, I was feeling like I had swallowed a ball of lead with my coffee that morning. And with every step I took in the direction of my office, the sensation kept intensifying, as if the ball were expanding and taking up more and more room inside me.

I hadn't been this ... *uneasy* ever since that awful call a couple of weeks ago when I had heard that Daniel was engaged. The one phone call where the lie had come to be.

But this was different, wasn't it?

This heaviness in the pit of my stomach had nothing to do with something I had blurted out in a moment of desperation and stupidity.

Although maybe it did.

Because as much as acknowledging that the way I felt had anything to do with how Aaron and I had left things on Saturday was the last thing I wanted to do, I had to. And as much as I refused to waste a second of my time worrying over it, I had done.

Which was absolutely ridiculous because why would I want last Saturday – or him – to take any space in my head? I had no reason to. Not consciously at least. We weren't friends. We didn't owe each other anything. And whatever he had said – or done, or looked like, or smelled like, or the way he had smiled or held me as we danced or even whatever he had whispered in my damn ear – should have bounced right off me.

But apparently, my mind had other ideas.

'Being your friend has always been the last thing on my mind.'

Those had been his words. He couldn't have said it any clearer.

Fine by me. I had never wanted to be his friend either. Except maybe for a couple of days when he had first started at InTech.

But that ship had sailed long ago. I had blacklisted him for a reason, and that was where he should have stayed. In my blacklist.

The only teeny-tiny problem was that I sort of needed him. And I . . . *God.* I'd deal with that later.

Shaking off all of Aaron's drama and burying deep that kernel of uneasiness so it did not grow into something else, I placed my bag on my chair, grabbed my planner, and made my way to the room where our monthly Breakfast & Broadcast was held. Jeff, our boss and all five teams that he coordinated attended. And no, we didn't have breakfast and watch the news. Unfortunately. It was just a meeting that took place once a month, where bad coffee and a really sad excuse for cookies were provided and where Jeff updated our division on the latest news and announcements.

Being one of the first in the room, I took my usual place, opened my planner, and went through a few reminders I had noted down for the week while the room filled out with people.

Feeling the soft brush of a hand on my arm and the light scent of peaches, I turned, already knowing who I'd find smiling down at me.

'Hey, Jim's or Greenie's for lunch?' Rosie asked in a hushed voice.

'I'd sell my soul for a bagel from Jim's, but I shouldn't.' Today was definitely not a salad day; my mood would plummet down even more, but the wedding was right around the corner. 'So, Greenie's.'

'Are you sure?' Rosie's gaze slid to the cookies displayed on the narrow table placed at the entrance of the room. 'God, those look worse than usual.'

I chuckled, and before I could answer, my stomach grumbled.

'Kinda regretting not having breakfast,' I murmured, looking at my friend with a grimace.

'Lina.' Rosie frowned, her voice holding a warning edge. 'That's not you, sweetie. That diet you have been on, it's just stupid.'

'It's not a diet.' I rolled my eyes, ignoring the voice in my head that was agreeing with my friend. 'I'm just watching what I eat.'

She cut me a look that told me she didn't believe me. 'We are going to Jim's.'

'Trust me, after the weekend I had, I'd let you take me there, and I'd raid the place, but it's gonna be a no.'

My friend searched my face, probably finding something in there because an eyebrow arched. 'What did you do?'

I leaned back on my chair, a little huff leaving my lips. 'I did not—' I stopped myself. I had done plenty. 'I'll tell you later, okay?'

Her eyes filled with concern. 'At Jim's.' With one last nod, Rosie shifted past me and went to the chair next to Héctor, her team leader.

When I caught the eye of the old man, I waved at him with a small smile, receiving a wink from him in return.

And then – catching me completely off guard, even when it shouldn't have – my Aaron radar went off. Warning me of his presence.

My heart lurched in my chest, and my gaze hunted him down.

He is not that good-looking. He's just tall, I told myself as I took him in.

Something in my ribcage sped up.

It was the tuxedo, because my body is surely not reacting to that button-down shirt and those pressed slacks, I thought as my eyes followed his long strides to the chair I knew he'd take a couple of rows in front of me and to my left.

Yeah, his face is certainly nothing to write home about, I reminded myself as I studied his hard and masculine profile, from his jaw to the dark line of thick hair framing his forehead.

See? I've got this under control. My body is back to normal. I didn't need the comfort of a cream cheese and salmon bagel.

But then Aaron looked back. His eyes met mine across the room. Finding me looking at him in a way I presumed was a little too intense for someone who had sworn she wouldn't pay him any attention only a few minutes ago.

I felt my cheeks flush a deep shade of red, and I'd bet I looked like my whole face was on fire.

And yet, the one who looked away first wasn't me. It was him. Aaron's eyes fell down and stayed somewhere ahead. Somewhere that wasn't me.

Something about that did not sit well with me. Something about the fact that he had just dismissed me so quickly bothered me more than ever.

But before I could delve too much into that, Jeff's voice pulled me right back. 'Good morning, everyone,' he said, and the low muttering in the room turned into silence. 'This Breakfast and Broadcast session will be fairly short. I need to run to an impromptu meeting I was called to in about thirty minutes, so don't get too comfortable, and have your fill of cookies before it's over.' Our boss laughed lightly.

Nobody bothered to move. Obviously.

'As you know, we are undergoing some important changes in the structure of InTech. A rearrangement of the responsibilities will take place – among a few other things, of course. Everything will have a repercussion on the structure of the company as we know it today. But this is not a reason to worry. Most of the changes will be integrated gradually and throughout the upcoming months.'

The screen that hung from one of the conference room walls showed an organizational chart of our division with our boss's name highlighted on top – Jeff Foster – and the names of the five team leaders right under his – Aaron Blackford, Gerald Simmons, Héctor Díaz, Kabir Pokrehl, and me, Catalina Martín.

There had been rumours – nothing more than corridor whispers – that something big was about to happen in the company. Something that would shake things up. But no one really knew what was about to come.

'Having said that,' our boss continued after clearing his throat, 'there is an announcement I'd like to make now, before any of it is officially released in a corporate statement.'

The man who my friend and colleague Rosie had referred to as a *silver fox* one time when she was a little tipsy, who was all grey hair and natural charm, seemed to hesitate for a moment. His hand flew to the collar of his shirt, tugging at it lightly.

Jeff pressed a key on his laptop, and a new slide was displayed on the screen. One with a diagram that was very similar to the one presented previously. Almost a duplicate, it was essentially the exact same, except for one single detail.

The name filling the blue square above the five team leaders in the Tech Division was no longer Jeff's.

That ball of lead I had been feeling since early that morning fell to my feet.

Our boss clasped his hands together, my gaze switching between him and the screen. 'I am pleased to announce that Aaron Blackford will be promoted to head of the Solutions Division of InTech.' Jeff's words entered my ears, travelling all the way to my head, where they seemed to bounce from one wall to the next, unable to be processed by my brain. 'Aaron has been one of the most consistent and efficient members I have ever had the pleasure to oversee, and he has proven himself worthy for this promotion time and time again. So, I have no doubt in my mind that he will do an amazing job as head of the division.'

Everybody had been shocked into silence. Just like me.

'It hasn't been decided when he'll take over all my responsibilities while I undertake a more advisory role for InTech, but I wanted to give you – the *Solutions* family – the news first. Even if it hasn't been officially announced yet.'

Jeff continued talking then, probably going through whatever was in the agenda of the Breakfast & Broadcast next. Or maybe not – I didn't know. I wasn't listening. I couldn't when his announcement was the only thing spinning in my head.

Aaron Blackford will be my boss.

My gaze shot to Aaron, who was leaning back in his chair. His gaze was fixed somewhere in front of him, his expression impassive. Even more than usual.

There was a pause and some clapping. With which my hands joined in automatically.

Aaron Blackford will be promoted to head of the division, and I just went on a date with him. A fake date but one to anyone looking.

For an instant, I was hurled back in time. To a past I had left behind and did not want to remember. Or relive ever again.

Shaking my head, I tried to assuage the whirlwind of unwelcome memories. No, I wouldn't think of that right now, not in front of everyone.

My gaze, which was still latched on to Aaron, studied his vacant expression.

This changed everything. Whatever was . . . between us.

It no longer mattered that he was my only option. It didn't matter anymore that no one in Spain would believe we were dating because we bickered and argued constantly. It did not matter that he had confessed he never wanted to be my friend and that I didn't know where that left us.

None of that mattered because, now, the deal was off. It had to be off.

I would not play charades with the man who was to be promoted to head of my division. My boss.

There was no way I'd put myself in a situation I had already been in, which had ended up so badly. For me. Only for me. So, even if all of it would be fake – had been fake last Saturday – I simply would not risk it.

The screeching of chairs brought me back to the room. I watched everyone swiftly stand up and scatter, Aaron included.

I met Rosie's gaze, gaping green eyes framed by dark curls.

Holy shit, my friend mouthed.

Holy shit indeed.

And she didn't even know all of it yet.

I caught a glimpse of Aaron's back somewhere behind Rosie, and a resolution that hadn't been there a moment ago solidified in my mind. Mamá had taught me better than to leave things hanging over my head. Ignoring and waiting for them to go away on their own wasn't the smart thing to do. Because they didn't. Sooner or later – and just when you least expected them to – they'd fall off right on top of you, and chances were, they'd take you down with them if you let them.

With newfound determination driving my body, I waved at Rosie and let my legs walk me out of the meeting room. My short limbs were on a mission, trying to catch up with the long strides of the man I was chasing.

In less than a minute, which wasn't long but about enough for my heart to start racing with a weird and strange anticipation, he reached his office. I entered only a few steps behind him.

I watched Aaron walk up to his chair and let his body fall onto it, his lids falling shut and his right hand reaching for his face. He rubbed his eyes.

He must have thought he was alone because I didn't think Aaron had ever allowed himself to look like this when there was someone around. So weary. *Real* and not that steel facade he always put on.

Just like it had happened on Saturday, the urge to comfort him rose again. And despite myself, I almost started in his direction and asked if he was okay. Thankfully, the little common sense I had around this man stepped in and stopped me from embarrassing myself.

Aaron did not want my comfort. He didn't even want to be my friend.

Standing on the other side of his desk, only that piece of functional furniture separating us, I finally made my presence noticed. 'Congratulations!' I blurted with a dose of extra enthusiasm that I regretted immediately.

Aaron straightened in his chair, his palm falling to the armrest. 'Catalina,' he said in a voice that, now, I could not hear without thinking of last Saturday. His gaze zeroed in on me, his features piecing back together. 'Thank you.'

'You deserve the promotion.'

He did. And beneath everything I was feeling in that moment, I was only happy for him. Genuinely.

He nodded in silence.

Grabbing on to my planner with both hands, knowing it was the only way I could keep myself from fidgeting, I hunted my disjointed mind for a way to voice what I had come here to say as we stared at each other in silence.

'I think we should . . .' I trailed off, still not finding a way to say it. 'I think it's better if we—' I shook my head. 'I know you probably don't have the time to talk. But I think we should do that.' I watched him frown. 'Privately.' That frown deepened. 'If you have the time, of course.'

I didn't want that door behind me closed because the idea of being in a room with Aaron made my heart do silly, stupid things that I was trying really hard to ignore. But it was the only way to ensure nobody would either come in or walk by and overhear us.

'Of course,' he said with his brows still furrowed. 'I always have time for you.'

That stupid lurch in my chest resumed.

Swiftly, Aaron unfolded his body from the chair and walked around the desk and then around me while I kept my gaze where he had been a few seconds ago. Standing there like a total dummy, I heard him shut the door, the noise echoing in the silent room.

'Sorry,' I mumbled as he reappeared in front of me. 'I could have done that myself. I just didn't—' I sighed. 'I didn't think. Thanks.'

This time, he didn't return to his chair. Instead, he leaned his body on the edge of the wooden surface of his desk. 'It's okay. We can talk now.'

Those blue eyes of his pinned me down, waiting.

'We can talk now, yes,' I repeated, squaring back my shoulders. 'I think we should do that.' I watched his head nod, feeling my skin clammy with trepidation. 'It would be good to clear the air after . . . all that's happened.'

'Yes, you are right,' he admitted. Bracing his arms on the desk, his hands grabbed on to the edge. 'I came into work today with the intention to get you after the meeting. Suggest that we could have lunch together and talk.'

Lunch together.

'But we never do that.'

Aaron sighed very softly. 'I know,' he said almost bitterly. 'But I wanted to take you anyway.'

I stared at him, finding it hard to ignore the effect his words had on me.

'I don't think I'll be able to now. My whole day has been side-tracked by the news.'

That . . . that was just as shocking as him admitting to wanting to have lunch with me.

'You didn't know Jeff would announce your promotion?'

'Not really. I didn't think that was going to happen anytime soon. Especially not today,' he confessed, sending about a million questions rushing through my mind. 'But that's not important now. You want to talk about us, I assume. So, let's do that.'

'But it is,' I countered, feeling outraged on his behalf and ignoring the way that us had made me feel. 'I think Jeff ambushing you like that is important. I can't imagine why he would do something like this. It's just' – I lowered my voice, realizing it had somewhat risen – 'unprofessional.'

The blue in Aaron's eyes simmered, now looking surprised himself. 'It is; you are right. And I'll talk to him about how much, trust me.'

'Good. You should.'

Something softened in his face, and I averted my eyes, letting them rest somewhere above his shoulder. Not wanting him to know I cared as much as I did. Simply because I shouldn't. We were still the same Lina and Aaron we had always been – certainly not friends – and about to be divided by a whole step in the hierarchy of the company.

Releasing one of my hands from the death grip I had on my planner, I scratched the side of my neck. My gaze still refused to shift to the left, where it'd probably connect with his. So, instead, it moved down, following the seam of the blue button-down that covered his wide shoulders while a thick silence wrapped around us.

'Listen, about our deal—' I started.

'On Saturday, I—' Aaron said at the same time.

Finally returning my eyes to his face, I found him gesturing for me to go ahead. I accepted the chance with a nod.

'I will say this, and I'll be out of your hair, I promise.' I exhaled through my nose, not paying attention to Aaron's frown. 'Now that you will become head of our division – which, again, is really great, so congratulations.' I let a polite smile tug at the corners of my lips. 'Things for . . . us will change.' I shifted on my feet, not happy with how that sounded. There was no *us*. Not after Saturday and not after this. 'What I'm trying to say is something that you have probably figured out yourself, but I just want to clear the air between us.'

Aaron's jaw clamped.

'Our deal is off. It was stupid, and now, it makes even less sense than it did. So, it's not a big deal. I helped you out on Saturday, but you don't owe me anything. Consider it payback for giving me a hand with the organization of Open Day, okay? We are even.'

I had expected to feel a big weight lift off my shoulders, but that was not what happened. Instead, it was as if my words had sunk me further down into the ground.

'We are even?' Aaron asked, his hands lifting from the oak surface and then falling right back again. 'What's that supposed to mean?'

'It means that you don't owe me,' I said with a shrug. Fully aware of the fact that I was repeating myself. 'You can forget about all this nonsense.'

His eyes filled with a dangerous mix of confusion and frustration.

'I think I'm being pretty clear, Aaron. You don't have to go through with your end of the deal. No flying to Spain, no wedding nonsense and pretending to be my boyfriend. No playing charades with me. That won't be necessary.'

'Your boyfriend?' he asked very slowly.

Ah shit. I hadn't used the word boyfriend the first time, had I?

'My date, whatever.'

'Have you found someone else? Is that what this is?'

I shot him a look. Was he for real right now? 'No, that's not it. Not at all.'

That muscle in his jaw jumped. 'Then, I'll come with you.'

I fought to keep the irritation off my face. *Why was he always so goddamn difficult?* 'You don't have to anymore.'

'But I told you I would, Catalina. It doesn't matter whether you think that we are even or not.' His voice was so sure, the way he said it so confident that it was hard not to doubt my decision. 'Saturday doesn't change anything.'

'But it does,' I told him a little too briskly. Aaron opened his mouth, but I didn't give him an in to talk. 'And your promotion does too, Aaron. You will be my boss. My supervisor. Head of our division. We shouldn't even be entertaining the idea of you coming to a wedding with me that takes place somewhere all the way across the ocean. The things people would say if they found out. I won't allow myself to be questioned—' I stopped myself, realizing I had said too much. 'It's just too . . .'

Ridiculous? Reckless? All of the above?

I shook my head, feeling light-headed and depleted. 'It's just not necessary anymore.'

But of course, Aaron wouldn't let anything go without a fight. 'I understand you being wary now that the news is out.' He shook his head. 'I didn't think it would happen this fast. But there's nothing I can do about that now. It doesn't need to change anything where we are concerned.'

He waited for me to speak, but instead of words rising to my lips, an avalanche of something different throttled down my throat.

Memories of a time when I had been stupid enough to get myself into a very similar position. One that hadn't involved a made-up relationship, but one that had been real. So real that the hurt over how it had blown up in my face was something I wasn't willing ever to relive or even get within shooting range of.

'That's a risk I won't take.' I heard my own voice, and I was aware that it had given away more than I would have liked. 'You wouldn't understand.'

'Then, help me out here,' he told me, something honest and open about his request. 'Make me understand. Give me that at least.'

My throat worked as I thought of those words that had been on repeat on my mind. 'No. That kind of treatment is one I reserve for friends.'

Something flashed across his face, and I expected him to snap back in the way he and I always did. But instead, he said, 'Catalina.' And it sounded all wrong and far, far from snappy. 'If I said that I didn't mean what I said on Saturday, it wouldn't change a single thing, so I won't.'

'Good,' I said, my voice coming out all wrong too. Although in a different way. 'Because it's okay if you don't want to be my friend. You don't have to explain or retract that. I've lived with that knowledge for almost two years now, and I'm fine with it.' Aaron's gaze sharpened, but I kept going, 'We are not ten-year-olds, heading into the playground for recess. We don't need to ask each other if we want to be friends. We don't need to be. Especially not now that you will be my boss. We shouldn't even be all that friendly. And that's fine. That's also why you're off the hook where our deal is concerned. I'll manage on my own.' As much as it was the last thing I wanted to do. But that was what single, lying maids of honor did – they attended weddings alone. 'This is not you going back on your word, Aaron. It's me releasing you from it.'

We watched each other for a long moment, my heart thumping against my chest while I told myself that what I was seeing in his eyes wasn't regret. Him feeling anything like that did not make any sense. Unless he regretted getting himself tangled in this whole mess. Now, that would be something I could understand.

Before I could give that any more thought, the ringtone of his phone blared through the office.

Aaron didn't take his eyes off me as he reached for it and answered, 'Blackford.' A pause. We stared at each other, his profile notably hardening. 'Yes, all right. I'll have a look myself. Two minutes.'

I watched him place the phone back on the desk, and then he straightened to his full height.

He searched my face in a way that made my neck and ears flush. As if the skin of my cheeks, nose, and chin hid the answers he was looking for.

'There is something you are not telling me,' he finally said. And he wasn't wrong. There was much I wasn't telling him. And it'd stay that way. 'But I'm patient.'

Something flopped against my ribcage. I didn't understand what he meant or why my chest felt tight all of a sudden.

'It's something important, and I need to go.' He stepped in my direction, both hands in his pockets and eyes still on me. 'Get back to work, Catalina. We will continue our conversation.'

Not more than a heartbeat later, Aaron disappeared through the door. Leaving me in his office, staring into empty space. Thinking how well he had already fallen into his new role, doubting there was something we had to continue talking about, and finding it really hard to believe that he had anything to be patient for.

Basically because, where we were concerned, neither of us had anything to wait for.

CHAPTER ELEVEN

Everything went downhill after that day.

As much as my intention had been to sort out the whole thing with Aaron, our conversation hadn't relieved me in the slightest. Sure, I had made it very clear that he was off the hook, but his words still hung over my head. They had for the last two weeks.

'*There is something you are not telling me,*' he had said. '*But I'm patient.*'

It was like waiting for a bomb to drop.

And on top of not knowing where we stood after that cryptic statement, I hadn't brought myself to tell Rosie about it. Yet. I would – as soon as I figured a contingency plan for my wedding situation. Which was only three days away. Three.

I eyed the analog clock I kept on my desk. It was eight in the evening, and I was not even close to being done with the day.

How could I be when nothing was going according to plan? I hadn't found anyone to replace Linda and Patricia, so I was still covering for them myself. I still hadn't figured out how I'd be entertaining our guests for the whole sixteen hours Open Day was planned to last. And I had found that our hopefully prospective client, Terra-Wind, had been getting cozy with one of our biggest competitors. Not because they were better than us, but because they were one of those consulting companies that offered their services at ridiculously low rates.

A crisis I had been dealing with for the last three hours.

'Thank you, Miss Martín,' a man in a dark suit spoke from the screen of my laptop. 'We will study your offer and come to a decision.'

I nodded. 'Thank you for your time,' I said, making myself smile politely. 'I look forward to hearing back from you, Mr Cameron. Have a good evening.'

Hitting End on the conference call I had been on with the representative of the decision board of Terra-Wind, I took off my headphones and closed my eyes for a moment. Jesus, I didn't even know how that had gone. I just hoped I had gotten through to him. My team was worth every extra penny, and Terra-Wind was a renewable company that had the resources and the potential to do something for the state of New York. I wanted this project.

Opening my eyes, I watched my phone flash with my sister's name, causing a twirl of mixed emotions. Any other day, I would have automatically picked up. But not today. I had already sent several of her calls to voicemail. If it were a real emergency, my whole family would have been blasting my phone.

'*Lo siento mucho, Isa,*' I said as if she could hear me. 'I don't have time to deal with another bridal apocalypse.'

I silenced my phone, placed it screen down, and moved onto the stack of résumés that HR had sent over for the vacancies I needed to fill. Two – I'd check a couple of them and take the rest home with me.

Four résumés later, I was dropping my trusty highlighter down. I let my back fall on the backrest of my chair.

My head was spinning, probably due to the fact that I had been working on mostly an empty stomach. Again. Because I had been dieting. Wrongly, most likely. Closing my eyes once again, I scolded myself for being that dumb.

But, as much as I hated myself for it, I couldn't stop thinking of standing in front of Daniel. My ex, the groom's brother and best man. Who, unlike me, was happily engaged. Or in front of *everybody*. I could already feel every single soul attending the ceremony watching me, watching us. Measuring my reaction and assessing me – from the way I looked to the way my lips would tug down and pale when I finally faced him. Looking for possible answers that would explain why I was still single after all this time while Daniel wasn't.

Did she ever get over him? Did she ever get over everything that had happened? Of course not. Poor thing. What happened must have really messed her up.

So, was it that silly of me to want to stand there and look good? Not just fine. Not just getting by. To everyone watching, I wanted to look complete. Beautiful, flawless, unaffected. I needed to give the impression that I had my life back on track. All figured out. Happy. With a man on my arm.

Objectively, I knew how stupid all of it sounded, how much I shouldn't be measuring myself in terms of having a man, looking thinner, or having clear skin. But, God, I knew that was what everybody else would be doing.

I shook my head, trying to banish those thoughts from my mind but only making it worse with the way my head kept spinning. My body was screaming at me for something, anything that would appease the hollowness in my stomach.

Water. That would help.

Grabbing my phone and slipping my badge on the pocket of my camel slacks, I stood on weaker legs than I would have liked and made my way out of the office. There was one of those water dispensers down the corridor. Three more missed calls from my sister. With the time difference, she'd be asleep by now.

Lina: Lo siento, bridezilla. 😜

I typed, and the text blurred for a second. I stopped walking, trying to get my eyes to focus back on the screen.

> Lina: Hablamos mañana, vale?

I continued, but the characters on the screen started dancing. My fingers lost all certainty, vacillating over the keyboard of the device. My vision doubled and then blurred, not managing to distinguish with any clarity the words I thought I was typing as they appeared on the text bubble.

A shaky breath left my lips as I attempted to hit Send.

Water. That's what I need.

My head lifted from my phone, and my legs resumed again, taking me a few feet down the corridor. I knew that the water dispenser was right there, probably about five or six steps ahead of me. But white spots scattered in front of my eyes, and everything blinked out for a second. White. Then, the fluorescent-illuminated corridor came back, narrowing, tunnelling away.

'Whoa,' I heard myself murmur.

I was completely unaware of the fact that my legs had kept moving forward until I had to balance myself with one hand on the wall.

'Oh *mierda*.' I stumbled.

My eyelids fluttered closed, and I could feel how all the blood in my face rushed down, leaving me woozy and unbalanced. I willed my eyes to open. But all I saw was white. A white and misty blanket that covered everything in front of me. Although perhaps, it was the wall. I couldn't be sure.

I . . . I messed up. Big time. Eight thirty. No one around. That kept echoing in my head as I tried to account for the signs that indicated I was going down. And I . . . dammit. I couldn't remember. Couldn't . . . think. My skin felt cold and clammy, and I just wanted to close my eyes and rest. I was vaguely recalling that being a bad idea when my limbs started giving out.

Then, I was lying down.

Good. That's good. I'll rest, and then I'll be better. I toppled to one side. *It's cold, but it'll . . . get . . . better.*

'Catalina.' A voice seeped through the haze. It was deep. Urgent.

My lips were cool and felt detached from my body, so I didn't answer.

'Fuck.' That voice again. Then, something warm fell on my forehead. 'Jesus, fuck. Catalina.'

I messed up. I . . . knew. I had done something wrong, and I wanted to admit it out loud to whoever was there, but all I achieved was a mumble that didn't really sound like . . . anything.

'Hey.' That voice softened, no longer sounding angry.

And I . . . I was so tired.

'Open those big brown eyes.'

That warm pressure I felt on my forehead moved down my face, spreading across my cheek. It felt good against my cool, damp skin, so I leaned on it.

'Open them for me. Please, Catalina.'

My eyelids fluttered open for an instant, finding two blue spots that made me think of the ocean. I felt a sigh escape my mouth, that hollow and void sensation receding for an instant.

'There you are.' I heard the voice again. Even softer now. Relieved.

As I blinked slowly, my vision started to return in flashes. Deep blue eyes. Hair as dark as black ink. The hard line of a jaw.

'Lina?'

Lina.

There was something funny about that voice calling my name. The one everyone called me.

No, not everyone.

I blinked some more, but before my eyes could focus on a fixed point, I was lifted in the air. The movement was slow, so gentle, that I barely noticed it at first, but then we started moving. And after a few seconds, the motion was enough to send my head spinning again.

'*Mi cabeza,*' I said under my breath.

'I'm sorry.' I felt the words rumbling against my side, becoming aware of how my cheek was resting against something hot and hard. Something with a heartbeat. A chest. 'Just stay with me, okay?'

Okay, I'll stay. And I burrowed into the chest, ready to lose myself in the exhaustion rocking my body.

'Eyes open, please.'

Somehow, I complied. I let them fall on a shoulder that looked terribly familiar as we moved. And gradually, my vision cleared. My head, no longer whirling, locked back on my shoulders. The sweat on my skin cooled down.

My eyes roamed around as recollection of what had happened ran through my mind. I had fainted, from not eating enough. Like a total dumbass. Sighing, I looked up, my gaze zeroing in on a chin that stretched into a jaw that was topped by lips that were pressed together tightly.

'Aaron,' I whispered.

Blue eyes met mine for an instant. 'Hold on. Almost there.'

I was in Aaron's arms. His left arm around my legs, hand spreading on my thigh. His right one around my back, his long fingers splayed across my hip. Before I could delve into that or focus on the comforting and amazing warmth emanating off him and into my skin, he was putting me down.

Confused, I looked around me. My gaze stumbled upon that horrible, disturbing framed artwork of a kid with huge eyes. I had always hated it, and I knew exactly where it belonged. We could only be in Jeff's office. He was the only person I knew who didn't find that frightening.

My ass settled on a plush surface, and my back followed, resting on something that felt a lot like a pillow. I placed my hands at my sides, noticing the fabric beneath my fingers. Leather. A sofa. Jeff had one in his office. It was one of those leather settees that looked all pretentious and classy.

Aaron's palm brushed my face again, and my attention returned to him. He was close, really close. Kneeling on the floor in front of me. His touch was comforting, but his expression didn't match the soothing quality of his fingers against my skin.

'Do you want to lean back?' he asked, an edge in his voice.

'No, I'm okay.' I willed my voice to convey the strength I wasn't feeling. His eyebrows draw into a scowl. 'You look so mad.' It was an observation that should have been kept to myself probably, but I guessed that, given the circumstances, I wasn't in a position to be picky with what left my mouth. 'Why are you mad?'

'When was the last time you ate, Catalina?' His scowl deepened, and he shifted on his knees, straightening his back. I watched him pull something out of his pocket.

I grimaced. 'Lunch? I think. Maybe more like brunch because I didn't have time to get breakfast, so I just had something at around eleven.'

His hand froze midair in front of me, allowing me to see that something he was holding. It was wrapped in white wax paper. 'Jesus, Catalina.' He shot me a look that would make anyone else cower. One that would definitely help with his soon-to-be new position.

But even if my tank was literally empty, I was still Lina Martín. 'I'm fine, Mr Robot.'

'No, you are not,' he shot back. Then, he very carefully placed on my lap what I already knew was a delicious Aaron Blackford homemade granola bar. 'You fainted, Catalina. That's really far from being fine. Eat this.'

'Thanks. But I'm okay now.' I looked down, my gaze getting acquainted with the gifted snack one more time. With shaky hands, I snatched it. Unwrapped it with clumsy fingers. 'Do you always carry these on you?' I hesitated, my stomach complaining for some reason.

'Eat, please.'

So odd, how he could say please and make it sound like a threat.

'Jeez.' I took a bite. Then, I spoke with a mouthful – because who cared? He had literally just picked me off the floor, white-lipped, sweaty, and on my way to dramatically passing out – 'I said I'm okay.'

'No,' he thundered. Pinning me down with a warning. 'What you are is a *dumbass*.'

I frowned, wanting to be upset but agreeing with him. He didn't need to know I was on his side.

'Stubborn woman,' he muttered under his breath.

I stopped chewing, making an attempt to stand up and stomp out of that office. He stopped me with oddly gentle hands on my shoulders.

'Do not test me right now.' That damn scowl was back with a vengeance.

I gave up under the soft grip of his large palms and let my body fall back.

'Eat the bar, Catalina. It's not nearly enough, but it'll do for now.'

Feeling the ghost of his hands on my shoulders, I shivered. 'I'm eating. No need to boss me around.' I averted my eyes and resumed chewing, trying not to think of how much I wanted those palms back on my skin. Or those long and big arms around me. I needed the comfort. My body felt stretched too long, my whole being chilled, my muscles overworked.

'Stay here. I'll be right back.'

I nodded, not looking up. I simply limited myself to chowing down the snack.

Only a few moments later, Aaron was back. All determined strides and stiff back. 'Water,' he announced, dropping a bottle on my lap. He placed my phone beside me too.

'Thanks.' I unscrewed the lid, chugging down a quarter of the bottle.

When I was done, I looked up again. Aaron was standing in front of me now. Still looking all angry and bunched up. I let my gaze fall from his face, feeling extra tiny, sitting there while he towered over me.

'So, I guess this will be your office soon. I hope they let you redecorate.' I eyed the horrible painting behind him.

'Catalina.' The way he said my name held a warning.

Ugh. I was not down for a lecture.

'That was so stupid. Not eating, risking hypoglycemia when the whole building is deserted. What if you had lost consciousness and no one was around to find you?'

'You were here, weren't you?' I answered, still not looking at him. 'You are always here anyway.'

A noise came out of his throat. Another warning. *Don't give me that shit*, it told me.

'Why are you not eating?' His question felt like a punch, right in my stomach. 'You always, always used to have something in your hand. Jesus, you used to pull pastries out of your pockets at the oddest and most inappropriate times.'

That had me looking up, meeting ice-cold eyes. I had; I was a snacker. That was part of the problem, wasn't it?

'Why are you not doing that now? Why haven't you done that for the last month? Why are you not eating like you usually do?'

Narrowing my eyes at him, I clasped my hands together. 'Are you calling me a—'

'Don't,' he hissed. 'Don't even try it.'

'Fine.'

'Tell me,' he insisted, his gaze hardening like stone. 'Why are you not eating?'

'Isn't it obvious?' My breathing quickened, every word costing me more and more effort to spit. To admit the truth. 'Because I want to lose weight, all right? For the wedding.'

He reared back. Appalled. 'Why?'

Most of the blood that had left my head earlier rushed back. Awful timing. Just like everything else about my life. 'Because,' I breathed out. 'Because that's what people do before an important event like that. Because I want to look my best, as much as you won't believe it. Because I'd like to look as amazing as I possibly can. Because, apparently, I have been going around, stuffing my face with pastries twenty-four/seven, and my body has definitely been storing it. Because I just . . . did it, okay? What does it matter?'

'Catalina,' he said, and I could hear in his voice how disconcerted he was. 'That's . . . ridiculous. You've never been like that.'

Did he think I couldn't possibly want to . . . look beautiful? 'What, Aaron?' I whispered, not finding my voice. 'What is so ridiculous exactly? Is it so hard to believe that from me? That I'm like that? That I care about how I look?'

His throat worked. 'You don't need any of that goddamn shit. And you are smarter than dieting like that.'

I blinked.

Then, I blinked some more. 'Did you just say goddamn shit? At work?' I lowered my voice. 'In Jeff's office?'

Now that I thought of it, he had dropped a few bad words earlier, hadn't he?

Looking down, he shook his head, his shoulders falling with something that looked a lot like defeat. 'Jesus,' he breathed out. 'Fuck, Catalina.'

Wow. 'All this swearing,' I said while I tried to search his face for whatever was going on with him. 'I don't think my ears will ever recover, Blackford.'

One of his hands went to the back of his neck. His head fell back, reminding me a lot of that moment I hadn't been able to forget. When he had followed that with wonderful laughter. When he had smiled freely. As brightly as one could smile. But he didn't do any of that now. He just gave me a tug of his lips, tiny little wrinkles in the corners of his eyes.

'You are cute,' he said matter-of-factly. 'But don't think you can play that card now. I'm still mad.'

Cute? Cute as in *cute* or cute as in small and funny and something you smiled at with fondness? Or perhaps cute as in—

I stopped myself. Closed my eyes for an instant, so I would just stop thinking.

'Are you feeling better? Think you can stand?'

Opening my eyes, I nodded my head. 'Yeah. No need to carry me around again.' Although the lurch in my chest at the thought reminded me how comfy I had been up there. 'Thanks.'

'I can if I—'

'I know you can, Blackford,' I interrupted him. If he offered again, I might take him up on it. 'Thank you for doing it earlier, but I got it under control.'

He nodded, stretching out his hand in front of me. 'Come on. Let's go. We'll grab your things and get you home.'

I didn't reach out for it with mine. 'I can—'

'Cut it out, will you?' He stopped me. God, we both were so freaking stubborn. 'Now, you can let me walk you out and drive you home' – he paused, like a total drama queen – 'or I can carry you out of this building and into my car myself.'

Holding his gaze, I lifted my hand and held it in the air, just a few inches away from his. I measured his words. Assessed my thoughts. Vaguely ignoring the way I'd love nothing more than to see him trying option number two. And what was far more disturbing than that was, I didn't think it was for the pleasure it would bring me to fight him on something like that.

'Fine,' I said, wrapping my fingers around his as well as I could, considering the size difference. 'No need to get your panties in a bunch, Blackford.'

He sighed. But then he pulled me up, doing something with our hands. Something that somehow changed the positions of our palms, which were now against each other.

A flutter took flight in the middle of my chest. And as we exited the office, I realized it'd soon no longer be Jeff's, our boss. This would become Aaron's office.

Soon enough.

Which should have been reason enough to immediately drop his hand and run in the opposite direction. It should have been enough to stop myself from welcoming the warmth of his palm or letting him take me home.

It should have. But ironically, I hadn't seemed to be listening to a whole lot of *should haves* lately. So, what was a couple more?

~

'Hello?' A distant male voice stirred me back to life.

Un poquito más, I silently begged as I fought to fall back into oblivion. *Un ratito más.*

'I'm Aaron.'

Aaron?

Eyes shut and every thought sticky and heavy, I halfheartedly tried to make sense of what was happening. Why was Aaron's voice sounding right beside me? I wanted to go back to sleep.

I vaguely recognized the characteristic dull vibration of an engine. *Am I in a car? A bus?* But we weren't moving.

A dream. Yeah, that made sense. Right?

Confused and overexerted, I buried deeper into the warmth of my bed and decided I didn't care if I dreamed of Aaron. It wouldn't be the first time anyway.

'Yes, that Aaron.' The male voice was no longer distant. 'Yes, I'm afraid so,' he continued. Every word bringing me more and more awake. 'She's asleep right now.'

I felt a featherlike caress on the back of my hand. And my skin flared back to life. Feeling way too real for this being a dream.

'No, everything is fine.' Aaron's baritone texture reverberated through my ears, and I found a weird comfort in recognizing it. 'Okay, I will tell Catalina to call you back.' A pause. Followed by a chuckle. 'No, I'm not one of those. I love meat. Roasted lamb in particular.'

Meat. Yeah. That was something I also loved. *We should eat meat together, Aaron and I.* My mind wandered away for an instant, thinking of juicy and crispy lamb and Aaron too.

'Okay. Thank you, and likewise, Isabel. Bye.'

Wait. *Wait.*

Isabel?

Isabel as in my sister, Isabel?

More confusion tugged at my still-foggy mind. I felt one of my eyes flutter open. I wasn't in my bed. I was in a car, which was immaculate. Obsessively so.

Aaron's car.

I was in Aaron's car. Not a dream.

And . . . *Isabel.* She had called me earlier today, hadn't she?

And texted me. And I had ignored all of it.

All at once, the events of the last hours snowballed down my mind, overwhelming my half-functional brain.

No. My eyes blinked fully open, and my body sprang up.

'I'm awake,' I announced.

As I whirled my head from one side to the other, my gaze

stumbled upon the owner of the car I had been napping in. He passed both his hands through his hair, looking as humanly tired as one could.

His head turned in my direction. 'Welcome back,' he said, looking at me strangely. 'Again.'

My heart squeezed. Why exactly, I didn't have the slightest idea.

'Hi,' I managed with my scattered brain.

'Your sister called,' Aaron told me, making my whole body tense. 'Five times in a row,' he added.

I opened my mouth, but my tongue didn't work through the words. Any words.

'It's okay. Something about a weird text you sent her,' he explained and offered back my phone.

I clasped it, grazing Aaron's fingers very briefly.

Feeling Aaron's gaze on me, I checked on the text. God, it was unintelligible. Alarmingly so.

Aaron continued, 'Then, she went on about the seating or the tables, I think? Maybe something about the napkins too.'

I looked over at him, catching one of his hands shooting to his hair again. The muscles on his arm flexed, and my still-sleepy eyes seemed to be absorbed by that motion and that motion alone.

'I'm sorry. I shouldn't have picked up,' Aaron said, bringing my gaze to his face once more.

'It's okay,' I admitted, shocking myself. 'If she called me at three or four in the morning, Spain time, that meant she was genuinely worried. She would have probably sent the New York City Fire Department to my place if you hadn't answered.'

Something odd shone in his eyes. 'I'm glad to hear that because your phone rang and rang. And you . . .' He shook his head lightly. 'You sleep like the dead, Catalina.'

He wasn't wrong.

Not even the arrival of the apocalypse – even if the very same

Four Horsemen were galloping in my direction, shouting my name – could shake me awake when I was deeply asleep. Which was ironic really because Isabel talking to Aaron on the phone was my idea of a world-ending event.

My eyes widened with a realization.

Aaron had talked to my sister. He had mentioned meat. Roasted lamb. Which was on the menu for the wedding. The connotations of that twirled in my weary head.

'Are you okay?' Aaron asked as I silently panicked.

'Yes,' I lied, forcing a smile. 'Super-duper okay.'

Aaron's brow arched. Maybe that had been a giveaway to how not super-duper okay I was.

'I told her you were fine, just asleep. But I think you should call her back tomorrow.' He pointed at my phone. 'Judging by the five-minute monologue in Spanish before I could even tell her it wasn't you on the line, I'd say she'll feel better when you do.' Aaron's lips twitched in what was the beginning of a smile.

'Yeah,' I murmured, a little too absorbed by his mouth when I should have been trying to manage a crisis. 'Okay.'

That smirk stretched into a lopsided smile.

Ah, man. Why did it look so good on him? He didn't smile nearly enough.

Which was *not* important.

What mattered was that Aaron had talked to my sister, and she never minced her words. Ever.

'So, Aaron,' I started, the words rushing out, 'when you talked to my sister, you told her your name. Right?'

He cocked a brow. 'Yes, that's what people do when they introduce themselves.'

'Okay.' I nodded my head very slowly. 'And how did you say that exactly? As in, *Hey, I'm Aaron.*' I dropped my voice, imitating his. 'Or like, *I'm just Aaron. I'm no one. Hello.*'

He tilted his head. 'I'm not sure I understand the question, but I'm going to go on a whim and go with option one. Although my voice sounds nothing like that.'

I exhaled through my nose, bringing the pads of my fingers to my temples. 'Oh, Aaron. This is not good. I'm . . .' I blinked, feeling myself pale. 'Oh God.'

Aaron frowned. 'Catalina' – his blue eyes assessed me, concerned – 'maybe I should take you to a hospital, get you checked out. You must have hit your head when you fell.'

He angled his body away, placing one hand on the steering wheel and lifting the other one to the ignition.

'Wait, wait.' I stopped him right before he started the car. 'It's not that. I'm okay. Seriously.'

He cut me a glance. 'I'm fine.'

He looked like he didn't believe me.

'I promise.'

His hands dropped, falling on his lap.

'But I need something from you.' I watched him nod. *Whoa, okay.* That was easy. 'I need you to tell me exactly what you told Isabel.'

'We talked about this. About a minute ago.' He brought one of his hands to the back of his neck.

'Just do it for me. Humour me.' I gave him a weak smile. 'I need to know what you said.'

The man looked at me as if I were asking him to take his clothes off and perform a choreographed dance in the middle of Times Square.

Which I'd be totally down for – but again, not important.

'Please.' I tried my luck with the magic word.

Aaron stared at me for a long moment. And somehow, I discovered that six-letter word turned out to be the key to making him do something for me without putting up a fight.

He sighed, falling deeper into the seat. 'Fine.'

'Oh, and be as detailed as you can too. Use her exact words if you can.'

He exhaled again. 'After she switched to English, she said that it was nice to meet me. That you'd better have a good excuse for not picking up because that text was scary. That the stupid hippie who was in charge of the flowers was going to ruin her wedding because, now, the linen of the tables wouldn't match her bouquet.'

That had me snorting. That poor florist was about to pay for his sins.

He continued, 'And that she'd see me in a few days. At the wedding.' That last part wiped all humour off me. 'Before that, she asked me if I was one of those hipsters who didn't eat meat. Because in that case, she would have to uninvite me to the wedding. Then, she added that she was joking and told me that I'd better be there if I knew what was good for me. Especially if I loved roasted lamb. I said sure. I do love lamb, to be honest. I don't eat it often enough actually.'

An ugly, loud, animal-sounding groan left my body.

'Mierda. Qué desastre. Qué completo y maldito desastre.' I brought my hands to my face, covering it with my palms and wishing that hiding from this stupid situation were as easy as that.

'She might have said something like that, too, when she thought it was you on the phone.' Then, with medical curiosity, he asked, 'What does that mean exactly?'

'It means shit. Mess. Disaster. Catastrophe,' I answered, my voice muffled through my fingers.

Aaron hmmed in agreement. 'That would definitely fit the tone of the beginning of the conversation.'

'Aaron' – my hands dropped to my lap – 'why did you tell her that you would be there? The wedding is only a few days away. I'm flying to Spain in three days.'

'We just went through this,' he said, sounding as exhausted as I felt. 'I did not tell her I'd be there. She assumed I'd be there.'

I shot him a glance.

'After what went down?' I told him, trying a new approach to the topic. 'After our conversation and how we agreed that our deal was off? You let her assume you'd be there.'

Had he forgotten about that? Because I had not.

'I told you we would talk about it.'

When? I wanted to ask him. While I was on my way to the airport? We were out of time to talk about anything.

'But we haven't talked, Aaron.'

Two weeks. He'd had two weeks to reach out to me. And as much as I had hated myself for it, a part of me had waited for him to do that. I had just realized it. Well, at least that explained why I hadn't brought myself to tell Rosie. Or my family. Yet.

I shook my head. I was so dumb. 'And we don't need to. We have nothing to talk about.'

Aaron clenched his jaw, not saying anything else.

My phone pinged a couple of times, but I ignored it. I was busy shooting daggers at Aaron.

Depleted of energy, I gave up and rested my head on the lush headrest of the copilot's seat. My eyelids shut, and I wished I could shut down the world too.

The sound of my phone going off again with a couple more texts brought my eyes to my lap.

I ignored it again. 'What am I going to do?' I thought out loud. 'In a few hours, Isabel will be calling everyone to tell them she talked to *Lina's boyfriend* on the phone.' I was screwed six ways from Sunday. 'I guess I could always tell them I broke up with you.' I released a long sigh. Then, I turned to look over at him. 'Not with you, you. But with—' I shook my head. 'You know what I mean.'

At that, Aaron straightened in his seat, further cramping the space inside the car.

Before either of us could say anything, my phone went off

again. I lifted it off my lap with the intention to silence it. *'Por el amor de Dios.'*

An alarmingly large number of messages flashed on my screen, confirming my suspicions.

> Isabel: I just talked to your BF. 😋 What a deep, sexy voice he has. Send pics, pls.

> Mamá: Your sister told me she talked to Aaron. If he wants a meatless menu, we can still talk to the restaurant and ask them to prepare a fish option. He'll have fish, right? That's not meat, is it?

> Mamá: Unless vegetarians eat chicken. Do they? Charo used to be flexotorian? Flexatarian? I don't remember. But she still had jamón and chorizo. You know I don't know about all those food trends.

> Mamá: If he does, we can also ask for chicken. Ask him.

Oh sweet baby Jesus. How in the world was my mother awake?

> Isabel: It's weird that I don't know what your boyfriend looks like. Is he ugly? That's okay. I bet he makes up for it in other ways. 🍆

> Mamá: Just let me know what he eats. It will be fine. I won't tell Abuela. You know how she is.

> Isabel: I'm joking, you know. I wouldn't judge your boyfriend by the way he looks.

> Isabel: Also, I won't ask for a dick pic because that's your business, but I won't complain if you want to show me one.

I groaned.

> Isabel: Joking again. 🤍

> Isabel: Not about the sexy voice though. That was 🔥

'So, that leaves us two options,' the man beside me said.

Whirling my head around and almost butting his in the process, I found him looking over my shoulder. Close — his mouth was so very close to my cheek.

I jerked my phone against my chest, the skin of my face heating up. 'How much did you get?'

Aaron — my prospective boss — shrugged his shoulders. 'Enough.'

Of course he did. This is The Lina Martín Show after all.

'At least, enough to advise against breaking up with me until you hear the options we are left with.'

This man had squeezed himself into my dilemma, right there in the thick of things. I should be mad. Furious. And I wanted to be. But that us, that knowledge of not being alone to deal with the whole mess I had in my hands — one that I had created and had snowballed into this complex web of lies that included him — made me feel a little . . . better. A little less helpless. A lot less alone.

'We?' I said, hearing the doubt in my voice. The reluctance to believe in what I was saying. The hope to allow myself to.

Aaron pinned me with a look I knew very well. This would be the last time he'd say whatever was about to leave his lips. 'I'm not going to force this on you, Catalina. Not when there is something that you are not telling me. Something that made you change your mind so drastically after Jeff's announcement.' He raised a hand, brushing the top of his hair back, as if he were readying himself for something. 'I told you we would talk, and we didn't. That's on me. There is an explanation, but it doesn't matter right now.' He let that sink in for a moment. And it did. It sank to the bottom of my stomach. 'We can make it work. We'll make it work if that's what you want.' He paused, and a breath got stuck in my throat. 'I'll make it work.'

I stared into eyes that gleamed with resolution.

I wanted that. I wanted this to work. He had been right when he declared he was my best option. Because he had been. Even before all of this happened. But things had changed a few days ago.

He is being promoted. He's becoming my boss. That is a deal-breaker. I learned my lesson with Daniel.

And now, it had all changed again.

Everyone back home will be expecting him. Now more than ever. It's too late to back down.

Perhaps ... if no one from work ever found out about our arrangement, there'd be no risk. No one had a reason to even imagine that we would go anywhere together, much less all the way to Spain for a wedding. No one had learned of the fundraiser. My mind kept picturing the same scenario over and over again. Filling me with dread. Me, landing in Spain with no one by my side. Alone. Stuck in the past. Smiled at with pity. Glanced at with sadness. Whispered about.

My blood dipped to my feet, reminding me of earlier, when I had almost fainted.

'What's option A?' I whispered, exhausted from trying to get to a conclusion on my own. 'You said we have two options. What's the first one?'

Aaron's expression assembled into one that was all business.

'Option A is, you fly home alone. As much as I advise against it, it remains an option.' Hearing that from someone who wasn't me sent a shiver crawling down my arms. 'I have no doubt that you will be fine. But that doesn't mean it's your easiest route to ... whatever you want to accomplish.'

'I don't want to accomplish anything.'

'That's something neither of us believes. But it's okay. Either way, you do have a second option. And unlike with option A, if you decide to go with option B, you won't be on your own. You'd be bringing backup.' He placed his palm against his broad chest. 'Me. You know better than most that a challenging project needs the right kind of backing and support to succeed. So, you take me, and I'll do exactly that. You don't have to face anyone alone. You are giving them exactly what you promised to them.'

Something lurched against my ribs. And I almost had to rub a hand against my chest to appease it.

'By bringing me as your plus-one and *boyfriend*, which is a part of this whole thing you very conveniently omitted telling me about, you tackle the problem at the source – showing up alone and single. As easy as that.'

Aaron Blackford had impeccably delivered his pitch. Straight to the damn point.

'Easy? You are crazy if you think this is going to be easy,' I murmured. 'If you can barely put up with me most of the time, imagine an army of Linas in all sizes and shapes. For three days straight.'

'I'm prepared.'

The question was, was I? Was I really prepared to take the leap and potentially risk history repeating itself?

But then Aaron spoke again, 'I've never been scared to work for something, Catalina. Even when all odds are against me.'

The way those words hit me was close to making me gasp for air. As if that statement had carried extra weight and taken a swing at me.

I'm being stupid.

No. I *was* decidedly crazy if what was about to leave my lips was any indication of the level of how much I had lost my wits. But hell, it wasn't like I hadn't agreed to this before.

'Okay,' I pushed out. 'You have been warned – twice. Now, I guess you are really stuck with this. We are stuck with this, you and I.'

'I wasn't the one calling it off, Catalina.' He was right; I could give him as much. And then he said, 'You were already stuck with me.'

I averted my eyes, not wanting to expose how that made me feel. 'Whatever you say, Blackford. I just hope we don't screw this up.'

'We won't,' he declared firmly. 'Or are you forgetting that when I put my mind to something, I never fail?'

I blinked, a little terrified of that last declaration. Oh hell, it would take a certain level of confidence, perhaps even madness, to pull this off anyway.

Ignoring how I could almost feel the relief lifting some of the weight off my shoulders, I finally let my gaze roam outside the car.

'This is not my street.' I did not recognize the area where we were parked. 'Where are we?'

'Picking up dinner,' he said, pointing out the window at a food truck covered in a colourful pattern that intertwined luchador masks with floral motifs. 'This place has the best fish tacos in the city.'

My stomach grumbled at the thought of fish tacos. Any tacos would obtain that reaction, frankly. But fish tacos? They were my guilty pleasure.

'Fish tacos?'

His dark eyebrows knit together. And I was so hungry that I could have kissed that frown. 'You like them,' he stated rather than asked.

I did. 'Actually I love them.'

Aaron nodded as if he wanted to tell me, *See?* 'You might have

gushed over them to Héctor a couple hundred times,' Aaron commented casually. To which I blinked. A couple million times rather
than a hundred. 'How many will you take? My usual order is three.'

His usual order?

'Three sounds good,' I confirmed rather absently while my mind
wandered away, picturing Aaron coming here as a regular. Ordering
his three tacos. Sauce dripping off his otherwise spotless fingers.
Perhaps some out of the corner of his otherwise unamused mouth.

Stop it, Lina, I scolded myself. *Tacos are not sexy. They are messy
and sticky.*

'I'll be right back,' he said as he unfastened his seat belt.

A couple of seconds too late, my fingers worked on my own seat
belt with the purpose of me going with him.

'Don't,' he ordered as he threw his door open. 'Stay in the car.
I'll bring them.'

'You don't have to mother me or buy me dinner, Aaron,' I
complained, not wanting him to feel like he had to feed me or
something. 'You have done enough already.'

'I know I don't have to,' he said, slipping out of the car. Leaning
down, his head peeked inside. 'I planned on coming here tonight
either way. You just happened to be in the car,' he explained as if
he knew I needed to hear it. He wasn't wrong. 'And you should eat
something. It'll be a few minutes.'

Giving up, I sighed. 'Okay.' Fumbling with my fingers on my lap
as he leaned away from the car, I called for him again. He stopped.
'Make it four then,' I requested with a small voice. Being stupid with
food was officially over. 'Please.'

Aaron looked at me in silence for a long moment. So long that I
wondered if I shouldn't have ordered an extra taco. When he finally
spoke, he did so quietly, 'Try not to fall asleep again, okay? I can't
promise there will be any food left when, or if, I ever manage to
wake you up.'

My eyes narrowed. 'You'd better not ever do that, Blackford,' I said under my breath a second after he smashed the car door closed and crossed the street to the Mexican food truck.

Not more than thirty minutes later, I held in my hands a warm takeout container that smelled absolutely amazing as I shut my apartment door behind me. Five tacos – Aaron had gotten me five and not four, like I had told him. With a side of rice with serrano peppers too. And he hadn't let me pay for any of it.

'I got you,' he had said.

After that, he proceeded to save his number in my phone and asked me to send him my flight details the moment I got home. Then, he'd made me promise I'd eat and go to sleep. As if that wasn't exactly what I had been dying to do.

So, without giving in to the panic that I'd surely wake up in tomorrow, I did exactly as he had said.

He. Aaron Blackford. My soon-to-be boss and even-sooner-to-be fake date to my sister's wedding.

Because just like he had said, he really did get me.

CHAPTER TWELVE

Hours left to board the flight to wedding-doom: twenty-four.

Level of anxiety: reaching emergency status.

Contingency plan: triple-chocolate brownie. A truckload of it.

If yesterday had told me anything, it was that I had been a total idiot with my health. And while I knew that stuffing my mouth with chocolate was a far stretch from that, I guessed I was a woman of extremes.

And that was exactly what had brought me to Madison Avenue. More specifically, to the only place in New York City that held the power to soothe the raging beast that was my anxiety right now.

'Do you want your order to go, Lina?' Sally asked from the other side of the counter. 'How is Rosie, by the way? Is she not joining you?'

'I wish she were, but I'm flying solo today.'

Last night, I had been on the phone with Rosie for about two hours. Telling her what I was about to embark on hadn't been easy, and she might have squealed – unnecessarily – and bugged me with more of that stuff about heated looks between Aaron and me she had clearly been imagining, but it was good, having my best friend back on my team. Even if that was Team Deception. Having her waiting in New York when I came back from my trip to wedding-doom with an understanding smile and the pint of ice cream I'd definitely need would mean the world.

'And no, thanks. I'll have my coffee and brownie here.' I paused, reconsidering that. 'Brownies – make it two, please,' I told Sally. 'I can indulge. I have the whole day to lounge and relax. I took the day off work.'

She methodically weighed the coffee beans. 'Oh, you must have really missed me if you are sticking around for so long,' she commented as she smiled at me over her shoulder. 'Not that I'd blame you. Who wouldn't miss me, right?'

I chuckled. 'Of course I missed you. You are my favorite barista in the whole world.' My eyes were tracking all her movements; I was already salivating.

'Oh. Now, you are saying that only because I have the goods, but keep going, please.'

I was ready to admit that and perhaps ask her to marry me, too, if that meant an endless supply of free coffee for the rest of my life. Then, I saw her gaze move somewhere behind me as she pressed the buttons that made the caffeinated magic happen.

An appreciative gleam appeared in Sally's eyes.

'Good morning,' she told whoever was behind me. Then, she gave me a mischievous glance before focusing on her new customer again. 'Same as always? Double espresso, no sugar?' She paused, and I felt the newcomer right behind me.

I frowned, something sounding very familiar about that order. Black, bitter, and soulless, just like—

'Coming right up, Aaron.'

My spine stiffened as I kept my head straight ahead while my eyes widened.

'Thank you, Sally.'

That voice. It belonged to the man who would be boarding a plane with me tomorrow. The one man who I would be introducing to my family as my dear fake boyfriend.

Turning slowly in his direction, I was welcomed by a pair

of ocean-blue eyes, wrapped in a serious expression I knew very well. My mouth opened, but I didn't get the chance to say anything.

'It's worse than I thought,' he said, scanning my face as his lips pressed into their usual thin line.

'Excuse me?' I scoffed, imitating him and gawking at him up and down.

'Your eyes.' He pointed in the direction of my head. 'They look huge in your face. Bigger than usual. Are you sure caffeine is a good idea? You seem a little rattled already.'

My huge and bigger-than-usual eyes narrowed. 'Rattled?'

'Yes.' He nodded nonchalantly. 'Like you'll flip any moment now.'

Biting back a couple of bad words, I took a deep breath to stop myself from flipping – like he had said – right there and then. 'First of all, I am calm.' That earned me a look that told me he wasn't buying it. '*Yes.* Not only calm, but also serene, mind you. Just like one of those ponds where the water doesn't even move.'

I turned away from him, taking in Sally, who was leaning against the counter, chin resting on the back of her hand, engrossed in my conversation with Aaron. 'I'm starting to miss you less and less, Sally,' I quipped and watched her smile widen as she straightened. I sent Aaron a side-glance. 'Aren't you supposed to be at work, Mr Robot? You know, instead of out and about, pointing out how rattled random women look?'

'You are not a random woman,' he countered calmly, and then he leaned on the counter. Right beside me. 'And I was, in the morning. But I have the rest of the day off.'

'A vacation?' I gasped theatrically. 'Hell must have frozen over if Aaron Blackford took a day off.'

He never, ever did.

'Half day,' he corrected me.

Sally placed both our orders on the counter. At the same time.

Which struck me as odd, given that I had placed mine more than a few minutes before Aaron.

I narrowed my eyes at her as she gifted me with an angelic smile. 'There you go, guys. Nothing but the best for my favourite customers. Double espresso, no sugar. And a flat white.'

That reminded me of something she had said earlier about Aaron having a *usual* order.

'How often do you come here, Aaron?' I queried. Not often, since I had never stumbled upon him in the past, considering how religiously I visited Around the Corner. 'How do you even know this place?'

There were Google Maps, Tripadvisor, Time Out, and a million other sites that could be behind his discovery. And yet ...

'Often enough,' he answered, pulling out his wallet from his pocket.

With my eyes still narrowed and tracking how his long fingers fumbled with his wallet, a memory flashed in my mind. I had talked to Aaron about Around the Corner. Or I had been talking to myself about it and Aaron had happened to hear it – whatever. It was the day he had shown up and helped me with the Open Day stuff. My back straightened with the realization.

'What's so surprising, Catalina? I pay attention when you talk. Even when you mumble to yourself. Which you do very often. But every once in a while, you do say something interesting.'

'Are you a mind reader or something?'

'Thankfully not. I'd be terrified to know what you were thinking most of the time.' He stretched his arm and handed his credit card to Sally. 'It's on me.'

Okay. First of all, terrified? And second of all, I mumbled? *Often?*

Watching Sally as she took the credit card snapped me out of my stupid shock.

'Wait,' I yelped. That got both Sally's and Aaron's attention. 'You don't have to pay for my order. I have my own money.'

'I'm sure you do, but I want to.'

'But what if I don't want you to?' I argued.

Sally's gaze jumped from me to the man beside me. I turned too, finding Aaron's calm expression.

'And is there any particular reason why you don't want me to, Catalina? Something tells me, if this were anyone else, you wouldn't even bat an eyelash at getting a free coffee and brownie.' He eyed the counter. 'Brownies.'

'Well, yes. There is a reason, smart-ass.' I took a step toward him. A small one. I lowered my voice. 'I owe you enough as it is, and I am not talking just about the fish tacos from yesterday, okay?' Our gazes met. 'I don't need you to put me into further debt.'

If the way his face changed was something to go by, that last part of my statement seemed to really bother him.

'You don't owe me a single thing,' he said with a scowl. 'Me buying you a coffee, tacos, or anything for that matter doesn't put you in my debt.' His head shook, a few of the usually perfectly-in-place locks of dark hair bouncing and grabbing my attention. The scowl fell away, replaced by a somewhat-distant look. 'Will you ever accept anything from me without putting up this big a fight?'

'That's . . .' I trailed off, not knowing what to tell him. 'That's not an easy question to answer, Blackford.'

He tilted his head. 'I see.'

Then, he angled his large body toward me, closing much of the distance that had been separating us. The motion had been unexpected, and my breath hitched with surprise. Hyper-aware of how close he had come, I stuttered. Suddenly not knowing what to say or if I was expected to say anything at all.

Aaron's arm reached out, the backs of his fingers gracing my temple. My lips parted, tingles spreading down my skin.

It was him who lowered his voice then. 'Always fighting me.'

I looked up at his handsome and stern face, his blue eyes assessing my reaction.

'Resisting me.'

My heart tripped, making my chest feel like I had just sprinted a mile or two.

Aaron's head dipped, his mouth coming close to where his fingers had been a few seconds ago. Almost as close as it had been when we'd danced. 'It's as if you want me to beg. Is that something you'd enjoy? Me begging?' His voice sounded so . . . intimate. Hushed. But it was his next words that scattered my thoughts all over the place. 'Is that what this is? You like bringing me to my knees?'

Whoa.

An extremely familiar heat climbed up my neck, spreading to my cheeks. Heating my skin. Then, it rushed back all the way down, making me way too warm in a matter of seconds.

Aaron's gaze held mine as something dipped in my belly. 'Let me treat you, okay? I want to.'

My lips dried and then pressed together as I tried to get ahold of the chaos rushing through my mind and body.

'Okay,' I breathed out, sounding all shaky and wrong. I cleared my throat. Twice. 'Pay for my coffee. I'm not interested in you begging or putting on any kind of show in the middle of the coffee shop.' I cleared my throat a third time, my voice still not sounding right. 'So, please, pay away.' I paused, trying to get my body back on track. 'And thanks.'

Aaron nodded, the start of a satisfied smile tugging at the corners of his lips. 'See? It wasn't all that hard, was it?' he pointed out. His lips inched further up, looking all smug and—

Oh wait.

Realization dawned. 'You were . . .' I couldn't believe this. Any of this. My reaction to him. The fact that he had just made me . . . hot, just for fun and giggles. 'You were just making a point.'

His lips twitched. 'Maybe I was,' Aaron said, finally stepping out of my personal space and turning away. He looked over at me, that tug of his lips still up. 'Are you disappointed, Catalina?'

I can't believe this.

And what was worse, this meant that he was aware of the effect he had on me. He knew what his proximity did to my senses. To my body. And he had just used it to win this stupid discussion.

I gaped at his profile as he brought his mug to his lips, looking all pleased with himself.

'You know what, Aaron?' I shrugged my shoulders, fighting the smile that wanted to break across my expression. 'I truly am disappointed.'

'You are?' That smug look fell off his face.

'Oh, so much. And you know what I do when that happens?' I turned to Sally. 'Sally, I'll have one of everything you have on display. And I changed my mind. I'll get everything to go, please.' My lips broke on what I hoped wasn't an evil grin. 'He insists on paying.' I pointed at Aaron with my thumb. 'So, please, let him do that before he chases away all your customers with I don't know what antics about him getting on his knees.'

'Oh, I wouldn't want that,' Sally said with a wink. 'You do like our lemon bars. Should I put two instead of one?' she asked as she grabbed one of the biggest containers.

I nodded. 'What a lovely idea. I do love them, and why not two blueberry muffins too? They look fantastic from here.'

Aaron remained by my side as he witnessed my little display. 'If you think I'm not elated to see you eat, then you don't understand how serious I was yesterday.'

I ignored the way that made me feel.

'But I still hope you are going to share.'

'I thought you were treating me, not the other way around.'

If I hadn't known him any better, it would have been easy to overlook the unfiltered amusement shining in his eyes. But it was right there.

And as I peered into that handsome face I had despised – perhaps unfairly, *okay, fine* – so often in the past, it hit me. I was just as amused, if not a little more. And we did not have only that in common. Both of us were doing an awful job at hiding it too.

But somehow, for the first time in history, neither of us seemed to care. We simply continued looking at each other as we stood there. Gazes locked. Both of us fighting what I knew were petty smiles. Hiding our amusement like a pair of stubborn idiots, waiting for the other to break and grin first.

'All right.' Sally's voice broke through the spell, making me turn abruptly. She was smiling. Brightly. 'Order packed and ready.'

'Okay, thanks,' I muttered. With a little bit of a struggle, I managed to gently hug everything to my chest. 'All right, Blackford. Thank you too. Always a pleasure doing business with you.'

'You really are not going to share, are you?'

'Nope.'

We stared at each other while seconds ticked by.

'I . . .' He trailed off, looking like he was changing his mind about something. My heart raced. 'I don't like running through the terminal. So, try not to be late tomorrow. It's not—'

'Cute. I know, Blackford. Bye.' Then, I turned on my heel and walked away.

First, he'd gone after my sweets, and now, this.

One day, I was going to throw something at that ridiculously symmetrical face of his. I truly was, but it was never going to be a brownie.

CHAPTER THIRTEEN

Aaron was never late. He wasn't programmed for that kind of careless behaviour.

I knew because I had been trying to be painfully earlier than him to every single appointment our calendars had in common for a little more than one year and eight months. Which could only mean one thing. He wasn't coming.

He had seen reason and realized how ludicrous our plan was.

My plan, which he had agreed to.

Or was it the other way around? At this point, I didn't know anymore.

Not that it mattered if he wasn't coming.

Because that was the only reasonable explanation as to why I found myself in the middle of the Departures terminal, under the huge panel that displayed the status and times of all the outgoing flights, cold sweat running down my back and no one by my side. At least, not the surly blue-eyed man who should have been here right about now.

Gaze roaming around, I let that sink in.

I am on my own.

A wave of sheer panic curled its way down my spine. Something else too.

Something that tasted a lot like betrayal. Which didn't make sense really. When it came to Aaron, I wasn't entitled to feel betrayed. Or abandoned. I also didn't want those emotions wreaking havoc in my head. Or my chest. Not when I was more than able to understand why he would get cold feet.

This whole thing was crazy anyway. Total nonsense. So, why would he go through with the insane plan I had concocted?

My eyes landed on the suitcase and the weekender bag pooled at my feet as I tried really hard to shove away the way I was feeling.

You are fine, I told myself. *Ignore that stupid, crushing sensation you have no business feeling and go check in your bags.*

The last thing I wanted to do was board that plane alone, but I would do it. I would face my family – and Daniel and his fiancée and the past I had left behind – and the consequences of my lie with my head held high. And I'd do it on my own, as much as I had allowed myself in the last forty-eight hours to trust I'd be doing it with someone by my side.

Dios. How had I let this happen? How had Aaron Blackford made himself indispensable in my life?

Bracing my hands on my hips, I remained where I was for what I promised myself would be one last minute. And just to be thorough, I vowed to myself again that I'd be fine.

The pressure building behind my eyes? Nerves. Going home had always filled me with equal parts of joy and remorse. With as much nostalgia as the pain that came with the memories. That was why I didn't go back all that often.

But that didn't matter. I was a big girl. Before Aaron, the plan had always been to do this on my own, so that was what I'd be doing.

With one shaky exhalation, I emptied my head and chest of every thought and fleeting emotion, and I let my arms drop from my hips as I reached for my bags.

Ya está bien. Time to go. Hell waits for no—

'Catalina,' a deep voice I'd thought I'd never be glad – not just glad, but also relieved, happy, freaking *elated* – to hear said behind me.

Closing my eyes, I gave myself a moment to get rid of the swirl of overjoyed and inappropriate emotions I had unsuccessfully tried to push away less than a heartbeat ago.

Aaron is here. He came.

Swallowing hard, I pressed my lips together.

I'm not alone. He is here.

'Catalina?' he called one more time.

Turning very slowly, I couldn't stop my mouth from finally shaping into what I knew was a wobbly smile. One that probably gave away every single emotion fighting to burst out of me.

Aaron's frown welcomed me, and I swore I had never been so happy to see that stubborn knot that wrinkled his brows together.

He came, he came, he came.

He tilted his head. 'Are you o—'

Before he could finish formulating that question, I landed on his chest with an *oomph*. Then, I wrapped my arms around him the best I could. 'You came.' The words were muffled against the soft fabric of whatever he was wearing. His chest was warm and wide and snuggly, and for a second, I didn't want to give a damn about how I had plunked myself onto him or how embarrassed I'd be about it later.

Because for better or for worse, I was hugging Aaron.

And he . . . he wasn't returning the embrace, but he was letting me. With his arms hanging at his sides, just where they had been when I launched myself at him. His chest wasn't moving much either. It felt a lot like hugging a marble sculpture, unyielding and hardened under my cheek, only that it pounded with a heartbeat. The latter being the only sign that I had not shocked him into cardiac arrest.

Because besides that, Aaron remained completely still. Taking one step back very slowly, I gazed upwards.

Okay, so he looked like a statue too. Perhaps I had broken him with my hug.

That would explain why he was barely blinking as he stared at me for a while.

Time in which the last minute started settling in. Desperately, I searched my mind for something to say, anything to excuse my brief and temporary madness that had resulted in me launching my body at his. I came up empty.

He finally broke the silence. 'You thought I wasn't coming.'

A part of me didn't want to admit it. Even when it was pretty obvious.

Aaron continued, accusation in his voice, 'You hugged me because you thought I wasn't coming.' His gaze was searching. As if he couldn't believe or understand what had just happened. 'You've never hugged me before.'

I stepped further back, fumbling with my hands and feeling a little overwhelmed by the way he was looking at me. 'I don't think it computes as a hug when one of the parties remains like a wooden stick, Captain Not So Obvious.' I decided right then that in my head, it hadn't been a hug. 'Plus, you were late, and you never are, so what did you expect me to think?'

As I backed away some more, putting the right amount of space between our bodies, my gaze finally managed to take him in completely. From head to toe. And ... yeah, from toe to head too. Because the soft fabric that had been pressed beneath my cheek a moment ago was a plain white cotton T-shirt. And the legs that had remained unmovable under my hug attack were clad in faded jeans. And the—

Are those tennis shoes on his feet?

Yes, they totally were.

I had no idea what I had expected him to wear, but it surely wasn't that. I hadn't been prepared for the image of Aaron standing in front of me in something that wasn't the long-sleeved button-down shirt tucked in his dress pants that I knew him in.

Aaron looked relaxed. *Normal.* Not like the aloof stainless-steel working machine I was around at work. The one that screamed at you to keep your distance.

No. Ironically, what I wanted was to press my cheek against his chest again. Which was absolutely ridiculous. And dangerous too. This new version of Aaron was just as dangerous as the one that smiled and laughed. Because I liked it. A little too much for the well-being of our plan. Or mine.

'Catalina,' Aaron called, forcing my gaze to return to his face.

Cheeks heating, I pretended I hadn't been ogling him. And appreciating what I ogled.

'Yes?'

'I asked if you were done with that?'

Mierda. 'Done with what exactly?' I scratched the side of my neck, trying to conceal my embarrassment.

'Panicking. About me not coming. Are you finally done with that? Because I am here now, just how I said I would be. And I wasn't late. You just happened to be shockingly early.' He tilted his head slightly and then added, 'For once.'

Eyes narrowed, I checked the time on my phone. 'Fine, you might be right.' I returned my gaze to his. 'For once.'

The right corner of his lips tipped up. 'Good. So, now that we have established that,' he started, and I did not like one single bit how smug he looked all of a sudden, 'do you think you are done looking at me like I have grown a second head too? Because I'd like to get going.'

Busted. 'Yep,' I squared my shoulders. 'Done with that too.' I reached for the handle of my carry-on suitcase. 'I just didn't know you owned normal clothes.'

Aaron cocked a brow.

My treacherous eyes swept him head to toe again. Dammit, he looked really, really good, all cosy and comfy.

I shook my head. 'Come on, Mr Robot. We have bags to check in,' I told him, forcing my eyes away. 'Now that you are here and all.'

Reaching for the weekender bag – which was filled to the brim – I lifted it off the floor, hung it off my shoulder, and tried to walk with as much grace as I could while probably looking a little bit like an overloaded Sherpa.

In one long stride, Aaron caught up with me. I watched his eyebrow rise as he gave me a sideways glance. 'How long are you planning on staying in Spain?' He eyed my two pieces of biggerthan-strictlynecessary luggage. 'I thought we'd be flying back on Monday.'

'And we are.'

Eyes wide, Aaron made a show out of looking me and my luggage up and down. 'That's how you pack for three days?'

I quickened my pace while I tried really hard not to *assplant* on the terminal's polished floor under the weight of the bag on my shoulder. 'Yes. Why do you ask?'

Instead of answering, his hand on my arm stopped my course. Without giving me a chance to complain, he delicately snagged my bag and placed it on his shoulder.

The physical relief was so immediate that I had to stop myself from moaning in response.

'Jesus, Catalina,' he huffed, looking back at me, horrified. 'What are you carrying in here? A dead body?'

'Hey, this is not a regular weekend visit to the fam, okay? Stop luggage-shaming me,' I said to the scowling man walking beside me. 'I had to fit loads of stuff. Make-up, accessories, hair dryer, hair straightener, my good conditioner, lotion, all the dresses I'm taking, six pairs of shoes—'

'Six pairs of shoes?' Aaron croaked, scowling even harder.

'Yes,' I answered quickly, my gaze hunting for the right check-in counter. 'One for each of the three different outfits I need, plus the pertinent three backups.' I paused, thinking of something. 'Please tell me you packed at least one backup.'

Aaron rearranged my bag on his shoulder, shaking his head at the same time. 'No, I didn't. But I'll be fine. You, on the other hand . . .' Another shake of his head. 'You are—'

'Brilliant?' I finished for him. 'Astute? Gifted in the art of packing? I know. And I hope you have enough clothes in that tiny suitcase you are carrying.'

'Ridiculous,' he murmured. 'You are a ridiculous woman.'

'We'll see who's the ridiculous one when something accidentally happens to your shirt, tie, or suit, and you have to wear one of my dresses to the wedding.'

A grunt reached my ears. 'Six pairs of shoes,' the scowling man in casual wear muttered. 'Ridiculous woman packing her own weight in clothes.' He went on, almost too low for me to make out.

'If it's too heavy for you, you can give it back. I was doing fine myself.'

His head shot in my direction, giving me a look that told me that wasn't an option.

Sighing, I accepted the help. 'Thank you, Blackford. That's very kind of you.'

'And you were not doing fine,' he countered back, making me want to take back my thank-you. 'You could have hurt yourself.'

Aaron veered to the left, and I finally tracked down the counters matching the airline we were flying with.

I followed him. 'I appreciate the concern, Big A. But I've got my own set of muscles.'

He brushed over my use of his nickname. 'Of course. You have to be stubborn on top of ridiculous,' he muttered under his breath.

I had to hide my smile. 'Said the kettle to the pot.'

With a last sideways glance, Aaron sped up, letting his long legs carry him away with his small and reasonable suitcase and my ridiculously brimming bag on his shoulder.

From my position a couple of steps behind him, I had no choice but to let my gaze travel down his backside. A not-too-small and certainly not-very-quiet part of me was a little in awe of how his jeans hugged those muscled thighs, which had once propelled him across a football field. That same part got a little louder when my eyes trailed up, catching how his biceps, which I knew had carried a brown melonlike leather ball across that very same field, were bunched as his arm held the weight of my bag.

Ugh. It was terribly disturbing how distracting Aaron's backside was now that I knew more of him. Now that I knew all these tiny little pieces of his life.

The ones I had found out about the night of the fundraiser, sure. But also those I had dug up when I googled him.

Yes, I had fallen prey to my curiosity. But just once. I had allowed myself to do that one single time.

And that level of self-restraint hadn't been easy to achieve. At least not considering how everything I gleaned from my little Google rendezvous had been stuck in the back of my head ever since I had indulged. Demanding to be acknowledged more often than I was ready to admit.

My mind seemed eager to hold on to the pictures of a younger version of Aaron – just as stoic, his shoulders as wide, and his jaw just as hard – dressed in a purple-and-gold uniform that made my heart rate grow a little quicker only thinking about it. Or the headlines proclaiming that he had been a known name back in that day. But what I'd had more trouble forgetting were the articles – and there had been more than a couple dozen – praising his performance and foreshadowing the player he would become. But hadn't.

So, why hadn't he? Why did the press coverage of his football career go for a few years and then stop altogether?

That was something I hadn't managed to find.

And it only fuelled my itch to know more. To learn more about this man I had thought I had all pieced together but that I was learning I couldn't have been more wrong about.

As if on cue, Aaron looked back at me. His brows rose on his forehead. 'Is something wrong?'

Caught a little off guard, I just shook my head.

'Then, come on. At this pace, we will never make it to Spain.'

'If only I were so lucky,' I mumbled. But then I shot forward, hurrying until catching up with him.

Once again, Aaron was right.

There were more pressing concerns to occupy my mind with.

Like the plane we would be boarding in less than a handful of hours.

Or the fact that once we did so, there was no turning back.

Because we were doing this. We were really doing it, and we had to ace it.

By the time we landed in Spain, my family needed to believe that Aaron and I were happily – hearts bursting, birds chirping, and flowers blooming – in love. Or at the very least, that we could stand each other for more than ten minutes without causing an international war to erupt.

And as much as I had no clue how we would ever manage to do that, I was sure of something. We, Aaron and I, would figure it out.

We had to.

CHAPTER FOURTEEN

'And you said the desserts were nothing to write home about. Well, this chocolate cake tells a different story, pal,' I talked over my surprisingly amazing in-flight dessert. 'Do you think I could ask for another serving?' I hummed in pleasure.

Heck, it was so good that I wasn't even ashamed to do that.

Not even with Aaron occupying the lush first-class seat beside me. Oh yeah, because, apparently, I flew in first class now. I still hadn't figured out exactly how I had let him ask for – or rather demand – an upgrade of my economy seat without even putting up a fight. But I knew it had included him throwing an arm over my shoulders and uttering the word girlfriend. Which, in hindsight, I knew had blindsided me enough to somehow nod like a fool and place my passport on the check-in counter.

He lowered the newspaper he had been hiding behind and revealed a cocked eyebrow. 'Pal?'

'Silence. I'm having a moment with my cake.' He sighed and returned to his reading.

Holding my spoon in the air, I hesitated before taking it to my mouth. 'You didn't have to do that, you know? Paying for the upgrade of my tickets is too much.'

I heard a noncommittal grunt come from him.

'I'm serious, Aaron.'

'I thought you wanted to eat in silence.'

'I'll give you back the money when we return from the trip. You are doing enough as it is.'

Aaron's sigh followed my words almost immediately. 'There's no need. I'm a member of the airline's Sky Club, and I have plenty of miles,' he explained as I finally took that last bite of chocolate heaven. 'And as I told you, this is time we can use to prep.'

When I finally devoured what had just become the highlight of my day, I wiped my mouth with the napkin, placed it back on the tray in front of me, and turned to Aaron. 'Which reminds me, break is over.'

He ignored me.

I poked the back of the newspaper with my index finger. 'We have to get back to work. Come on.' Another poke. 'Time to prep.'

'Do you have to do that?' Aaron pleaded from behind it.

'Yes.' I poked the newspaper a few times, making it impossible for him to keep reading. 'I need your full attention. We have only gone through a few of my family members, and we are running out of time.' I tugged at one of the corners. 'Do I have your attention?'

'You don't need to do any of that.' He lowered the large black-and-white-printed pages with a brisk motion. 'You always have my undivided attention, Catalina.'

That made my finger halt in the air.

'Ha.' I narrowed my eyes. 'Cute of you to try to buy me with cheap tricks.' I levelled him with what I hoped was a serious look. 'Don't think you are going to get out of it, sweet-talking me into leaving you alone. The international relationships of the United States of America are not important right now.'

With a reluctant nod, Aaron folded it meticulously and set it on top of his tray. 'All right,' he said, blue eyes focusing completely on me. 'No distractions. I'm all yours.'

All yours.

My breath got stuck somewhere between my lungs and mouth. 'Groom and bride?' I managed to get out.

'Gonzalo and Isabel.' He rolled his eyes, as if I could do better at testing him.

Challenging me.

'Trio of cousins, who you will not listen to a word that leaves their lips?' I paused and then tilted my head. 'Especially if it starts with, *Hey, do you want to hear something funny?*'

'That would be Lucas, Matías, and Adrián.'

He hadn't hesitated. Well, good. Those savages were dangerous; you never knew what would come out of their mouths. Or them in general.

'Parents of the bride and your supposedly future parents-in-law if you were serious about me, which you totally are?'

'Cristina and Javier,' he answered immediately. 'I should be polite but address them by their first name, or they will be offended and think I'm a pretentious ass.' Aaron paused after repeating my earlier words exactly. He adjusted his big body in the more than spacious seat, making it look smaller and cramped. 'Javier is a university History professor and speaks English fluently. Cristina is a nurse, and her English is . . . just not as good. However, she is the one I should be more wary of. Even when it looks like she doesn't understand me, chances are, she is still weighing my every word.'

I nodded, secretly impressed. He was acing all my questions – for the second time. Not that I was surprised. He had proven in the past that his determination knew no limits when it came to success, no matter the task. Aaron didn't half-ass things; he delivered the best results. Always.

Good. He was going to need all his determination with the Martín family and the rest of the wedding party.

But that didn't mean I was completely satisfied. Not yet. 'Parents of the groom?'

'Juani and Manuel,' Aaron shot back quickly.

Nodding my head, I watched his mouth open, knowing what he

was going to add before he said it. Those were the parents of the groom's brother too. Who was my ex.

'Okay, next question,' I rushed out before he could speak. 'Cousin who you must avoid at all costs unless I am with you to control the situation?' Turning in my seat, I faced him completely.

In an attempt to see how he worked under pressure, I schooled my face with my most assertive expression.

Aaron's jaw twitched, and he looked distracted.

Dammit. Was he hesitating? He mustn't.

I was about to voice an objection when he recovered, beating me to it. 'Charo.' The name of my cousin sounded different from Aaron's lips, the word adorned with his strong American accent.

And I would have instantly criticized his pronunciation, if not for what he did next and the shock that it induced in my body.

His arm rose in the air, his big hand reaching for my face very slowly. My eyes switched from that hand to his face, finding his gaze fixed somewhere just above my chin. And then, before I could stop what was about to happen, his thumb made contact with my skin. Very softly.

He was brushing my cheek. Very close to my mouth.

All and every complaint died and went up to heaven the moment his finger swiped over my skin.

He started talking again, looking engrossed by the motion of his thumb. 'Charo,' he repeated distractedly.

While I . . . I simply remained frozen in place. Feeling how that simple contact against my skin seemed to awaken little fires all across my body.

'You said I must run away from a red-haired woman with inquisitive green eyes and little to no shame. And that would be Charo.'

How such a gentle contact could scorch my skin so effectively was something that I . . . couldn't understand. My lips parted, a shaky breath leaving them.

Only then did Aaron's eyes look up and meet mine.

My blood swirled, rising to my neck, my cheeks, my temples. Spreading out as I held his gaze, the blue in his eyes turning a little darker.

When Aaron looked away, just as he retrieved his thumb, I felt myself relax. But it was short-lived because as soon as my gaze fell down and found his hand as it hovered in the air, I discovered with horror that there was a smudge of chocolate on his thumb.

Chocolate which had been on my face less than a couple of seconds ago.

Oh Lord.

And yet, what almost knocked me off my seat and onto the carpeted floor of the aircraft turned out to be something else entirely. Not the knowledge that I had been talking for a small eternity with cake hanging from my face. Nope. Or the knowledge I had done so in front of Aaron, who would probably use that against me in the future. No. What almost knocked me on my ass, if not for the seat belt, was Aaron parting those lips that were so often pressed in an unamused line, and licking the chocolate clean off his thumb.

Chocolate that he had just retrieved from the corner of my mouth.

A riot of emotions burst inside my belly as I watched his throat gulp it down, appreciation flashing through his face.

And I . . . *holy shit.* I just stared at him, completely . . . enraptured. Utterly shocked.

I should have been appalled. But I wasn't. My brown eyes were now fixed on Aaron's mouth, noticing how all the heat that I'd felt in my face travelled around my body to all kinds of interesting places, all the while keeping my eyes where they were. On his lips.

Out of my peripheral vision, I made out how Aaron cleaned his hand methodically on the napkin that rested on my tray.

'You were right; the cake was that good.' He cleared his throat, as if nothing had happened. 'As I was saying, we should avoid your cousin Charo.'

When my gaze somehow managed to make it back to his eyes, I felt all kinds of hot, bothered, and weird.

'You stressed how important it is that Charo doesn't suspect us. Our deal.'

Barely listening to what he was saying, I watched his hand lift in the air again. Then, his thumb was brushing the edge of my lips one more time. This time, I felt it twice as intensely. His touch twice as gentle. My eyes fluttered closed for an instant.

'I think you got all the chocolate.' My voice was so breathy that I barely recognized it. 'Thanks.'

'Just wanted to be thorough,' he answered quietly as his gaze lifted from that goddamn spot close to the corner of my lips to my eyes. 'Next question?'

'Best man?'

I squirmed in my seat, uneasiness replacing all the earlier tingly warmth. Perhaps because that was a topic that didn't wake up the fuzziest of feelings in me. Or maybe because of how unsettled I was by what had just happened. I couldn't be sure, but I held my breath as I waited for his answer.

'Daniel.' Aaron's gaze held mine. 'He's your ex and the groom's brother.'

I nodded my head once, unable to do much more than that.

Aaron rearranged himself in the seat, dipping his head so we were at eye-level. 'You haven't said much else about him. Is there anything besides that, that I should know?'

He regarded me quietly, almost expectantly, and I could really tell I had all his undivided attention. Just as he had said earlier. Although this time, it wasn't a trick. The need to open up to him and tell him everything manifested itself, making me doubt myself.

'No. That's all.' I lowered my gaze to his hands, which were resting on his lap. 'He's my ex and Gonzalo's older brother by a few years. Isabel and Gonzalo met through us, when we started dating. And . . . that's about it.'

If I were smarter, I'd tell Aaron the whole story.

But lately, I'd seemed to excel at making only stupid decisions. So, that was all I gave him.

In my defence, facing the catalyst of my current predicament was going to be hard enough. I did not want to spend my time talking about Daniel because that meant going back down memory lane, which had consisted of bad choices and heartbreak.

So, no, it wasn't something I was happy to casually chat about regardless of how crucial it was for the show we were about to put on. Even if a part of me refused to acknowledge just how small I would feel, showing Aaron that piece of myself, and even when I knew that I was lying to him. Lying again. It was a lie by omission, sure, but it had the potential to bite me in the ass later. Just like any lie would.

'You can trust me,' he said softly.

Maybe I could. But that didn't mean trusting Aaron with that would ever come easy to me. That fragment of my life had been locked up for a long time – perhaps so long that the chances were the lock had grown rusty and withered and there was no working it back open. That would explain how I had gotten here. Somewhere across the Atlantic Ocean, sitting next to a man I usually struggled to share the same air with without wanting to throw something at his hard head, but who had somehow happened to be the one man in New York City in the position to fill in as my made-up boyfriend.

'What's my *abuela*'s name?' I kept my gaze low, anywhere but on his face. I didn't think I wanted to get a single clue as to what he was feeling at that moment. I didn't think it would make me feel good.

'Catalina,' Aaron said my name with something that sounded a lot like pity.

I hated it. 'Incorrect,' I snapped. 'My *abuela*'s name is not Catalina, Aaron. You need to know the name of my only living grandmother.'

I was deflecting, but that didn't change the facts. He really had to know the name of my *abuela*.

'So?' I pressed. 'What's my *abuela*'s name?'

Aaron dropped his head on the plush headrest, closing his eyes for a second. 'Your *abuela*'s name is María, and she doesn't speak one word of English, which shouldn't trick me into thinking that she is harmless. If by any chance she shoves food in my direction, I'm to keep my mouth shut and eat.' Aaron's words rolled off his tongue, as if he had been practising this speech for weeks.

'Impressive.' I nodded my head.

He took a deep breath and looked at me, pleading. 'We have gone through this a thousand times, and you are giving me a headache.' His eyebrows knitted. 'You need to relax. I need to rest. Let's do that. Do you think you can be quiet for a few hours?'

'First of all, it was only three times.' I showed him with my fingers, just to be thorough. 'And we are not even done with the last round of questions. And secondly, I am completely and absolutely relaxed. I am cooler than a cucumber, Blackford. I just want to be sure that you don't screw up and mix up basic info. You are my boyfriend—' I stopped myself, hearing what had just left my mouth. 'That is the part you will play in this whole Spanish love deception. My made-up boyfriend. So, you should at least know the names of my immediate family, so no one can sniff that you and I are not a real thing. And trust me, they'll know if you so much as hesitate.'

That earned me a scowl.

'Yes. Do not look at me like that,' I told him, pointing my finger at his frown. 'In Spain, cousins and second cousins are immediate family too, okay? Same goes for uncles, aunts, and great-uncles and great-aunts. Sometimes, neighbours too.' I paused in thought. 'Oh, maybe we should go over the physical descriptions again—'

'No,' Aaron cut off my suggestion, his voice sounding more frustrated by the second. 'What we need to do is rest. And if you don't want to do that, then you should let me rest. Do you want me to be all grumpy when we land?'

'You are always grumpy.'

His scowl deepened. 'Do you want me to be so tired that I'll be extra grumpy and make a bad impression?'

'Is that a threat?' A gasp left my lips.

'No,' he said, taken aback by my accusation. 'But it is a possible outcome if you don't let me sleep.'

'But it will be just one more time. It can be quick. Just first cousins?' I bargained with a pout.

Aaron sighed dramatically.

'Or maybe we should go over basic stuff, like my favorite colour, the movie that makes me cry, or what I'm most afraid of.'

Aaron deflated in his seat.

I opened my mouth, but Aaron cut the air with his hand, stopping me. 'Coral. *P.S. I Love You.* And snakes or anything that looks remotely like one.'

Well, that . . . was one hundred percent correct.

Then, he closed his eyes, shutting off the world. And me.

Rendered speechless, I rested my head on the seat, imitating him, as I told myself I didn't want to think about how he had been right. On all of those three things. But the silence only turned every other thought and worry in my head louder and louder.

That earlier emotion was back, making me feel squirmy and nervous and causing me to lose control of the little restraint I usually tried to keep up around Aaron.

'I just want to make sure everything goes perfectly.' My voice came out weak. 'I'm sorry if I am giving you a headache.'

Aaron must have heard something in my confession even if I wasn't sure my words had been loud enough to reach him over the buzz filling the cabin.

His eyes snapped open, and his head turned in my direction. 'Why are you so sure I will mess up?'

That question seemed sincere. And that only made the knot in my chest grow.

Did he think all I worried about was him failing at remembering my *tía-abuela*'s name?

The real impostor was me, not him. 'It's not that.' I shook my head, unable to find the right words. 'I . . . I want them to believe I'm happy.'

'Are you not happy, Catalina?' His gaze searched mine with that intensity of his that I was slowly starting to believe would eventually expose all my secrets.

'I guess I am,' I exhaled, sounding more sombre than I wanted to give away. 'I think I'm happy. I just want everyone else back at home to believe that I am. Even if the only way to accomplish that is this way' – I waved my hand between the two of us – 'if you look the part. If we do. Only if everyone back home believes that I'm not lonely and single because I'm broken.' I could see him piecing something together, so I filled in the silence. 'We need to make them – all of them – believe that we are deeply, utterly, and completely in love. If they find out about our arrangement, they won't let me live it down. It will be humiliating. Probably a million times worse than attending the wedding alone and having them pity me until the end of my days.'

If they discovered that I had convinced someone to act as my boyfriend, someone who wasn't even a friend, I would only manage to confirm what they already believed about me. That I was the broken, stuck, and pathetic Lina they saw.

Aaron's eyes sparked with what looked like understanding. As if something had finally clicked together. The truth behind my motivation perhaps? I hoped not. But whatever it was, it was short-lived because we were interrupted.

His attention shifted to the flight attendant hovering right above our heads.

She directed a radiant smile at him. One he didn't reciprocate. 'Would you like something to drink, Mr Blackford? Miss Martín?'

'Two gin and tonics, please,' he said without so much as a second glance at the flight attendant. 'That okay, baby?'

My head reared back at that last word. *Baby*. 'Yes, sure,' I whispered, feeling my cheeks heat immediately.

Okay, that had … that had been … I had never been *baby* to anyone. And judging by the quick flutter in my stomach, I had kind of liked it. Oh boy. I had actually liked hearing that. Even if it had been fake.

'Thank you, erm …' I stole a glance at the flight attendant, who was eyeing Aaron in an appreciative way. 'Thank you, boyfriend.'

The woman nodded at us with a tight-lipped smile. 'I'll be back with your drinks.'

'You know,' Aaron started in a hushed voice once she was gone, 'you are worried about me messing up and mixing up dozens of Spanish names that I've heard for the first time today, and yet you overlook that calling me boyfriend will probably give it all away rather quickly.'

'Dozens of names?' I hissed. 'More like a dozen.'

Aaron cut me a look.

'A couple dozen, tops. But you might be right,' I admitted, earning a shocked look from him. 'What pet name would you like me to call you?'

'Whatever makes you the happiest. Just pick one.'

In that moment, the effect of the *baby* came back with a vengeance. 'I don't know,' I said, kicking that one out of my head. 'I guess one in Spanish makes sense. *Bollito? Cuchi cuchi? Pocholito?*'

'*Bollito?*'

'It's little bun.' I smiled. 'Like those bread buns that are spongey and shiny and so cute that—'

'Okay, no.' He frowned. 'I think it's better if we stick to our names,' he said, taking both drinks from the attendant who had just reappeared and placing mine in front of me. 'I don't think I can trust you to pick one in Spanish without knowing what it means.'

'I'm very trustworthy – you should know that by now.' I brought a finger to my chin, tapping it a few times. 'How about *conejito?* That's little bunny.'

With a long sigh, Aaron let his massive body fall deeper into the seat.

'You are right; you are not a bunny.' I paused. '*Osito?*' I made a show of looking him up and down, as if I were testing the name on him. 'Yeah, that one is way more fitting. You are more of a bear.'

What was very close to a groan got stuck in Aaron's throat. He lifted his glass to his lips and almost downed half of it. 'Just drink and try to get some sleep, Catalina.'

'Okay.' I turned away, snuggling in my seat and taking a sip of my drink. 'If you insist, *osito*.'

From the corner of my eye, I saw Aaron finishing up the rest of his gin and tonic.

Not that I blamed him. We were definitely in need of some liquid courage if we wanted to survive this.

CHAPTER FIFTEEN

Going through the motions of disembarking the aircraft, getting through customs, and picking up our luggage felt a little bit like one of those strange dreams where everything around you felt fuzzy and unreal, but there was a part of you, deep down in your conscious-ness, that knew it wasn't real.

Only this time, it was. And the loud *thump, thump, thump* in my ears was evidence of just how much.

And yet, as much as that part of me kept repeating that I would wake up while my heart kept screaming that I already was awake and that this was really happening, the moment the Arrivals gate came into view, my whole body froze with realization.

My suitcase wheels screeched against the floor as my two feet became rooted to the spot. Breath stuck in my throat, I watched the gates opening and closing, letting out whoever had been walking ahead of us.

I glanced at Aaron, who had been walking beside me but was now a couple of steps ahead. My overpacked bag hung off his shoulder again.

'Aaron,' I croaked, that *thump, thump, thump* growing louder and louder. 'I can't do it.'

Feeling as if my lungs had been filled with cement, I brought a hand to my chest. *'Ay Dios.'* I heaved. *'Ay Dios mío.'*

How had I let this get so far?

What was I going to do if everything blew up in my face? What if I made it all worse?

I was crazy. No, I was plain stupid. And I wanted to punch myself in the face. Maybe that would snap me out of it.

My gaze roamed around desperately, probably looking for an escape. A way to get out. But I couldn't see anything past those gates that separated us from my parents and kept swallowing passenger after passenger.

'*No puedo hacerlo,*' I muttered, not recognizing my own voice. 'I can't do this. I just can't go out there and lie to my whole family. I can't. It won't work out. They'll know. I'll make a fool of myself. The fool that I am because—'

Aaron's fingers found my chin, tilting my face up to meet his gaze. 'Hey.' The blue in his eyes shone under the fluorescent light illuminating the terminal, snatching all my attention. 'There you are.'

Not able to voice a single word more without completely losing my shit, I shook my head lightly. His fingers remained where they were.

'You are not a fool,' he told me as he kept staring into my eyes.

My lids fell closed for a moment, not wanting to see whatever he was looking at me with on top of everything I was barely keeping at bay. 'I can't do it,' I whispered, opening my eyes and meeting his gaze.

His voice hardened. 'Catalina, stop being ridiculous.' Contrary to the gentle grip of his fingers, his command was blunt. Insensitive, considering he was talking to a woman on the verge of flipping out.

But something in it forced me – enabled me, I realized – to take the first full breath in the last couple of minutes. So, I did exactly that. I breathed in, and then I breathed out. All the while, Aaron looked me straight in the eye with something that should have made my anxiety shoot back to the roof but that instead brought me slowly back.

'We've got this,' he said with confidence.

We.

That simple two-letter word somehow sounded a little louder than the rest.

And then, as if he had been waiting for me to be ready to hear it, he went for the killing blow. 'You are not on your own anymore. It's you and me now. We are in this together, and we've got this.'

And somehow, for a reason I knew I would never be able to explain, I believed him. I didn't question or fight him.

Neither of us said anything else. My apprehensive brown eyes held his determined blue ones, and some kind of silent understanding passed between us.

Us. Because we, Aaron and I, had just become an us.

Aaron's fingers dropped from my chin and wrapped around the hand that hadn't been clutching my chest.

He squeezed gently.

Ready? he asked me without words.

I took one last deep breath, and we headed for the doors that opened to the Arrivals terminal of the small Spanish airport.

To my parents.

To this outrageously ludicrous farce we were about to embark on.

To this ... what had I called it before? Oh yeah, to this whole Spanish love deception we had planned.

Because we, Aaron and I, got this. He had said so. And I believed him.

I just hoped, for both our sakes, that he was right.

~

'Papá, for the last time, we are more than okay here.' My eyes searched the small room for my fake boyfriend, looking for backup.

The corner of his lips tipped up.

'Maybe if we move Abuela to your sister's place,' Papá continued, 'you two could take the big guest room in the house. Although I am not really sure if Tío José and Tía Inma will be sleeping there. Wait, let me call—'

'Papá,' I cut him off, reaching out to pat his arm. 'It's okay. This apartment is more than okay. You don't need to move us to the house. Leave Abuela alone.'

A wave of nostalgia and familiarity hit me right in the gut. It had been so long since I had come home; all of it felt as familiar as breathing, and at the same time, it was like a memory I had not revisited in a long time. My dad and his good heart, always so accommodating. Caring too much. Trying to make everybody feel at home even if it meant going through the bedroom Hunger Games. I had been so preoccupied with dreading the moment that I had forgotten they were my family. My home. And, God, despite everything, I had missed them with all my heart.

My mom shifted from the entrance of the cramped bedroom, assessing the situation. '*Ay, cariño*, your father is right. *No sé . . .*' She hesitated, looking for the words. '*Este hombre es tan alto y . . . grande.*' Her gaze landed on Aaron, travelling from his head to his feet and back up again, while she shook her head with a mix of awe and scepticism.

I thought I had seen that start of a smirk on Aaron's lips inching higher, which earned him a questioning look from me.

'I know what *grande* means.' That little bend of his lips was there until he turned to my mother, squaring his expression. 'I appreciate your concern, Cristina. But we will be perfectly fine, sleeping here. *Muchas gracias por todo de nuevo.*'

Together with my mother's, my jaw almost dropped to the floor for the second time today. The first time had been earlier in the airport, where I had first learned that Aaron did speak enough Spanish to introduce himself to my parents in my mother tongue. With barely an accent.

Quickly after, and while my jaw stayed right where it was, the grin that was reserved for a very limited number of people came alive in Mamá's face.

Then, I watched her release a breath, half-wonder and half-resignation. As if she was fine to accept Aaron's statement without putting up any kind of fight as long as he kept talking in Spanish. Which was something she reserved for very few too.

My very lucky and very much fake boyfriend gifted her with a polite smile.

'Catalina doesn't take that much space anyway,' Aaron suddenly said. 'We will find a way to snuggle in. Right, *bollito*?'

My head swirled in his direction. 'Yes,' I gritted out. 'We will snuggle right in.'

Promising myself he'd pay for that later, I looked at my dad in horror. Much to my dismay, I found him grinning. My mom, on the other hand, just nodded, her eyes flitting from Aaron to me, assessing our difference in size and height.

Which, thankfully, wouldn't be a problem. The convenient apartment that my parents rented during the high season to vacationers had two bedrooms. Just like everything about the flat, the rooms were small and functional with only what was strictly necessary. But that meant that we, Aaron and I, wouldn't be doing any *snuggling*. We were not even going to be sharing a room.

Thank the heavens.

Which reminded me, it was time for my parents to leave.

'Okay, you two. Thank you, but this is enough of a welcome,' I said, walking up to them and pushing them lightly toward the door. 'We have suitcases to unpack and a bachelor-slash-bachelorette party to get ready for.'

'*Vale, vale*,' my mom said as she grabbed my dad's arm. 'You see, Javier? They want to be alone.' Her eyebrows did a little wiggle. '*Ya sabes.*'

My dad muttered something unintelligible, showing that he had no interest in finding out why.

So, I ignored my mother's innuendo, and after wrapping my parents in a big hug, I shooed them out the door. In the meantime, Aaron politely thanked them again – in Spanish, for my mom's benefit – and remained in the corner, where he had been standing.

With my parents finally gone, I turned to Aaron and found him placing both of our suitcases on the bed. He unzipped his and started extracting pieces of clothing and toiletries.

'Actually, you don't need to do that,' I told him, not bothering to open my bags.

Aaron cocked an eyebrow.

'We will sleep in separate rooms,' I explained.

'Oh?' That was the only thing that came from him.

Ignoring that puzzled look he had just shot me, I made my way to the hallway to lead him to what would be his room.

With his very own bed.

Right behind me, Aaron stepped in the space only a few seconds after.

'Ta-da!' I gestured with my arms. 'Here's your room. Your dresser. Your bathroom is out in the hall though. And, yeah, that will be your bed.'

I pointed at the twin bed as I took in its ridiculous dimensions. The room was much smaller than I remembered.

Glancing at Aaron, who was right by my side, I found him inspecting the bed with his arms crossed over his chest. Just how my mother had done a few minutes ago, I eyed him up and down.

Yeah. That was not going to work.

'All right,' I said, accepting he would never, ever fit there. 'I'll change rooms with you. Take the other one; it's bigger. I'll take the twin.'

'It's okay, Catalina. I'll sleep here.'

'No, you won't. You won't fit in that tiny bed,' I pointed out the obvious. 'Not even diagonally, I don't think.'

'It's fine. Go unpack your things. I'll make it work.'

'You won't. There's no way you can sleep here,' I insisted, ignoring the dirty look Aaron sent me over his shoulder.

'I will.'

Stubborn, hardheaded man, I thought.

'You are the only hardheaded one here,' he said.

I narrowed my eyes at the mind reader. 'Well, if you want to be my pot, I'd gladly be your kettle.' I pointed at the bed. 'Prove it. Show me you fit in there, and I'll leave you alone.'

Aaron sighed as he uncrossed his arms and brought a hand to his face. 'Would you just—' He stopped himself, shaking his head. 'You know what? This one time, I'm going to humour you. Just to avoid wasting away both our lives, arguing over this until we are rolling on matching wheelchairs.'

He was wrong; matching wheelchairs was something that would never be in my plans where Aaron Blackford was concerned.

In two strides, my fake and very tall boyfriend was right in front of the modest twin.

He won't fit. I was sure of it. So, I leaned back and waited for him to prove how right I was.

As soon as Aaron climbed onto the tiny piece of furniture, the mattress bounced a little too wildly under his weight. With a loud squeak, he adjusted his body, lying on his back. Changed his position a couple of times as the mattress complained under his weight. Nothing.

He. Did. Not. Fit.

Taking in the clearly larger-than-the-bed man in front of me, feet dangling off of the frame and glaring at the ceiling, I couldn't help but let the grin I had been fighting finally break free.

It wasn't the fact that I had been right all along. Nope. The

satisfied and toothy smile that split my face had everything to do
with the grumpy Aaron who was lying diagonally on the tiny twin
bed with a scowl that went for miles. The best part was that he
had humoured me and proven it, just because I'd told him to. Just
because we were equally stubborn.

And that only made me grin wider.

Walking closer, I didn't turn down the megawatt smile as I looked
down at him. 'Comfy?'

'Very.'

'I just bet you have never been this comfortable in your life.'

He rolled his eyes. 'Fine,' Aaron said as he sat up, the springs in the
simple and – let's face it – most likely cheap mattress creaking loudly
under his weight. 'So you were right,' he continued as he moved to
the edge, trying to leave a bed that seemed to be turning into quick-
sand, swallowing each of his movements. 'Now, if you would just—'

Before I could even realize what was happening, the structure of
the bed gave in with a big bang, engulfing part of the mattress and
Aaron along with it.

A gasp shot out of me as my hands flew to my mouth.

'Jesus fucking Christ,' Aaron growled.

'Oh my God, Aaron.' The cackle that left my mouth as I stared at
the grumpier-than-ever man sitting in the middle of the box spring
catastrophe was probably heard all the way to New York City.

He didn't look anywhere near okay if the way he glowered was
any indication.

But I asked anyway, 'Are you okay?' I tried to sober down; I did.
But I couldn't hold in the laughter. So, I laughed.

Then, I laughed louder.

'Yes. All good,' he grunted. 'Nothing I can't handle.'

'Okay, but just in case . . .' I stretched my hand to help him out,
but both of us froze when a holler came from the entrance door of
the apartment. A voice that sent shivers down my spine.

'¡*Hola!*' a pitchy shrill tone called.

Was that . . .

'¿*Hay alguien en casa?*' that voice I realized I knew – and I was related to – called again.

No.

The woman whose red hair I was almost certain was about to make an appearance in about two seconds asked if there was someone at home. As if she hadn't probably known already.

Charo. My cousin Charo was in the apartment. And judging by the quick clicking of her heels, she'd be in the room in about—

'*Ay, pero mira qué bien.* Someone is christening the bed.' A giggle that was not adorable and was outright evil instead reached my ears from behind me.

Understanding flashed through my fake boyfriend's face.

Not caring to wait for my response, my cousin continued babbling, 'Look at this mess.' She tsked. 'After being single for so long, one would think you were out of practice, *Linita*.'

I grimaced. Way to put it out there, *prima*. My eyelids shut on instinct, and I felt a blush climbing up my throat.

'Because, really, how many years have gone by since the whole thing with Daniel exploded? Three? Four? Maybe more.'

Oh sweet Lord, I wanted to disappear. I couldn't believe Charo had gone straight to that after barely saying hello. And in front of Aaron. I didn't want to look at him. Didn't want to look in his direction for that matter. Couldn't that busted and mangled bed swallow me up too?

And just like that, my wish was granted.

Aaron tugged at my arm and pulled me right with him, ripping a squeal out of me. Right onto the chaos that used to be a twin bed. My body ended up sprawled half on top of him. Not for long though because before I knew what was really happening, his large and meaty arms flipped me onto his lap. Turning me to face my cousin Charo and causing my body to go as stiff as a broomstick at the change of positions.

Holy shit, I am on Aaron's lap. Back to front. Ass on . . . yeah. On his lap.

'I'll take the blame for all this.' His deep voice came from very freaking close behind me as I slowly recounted all the body parts I felt pressed against my own much softer ones. Thighs, chest, arms, all hard and flushed against my back. Against my ass. Against my own thighs and . . . I had to stop thinking of body parts. 'Hard to resist myself really.' My fake boyfriend's words entered my ears at the same time I noticed the muscles underneath me flexing. 'Right, *bollito*?'

Oh my God.

He was . . . I was . . . I just—

'Right,' I croaked, '*osito*.'

Charo beamed at us, one hundred percent satisfied with the show. She had just gotten to the apartment and already obtained a story I'd be hearing about for the next ten years. The time Lina and her boyfriend broke that twin bed. I bet she'd add stuff that never happened, maybe that she had seen Aaron naked or something.

A mental image intruded my mind. One of Aaron. Sans clothes. With all those muscles I was feeling—

No. No. No.

'*Ay*, look at you two,' my cousin said, bringing her hands under her chin. 'You look so adorable together. And, Lina! I never thought you'd be this kind of crazy.' Charo wiggled her eyebrows. Aaron's hand landed on my knee, the contact branding the skin under my jeans. God, I could feel him all around me. If I relaxed my spine, I'd snuggle right into him.

That warm palm squeezed my thigh.

I kept losing my focus, and now, Charo seemed to be waiting for me to say something.

'Oh yeah.' I recapped as fast as I could. I needed to get out of here. Off Aaron. The position we were in was too distracting. In a very, very, very bad way. 'Erm. Yes, crazy. Oh, you bet! This is all super crazy,' I said, squirming in Aaron's lap as I unsuccessfully tried to make my way out of the man-sized black hole that had sucked me in. 'It is crazy because I am super crazy. Crazy about him, that is.' I squirmed some more, realizing I might be stuck somewhere between his large thighs. *Keep talking.* 'Like, so crazily in love, it's even crazy, you know what I mean? So crazy–'

'I think she got it,' my fake boyfriend whispered in my ear, sending a stupid shiver rushing across my whole body.

I kept shifting further in his lap, ignoring how everything I felt underneath me – or my ass, more specifically – was solid and warm. No, hot. It was hot. Muscles upon muscles upon more muscles. Some of them becoming harder with every useless effort I made.

Oh my gosh. *Oh Dios mío.* Was that . . . no. It couldn't be. Aaron couldn't be . . . aroused.

Desperate, I tried to propel myself off him one more time, obtaining a little grunt from Aaron's lips. It landed on the back of my neck as a puff of air.

'Stop,' he breathed in my ear. 'That's not helping with the situation.'

I immediately obeyed, forcing my body to relax into him. *Okay, I have this. Think of it as a chair. A throne. Not Aaron. Just a hard man-sized throne.*

I gave my cousin a fake smile. 'So, what are you doing here, Charo?'

'Oh, I was going to stay with a friend for the wedding weekend, but the bathroom in his apartment flooded or something, and I have no choice but to sleep here instead,' she explained with a little wave. 'I'm sure you thought you had the place to yourselves, huh?' She wiggled her eyebrows again. 'I swear I won't be in the way. You won't even notice I'm here.'

There was only one way we wouldn't notice Charo snooping around, and that involved hard-core narcotics.

'Great. Well, we should really unpack and let you do the same,' I announced from my position on my Aaron throne. I cleared my throat. 'Yeah, all right. Let's do that,' I added, neither Aaron nor me moving. I cleared my throat very loudly. 'Don't you think we should get going, *osito*?'

Before I could ask, Aaron's big hands were on my waist, and I was lifted off his lap and then up in the air. With shaky legs, I landed in front of my cousin.

Whoa, okay. So, it could have been that easy.

Aaron – who had mysteriously regained his usual agility – followed suit, leaving behind him the spring and wood disaster.

'I haven't introduced myself.' Aaron stretched out one of the hands that had been wrapped around my waist a little more than a second ago. The one hand that had squeezed my thigh. '*Soy Aaron. Un placer conocerte.*'

My cousin – who I suspected had already requested all of Aaron's available information from my mother – took his hand and pulled him to her. '*Ay y habla Español! El placer es mío, cariño.*' She planted one kiss on each of his cheeks.

Yeah, I was sure she hadn't been lying when she said the pleasure of meeting him was all hers.

After my cousin released Aaron, who looked a little dumbfounded, she engulfed me in a hug too. 'Come here, *prima*. I have kisses for you too.' And she added in a whisper so only I could hear it, '*¿Dónde tenías escondido a este hombre?*'

Where were you hiding this man?

I chuckled. 'Oh, *prima*, if you only knew.'

Stepping away from my red-haired relative, I was startled by the contact of Aaron's palm on the small of my back.

I jumped back, right into his front.

Aaron looked down at me, a question in his gaze. 'Go ahead to our room and start unpacking. I'll take care of this mess for your cousin.'

That was ... so very thoughtful. I had forgotten about it. Apparently, leaving my cousin to deal with a broken twin bed wasn't high on my priority list.

'*Uy*, no, no.' Charo intervened before I could apologize. 'I will call Tío Javi,' she said, referring to my dad as Uncle Javi. 'You two go and settle in. I'm sure you are exhausted from the trip. Just make sure not to break the other bed too.' She accompanied that with a cackle. 'I can take the blame for this one, but yours? That would be an awkward conversation with your dad.' Then, she winked.

Without more than a thank-you, we shuffled back to what would be our room.

Our room, which we had to share now.

Dammit.

We'd better unpack and try to get comfortable. If that had been any indication of what was ahead of us during the upcoming days, my fake boyfriend and I were in for a messy ride.

Suitcases almost empty and all wedding attire already hanging in the closet, I sent a sideways glance at the bed in our room. I had been doing that for the last fifteen minutes.

I'll be waiting here, it seemed to sing, making me wish it would magically crumble down and disappear too.

'Stop worrying. I can sleep on the floor if it makes you that uncomfortable.' Aaron looked at me, eyebrows creased.

'I'm not worried,' I lied.

Sharing a bed with Aaron was something I hadn't expected. Or planned for. My parents had said only we would be staying in the apartment. Most of the guests were from the region, and the ones who weren't would be arriving only for the big day.

'We are adults, and we have known each other for almost two

years now. We can be civil and share the bed. At least it's a double. And it's standing up.'

'I'll tell your parents that I will take care of the other one. I'll pay for the damages.' There was something in his voice. He sounded pensive and almost . . . embarrassed?

'You don't have to, Aaron.' And I meant it. 'It wasn't your fault. The bed had lasted more than it should have, really. These things . . . happen.'

Grabbing a couple of shirts off my suitcase and unfolding them, I pondered my own words. Never in my life had I witnessed that firsthand, but hey, these things did happen. Maybe to Aaron they had. Maybe he had destroyed dozens of beds. Reducing them to a mess of wood and springs. He was a large man, one who was built too. Beds could very well give out and burst under his weight. Maybe if he moved around too much. Or if he dropped his body on them with certain force. Or if he engaged in activities that tested the resistance of the frame and springs and—

No, no, no. I kicked out of my head that image of a sweaty and naked Aaron doing—

No.

'Okay,' Aaron said, zipping closed his emptied suitcase. 'And if you are sure we can share the bed, then we will. With a little luck, this one won't shatter too.'

A whole new mental image ambushed me. One very similar but that now included me and—

Nope. I needed to stop this nonsense.

'It's settled then,' I said, getting rid of those unwanted thoughts and ideas. 'No sleeping on the floor. We can't risk getting caught, having Charo around. Couples share beds.'

'And we would get caught exactly how? Does your cousin go around, entering bedrooms she doesn't sleep in?'

'Well, Aaron, I really wish I could tell you she didn't, but I would be lying.'

Years had taught me that Charo was unpredictable.

'So' – I changed the subject – 'in a couple of hours, we will be meeting the youngest members of the Martín clan for phase one of the bachelor-slash-bachelorette party.'

'A little briefing, please?' he queried. Aaron had finished unpacking – which I hadn't – so he leaned his back on the wardrobe that was in the corner of the room and gave me his full attention.

'You'll be delighted to hear that we will spend the day outside, enjoying the warmth of the Spanish sun on our skin and doing something that has nothing to do with sipping mimosas and getting massages. Which was my idea.' I walked to the narrow dresser and grabbed a neat stack of towels. 'My maid-of-honour duties were overruled by one of my youngest cousins, Gabi.' I placed the towels on the comforter. 'And that means only one thing.' I paused dramatically. 'The Wedding Cup.'

'The Wedding Cup?' A chuckle left Aaron's lips.

Strangely, that little noise made me want to smile. I ignored it and gave him a rundown of how we'd be occupying our day instead.

'In the Wedding Cup' – I sighed – 'Team Bride, which is composed of all the females invited to the bachelor-slash-bachelorette party, competes against Team Groom, which will be composed of the male ones.' I said that last part with sarcasm. 'Real refreshing, huh? Boys against girls, competing in a series of games and activities. Yay.'

Aaron nodded, not taking any side. 'I can tell, you are very excited. But please continue.'

I sent him a look. 'The team that collects more points will secure the win and obtain the Wedding Cup.'

'And is this cup a physical trophy or just a symbolic reward?' Aaron asked, and I could tell he was trying to take this seriously. Unsuccessfully. He could barely contain his amusement.

'Listen' – my arms went to my hips in an attempt to make myself look imposing – 'I told you I was not in control of this. I am more of a representative maid of honour. My cousin Gabi is one of those fitness-obsessed people, and she organized the whole thing. So, just be glad that you are not stuck with me on your team.' Picking up my toiletry and make-up bags, I walked to the modest en-suite bathroom as I kept absently filling Aaron in while I placed all my things on the narrow space available. 'I am not happy about this, okay? If it were up to me, we would be at a spa while you guys went somewhere to do ... guy stuff.'

'Guy stuff?' I heard Aaron's voice coming from the bedroom.

'Yeah, punch your chests, drink beer like it's the end of your lives, or go to a strip club. What do I know?' I shook my head, knowing I was being a little too stereotypical. 'But no,' I continued, placing a travel-sized container of shampoo on the counter. 'We couldn't be so lucky. Funny enough, the one on board with this thing is Gonzalo. Who would have thought? A stupid competition over enjoying his last day as a bachelor away from his bride. Not that I'm shocked. Gonzalo has been crazy about my sister since the moment he laid eyes on her. So, why would he want to spend a day away from her?'

What they had was the real stuff. Honest, devoted, palpable love. The one that transcended distance, differences, and obstacles. The kind that was meant to be written about in books. Thinking of it filled my chest with warmth and longing for something I didn't know whether I'd ever be able to find.

'Anyway, Gonzalo is the Wedding Cup's biggest cheerleader. And something tells me, he'll be more than thrilled when he sees you. He'll holler and bro-hug you, and you'll be his new best friend. I can tell. Gon is so competitive, always has been, so he'll be over the moon to have the closest thing to a freaking Greek god on his team. Straight out of Olympus.' I snorted.

Aaron did look a little like one of those sculptures. All stoic with smooth and symmetrical lines. Gonzalo would love Aaron on the—

Hold up.

What did I just say?

My eyes closed at the realization that I had called Aaron a god. A Greek one. Out of Olympus. Out loud.

Oh, please, bathroom walls, be thick and soundproof. Please.

Sensing his presence somewhere behind me and considering the dimensions of both the room and en suite, I remained very still.

I opened my eyes and looked at his reflection in the mirror in front of me.

Aaron was leaning on the doorframe.

Inhaling a deep breath, I let my eyes travel around the counter, taking in everything and making my way up until finding Aaron's gaze in the mirror.

'Chances of you not hearing me from the bedroom?' I ventured.

'It depends.' I watched his throat work, swallowing. 'How good hearing do Greek gods have?'

I had two options: own it like the grown-up woman I was, or ignore this had just happened and be a total chickenshit.

Rearranging every item I had just placed on the shelf in silence, I opted for the latter, all the while feeling his gaze following my every move.

A moment later, I sensed Aaron turn around, but before he walked away, I called out, 'Oh, and, Aaron?' I watched the reflection of his back in the mirror. 'The losing team has to perform a choreographed dance tonight.'

No answer came from him, but when he finally took a step away, I could perfectly imagine the competitive gleam coming alive in his eyes.

CHAPTER SIXTEEN

I stood with my hands on my hips, getting a little lost in the palette of blues and greens that painted the view before me.

When people thought of Spain, they thought of jammed beaches under the merciless summer sun. They thought of tables loaded with jars of *sangría*, pans stuffed with *paella*, and a payload of *tapas*. They most likely thought of some dark-haired dude serenading the evening with impossibly masterful fingers strumming a guitar too. And in a way, they were not completely wrong. One could find that in Spain. But it was only a small part of what represented my home country. One that sadly didn't even cover ten percent of what it offered.

The small city where I had come from stood on the most northern coast of the peninsula, wedged between the often fierce and ivory-topped Cantabrian Sea and a range of emerald mountains.

Contrary to general belief, the country wasn't bathed in sun throughout the whole year either. Particularly not the northern regions. Nope. The north of Spain was known for granting its inhabitants the chance to experience all four seasons in the span of a few hours, any day of the year. Which made it possible for the vegetation to grow wild and lush, engulfing pastures and hills and creating an image very few thought of when it came to Spain. So, yeah, summer wasn't all that great in the north. But surprisingly, today the sky was clear, and the breeze from the sea was gentle. It brought me back to a time when, in days like these, we would try to make the most of it, as if our lives depended on it. From dawn till dusk. Isabel and me. *Las hermanas Martín*. The Martín sisters.

Taking a peek at the group of people who had gathered today for the Wedding Cup, a little part of me wondered what was going on inside Aaron's head. What had been his first impression of the place that had seen me grow up? Of my people?

Introductions had gone better than good. If Spaniards were known for something, it was their openness and hospitality. Nobody had seemed to bat an eyelash at my fake boyfriend. Not more than the awkwardness of having a *guiri* – what we called tourists – and therefore having to use their rusty English.

Only the youngest generation of both the bride's and groom's families, their partners, and some of our closest friends were here. Except for our barbaric and free-spirited cousin Lucas, who no one knew where he had disappeared to this time. And the best man – otherwise known as Daniel, my ex, my first and only relationship, or the man my family believed I had never gotten over. He had not arrived yet.

'*Aquí está mi hermana favorita.*' My sister's voice reached me a heartbeat before I was tackled from behind.

'I'm your only sister, idiot. Of course I'm your favourite.' I wrapped my hands around her forearms, which were resting on my collarbone.

'Forget about technicalities. You are still my fave.'

Sticking my tongue out, I looked at her over my shoulder. If not for our heart-shaped faces, we wouldn't look anything alike. Isabel had always been taller and leaner than me. Her eyes had little green speckles to the brown we shared – something I had always been envious of – and her hair was curlier and darker, just like Mamá's. But the differences didn't stop there. Where my sis was this puzzle piece that fit anywhere at the first try, I had always seemed to struggle with finding my place. Somehow, I always managed to be missing a little corner or have an extra edge that pushed me to keep trying somewhere I might fit better. That pushed me to keep looking for that place to call home. Because that was no longer Spain for me. But neither was New York, as much as I had Rosie and a career I was proud of. It had always felt . . . a little lonely. Incomplete.

'Hello? Earth calling Lina,' she said, coming to my side and tugging at my arm. 'What's up with you today? Why are you hiding here?'

I had been doing that, hadn't I? Even if only for a few minutes. My big sister knew me far too well, so I made a note of being extra watchful around her with Aaron. If there was someone who would see through the deception, it would be Isabel.

'Not hiding.' I shrugged my shoulders. 'I was just trying to have a moment of peace away from the bridezilla. I heard she almost ripped the groom's head off because he'd bought the wrong shoes.'

I stepped away and turned, so I could face her.

'You heard that right.' My sister and bride-to-be brought a hand to her chest, feigning dismay. 'I let him pick one thing, Lina. One. And he came home, all proud and happy, with a pair of shoes that made me question my taste in men, really.' She shook her head. 'I was this close to uninviting him to my wedding.'

'*Our wedding*, you mean.' I laughed.

'Yeah. Didn't I say that?' The corner of her lips tugged up with mischief. 'Anyway, I think we still have about an hour or so until lunch break. Are you ready?'

A look passed between us.

'For my death? Always.'

'Come on, drama queen,' Isabel said, linking our arms and pulling me in the direction of the group. 'Time to go back. Gabi sent me to fetch you. There's a schedule, you know.'

I pouted.

'Oh, stop that. It'll be fun.'

'It hasn't been, and it won't be,' I said, dragging my feet but following her because what choice did I have? 'Gabi has turned into this cute but terrifying sports mogul, and everyone is scared of her.'

Isa snorted. 'It's not that bad. Plus, we might still win. We are only three points behind those stupid suckers.'

'Did you just call your fiancé a *stupid sucker*?'

'Fine, we are only three points behind Team Groom. Better?'

'Better. But' – I shot her a humourless glance over my shoulder – 'they are still going to smash us like cockroaches.'

Shaking my head, I thought of how unathletic Team Bride was compared to our male counterpart. The points we had collected were lame pity points Gabi had given us to keep the team motivated. Well, everybody else on the team but me. Motivation had left me long ago. I was ready to call it a day and go stuff my mouth with food. My jet-lagged body had flipped the hungry switch, even before we started running around with this nonsense.

'You can blame yourself for that.' My sister's index finger added to her accusation. 'You brought Clark Kent's doppelgänger to the party.'

'He does look like him, doesn't he?'

Isabel nodded. 'And by the way ...' She paused, and before I could dodge it or be prepared for it, she tugged at my ponytail. A little too hard.

'Hey!' I grabbed my hair and moved out of the trajectory of other possible attacks. 'What the hell was that for, bridezilla?!'

'Don't be a baby; you deserved it. How dare you keep that' – Isabel pointed at Aaron, making me smack her hand down – 'hidden from me!'

'Isabel,' I warned.

She went on, ignoring me and waving her index finger in my

fake boyfriend's direction, 'When my sister starts dating someone, I expect a full report. Vivid descriptions, photos, videos, oil paintings – I don't care. Even those dick pics I mentioned, which you never sent.'

'Isabel.' I lowered my voice. 'Shut up. He will hear you.'

We were only a few feet away from the group.

She cocked an eyebrow and then tilted her head slowly.

Dammit.

'He's dating you. What's the big deal with him hearing you talk about it with your sister? You've seen his penis. We are allowed to discuss it.' She rolled her eyes. 'Actually, I think we are expected to do that. I'm sure he's talked to his friends about your bubbies.'

I cursed under my breath.

She stared at me, inspecting my reaction.

I looked nervously in Aaron's direction. Our gazes met. Those blue eyes, which always seemed to find me, held mine for a long moment.

Jesus, did he hear that?

Shaking my head very lightly, I returned my gaze back to my sister.

'You know,' she said, shrugging her shoulders, 'you only mentioned him a couple of times, so I was convinced it wasn't that serious. But I'm not so sure of that anymore.'

'What do you mean?' My heart sped up as I feared what she might say.

We had barely had any time to act all snuggly and lovey-dovey or however a boyfriend and girlfriend were supposed to behave. The Wedding Cup shenanigans had consumed all our time and energy.

'Well, for one, he's here,' Isabel pointed out. 'You bringing him home – to meet Mamá and Papá and basically the entire town – tells me that he's not just anyone. There must be something special about him. You wouldn't bring someone you were casually seeing or dating. Not even if they looked like he does. You don't trust people easily anymore.'

Stumbling over my own thoughts, I came to a stop.

Her words had smacked me right in the face. Emptying me of anything I could say.

Impostor. The accusation took shape in my head. How could it not when I was a big, fat liar?

Isabel took my silence as a sign to keep talking. 'Then, there's the way his eyes have been on you the whole time we've been here.'

Whoa, what?

'It's been only, what? A couple of hours? And he's still absorbed by you, watching and following every single move you make, as if you were pooping rainbows and leaving behind a trail of glitter. It would be disgusting if I wasn't in love myself.' She patted my hand. 'And trust me, sis, you all red and blotchy? Not that cute.'

My head whirled in Aaron's direction again. He was chugging water from a bottle, not looking half as physically exerted as everybody else. Even after carrying Team Groom on his back along with Gonzalo. As I got lost in the way his arm stretched and his throat worked down the water, I wondered if my sister had imagined all that or if Aaron's acting was that amazing. Maybe I hadn't given him enough credit.

'Anyway,' she added as we finally reached the group, 'you'll have to catch me up on this and tell me all the dirty details. Don't think that just because I haven't drilled you for them, I don't want them.' Isabel warned me with a look that told me she'd bug me until I broke under the pressure. 'But until then, just keep doing whatever you are doing.' She winked. 'Because, *hermanita*, he has it bad.'

A snort involuntarily escaped my lips. 'Yeah, sure.'

Isabel quirked an eyebrow.

Oh shit. 'Of course he has it bad, Isa.' I waved my hand. 'He's my boyfriend,' I tried to assure her, not sounding anywhere close to convincing.

So, I quickened my pace and left my big sister behind before I led her to uncover the whole farce. Thankfully, as soon as I reached the group, Gabi was already wielding her printed schedule and trying to gather everyone closer. In a perfect circle.

Rolling my eyes at that, I watched my cousin and Wedding Cup mastermind start shouting out orders in Spanish while we all tried to ignore how Gonzalo snagged my sister from behind and engulfed her in an embrace that included more than a fair share of inappropriate groping and fondling.

'Yikes,' I muttered under my breath. 'That's my sister.'

But at the same time, something squeezed in my chest. I realized that a small part of me observed the public display of affection with something that felt a lot like longing. And that compressing sensation bothered me; it awoke a very particular set of questions I had no answers to. All of them revolving around the same thing.

Would I ever find what Gonzalo and Isabel had? Would I ever allow myself to?

Would I ever be so head over heels, crazy in love that everything else would fade to black noise?

My gaze searched for Aaron, not because I wanted him to emulate Gonzalo, but because maybe everyone else expected him to. Not spotting him anywhere in the less-than-perfect circle of people around Gabi, I grew a little concerned as she shot more and more instructions to the group. His head would roll if he didn't get here ASAP.

A light touch on my arm grabbed my attention. Turning my head, I was welcomed by a pair of blue eyes that regarded me with something strange.

'Here you are,' I whispered loudly while Gabi kept going at it in the background. 'I was scared for your well-being. Where did you go?'

'I've been right here the whole time.'

That strange quality was still there. But I brushed it away. I had no time to inspect whatever I'd thought I saw in Aaron's eyes. Instead, I focused on how good he looked in his nylon shorts and short-sleeved henley.

'Are you having fun?' He offered me a bottle of water, pushing it gently in my direction.

'Oh, thank you.' I reached for it with both hands, managing to brush my palms along his fingers somehow. Sparks travelled all the way up my arms, making me retrieve my hands quickly and hold the bottle to my chest. 'That was . . . sweet. Very boyfriend-like of you.' I looked up at him, finding him frowning. I didn't give him the chance to complain. 'And not too much fun, to be completely honest,' I admitted with a small pout. I had been serious when I told my sister that I was ready to call it a day. 'Thank God we are about to be done here. Otherwise, I'd have to fake breaking a leg or a wrist.' I lowered my voice. 'Or knocking off Gabi with something.'

'I hope we don't get to that point.' The right side of his mouth tipped up. 'What's left then?'

'Well, Gabi saved the best for last.' I sighed. 'Now comes the real competition.' I gestured with my hands, as if I were unveiling a huge surprise. 'The star of the Wedding Cup: the soccer match.'

Aaron hummed, lost in thought for a short moment. 'I don't think I've ever played soccer.'

I perked up. 'Never, ever?' I watched his head nod. A chance to win. 'Like, not even once?'

'Not even once,' he answered. His mouth opened and then clamped down when Gabi hushed us in the distance.

Jesus, that woman needed to cool down. We straightened and faced away from each other.

Aaron lowered his voice, speaking from the side of his mouth, 'You think that will be a problem? She seems . . . a little strict.'

'Oh, I wouldn't worry about her.' I waved my hand, keeping my eyes up front. 'You, on the other hand? I'd worry about getting the hang of it in time.'

Out of the corner of my eye, I sensed Aaron glancing over at me quickly.

'And what happens if I don't?'

My smile turned lopsided. 'Then, Team Groom will lose. Miserably.'

I didn't think that would happen, but Aaron had admitted to something he wasn't amazing at. And that was new. I stole a quick glance in his direction; he had tilted his head and crossed his arms over his chest.

'If you end up sucking at soccer and messing up, everybody will blame you. But it's okay; you can't be good at everything.'

He didn't move or say anything.

'And you couldn't be scared of dancing with the rest of the guys, right?' Another quick look allowed me to see the word challenge written all over his face. I snickered. 'Oh, maybe you are. I didn't peg you for a chicken, but it kinda looks good on you. Maybe I should call you *pollito* instead of *osito*.'

His head turned very slowly. My gaze remained on him as I helplessly forgot about Gabi.

'Did you just call me a chicken?' he said, the blue in his eyes flaring. 'In two different languages?'

'Oh, you bet I did. I would be scared too. Our team is strong.' It wasn't. 'And just so you know, I make for a wonderful central defender.' I didn't. 'But maybe you don't know what that means. It's okay. Just know that some used to call me Ruthless Lina.' Not exactly true either.

Of all sports involving balls, soccer was probably the one I sucked at the least. Although if I had ever been called ruthless, it wasn't because I excelled at playing the game, but because I ruthlessly ate the floor.

'Central defender, huh?'

I nodded. He didn't need to know the truth.

Aaron dipped his head, his voice dropping too. 'Are you trying to impress me with sports lingo, Catalina?'

The way he had said my name was new. I couldn't explain how, but it had been different from any other time he had voiced those four syllables. And it sent a shiver dancing down my arms.

'It's sexy, but don't ever feel like you need to impress me. I already am.'

My lips parted. I thought my breath had hitched too. *Sexy*. Had he really said that out loud? My eyes searched his face for any trace of sarcasm or evidence that it had been a joke. But before I could find anything, a commotion broke behind us.

Turning, I discovered the newcomer responsible for it. The moment I got a glimpse of the head of dark blond hair I knew – or had known – so well, a heavy weight dropped to the pit of my stomach.

My ex was here. Daniel. Or at least, an older version of the man I remembered. Back when we had dated, he could have been mistaken for a guy my age. But that had changed. In the time since we'd last seen each other, the way he looked had caught up with his years. And he had aged well. Time had treated him kindly. The Daniel who was striding in my direction was an attractive forty-year-old, a man who moved with the confidence that only someone who stood in front of a class filled with college students every day would have.

Although he had always had that confidence, hadn't he? Wasn't that exactly what had led me to crush on my professor in the first place? It was during that very first lecture I attended. He walked in, cleared his throat, and flashed that dimple. It didn't take more than that. I had been a goner.

A lame, pathetic goner, crushing on her Physics professor. Or so I had thought, but then, by some magical turn of events, he had reciprocated my attention. He did more than that. And I had believed we had something real. Something lasting, just as Gonzalo and Isabel did.

And then everything had blown up in my face. Not in our faces, no. Daniel had been spared the nightmare.

'Is that Daniel?' Aaron's low, hushed question returned me back to the present.

I turned to him briefly, not finding my words so I just nodded. My attention jumped back to where my ex was, and as I watched how he hugged and clapped his brother's back, I felt Aaron stepping closer to me. I didn't move. I was rooted to the floor.

Aaron closed some more of the distance between us, positioning himself to my side, right behind me. And I was shocked at the warmth that his body radiated on my back and how his proximity quashed some of the uneasiness. It reassured me. He did. And I didn't understand how or why, but I didn't have the time to pick that apart. Not with Daniel and everybody else there. So, I just held on to it.

I stood there and watched how the best man started the round of greeting everyone with kisses and hugs. Around the group he went, and I swore there was something suspended in the air as he did so. As if every single person around me was holding their breath until the moment Daniel reached me.

Hating how the atmosphere seemed to thicken with every pair of eyes that turned to me, I reminded myself that I had already been expecting that kind of reaction. Everybody knew what had happened between Daniel and me. How ugly it got and how hard it was for me. And most of them had pitied me back then. I knew most still did in this moment, and some always would.

Daniel took that one last step towards me, causing a churning sensation to twist my stomach in knots.

'Lina.'

It had been ages since I had heard my name from Daniel's mouth. It brought everything right back, the good moments we had shared – and there had been really amazing moments – all that joy that came hand in hand with a first love you foolishly thought was going to last forever, but also all the pain at having that turned into an ocean of hurt. Because, sure, Daniel had been the one to break my heart, but the real damage had been done by everybody else. By everyone who had learned of our relationship and tarnished it with stupid and poisonous rumours that—

No. Not the time to think of that.

Daniel placed a hand on my upper arm and planted a kiss on my cheek. If it hadn't been for Aaron's warm palm, which had somehow landed on the small of my back, I would have stumbled backwards. That was how off guard that friendly kiss had caught me.

My gaze roamed around the group, confirming that every person present had their eyeballs turned on us.

Daniel seemed oblivious to all the gawking, smiling at me like we were old friends being reunited after years of not seeing each other. Which was the exact opposite of how I felt.

He looked me up and down. '*Dios, Lina. Cuánto tiempo. Mírate. Estás*—'

'Daniel,' I cut him off. 'This is Aaron,' I blurted out, pulling away from him and nestling myself a step further into my fake boyfriend and personal human-sized shield.

Daniel's furrowed eyebrows signalled his confusion. Probably because I had switched to English more than because I was introducing him to someone I was supposedly dating.

'Hi. I'm her boyfriend,' Aaron said politely, stretching his hand in front of him. '*Su novio*,' he clarified in Spanish for Daniel's sake. Which was completely unnecessary and kind of cocky, and in some parallel reality, it would have pulled a snicker out of me. But my lips remained pressed into a tense line. 'It's nice to meet you, Daniel.'

My ex and sister's fiancé's brother stared at Aaron for a brief moment and then broke into a wary but amiable smile. '*Sí, claro.* Nice to meet you, Aaron.' Daniel finally took Aaron's hand and shook it. 'I'm an old friend of Lina's.'

Something pulled tight in my stomach at Daniel's definition of what we had once been.

As soon as both men unclasped their hands, Daniel returned his attention to me, and Aaron's palm returned to my back.

'How have you been, Lina? You look so ... different.' Daniel's smile widened. 'Different, but good. You look amazing actually.'

His eyes kept assessing me, as if he couldn't believe that it was me. And I wasn't really sure how I felt about that, so I forced myself to smile in return.

'Thanks, Daniel. I have been fine, busy with work and ... life.'

'That's right.' My ex nodded his head. 'You are living the life in New York City. I always knew you had the potential to do great things, to get very far in your career.'

He had been my professor for a whole year before we started properly dating, and during that time, I had been a highly motivated student. An overachiever. Things had changed after that.

'And you did.'

'Thanks,' I muttered. My mind filing away all kinds of complaints. 'It's not that big a deal.'

Aaron cleared his throat lightly. 'It is,' he said softly. So much so that I thought he had said it just for me. But then he kept going, 'Lina leads a considerably large team of people in one of the most successful engineering consulting companies in New York. That is, by all standards, a big deal.'

'Wow.' Daniel smiled tightly. 'That's amazing, Lina. It is.' His lips turned somewhat more relaxed. 'Congratulations.'

I muttered my thanks, still feeling flushed over Aaron's words. There was a long and awkward moment of silence, and then Daniel's eyes flashed quickly between Aaron and me. 'So, this is him, huh? The American boyfriend.'

My head reared back, shocked by Daniel's word choice. With my shoulders tensing, my mouth opened with the intention of asking what that had been, but I felt Aaron's hand trailing up my back, stopping at the nook between my shoulder and my neck. His thumb brushed the skin there very gently. That touch – that thumb caressing the side of my neck – almost made me forget about who was in front of me and what he had said or if he had talked at all. His finger swiped right and left one more time, making a shiver run down my spine.

Closing my eyes briefly, I pulled myself back into the conversation and decided to ignore Daniel's last comment. 'Congratulations on the engagement.' I made my lips tug upwards. 'I'm very happy for you, Daniel.'

Daniel's eyes, which had been somewhere where Aaron's palm was, met mine. He nodded and flashed that dimple I had been so familiar with in the past. 'Thank you, Lina. I'm extremely grateful she said yes. It's not that easy to deal with me sometimes. I get lost in my head a lot when I'm working,' he said, slipping his hands in his pockets. 'Well, no need to explain that to you. You know that already.'

Yes, I did. Everybody here knew I did too. He hadn't needed to point that out. Not after downgrading our past to *old friends*.

My fake boyfriend's palm spread and shifted down my shoulder, his fingers trailing down my arm and reaching my hand. It was so very distracting, the way he touched me. And yet, he managed to keep me grounded, all at once. Every time my head had threatened to roam away, Aaron had pulled me right back before my feet could lift off the floor. Those gentle brushes against my skin had that power, I realized. And judging by the way my voice came out when I spoke next – breathy, weak – they also came at a price.

'Well, I wish you two the best.' And despite myself, I meant that. 'Will she be joining us today?'

Aaron's fingers wrapped around mine, awakening in me something that urged me to turn around to look at him. I suppressed it, keeping my gaze on Daniel.

'Unfortunately, Marta won't be able to make it. A last-minute work thing. She's also a professor, and she was called to a conference to cover for a colleague.' Daniel shrugged his shoulders.

And I made a note to talk to my sister later. I was under the impression the bride would know if someone had cancelled.

'It's all good though.' Daniel's eyes jumped to Aaron's hand one more time, his expression distracted. 'Attending a wedding alone is not all that dramatic. Plus, I wouldn't want to make it about me.' My ex pinned me with a look.

And was that . . . accusation that I saw in his eyes?

'I . . .' I trailed off, second-guessing myself. My cheeks burned, and I couldn't do much else but gape.

'Then, why waste more time talking about it?' Aaron managed to flatten his voice, about enough to sound bored. But I knew better. 'I'm excited to see what comes next,' he surprised me by saying. Then, his fingers squeezed mine. 'Lina was telling me that Gabi saved the best for last. Right, baby?'

He leaned and brushed his lips over my shoulder. Very softly. Impossibly lightly. But it made my body come alive.

'Right,' I breathed out. Urging the shock out of my expression.

God, I could still feel the imprint of his lips on my shoulder.

The touch somehow spreading out across my skin.

'Oh, and what's that?' Daniel asked. Or at least, I guessed he had because my mind was somewhere else.

Aaron kissed me. On my shoulder.

The temperature of my whole body had probably risen a couple – or ten – degrees.

It's good. This is what couples do. They kiss each other. On multiple body parts. Like shoulders.

'The soccer match. We'll be starting in a few minutes, I think,' I heard Aaron explain. 'Lina has promised me to show me all her moves. I won't lie; I'm equal parts intrigued and terrified.'

Trying to look the part, I leaned my head on Aaron's chest. And I almost slipped to the floor when I felt him brush another kiss on my hair.

'Yeah.' I said, my breath getting stuck somewhere in my throat. 'Ruthless Lina is about to make an appearance.'

Aaron chuckled, and I felt his chest vibrating under my temple. The hand that wasn't holding mine came to rest on my hip, sending electrical shocks through all nerve endings in my body.

Breathe, Lina. He's supposed to act like this.

I forced myself to remain still when, in reality, I wanted to do everything else but that. Like forgetting about Daniel and asking Aaron what in the world he was doing. Why had he kissed my shoulder? Or the top of my head? Could he please do that again just so I could check if my reaction had been a one-time occurrence or if that was the way my body reacted to his touch?

Daniel's mouth opened and closed, as he was probably feeling uncomfortable at our display of affection.

Of fake affection, I reminded myself.

My ex and former professor looked up, someplace where Aaron's head towered over mine. Something flashed across his face, too quickly for me to grasp its meaning. Then, he nodded and directed a small smile at me.

Not really understanding what had just gone down before the two men, I finally allowed myself to look up at Aaron.

And ... nothing. Just one of his blank expressions in place. Someone called Daniel's name in the distance. My head fell just in time to watch my ex walk away, all the way to where Gonzalo was standing. He took his place beside his brother.

Still feeling the weird tension in the air, I drew a shallow breath.

Ugh, that had been really awkward. I felt like I wanted to shake myself, so I could get rid of the yucky sensation that stuck to my skin. But that would have rid me of all the tingles I was still feeling too. That would also mean that I had to disentangle myself from Aaron's arm and chest and body, and . . . I didn't know if I wanted to do that.

You do, dumbass. This is not real.

And I needed to remember that before I did something really stupid.

~

If the chaos around me was anything to go by, I'd say we had a little situation on our hands.

'*No me lo puedo creer,*' my cousin cried in the middle of a less-than-perfect circle of people, throwing her arms in the air like the world was coming to an end. '*No podemos jugar así. Se cancela todo. Esto un desastre. No, no, no, no.*'

She grabbed a few of the T-shirts from the open box at her feet and hurled them at the floor.

Whoa.

'*Esos malnacidos—*'

'*Cálmate, prima,*' Isabel interrupted, telling her to calm down. '*Qué importa. Son solo unas camisetas.*'

Our cousin gasped and then hissed something really nasty at my sister, who barked right back at her.

Aaron leaned to his side and then lowered his voice. 'What's going on? Should we run?'

I stifled a snicker. I didn't want to anger Gabi any more. She was either about to cry or turn full-on She-Hulk, and no matter what, we'd have to deal with the fallout.

'There's been a mix-up with the T-shirts for the soccer match.' I sighed. 'Apparently, they sent the ones for the Team Groom in the smallest size instead of the largest.'

'Can't we play with what we are wearing?' the poor soul that was my fake boyfriend asked.

Gabi's head spun toward us. *'Qué ha dicho?'* she screeched.

'Nada.' I held my hands in the air. Then, I turned to Aaron. 'Keep your voice down. Didn't you see how she got when my cousin Matías asked why she hadn't thought of handing out the shirts earlier today? Or when Adrián said it would have been smart to double check the sizes before today?'

Aaron's lips pursed.

'Exactly. Good thing my sister intercepted her before she got to them. They are tough guys but it would have been a carnage either way.' I shook my head. 'You are tough too, but I need you in one piece, okay?' I stopped myself, realizing what I had said. 'We are expected to dance at the wedding.'

'I'm not going anywhere,' Aaron said from my side. 'I can survive your cousin. I could put us both into safety too. Just say the word.'

I averted my eyes and glanced in Gabi's direction. A red-faced Isabel was trying to jerk the box out of Gabi's grip. And my cousin was tugging at it quite ... violently, if I had to pick a word.

My sister yelped, and then she stepped back and brought both hands to her head. 'No, no, no, no.' She walked to the center of the circle, waving her hands in the air. 'We will play the soccer match. That's it,' she announced and then turned to Gabi. 'I am the bride, and you guys are obligated to do as I say.'

I snorted at that, which earned me an extremely threatening glance from my sister. I stiffened.

Jesus, this wedding would be the end of all of us.

My sister turned to our cousin. *'Gabi, no es el fin del mundo.'* *It's not the end of the world*, she told our cousin. 'You' – she turned to me again – 'for my next wedding, we are sipping margaritas.'

I bit back a laugh, but yep, I wholeheartedly agreed.

'All right. It's summer, the sun is shining, and I just had the best idea.' She paused dramatically, looking around the circle of people. 'Team Groom will play . . . shirtless!' Her arms rose in the air.

Nobody spoke.

'Come on, gentlemen.' Isabel's tone hardened. 'It's always the ladies undressing and showing some skin. This time is up to you to show off those wedding bodies.'

More silence.

Isabel glanced at her groom, who, just like everybody else, was still chewing on her suggestion.

She widened her eyes and swirled her finger in the air, instructing Gonzalo to snap out of it. 'Do something!'

My future brother-in-law perked up. 'Ah!' The groom shed his shirt, revealing his chest in all his dark-haired glory. He threw his arms up. 'Well said, *cariño*!' he roared. 'Come on, gentlemen. Shirts off.'

My sister rewarded her fiancé with a holler and some enthusiastic clapping.

Daniel, as the best man, took off his shirt next. Almost reluctantly, from the way he shook his head. My gaze involuntarily took him in. It wasn't a shock, seeing how, despite not being anywhere close to being buff – which he had never been – he was still in really good shape. And yet . . . I felt nothing. No stirring anywhere in my body.

The group's amusement grew as more of Team Groom's members followed Gonzalo's and Daniel's lead. Well, nobody present was really complaining, probably fearing my sister's reaction, who, at this point, was cheering at every newfound shirtless male. Even Gabi's frustration at losing her grip of the group's control decreased as the atmosphere turned lighter.

That was, until Daniel opened his mouth and brought down the fun atmosphere.

'What about you, American boy?' Daniel pointed at the still fully clothed man standing beside me. 'Are you sitting this one out?'

American boy.

My eyes widened. He had just called my boyfriend – *fake boyfriend*, I corrected myself. Had my ex just called my *fake* boyfriend a *boy*?

Sure, Daniel was about eight or nine years older than Aaron.

But calling him a boy?

My head swivelled in Aaron's direction.

Just in time to see his reaction. His jaw relaxed, the start of a . . . smile playing on his lips.

Then, he didn't hesitate. Calmly – scarily so – my fake boyfriend levelled Daniel with a look that would make anybody run for the hills. The look that had earned him his reputation back at work. It was the one he brandished as a warning sign. And it meant trouble. Serious business.

Holding my breath, I watched Aaron's fingers reach for the hem of his shirt.

Oh my God, he's gonna do it. My fake boyfriend and future boss is undressing before my eyes.

He pulled it up, and in one swift motion – worthy of one of those perfume ads where everything, except the compelling and otherworldly model in the frame, blurred into the background – Aaron peeled off his shirt.

I blinked.

Madre de Dios.

Aaron was . . . he was . . .

Fuck.

He was . . . gorgeous – no, he was *more* than just that.

Aaron was a freaking sight to behold.

And his unbelievable, out-of-this-world, ad-worthy upper body was so flawless that it made me want to weep.

I was a shallow, shallow woman. But I didn't care.

As my gaze gobbled Aaron in all his shirtlessness, I felt the air being punched out of my lungs. I'd thought I had always been impressed – almost fascinated, if I was being completely honest – by his height and size. But if there was something more impressive, more fascinating than that, it was his height and size decked with hard muscles of all sizes and types.

Jesus Christ. Were his abs sculpted in stone?

My stupid, hungry eyes travelled from his broad shoulders to his chiselled chest and then kept going down, taking in slabs of abs that my imagination would never have been able to fabricate in such perfection. And how his strong arms looked bare, corded with powerful muscles? I would never have been able to imagine that either. Frankly, I almost wanted to poke the man to check if it was all real.

Those boring dress shirts did him no justice. That casual outfit he had worn to the flight hadn't either. Not even the tux he had worn to the fundraiser did his body any justice.

He was ... too ... beautiful.

Yeah, I was ogling at that point, and I didn't really give a damn. Not this time. This was a historical moment. I had a flawless, shirtless Aaron standing in front of me, probably for the first and only time ever. And I wanted to commit this image to memory. Even if it haunted me for the rest of my life, I'd live with it.

Loud cheering and clapping broke through the vacuum I had been sucked in. Blinking, I realized Aaron's eyes were on me. Our gazes met. There was something intent and hungry behind that deep ocean blue. Something barely controlled. That, or I was seeing my own emotions reflected and looking back at me.

Cheeks flushed, I was completely and utterly unprepared for what the half-naked man in front of me did next. Aaron's eyes twinkled under the Spanish sun, one corner of his lips curled, gifting me with a full-fledged smirk, and then he winked.

A single, quick, playful wink.

That was all it took for my insides to melt into a puddle. Brain, chest, lower belly, and everything in between liquefied and gathered at my feet.

Nope. I hadn't been unprepared for that. I had been completely defenseless.

Aaron placed his hands on his hips, looking somewhat satisfied, and returned his gaze ahead, to where Team Groom was gathering to start the soccer match, as if he hadn't just made parts of my body dissolve into a goo I didn't know what to do with.

That flawless, shirtless, blue-eyed bastard. Throwing me off-balance like that.

I had been so caught up in all that, that I hadn't noticed Daniel's apprehensive gaze. It bounced a couple of times between Aaron and me before finally settling on the man he thought I was dating. Not for long though. A moment after that, Daniel turned, clapped Gonzalo's back, and started toward the improvised soccer field.

Before joining the rest of the guys, Aaron stepped close to me, stopping only when the point of our sneakers touched. He leaned in, his mouth dangerously close to my ear, as if he were about to tell me a secret just meant for me.

My throat bobbed.

'What do you think?' he asked, his words tickling the shell of my ear.

'You are . . . okay,' I mumbled like a total idiot.

I heard his chuckle. 'Thank you, I think. But I wasn't asking about that.'

Oh.

'I'll take the compliment though. For now.'

'What-what did you mean then?'

'I think that so far, we are doing a good job. What do you think?'

Oh, so he meant that. The charade, of course. Yes, that made more sense.

I nodded my head.

'We make a good team, Catalina.' And there it was, my name again. Voiced in that way that was all . . . new.

I cleared my throat, trying to ignore the fact that my face was about a palm from his flawless and bare pectoral. 'We do,' I murmured.

Aaron lowered his voice. 'I had no idea we would walk into that.' He cocked his head. 'Caught me off guard, but it's okay. I'm starting to understand.'

Confusion swirled in me. There was nothing to understand. Granted, there was a part I hadn't told Aaron – which wasn't the smartest way to go about it – but that remained in the past. It didn't affect our goal here.

'Just keep doing what you are doing,' I told him, swallowing the lump stuck in my throat. 'Focus on pretending you are crazy about me, all right?'

I heard him hmm; it was a low and short-lived sound, but it was enough to make me step back, so I could look at his face. His eyes held that determined edge I knew so well.

'Trust me, I am focusing only on that.'

Before I could say anything else, Aaron started jogging back. 'And remember,' he called from a distance, 'all is fair in love and war, *bollito*.'

Almost everybody around turned their eyes on me. My gaze met my sister's, and she was grinning so widely that I was scared her mouth would inevitably be hurting on her wedding day.

Reluctantly, I smiled back at all the onlookers, pretending I was cool and chill and not trying to gather my wits. 'Oh, he's so silly,' I told them. 'No need to remind me, *cosita mía*!' I called back to Aaron.

But Aaron had already shot off, running after the rest of his team. Leaving me standing there, watching how all the polished muscles on his back danced with each stride he took, and wondering what the hell that was supposed to mean.

My eyes narrowed.

'All is fair in love and war.'

It was in a way, I guessed. What I had trouble making sense of was, how did that apply when love was fake, and adversaries were left no choice but to join forces?

CHAPTER SEVENTEEN

Against all odds, we were close to the end of the soccer match, and both teams were tied.

One would think that having to play against a group of shirtless dudes was disconcerting. But I was related to a big chunk of them. I had already seen everything there was to see about one of them – Daniel. And out of the two remaining men, one was about to marry my sister. So, that reduced my distractions considerably.

My main and only source being just one.

One that I usually did a pretty good job of ignoring when we were in our real-world roles. Contrary to the roles we were currently playing, where I, as the girlfriend, was allowed to gawk. And where Aaron, as the boyfriend, was apparently allowed to look like a man shooting a *Sports Illustrated* cover.

Because that was exactly how a sweaty, shirtless Aaron looked, running across the green field after the ball.

And that was exactly where my two very shallow and very stupid eyes had been all the time. Following him around like two dumb bugs irremediably drawn by an irresistible light. And just like the bug, my eyes had no self-preservation instinct. By the end of the day, the images would be burned into my retinas, and there'd be no way I'd ever be able to get rid of them.

Hell, I already felt a little like a charred insect. Sweat was running down my back, and my skin was on fire from being under the sun. On top of that, my hunger had turned into starvation, and no matter how hard I tried to stay focused on the game, my attention always shifted to Aaron's long legs, striding from one point to the next. To how the muscles across his torso strained and relaxed as he moved. To the little drops travelling down his chest, across those glorious pecs. To how my blood seemed to simmer and swirl every time our gazes met.

So, yeah, I felt icky and bothered and hot. In no particular order.

And yet, somehow, Team Bride had still scored as many goals as the guys. Baffling really, but what did I know? I had been too busy, ogling my flawless, glistening fake boyfriend.

Gonzalo's voice boomed across the field, all the way to where I was. '*Vamos!* They cannot win this!' He accompanied each of his words with an aggressive clap. 'Five minutes! We've got five minutes, guys! We need to win this shit!'

As the men regrouped on their side of the field, I noticed how Daniel approached Gonzalo and Aaron, gesturing with his hands and pointing at our goal.

'*Madre mía,*' Isabel said from her position as our goalie, a few steps behind me. 'I think they are making strategic changes. This doesn't look good, *hermanita.*'

As I took in the men's motions and consequent change in positions, my sister's suspicions were confirmed.

'We are screwed, Isa,' I assessed without turning to her. 'They are switching Aaron to the front. They are using him as a striker.'

'*Mierda.* Clark Kent is going to be the one attacking?' My sister came to my side and narrowed her eyes in the direction of our opponents. 'Quick, take off your shirt too. That will distract him.'

I scoffed. 'What? No.'

'But, Lina—'

'I'm not taking my shirt off. What the hell are you talking about?'

'But your bubbies will distract your boyfriend.'

'They won't, trust me.' Realizing what I'd said was not exactly girlfriend-like, I explained, 'He's already seen all there is to see. So, forget it.'

'Then, dance or wiggle. Do whatever rocks his boat.'

I crossed my arms over my chest. 'No.'

'Fine. Then, we are going down.'

'Not without a fight,' I assured her and then brought my hands to my mouth and proceeded to rally the rest of the team. *'Vamos, chicas! Todavía podemos ganar!'*

My words of encouragement were naive; there was no way we could still win the match. Not with Aaron striking. And certainly not if I flashed him, like Isabel had suggested.

Turning back to my sister, I pointed a finger at her. 'Remember this moment when the losers, which no doubt will be us, are dancing for everyone tonight. Next time, if you want to bet and jeopardize my rep, pick quiz night. Not stupid soccer. Now, let's try to finish this with as much dignity as we can.'

As I faced the other team, all the guys clicked into action. My gaze focused on the ball, passing from one player to the next, all of them leaving every Team Bride member helplessly behind. Soon enough, I was witnessing how the ball landed at Aaron's feet, who, for his hulking size, moved with incredible agility and skill.

For someone who had never played soccer before, he had gotten the hang of it pretty damn fast.

Aaron's looming figure approached me swiftly, eating away the distance. Way too quickly for my brain to order my limbs to kick into action.

Mierda.

In an attempt to stop him in any way I could that didn't involve getting naked, I launched myself in his direction with the purpose of intercepting the ball. Or him. Anything would do. Unfortunately, that intent landed nowhere near where I'd expected. Just when I was about to reach him, my foot got caught in a little bump on the grass, causing me to trip and be catapulted forward.

So much for ending this with dignity.

As I braced myself for a painful landing, my eyelids shut involuntarily. I was swallowed by darkness, counting the seconds and milliseconds left for the upcoming crush against the grass. *Three, two, one . . .*

Nothing. Impact never ensued. One moment, I had been flying, eyes closed and about to face-plant on the floor, and the next, I was somehow suspended in time. No, I was suspended in the air. Not understanding how, I blinked my eyes open, just as a *humph* was punched out of my lips.

My midsection landed against something hard.

Then, I was greeted by the sight of glistening, smooth skin. A flawless back. My gaze trailed down, taking in a tight backside in sports shorts, followed by a pair of muscled calves.

Understanding sank in as I realized I was hanging off someone. Particularly off someone's shoulder – Aaron's shoulder to be one hundred percent exact.

What in the—

Everybody seemed to be on board, if the clapping and cheering around us were any indication. Ignoring the little commotion behind us, Aaron rearranged me on his broad shoulder, gripping my waist gently but firmly. A complaint rose and died in my throat as he shot off, running.

'Aaron,' I screeched with urgency.

He was running with me hanging off him like a goddamn human-sized potato sack.

With every stride, the symmetric and strained strings of muscle on his back moved. His backside too. Distracting me.

Dammit, Lina, no. Focus.

'Aaron,' I repeated, being ignored again. 'What. Are. You.

Doing?' My speech was interrupted with each bounce of his body. With each stomp of his long legs, guiding the ball in my sister's direction. 'Aaron Blackford!'

He chuckled. Then, he patted the back of my thigh. 'I couldn't let my girlfriend fall to the floor now, could I?' the bastard said calmly, not sounding one bit out of breath.

'Aaron,' I howled. 'I swear to Lucifer—'

He bounced a little extra hard, cutting my words. His hold on my waist tightened. Sending a wave of awareness down my legs. His other palm held the back of my thigh still, his fingers spreading across my skin. God, everything I felt under me was hard and warm.

Dammit.

I couldn't believe it, but I was mad and . . . and . . . and . . .

Shit. I was a little turned on by the display of strength.

That last thought had barely registered when Aaron's grip on my waist shifted, securing me with his whole arm. I could feel his biceps against my side. My blood swirled, and it had nothing to do with being upside down.

'Brace yourself, girlfriend. I'm going to win this thing and put some food in you before you eat my head off.'

'There's no stopping that from happening. *Boyfriend.*'

Wishing I could know how close Aaron was from delivering the killing goal, I twisted my body upward as much as I could. Behind us, phones were out, recording the whole damn thing.

Oh Lord, please don't let this end up on TikTok.

One last bounce, and chaos erupted as Aaron's strides came to a stop.

'Put. Me. Down.' I punctuated my words by attacking his back with my weak fists. Judging by his lack of reaction, I doubted he was even feeling it.

'Hey.' He turned around, giving me a view of my sister, who was still under the goal.

She might have just been scored against, but she was smiling.

Aaron continued, 'I knew you were bossy, but I didn't know you were this violent.'

'You haven't seen anything,' I gritted through clenched teeth while he remained casually standing there, unaffected by the weight of the woman he had tossed over his shoulder.

His chest shook under my hips and thighs. Was he laughing?

The nerve of him.

The situation called for extreme measures. So, with all the skill I could gather, I stretched down until my hand reached his backside and pinched his butt.

Yep. I, Lina Martín, had just pinched Aaron Blackford's butt. And I regretted it immediately.

One, because it was Aaron's butt cheek I had pinched. And how could I ever come back from doing something like that when I had to see his face at work – every working day of every week – and he'd soon become my boss?

And two, because it had been so smooth and firm that I wanted to do it a second time, just to be sure that an ass that hard was real. I wanted to double-check if a butt could really have that many muscles.

And that, together with reason one, made me question my sanity.

As that spun in my head, I realized that Aaron had noticed my unfriendly pinch. I knew because he had instantly frozen. My fake boyfriend's body – which was still underneath my hips, stomach, and legs – had gone very, very still from the moment my fingers came into contact with his ass.

Tempted to pinch him again to check if he was breathing or if I had shocked him as much as I had myself, I waited.

With astonishing care, his hands moved to my waist. Aaron lifted me from his shoulder, positioning my front against his chest, still holding me so my feet wouldn't touch the grass. Our heads were at the same level, our gazes irremediably meeting.

His face was this unreadable blank mask again, as if I had pinched all emotion out of it.

I realized I preferred playful Aaron to the one who hid whatever he was feeling. But that moved into the background as I recounted the nonexistent space between our bodies from our chests down.

I was feeling a little light-headed, so my arms braced themselves on Aaron's shoulders. Our eyes never breaking contact. I didn't think either of us blinked either.

Aaron rearranged my body in his arms, and with the change of position, I could feel the swaying of his chest against mine. I could feel the sweat on his skin under my hands and arms too. But above all, I was enraptured by those blue eyes that gleamed like diamonds under the punishing sunlight. My breath got stuck in my throat, not going anywhere. Just like I was.

Never in a hundred years would I have imagined myself in this position. Being held by a shirtless Aaron and not wanting to run as far and fast away as I could. But shockingly, I wanted to do the exact opposite; I wanted to take my time inspecting every inch of sweaty, bare skin I could see. I wanted to stay right where I was, perhaps maybe even let him carry me everywhere for the rest of the day.

And that admission scared me. No, it terrified me.

Or it should have because in that precise moment, I couldn't find it in me to care for anything besides the wild beating of my heart, thumping directly against Aaron's skin.

When Aaron finally spoke, his voice had a breathless texture, 'You pinched my ass, Catalina.'

I had. And I was sorry. Sort of.

Which didn't excuse the shameless, outright joyful grin that broke out on my face. I barely recognized myself in that moment, barely understood the need to smile that big and make him pay me back with one of his own. Perhaps a laugh too.

'I plead the Fifth,' I managed to say through my ridiculously silly smile. Still held in his arms. 'Plus, if by any chance, someone might have pinched your butt, you might have totally deserved it.'

'Oh yeah?' The corner of his lips twitched.

Almost there. 'Yep. One hundred percent well deserved.'

'Even if I'd saved that hypothetical person from a boisterous fall?' Aaron's eyes wrinkled with the smile I was looking for, his lips remaining mostly flat. Still.

'Boisterous? I was merely going to brush the floor. Very delicately, mind you.'

'You are a ridiculous, impossible woman, you know that?'

I knew, and I was ready to admit that, but then Aaron went ahead and gave me that grin I had been craving. His lips split, and his mouth gave way to a handsome smile that changed his face completely. One that I had seen only once before and that made my heart go all crazy in my chest. My eyes probably twinkled too.

He was right; I was ridiculous. This whole thing was so very ridiculous.

'Hey, guys.' Daniel's voice came from somewhere nearby, tearing through the moment and causing the little happy cloud I had been in to vanish. 'Food is on the table, and we are all about to start. Come on.'

As I heard what I assumed were Daniel's footsteps walking away, I knew my grin had extinguished.

Had that moment we had shared been all for Daniel and everybody else's sake?

Probably. No, most certainly. That was what couples did. Playful touches, wide smiles, heated glances.

And that made me feel ... a little dumb. Made his smile worth a little less. And made mine a very foolish one.

I guessed it was a good thing that Aaron's handsome grin had disappeared too. Although, even with Daniel there, his gaze had never left mine. And it didn't either when his arms shifted the hold on my waist and slid me down his body. Or so I told myself because as I went down, my eyelids might have fluttered, making it hard for me to see much as I was pressed against each hard plane, bulge, and slab there was in Aaron's chest.

My legs landed on the ground without much confidence. Dizzy from the overwhelming sensation dancing down my body, I was grateful for Aaron's hands remaining on my waist.

Once he seemed sure I wouldn't topple down, he let go of me. But not without tugging a little strand of hair that had come out of my ponytail first.

My heart proceeded to do the toppling down in that moment.

Even more so when his head dipped slowly. 'Not bad for a Greek god, huh?' His voice was not nearly as playful as a few moments ago. Right before Daniel had burst my bubble. But Aaron accompanied that with a wink.

That drew a tiny little smile out of me, and I had to shake my head to hide it.

Who is this man who goes around, throwing winks and smiles at me?

My future boss – that's who.

And wasn't that reason enough to start thinking about having a one-on-one with that flutter in my chest? The fact that this whole thing was a charade was reason enough already. But he'd soon be promoted to head of the division – my division – and I had to remember that.

'Come on,' he said when I remained quiet. 'I told you I'd put some food in you, and I am a man of my word.'

Yes, he was. And I shouldn't forget that either.

Aaron had promised he'd play the role of my boyfriend and that he'd do it wonderfully. And so far, he'd done such an excellent job that he was starting to convince even me that he was a different man from the one I had known in New York.

CHAPTER EIGHTEEN

Stopping myself from crawling under the table was becoming a real hardship. But if Isabel kept up the *Aaron and Lina* questioning for a little longer, I'd have no other choice but to do exactly that. Otherwise, my last resort would be to knock down the bride with one of the metallic trays containing the variety of *pinchos* we were snacking on. It would be a waste of food, and it was her bachelorette-slash-bachelor party, but it'd be the only way. She was a resilient woman; she'd recover in time for the wedding.

We stood in one of the most frequented bars – *sidrerías* – of my hometown, surrounded by the characteristically loud chatter of people and the sour smell of spilled *sidra* – the regional apple cider. These were establishments that one could find in every corner of any city or town in this region of the north of Spain. People gathered around in groups of all sizes and ages. Some stood around tall tables, just like we – bride, groom, best man, Aaron, and I – were doing. Others had been seated to have dinner, and some were leaning on the bar, chatting animatedly with the waiters.

Willing my lungs to take a slow, deep, and calming breath, I tried to order my thoughts, so I could dodge the last one of Isabel's questions.

'Come on. There has to be more to the story of how you two met.' Isabel's eyes shone with curiosity, bouncing from me to my very stoic fake boyfriend, who stood close enough to my side to steal a fair chunk of my focus. 'You are playing really hard to get, Lina.'

'That's the whole story, I promise.' Sighing, I averted my eyes to my hands, which were lying on the smooth surface of the table. My fingers were busy playing with my empty glass. 'Aaron started working for InTech, and that's how we met. What else is there that you want to know?'

'I want the details you haven't told me.'

I could tell my sister was about to start whining in that annoying and persistent way that had never once failed to break people and make them give her whatever it was she wanted. I had been there myself – many times.

She tilted her head. 'Hey, if you guys experienced lust at first sight and started hooking up and then dating, it's okay. Nothing to be ashamed of. Plus, it would explain that bed-breaking rumour going around.'

My lips parted, and my eyes widened. 'Charo works faster than I thought,' I muttered.

I sensed Aaron shifting by my side, closing the small distance between our arms.

But I didn't turn to look at him as my sister continued, 'I'm not Mamá, Lina. You can tell me.' My sister batted her eyelashes, and I heard how Gonzalo cleared his throat. 'Or share with the group – fine, whatever.' She rolled her eyes at her fiancé. 'Come on. We are listening. Did you guys hook up first? And if so, how many times?'

Daniel, who had been oddly quiet for someone who was supposed to be having a good time, sighed noisily. 'I don't think there's any need to share that with the group.'

My gaze swivelled in his direction, finding him with a deadpan expression.

'Thanks, Dani,' Isabel gritted out between her teeth. 'But I'll let *my* sister decide if she wants to share her sexcapades with the table.'

Oh Lord, did she just call it sexcapades?

At the change in Isabel's tone, Gonzalo wrapped his arm around her shoulders and tugged her against his side. I watched Isabel's body relax immediately, letting go of what I knew were years of contained animosity toward her fiancé's brother.

Sighing silently, I felt a pang of guilt slice across my chest. It was unprecedented, and I had no reason to feel responsible for the situation, but at the same time, it was hard not to let some of the weight fall on my own shoulders.

In an ideal world, the best man wouldn't be my ex. In that same world, I wouldn't have panicked when learning that he was engaged while I seemed to be stuck in time and alone, and I wouldn't have felt the need to lie to my family and tangle myself into the web of deception I had woven. Perhaps, in that ideal world, the man by my side would be there because he loved me and not because I had struck a deal with him.

But those scenarios were hypothetical and therefore unreal. Unattainable. And each of them painted a picture that was far from the truth. In the real world, there was a consequence to every decision I made. To every choice that I ever took. A perfect world where life happened neatly and ideally didn't exist. Life was messy and often hard. It did not wait for anybody to be ready or to expect the bumps on the road. You had to grab on to the wheel and steer your way back to your lane. And that was all I had done. That was what had brought me to where I was. For better or for worse.

It was unfortunate that the one man with whom Gonzalo shared DNA was not only my ex, but also the man who had been the other half of the relationship that was the catalyst for me leaving everything I had once called home. But I had made the choice to date him. My university professor. The man who would introduce my sister to the love of her life.

Because life wasn't ideal. It turned and bent. It spun you out for a minute and swung you right back in the next.

Contrary to what most believed, when I had applied for the

programme abroad that had taken me to New York, a year after everything had blown up in my face, I hadn't been escaping Daniel; I had been escaping the situation that my relationship with him had thrust me in. Granted, in the process, he had also broken my heart. And that was what everybody saw. The scolded, heart-broken runaway. But the damage went beyond a simple breakup. After that, I went through the worst year of my life. I almost quit uni and threw away my education. My future. All because people, those I had considered friends at some point, spun disgusting lies about me. And it hadn't only scarred me; it had also impacted my family.

For one, that sadness that everybody had regarded me with stuck to me across time. And the very few times I had come back home, single, it had thickened until solidifying into something that I carried with me.

Even my parents in a way. I could tell they were scared I'd never bounce back from it. Which was stupid. I was over Daniel. My singlehood had nothing to do with that. I simply ... struggled to trust somebody enough to give myself completely. I managed to keep myself one or two feet from anything that had the potential to hurt me. And that always ended one of two ways. I either walked away, or I was the one who was walked away from. But at least, I did come out of it wholly.

As for Isabel, she had gone from loving Daniel for giving her Gonzalo to threatening the best man's balls. Repeatedly. And while she turned into my fiercest protector and cheerleader, the breakup never shook the foundation of her own relationship. Which was evidence of how much they adored and loved each other. Besides, over the years, she had come to accept that even if Daniel had been at fault for a part, he hadn't done anything besides being willing to break some unspoken rule about dating a former student. Society had done the rest.

Which didn't give me – or Isabel or Daniel – the right to force Gonzalo to pick a side. Something that Isabel had come to terms with. Eventually. In her own way.

'There were no sexcapades, Isa.' I shook my head lightly, trying to shove all those thoughts and memories away.

'Not even one? Come on. You guys work together. And I saw you during the soccer match. You—'

'It was a very boring and uneventful meeting,' I interrupted her. 'Get your mind out of the gutter.'

Isabel's mouth opened, and I was left with no choice but to elbow my fake boyfriend.

Maybe Aaron's confirmation would appease her.

'Correct,' he said, and I could hear the amusement in his voice. 'No sexcapades took place.'

I watched my sister's lips clip closed.

'Unfortunately,' he added.

My own mouth was the one clamping down then. Or it fell open and to the floor – I didn't know.

Don't look at him. Don't look shocked. This is all part of the deception.

Focusing on my sister, I ignored Aaron's last comment and smiled – hopefully naturally.

Isabel reached for the bottle of *sidra* and poured a *culín* in my glass, filling only the bottom of it. Exactly how tradition stated *sidra* had to be served. Once she had served me a *culín*, Isabel proceeded to do the same with Aaron's glass. 'You are not telling me something.' Her eyes narrowed to thin slits as she pushed our drinks in our direction. Then, she levelled me with a look. 'I can see it in your eyes. Drink.'

I didn't think she was bluffing. Lying wasn't something I was particularly good at, and my sister had the sibling ability to see right through me.

My palms started sweating. My sister was onto something. And I needed to start talking, give her anything.

I downed the contents of my glass in one single gulp – exactly how tradition specified too.

'Fine, okay.' I placed my empty glass on the table. 'All right, so the day Aaron and I met ...' I started, my eyes unconsciously jumping to Aaron's face and finding him looking at me with a new kind of interest. I returned my gaze to Isabel. 'It was a cold and dark November 22—' I stopped myself, feeling the need to explain why I remembered the date so accurately. 'I remember because it was the day of my birthday, not because—' I stopped myself again. Then, I shook my head. I had barely started, and I was doing an awful job already. This was why I should never, ever lie. 'Anyway, it was November.'

Aaron's hand brushed my back very softly. The touch unsettled me at first, but then it magically instilled confidence in me. Just how he had done earlier that day. How he managed to do that, I didn't know. But when he moved his fingers over the fabric of my thin blouse, right above my shoulder blades, I felt a little less like a fraud.

'But that isn't important, I guess,' I continued, and I had to clear my voice lightly because it had come out a little shaky. 'When I first met Aaron, it was the day he was introduced as a new team leader by our boss.'

Aaron's touch turned loose and airy, and then it stopped altogether.

Trying to keep my head on the story and away from the dainty trail of goosebumps he'd left on my skin, I continued, 'He entered through that door, all cold confidence and determination. Looking larger than life with those long legs and broad shoulders, and I swear everybody in that meeting room fell into silence. I could imme-diately tell he'd be that kind of man everybody ... respected – for lack of a better word – without more than a word or two being spoken. Just by the way he looked around, assessing the situation. As if he were looking for possible threats and coming up with a way to eliminate them before they could manifest. And even then, everyone seemed to be charmed by the new guy.'

I remembered perfectly how everyone had first gaped at the handsome and stern new addition and then silently nodded in appreciation and awe. Me included at first. I'd never admit it, but back then, I had gotten as far as thinking I could let that deep voice of his lure me to sleep every night, and I'd be content for the rest of my days.

'So, yeah, every single one of my colleagues was pretty much enraptured. Not me though. I wasn't fooled that easily. All throughout Jeff's and Aaron's speeches, I kept thinking about how nervous he must have been. I kept noticing his shoulders inching higher and his gaze growing ... unsure. As if he were holding himself from bolting out that door. So, I came to the conclusion that he wasn't as standoffish as he looked, standing there. He couldn't be. It was just nerves. One couldn't possibly give off that vibe on purpose. It was his first day, and that was some intimidating shit. I thought he just needed a little push in the right direction. A little friendly welcome to fall into place.'

And then I proceeded to do a very dumb and impulsive thing. Just as I always managed to do. 'And I couldn't have been any more wrong.' I chuckled bitterly. 'Maybe Aaron wasn't nervous – I wouldn't know. But he didn't need any kind of push. He was not looking for friends. And he certainly was aware of what impression he was making.' I returned back to the present in that moment, and I was greeted by three pairs of confused eyes. My throat dried out. 'I mean, that obviously changed. Eventually,' I added quickly in a less-than-convincing tone. 'Because we are super in love, so yay!' Throwing my arms in the air, I cheered, trying my best to get the control back, but the gesture landed nowhere near where I'd wanted it to.

Isabel's face fell slightly, and right before her frown could fully form, Aaron surprised me by coming to my rescue.

'Catalina isn't wrong. That day, I was a little nervous,' he confessed, and my head swirled in his direction.

Aaron's gaze was on my sister, which was good because we were
in desperate need of some damage control that required all his
attention and charm. But also because I didn't want him to see my
expression as I watched him. That trip down memory lane had left
me a little too raw to hide how I really felt about that day.

'I didn't have any plans or hopes of making friends, not during
that first meeting and not any day after,' he continued.

Well, that wasn't a shock to me, not after almost two years of
enduring the consequences of that position.

'And I was plenty obvious about it. The last thing I wanted was
someone getting the wrong idea and thinking I was there for anything that wasn't doing the best job I could. And in my book, that is
not compatible with telling jokes and exchanging family tales. That
day though, Lina showed up in my office. A little after five p.m.' He
looked down at his hands, and his eyelids sheltered the blue in his
eyes for just a heartbeat.

For a reason I couldn't explain, my heart raced in my chest at the
memory. *Embarrassment*. It had to be the physical reaction at reliving
that embarrassing moment through Aaron's words.

'Her cheeks were flushed, and there were some snowflakes still
clinging to her hair and coat. She was carrying a gift bag with a
ridiculous pattern of tiny party hats printed on it. As I took her in,
I was certain that she had gotten the wrong office, that she couldn't
possibly be there, carrying some kind of gift for me. Maybe she was
looking for the guy who had sat there before me.'

I watched his throat work as his words held his audience's
attention.

'And I was going to tell her, but I didn't stand a chance. She
started babbling some nonsense about how cold New York was
in winter and how irritating people turned when it snowed, how

chaotic instead of peaceful the city actually was. "As if it's my fault that New Yorkers hate the snow," she said. "It's like the cold numbs their brains, and they turn stupid."' Aaron smiled sheepishly. Very briefly, one moment there and the next gone.

And I kept staring at his profile, eating up his words and how they sent me right back to that day.

At that point, my heart banged against my chest with growing urgency, as if it were a wild thing, asking to be let out. Begging to ask all the questions taking shape in my head and threatening to do it itself if I didn't.

'She placed the bag on my desk and then told me to open it. But the cold must have numbed my brain, too, because instead of doing that, I kept gawking at it. Petrified and ... intrigued. Staring at it and not having the slightest clue as to what to do with it.'

He had done that, and his reaction had made me panic and jump into crisis-control Lina. Which had been my second mistake that day.

'When I didn't reach for it, she shoved her hand into the bag and pulled the contents out herself.' Aaron chuckled, but he wasn't laughing. Because the curt noise was almost sad.

I wasn't laughing either. I was too busy chewing on the fact that he remembered everything. All of it. In detail. My chest filled with more questions.

'It was a mug. And it had a joke printed on it. It said, *Engineers don't cry. They build bridges and get over it.*'

Someone laughed then. Isabel or perhaps Gonzalo – I wasn't sure. With all that crazy banging, my heart had somehow moved up my throat and to my temples, so it was hard to focus on anything besides its beating and Aaron's voice.

'And you know what I did?' he continued, bitterness filling his tone. 'Instead of laughing like I wanted to, instead of looking up at her and saying something funny that would hopefully make her give me one of those bright smiles I had somehow already seen her give so freely in the short day I had been around her, I pushed it all down and set the mug on my desk. Then, I thanked her and asked her if there was anything else she needed.'

I knew I shouldn't feel embarrassed, but I was. Just as much as I had been back then, if not more so. It had been such a silly thing to do, and I had felt so tiny and dumb after he brushed it away so easily.

Closing my eyes, I heard him continue, 'I pretty much kicked her out of my office after she went out of her way and got me a gift.' Aaron's voice got low and harsh. 'A fucking welcome gift.'

I opened my eyes just in time to watch him turn his head in my direction. Our gazes met.

'Just like the big jerk I had advertised myself to be, I ran her out. And to this day, I regret it every time it crosses my mind. Every time I look at her.' He didn't even blink as he talked, looking straight into my eyes. And I didn't think I did either. I didn't think I was even breathing. 'All the time I wasted so foolishly. All the time I could have had with her.'

If I hadn't been leaning on the tall table of the *sidrería*, I would have fallen to the floor. My legs weren't able to support my weight any longer. My body had somehow numbed. Aaron looked at me – no, he looked into me. And in return, he let me do the same. I couldn't know how, but I swore, in that moment, he was laying bare a little piece of himself in front of me. He was trying to tell me something I didn't think I had the ability to process. Or was he? Was he begging me to remember that this was all a farce? Or was he begging me to remember that even if it was, his words still held part of the truth?

But that couldn't make any sense, could it?

No. Nothing did. Not me wondering and not whatever I thought I had heard in his words or seen in his eyes.

Certainly not the way my heart had broken free and turned into a wrecking ball, demolishing everything it found on its way and leaving nothing more than a trail of shambles behind.

'And what happened next?' a familiar voice asked.

'Then,' Aaron answered, and his hand rose, the backs of his fingers brushing my cheek, 'I acted like a fool – an idiot, depending on who you ask – for a little longer.'

My eyelids hid my eyes, breaking off the contact. I could feel my blood pumping through my body. The imprint of the ghost of his touch right beneath my cheekbone.

'And eventually, I somehow managed to make her give me the time of day. I talked her into believing that she needed me. Then, I showed her – proved to her – that she did.'

My eyes were still closed. I didn't trust myself to open them.

I didn't want to see Aaron. His face, his lips, the serious line of his jaw. I didn't want to see if there were any secrets in the depths of the ocean in his eyes.

I was terrified of not finding a single thing there. Of finding something. Everything, anything. I ... was simply terrified. Confused.

Then, someone started clapping. And I heard the unmistakable voice of my sister.

'You,' she said when I blinked open my eyes. Isabel's voice sounded shaky with emotion and anger. All at once.

Not that I cared at that moment. I was looking into Aaron's eyes again. And he hadn't lifted his gaze off me.

What is happening? What are we doing?

My sister continued talking, 'That was so beautiful, Aaron. And you, Catalina Martín Fernández,' she used our two last names, which meant trouble. 'You are no sister of mine any longer. I can't believe you kept all that from me. You made me talk about sexcapades and lust when the truth is so much better than all that superficial crap.'

The truth. That little word soured my stomach.

'Good thing your boyfriend has better sense. You are so very lucky he's here.'

Aaron kept his eyes on me when he said, 'See? It's a very good thing I'm here.'

That sent my heart into doing another cartwheel.

'Oh, Aaron.' I heard my sister exhale shakily, and I could tell she was about to cry. Or kick my ass. It could be either one of those. 'You have no idea how happy this makes me. It's the best wedding gift I could ever get, seeing my little sister finally . . .' Her voice wobbled. 'After all this time, it's just . . .' A hiccup. 'Oh, man. Why am I crying when I want to kick her ass? It must . . . it must . . . be . . .' She hiccupped again.

Oh dear Lord.

Tearing my gaze off Aaron, I reluctantly turned to my sister.

She was full-on bawling. And she looked pissed off too.

'It must be all this wedding pressure,' I thought she mumbled.

Daniel, who I had completely forgotten about, said something under his breath and reached for the bottle of *sidra*. It was empty, so he placed it back on the table and bolted in the direction of the bar.

'*Ven aquí, tonta.*' Gonzalo pulled my sister into his arms, tucking her head under his chin. Then, he mouthed over her head, *More alcohol.*

Yep. Only that would save the night if the bride was weeping. Especially when it was over a story that wasn't true.

Because it couldn't be.

It was all a lie. A deception.

Aaron had played with the truth. Just how I had asked him to do. He had adorned it, altered it so it fit this charade we were starring in. It was nothing more than that. We were still the same Aaron and Lina who had left New York.

And on that note, Aaron would still be promoted to my boss.

Did you hear that, stupid and delusional heart? No more weird business. Where Aaron Blackford was concerned, it was all an act.

~

By the time we rolled into the next spot, the club — and giving that name to the modest and scrubby bar that doubled as a club at midnight was a stretch — I was ninety-nine percent sure I might have crossed the tipsy border and walked right into drunkland.

The remaining one percent was divided. With all that *sidra* pumping through my veins, it was hard to discern if the way I felt had everything to do with the alcohol or if it was partly due to the man who had been watching over me like a hawk.

Aaron had stopped drinking at some point between Isabel's waterfalls show and the arrival of the rest of the bachelorette and bachelor party to the *sidrería*. Which I wasn't sure was a good thing. He was completely sober, and that meant, tomorrow, he'd recall every single detail of the night. And that wasn't good. Not when every time he touched me, my body came openly alive, and then I proceeded to melt to the floor. And definitely not when every time he dipped his head to ask me if I was doing okay or if I was having fun, my heart decided that my chest wasn't roomy enough and plunged itself to the pit of my stomach.

As for the rest? Well, I was mostly preoccupied with the way the loud music was filling my ears and spreading all the way to my hips and feet as we navigated the crowded and dark interior.

Moving forward into the sea of bodies with the rest of the party in tow — or not because chances were, we had lost them — I was unexpectedly shoved back a couple of staggering steps. Aaron, who had been walking very close behind, intercepted me. His arm came around my waist, and his palm landed on my hip.

In one swift motion, he had me secured against him.

Just like I had experienced about a hundred and twenty times that night, all my nerve endings were instantly charged with electricity the moment my back came into contact with his front. Every inch of my skin that was flushed against him heated. Even through the thin fabric of my blouse and his button-down.

His long, strong fingers squeezed my hip.

Turning my head to look up at his face, I didn't care that my lips had parted and that my eyes probably looked hazy and a little clouded. Just how I felt. But then again, it wasn't like I could conceal it. For whatever reason – the alcohol in my system or Aaron's closeness – I simply couldn't hide it.

So, instead, for the first time, I let myself enjoy it. Let my whole focus be on him. On all the points where our bodies touched and on the way he looked down at me. I *focused* on Aaron and on the way he was holding me against him as we blocked the way further inside the bar.

Keeping our gazes locked over my shoulder, I allowed my back to relax into him. And something danced in the blue of his eyes. I thought he was going to smile, but his mouth pressed into its serious line.

'You got me,' I said over the blaring music. 'My saviour. Always coming to my rescue, Mr Kent.'

A part of me knew that was mostly the alcohol talking. But Aaron didn't answer. His lips remained sealed as I watched his throat work. Someone behind him called us. Or perhaps it had come from the opposite side of the overcrowded bar. I didn't know, and I didn't care. I was going to tell Aaron to ignore it, but then he somehow tugged me into his side. Wrapping a large hand around mine at the same time.

I liked that. Far too much. So I didn't complain.

Aaron guided me through the place as if he were the one who had spent countless nights here when he was younger. The bar was every bit as gloomy and packed with swirling bodies as I remembered.

The music still boomed too loudly, and the floors were sticky with spilled drinks.

I loved it.

And I loved that Aaron was here with me tonight too. I loved that he protected me from those who accidentally – or drunkenly – pushed and shoved.

I loved many, many things right then. And I had the need to tell him.

Stopping, I turned around and went on my tiptoes, hopefully going somewhere near Aaron's ear and not his armpit or something because that would be really embarrassing. 'Don't you love this place? I do. It's nothing like New York's fancy-schmancy clubs, huh?'

Aaron leaned down, his lips hovering over the shell of my ear. 'It's very . . . authentic.' He paused but didn't retrieve his mouth from that spot. A shiver crawled down my back. 'At first, I was a little wary. I'm not gonna lie.'

I felt the corners of my lips tugging up. Yeah, the place was definitely not Aaron's style.

'But now . . .' he continued, and his lips brushed the sensitive area below my ear, making me melt and come to life, all at once. 'Now, I think I could stay here until the sun comes up. Maybe even a little longer.'

My lips parted, but as I was ready to speak, someone pushed me, and the words were ripped off my tongue. I was shoved further into Aaron's body, this time front to front. And I immediately felt against me all the hard planes and lean muscles I had witnessed shining under the sun that morning.

Something beneath my skin quickened, almost like a zap.

My body urged me to obliterate the last inch of space between us. It was crazy how much I wanted to do that. I felt the urgency in my blood. As if my heart were pumping pure madness throughout my body. Making me reckless. So much so that my arms lifted of their own accord, my hands linking behind Aaron's neck. I watched his eyes widen for just a heartbeat, and then something simmered and flared in his gaze. That blue blaze wiped clean the surprise, replacing it with something that looked a lot like hunger.

Everybody else around us was dancing to a beat that my hazy mind seemed to remember from something. It was Latin; it was decadent and fun and what summer nights in Spain were usually made of. Without really knowing how, my hips started moving. Aaron's hands shifted to my waist. And we were dancing. The memory of doing that with him not so long ago blindsided me for an instant. How ironic it was that we'd found ourselves in the same situation so soon after and that we seemed like completely different people.

It didn't make sense.

But I didn't care. Not tonight.

My fingers played with the short strands of hair at Aaron's nape as our hips swayed to the Latin beat. So soft – his hair was so very soft. Just how I had imagined. I pulled a little on the strands, not knowing why. In answer, Aaron's fingers tightened on my waist, causing my blood to swirl and heat, gathering in all kinds of interesting places.

Without being able to stop myself, I went up on my tiptoes again, not needing an excuse to examine his face closer. He wasn't frowning or smiling, but there was something about his features that made him look different. Unbound. Yes, that was it. There wasn't a trace at all of that restraint I was so used to seeing in him. And to me, that made him look as handsome as he had ever looked.

Maybe I should tell him.

My lips parted with the words, and I watched his gaze dip to them. The look in his eyes released a flock of butterflies low in my belly.

'Aaron,' I said, but I was distracted by the way he was looking at me. I didn't think I was dancing anymore. What was I going to say?

'Do you trust me, Catalina?' he asked me.

Yes. The answer flashed across my mind, but I didn't voice it. There was something that had intercepted the three-letter word. Something I was vaguely aware I needed to remember.

Aaron's fingers spread, and his thumbs trailed across the fabric of my blouse. One of them slipped beneath the hem. The simple contact sent a wave of pure awareness across my skin.

'You don't, not yet,' he said against my ear, and then his lips hovered above my cheek, causing my breath to hitch. 'But you will trust me; I'll make sure of it.'

I . . . I didn't think I understood that. Not then and probably not anytime soon. But what did that matter when his mouth was so close to mine? When his lips were dancing across my jaw, barely making contact, which only drove me crazy. If I moved, if I just tilted my head and—

A squeal and a hand landing on my arm burst whatever thought had formed in my head.

And the next thing I knew, I was being dragged away from Aaron. Another loud screech hinted at who was behind me, pulling at my arm.

'*Lina, nuestra canción!*' my sister yelled over the music, stopping us both at a narrow opening, where there was some space.

Our song?

My ears took the song blasting through the speakers as my brain worked out the situation slowly.

It was impossible not to recognize the beat. How could I not when that infamous video of my sister and me dancing to this very same song had been played over and over at family gatherings and Christmases for the last twenty years? Both the music and the choreography were ingrained in my brain forever. '*Yo Quiero Bailar*' by *Sonia y Selena* was playing, and that only meant one thing.

'Time to pay up!' Gonzalo cheered.

That was followed by everyone else making as much space as they could around Isabel and me as the rest of Team Bride assembled behind us to deliver the payout for losing the Wedding Cup.

My body came alive with the familiar beat.

'You'll pay for this, *bridezilla*,' I yelled over the music as we looked at each other, readying our positions to start the infamous choreography.

'Me?!' she yelled back as we moved our butts in sync. 'You'll thank me later.'

We swirled with our arms up and then shimmied our way down.

'What do you mean?' I demanded as we bumped our hips, following through with the stupid dance.

I was aware of the rest of our improvised array of backing dancers from Team Bride somewhere behind us. They were replicating our moves as well as they could. To their credit, I didn't think my sister's – or my – drunken attempts were that easy to imitate.

'What I mean is . . .' Isabel said as we came closer again, faced each other, and high-fived over our heads. Then, we started lowering our bodies to the floor with the beat of the song, making our way down in a way that was supposed to be seductive and probably ended up being unnaturally clumsy. 'If your boyfriend's smouldering eyes are any indication, you are so going to get extra laid tonight.'

Her words had barely entered my ears and registered when I almost landed on my ass.

My head shot to the side, taking in our audience and immediately landing on a very particular set of eyes. Smouldering eyes, as Isabel had just put it. And as my body went through the motions, relying on only muscle memory, I couldn't tear my gaze away from that pair of piercing blue eyes.

I executed the routine almost absently, not able to look anywhere else. Magnetized by those two blue spots that seemed to be ignited with light. And while I could blame the alcohol running through my bloodstream, I couldn't figure out what his excuse was.

He ate up every ridiculous and silly motion as if he were contemplating something that was more than a routine created by a pair of teenagers a bunch of years ago. He looked at me as if I was more than a grown-ass woman executing a goofy and wacky dance. Like he couldn't get enough. Just as if he were about to part the crowd and close the distance between us so he could drink in even the smallest of my motions.

I had never been looked at that way. Not ever.

When the song came to an end and transitioned into the next hit from a decade ago, whatever was passing between Aaron and me churned low in my stomach. With urgency. So much that it made me dizzy and flustered and about to crawl out of my skin.

The memory of my body flush against his flickered through my mind. That had only happened a few minutes ago.

My heart raced in my chest as I tried to gather myself, to control my breath. Sweat dripping down my back and arms, an overwhelming sensation made its way across my whole body.

I needed air, fresh air. That always helped.

'I'm going outside for a second,' I told Isabel as I wrapped her in a quick hug.

My sister nodded, distracted by the song playing, which happened to be her new favourite tune in the world. I veered for the door, not daring to look back at Aaron. I couldn't. I just . . . couldn't.

I needed to order my thoughts.

Once I made my way through the sea of dancing bodies, I stepped outside. The night was warm and humid, and I welcomed the breeze from the sea hitting my skin.

The relief was instant but short-lived. Now, my legs seemed to weigh about a hundred pounds each.

But I'd take that over everything I had been feeling back inside.

I also regretted every drink I had had tonight. Maybe with a clearer mind, I'd be able to understand whatever the hell was going on. Particularly why my heart seemed to be plotting against me.

Letting myself fall onto the side of the road, I sat, so I could rest my legs. This was a pedestrian area, and only resident cars were allowed to drive through. Given the time, almost three in the morning, chances of being run over were low. So, I took my time, trying to appease whatever was still making my skin flush and tingle.

Eyes shut and elbows on my knees, I focused on the muffled music coming out of the bar.

The door behind me opened and closed quickly after.

I knew he was there before he said anything. He didn't need to. I was attuned to him, it seemed. To this quiet man whose presence always spoke to me far louder than his words. Not turning back, I listened to his heavy footsteps as he walked to where I was, sitting on the lukewarm pavement of the sidewalk. Aaron let his body fall into place right beside me. His long legs stretched ahead, taking possibly two times the space mine did.

A bottle of water fell softly on my lap.

'You'll probably want to drink that,' Aaron said.

The overwhelming sensation that had pushed me to walk outside had not dissipated yet, hampering my thoughts.

He nudged my leg with his knee, encouraging me.

I regarded the bottle still on my lap. I was so freaking exhausted all of a sudden, and my arms felt too heavy to reach for it and open it. My whole body felt like that. And Aaron was sitting so close, all big and warm, so inviting for me to lean my head on his arm and close my eyes for just a minute. Just one really short nap.

'No sleeping, baby. Please.' Aaron snagged the bottle from where he had placed it, opened it, and shoved it back in my hand. 'Drink up,' he said softly.

Another nudge of his leg.

And what a beautiful leg that was. He probably had more muscles on his quadriceps alone than I had on my whole body. Bringing the bottle to my lips, I took a big gulp of water as I continued my perusal.

That is a very good-looking right thigh, I thought as I returned the bottle to my lap.

A little chuckle had me glancing at the man responsible for it.

His lips bent in a lopsided smile, distracting me.

'Thank you,' he said, his smile stretching. 'Nobody has ever complimented that particular part of my leg.'

I frowned.

Did I say that out loud? Ah Hell.

Looking at him, still in silence, I opted to drink some more water. My brain was clearly dehydrated if I was going around, voicing whatever crossed my mind.

'Feeling better?' Aaron asked from my side.

'Not yet,' I gave him a wobbly smile. 'But thank you.'

His frown made an appearance, wrinkling his forehead. 'I'll take you back to the apartment. Come on.' The legs I had been so busy admiring flexed, ready to push his body upward.

'No, wait.' My hand landed on that very good-looking – and oh, really hard – thigh, stopping him. 'Not yet, please. Can we stay here just for a little while?'

Aaron's blue eyes seemed to assess something, probably my state. But his big body stayed put beside mine.

'Thanks.' My gaze fell back on his stretched legs again. 'There's something I need to tell you. A confession.' I didn't look back at him, but I sensed him tense. 'I googled you, just once. But I did.'

Aaron seemed to ponder that for a moment. But he didn't comment on it. Instead, he snatched the bottle of water from my grip, opened it, and indicated to me to drink some more.

I complied and downed the rest of the contents. Then, he

retrieved the empty bottle, and I thought I heard him mutter something, but I wasn't sure.

'I found lots of stuff, you know. That's why I only allowed myself to google you one single time,' I admitted with a sheepish smile. 'I was scared of finding something that would change what I thought of you.'

'And did you?'

'Yes, and no.' Had what I found changed the image I had of Aaron? I didn't think I could answer that. 'I probably scrolled down photos upon photos of you until Google had nothing else to show me.'

'That's a lot of scrolling.'

'I guess.' I shrugged my shoulders. 'Do you want to hear about what I found?'

He didn't answer, so I told him anyway, 'There was this one image of you in the middle of the field; your back was to the camera, and you had your golden helmet hanging off your hand. I couldn't see more than your back, but I swear I could tell what your face looked like. I could picture in my head how your eyebrows were wrinkled on your forehead and how your jaw was bunched up – the way you do when you are upset but you don't want to show you are.'

Aaron had gone quiet, so I stole a glance at him. He was looking at me, and there was something that looked a lot like shock in his expression.

But I was no-filter Lina tonight, and I didn't seem to care about talking or revealing too much. 'Then, there were the articles,' I went on. 'There were more than a few, and they all praised you as a player. As an NFL promise. But then it all stopped. It was as if you had dropped off the face of the earth.'

Aaron's eyes looked vacant, as if he were no longer there with me, sitting on the sidewalk in the Spanish town that had seen me grow up.

I continued, not because I wanted to press him for details, but because I somehow couldn't stop from explaining myself, 'I don't think there are many football promises who hang the helmet for the not-so-glamorous life we lead as engineers for a medium-sized technology company.' I didn't know much about how college football worked, but the little I had read during my googling session told me I wasn't wrong. 'Ever since you told me about it, I have been wondering what could have possibly led you to make such a decision. An injury? Burnout? How does someone jump from one side to the other?'

I brushed my fingers across his forearm. I thought it would startle him, but it didn't. Instead, his other hand wrapped around mine, and then he placed our interlaced fingers on his thigh.

'It's okay if you don't want to talk about it.' I squeezed his hand. It really was okay, but that didn't mean I didn't feel somehow disappointed. 'If you don't want to tell me.'

Aaron didn't say anything for a long moment. I used that time to come to terms with the fact that he'd never open up to me. Not that I'd blame him. I hadn't been completely honest with him about my past either. But as much as I tried to tell myself otherwise, the falling sensation in my chest made it hard to ignore how I really felt. I wanted to know. I wanted to unearth and learn everything about his past because I knew deep inside me that it was the key to finally understanding the man he was today. And him not letting me in only reminded me that I wasn't different from anybody else.

'Catalina,' he finally said, and he followed that with a deep and tired sigh. 'I want to tell you. I'd gladly tell you everything about me.'

My heart decided to resume all those shenanigans I had been dealing with that night. *He'll tell me everything about him.*

'But you are barely standing on your own feet. You are in no condition to stay with me for a complete conversation.'

'I'll stay with you,' I said very quickly. 'I'm not that drunk. I will listen, I promise.' Even though I was feeling slightly better, the likelihood was that I'd fall on my face if I moved too fast. But that wouldn't stop me. 'I can prove it. Look.' My legs pushed my body up, propelling me in a rather wobbly way. But that didn't matter. I'd prove to Aaron I was completely fine.

I wasn't going to let the chance slip through my slightly intoxicated fingers or legs—

A pair of big hands cut my trajectory, holding me by the waist.

'Easy there. Let's keep the standing to a minimum,' Aaron said as he effortlessly returned me to my former position, right beside him. Perhaps a little closer to his body. Which I wouldn't complain about. 'Do you want to know that badly?'

'Yes. I want to know everything,' I confessed, following no-filter Lina's lead again.

A humourless laugh left him. 'I never planned for this to happen this way.'

My hazy brain didn't really understand that, but before I could ask, he continued, 'I always played football. That was all I knew for almost two decades. My dad was sort of a big deal in the coaching and management world back home, in Washington.' Aaron shook his head, those dishevelled, short locks almost flickering under the soft light of the street. 'He knew how to spot potential, had done it a million times. He was known for that. So, when he realized I had that raw talent he talked about so much, it was as if all those years of his career had been preparing him for that. For having a son he could mould into the perfect player from the very beginning.'

'He coached you since you were a kid?' I murmured.

Aaron flexed his legs and leaned his elbows on his knees. 'More than that. He turned me into his own personal project. He had this kid with potential for becoming everything he had dreamed of, right at home. And he had the tools and the experience to make that possible. There was no room for failure. He worked hard on turning me into this flawless football machine, which he had carefully assembled together since the moment my legs were strong enough to run after a ball and my hands were large enough to hold one.' Aaron paused. He was facing the gloomy street in front of us, and I could see how his profile turned hard. 'We both worked on that. And for the longest time, I thrived on it.'

I found myself shifting closer to him until my arm and shoulder were completely flush against him.

'How did that change?' I asked, letting my body lean a little on Aaron's side. 'When did you stop enjoying playing?'

He looked at me out of the corner of his eye, something softening in his expression. 'That photo you mentioned earlier?' he asked, and then he faced away from me, staring into the empty street in front of us. 'That was the last game I ever played.' Aaron paused, and I could tell he needed a moment to gather himself from the way his voice had sobered. 'That happened exactly one year after my mom passed away.'

My heart squeezed in my chest, and I felt this urge to wrap my body around him, so I could shield him from the pain in his voice. But I limited myself to grabbing his warm hand and slipping my fingers between his. Aaron brought our interlaced hands to his lap.

'In that moment, as I stood there, watching the crowd and my teammates celebrate a victory I couldn't bring myself to care about, I decided I'd pull out from the draft. And I did.'

'That must have hurt so much,' I told him, my thumb caressing the warm skin on the back of his hand. 'All of it, losing your mom and letting go of something you had worked all your life toward.'

'It did, yeah.' His head dipped, and I watched him look at our intertwined hands. 'My dad couldn't understand it. He wouldn't even try.' A bitter chuckle left him. 'My football career had turned into the perfect escape, following Mom's diagnosis. Instead of that consolidating our father-and-son relationship, it turned us into coach and player instead. Nothing more than that.'

More loss. My heart broke for Aaron. I squeezed his hand and then very slowly leaned my head on his arm.

He continued, 'He said I was throwing away my life. My future. That I would fail. That if I did drop an opportunity that would change my life, he didn't want to have anything to do with me. So, I graduated and left Seattle.'

Aaron still held my hand in his lap; his fingers had tightened around mine as he talked. I kept the side of my head on him as I felt my other hand fly to his forearm. It was the only way I could express how sorry I was for what he had gone through without engulfing him in a tight hug I wasn't sure I'd be able to let go of. At least, not for the rest of the night.

'It must have been so hard, growing up, limited by someone else's idea of what you should and should not be.'

He absently played with my fingers, the soft caresses of his skin against mine causing tingles to crawl up my arm. 'I realize that now, in hindsight. I never noticed while it happened; it was just how things were. I was given a set of goals, and I simply went with it,' he explained, his thumb trailing up my wrist. 'I was never unhappy – at least, not until I realized that perhaps I wasn't com-pletely happy either.'

'And now? Are you completely happy now, Aaron?'

Those soft brushes of his fingers against mine came to a stop, and he didn't hesitate when he answered, 'Completely? Not yet. But I'm working my fucking hardest on getting there.'

CHAPTER NINETEEN

For anyone witnessing my foolish attempts at reaching the bedroom, it would have been pretty obvious that I was about to face-plant on the floor. And they wouldn't be wrong. It was a wonder I was able to move at all, considering my feet barely lifted off the ground with all the dragging they had been doing.

Ironically, and contrary to the story my body told, I didn't think I had ever felt more awake than I did as I crossed the threshold of that door.

My head was working at full speed. Processing everything Aaron had told me about his past. I kept spinning and turning even the tiniest pieces of information until I was completely sure I had them pinned down securely so they wouldn't flee my memory.

Never mind that my legs wobbled with every step I took and exhaustion throbbed through my body. Aaron's confession – because it had felt like he was unveiling something he had kept guarded and locked away from sight – had created a little riot in my head.

And my chest. Definitely my chest too. The organ that resided there had constricted and squeezed, and I was still trying to come to terms with the fact that I wasn't supposed to feel that way. Or to act on it. A part of me missed being drunk or tipsy enough not to care, but after all the water Aaron had insisted on me gulping down and the fact that I hadn't touched a drink after we went back inside the infamous bar, I didn't have the luxury of that excuse anymore.

It was past five in the morning, and the effect of the alcohol had faded to a very low buzz that indicated tomorrow wasn't going to be much fun.

I didn't realize I had been standing in the middle of the bedroom, staring into empty space, until Aaron closed the door behind him. When I turned, my gaze immediately fell on the glass of water in his hand.

I watched him walk to the nightstand, where I had placed a few of my things, and set the glass there.

'That for me?' I knew the answer, but the small gesture turned something inside of me to mush. Just like every time he had watched after me tonight. It just . . . didn't feel all that small anymore. 'If you keep taking care of me this fiercely, it's going to be really hard to go back to real life.'

Perhaps I shouldn't have said that, shouldn't have phrased it that way, but after everything that had happened tonight, the careful grip I tried to maintain around Aaron seemed to be loosening.

Aaron nodded, his expression turning somewhat more serious. But he didn't comment on what I had said. Instead, he unbuttoned the top of his shirt and then changed his mind and started fumbling with the wristband of his watch.

Feeling my legs wobble – for all the wrong reasons – I walked to the edge of the bed and sat on top of the simple and silky comforter. Stopping my body from melting into it right away, I exhaled tiredly, releasing some of the tension in my shoulders. But before I could completely relax, my spine stiffened with a realization.

The bed.

We would be sharing this very same bed tonight.

That fact had somehow fled my mind until now. And its return did strange things to my belly. Things that were not strange in a funny way, but in a rather exciting way. Things that heated my skin.

Well, if I was feeling this way and we hadn't even gotten into bed yet, I couldn't even begin to imagine what would happen when I found myself tucked under the same comforter as Aaron. His large body and my much smaller one sharing and crowding the modest space the mattress offered.

And I . . . *oh, shit.*

In an attempt to distract myself, I occupied my hands, taking the flats off my hurting feet. Once I was done with that, I rubbed my temples, telling myself to chill the heck out because this was okay. We were adults. About to share a bed. So?

'How bad is it?' Aaron asked from where he stood still at the other end of the bed.

I chuckled, but it came closer to the sound that someone who was choking would make. 'Well' – I cleared my throat – 'I feel like I was run over by a stampede of very angry and very heavy antelopes that were in a rush to get somewhere.'

Aaron appeared in my field of vision, coming to a stop in front of me. 'Are you referencing Mufasa's death?'

My fingers stopped working, hovering above my temples. 'You like *The Lion King*?'

'Of course.'

'Any other Disney movies?' I was tempting my luck here. Aaron's expression remained serious. 'All of them.'

Shit. 'Even *Frozen*? *Tangled*? *The Princess Frog*?' I asked, and he nodded.

'I love animated movies. They take my mind off things.' He dipped his hands in the pockets of his jeans. 'Disney, Pixar . . . I'm a big fan.'

This was too much. First, he'd opened up about his childhood earlier today, and now, this. I wanted to ask how and why, but there was a more pressing issue. 'What's your favourite?'

Please don't say the one that will send my heart into cardiac arrest. Please don't say it.

'*Up.*'

Fuck. He had said it. My heart struggled there for a moment. And that little spot that had been softening throughout the night got a little bigger.

'Oh.' The word breathily left my lips. It was all I managed.

My eyes closed, and my fingers resumed massaging my temples. Although maybe I should have been massaging my chest.

'That bad, huh?' He seemed to be gauging something when I looked back at him. My sobriety most likely.

'Don't worry.' I waved my hand. 'I'm okay. I'm not drunk by now. I promise I won't puke all over you tonight.'

That didn't earn me much of an answer, making me cringe over my choice of words.

Without further comment, Aaron disappeared into the tiny en-suite bathroom, leaving me to deal with my awkwardness and thoughts.

Which mainly centered around Aaron – watching animation movies in the privacy of his home, particularly Up and perhaps finding a kindred spirit in Carl – and the damn bed again.

I stood up slowly.

My gaze followed the geometric pattern that crisscrossed the comforter, all the way to where the pillows lay. *Our heads will be there, only a few inches apart.* Everything I was feeling was slowly replaced by a weird mix of anticipation and something . . . new.

I needed to keep my cool. It was just a bed. We were two adults who could sleep next to each other. We were . . . friends now? No, I didn't think we were. But we were not just colleagues either. Even forgetting about the fact that he'd soon be my boss, I didn't think we only qualified as two people who worked together, argued on a regular basis, and struggled to tolerate each other for more than ten minutes. Our deal – this love deception game we were playing – had pushed us out of that meticulously labelled area we had been in. Shoved us right into a completely new and uncharted territory. And now, we were more than whatever we had been. We were ...

We were about to share a bed. That was the only thing I knew for sure.

That, and the fact that I needed to stop overthinking it. What I needed to be was ... unaffected. Yeah. If we were going to share a bed, I needed to stop behaving like it was a big deal. Even if it was. Because it motherfreaking was. Aaron had been showing me just how much with his soft but unwinding touches and these little pieces of himself that were just as provoking.

What had Rosie told me once?

'Set your goal free into the universe. Visualize it.'

That was exactly what I needed to do.

So, I visualized myself as impassive. Unconcerned. Unimpressed. I was a block of ice in the middle of a blizzard. I'd stand solidly. Immovable and cold and calm.

Yeah.

Walking to the closet with that in mind, I pulled out my pyjamas, which consisted of shorts and an old T-shirt with *Science Rocks* in bold yellow letters. A part of me regretted not putting more thought into it now that the room arrangement situation had changed. Another much smaller part thought that Aaron would appreciate the message in the shirt. That maybe he would give me one of those lopsided smirks that—

No. Those were not thoughts a block of ice would have.

Aaron walked out of the bathroom in silence, still dressed in his button-down, which now had two new undone buttons – which, I reminded myself, did not affect me – and headed directly to his side of the closet. Returning the silence, I slipped into the bathroom, so I could change and wash up.

Once done with that and clad in my jammies, I filled my lungs with a deep and hopefully energizing breath and returned to the bedroom.

I didn't know what I had expected to find, but I was surely not prepared for the sight of Aaron in only a pair of sleeping pants. They hung low on his hips – so low that I could see the waistband of his underwear – and they were a dark shade of gray that complemented his skin.

My gaze trailed up, and there it was. That glorious chest that I had witnessed shining under the sun with droplets of sweat that—

Jesus, no, no, no.

I needed to stop gawking. Eating him with my eyes as if I had never seen a naked chest before. It couldn't be healthy. Good for my mental health.

Turning away from him a little too briskly, I fumbled with my discarded clothes. Out of the corner of my eye, I watched him slip on a short-sleeved shirt.

Good. That was definitely good. *Cover those chiselled pecs and abs, stupidly flawless man who loves Up.*

I opened the drawer of the narrow dresser and stared into it. Realizing I didn't need anything from there, I closed it again. I threw open one of the wardrobe doors and realized the same damn thing. Cursing under my breath at my evident show of stupidity, I sensed Aaron move behind me.

My hands twisted the clothes I was holding into a ball.

A soft brush on the back of my arm derailed my inner pep talk, immediately lighting on fire my attempts to convince myself I was *cool* and *unaffected*.

'What's wrong?' He skimmed those fingers up and down the back of my arm. 'You are fidgeting.'

'Nothing is wrong. I'm okay,' I lied, and I heard my own voice shake. 'I'm . . . cool.'

I so wasn't.

Aaron flickered his fingers one last time across my skin as I remained with my back to him. It felt like he was waiting for something, and when the silence that followed my comment stretched, he sighed. 'I'll sleep on the floor.'

His voice had sounded all wrong, so I finally turned to face him. He was walking away, so I reached for his arm, wrapping my slender fingers around his wrist. I could feel his pulse against my skin.

'Don't,' I whispered. 'I told you, you don't have to. We will sleep on the bed. Both of us.' I swallowed the lump that had formed in my throat. 'That's not what I'm worried about.' And that wasn't a complete lie. I knew that Aaron would gladly sleep with half his body hanging off that bed if I so much as looked slightly uncomfortable. Hell, he'd sleep on the floor if I let him. 'I'm just . . .' I shook my head, not knowing how to finish that statement. Not daring to.

It's not you in bed with me that I'm scared of, I wanted to tell him. It's me and everything that's going on inside my head and that stupid organ in the center of my chest – that's what I'm scared of. It's me and what I could possibly let myself do, that I'm terrified of. It's this whole charade we have been executing that is messing with everything I thought I knew.

It hadn't even been a day since we had landed in Spain, and I felt like everything between Aaron and me had changed more in twenty hours than it ever had in almost two years.

How could that be possible?

'Tell me what's going on inside your head; you can trust me.' He lifted his free hand and cupped my face in his palm. 'Let me show you that you can trust me.'

Oh God, I wanted to let him do that. Badly.

But it felt like jumping off a cliff. Bold. Too reckless. It petrified me.

Meeting his gaze, I realized I could drown in the blue of his eyes if I allowed myself to. Which only fuelled my fear. Long gone was that block of ice I had preached about a handful of minutes ago.

That simple gesture – his warm hand cupping my cheek – melted me to the ground. Dissolved me into nothing more than water. He had that power over me.

'I don't know how.' I leaned my face into his palm. Just for a heartbeat. That was all I allowed myself.

Then, Aaron's touch was gone, and the forgotten clothes that I still held under one arm were snagged out of my grip. He placed them somewhere else. The floor, the dresser, the bed – I didn't know, and I didn't care. Not when a very particular emotion had solidified in his gaze. Determination.

Deep in my gut, I knew he was going to show me that I could trust him. That perhaps I could jump, and it would be okay. That maybe he wouldn't let me drown like I felt I would.

Something settled in the air around us. Something thick and sultry changed the atmosphere in the small room.

'Close your eyes,' he requested. Although it hadn't been a question. Not really.

It didn't matter because my eyelids fell immediately shut.

For the first time in my life, I did exactly as Aaron had said without putting up a fight. Not a single bone in my body was willing to do anything else but follow his directions. Letting him show me whatever he was after.

Taking the weight of answering his question off my hands.

Eyes closed, I felt him stepping closer, his proximity like a warm blanket I wanted to wrap myself in.

With each lingering moment that passed, where I waited, every other sense gradually heightened. I could hear my heavy breathing, feel my chest heaving up and down, sense the way my blood was being pumped through my body, reaching my temples with growing intensity. I could feel the warmth radiating off Aaron's large body in waves that seemed to be in perfect sync with my heartbeat.

And as his silence crowded the space between us, I kept waiting. In the darkness that had swallowed me, I anticipated his words, his touch, his next move like I had never anticipated anything in my life. Like I was ready to come out of my skin if he didn't follow up that first command. Hating and relishing in every second that separated me from whatever was going to come next.

'Once, I told you I was patient.' Aaron's breath fell on my temple, sending a rush of sensation along the back of my neck. 'That I wasn't scared to work hard for what I wanted.'

Closer. He was much closer than I'd thought, his proximity warming my skin even though not a part of our bodies touched. I could change that. I only needed to lift my hand, and I could be brushing those lips that were so close to my ear with my fingers. Or I could push him away and end this torture.

But then he continued, 'I might not have been completely honest.'

I did neither of those two things. My hand didn't reach out or push him away. Instead, I let the anticipation simmer in my blood. I let him take that choice away from me. And just as if he could read me like an open book, he did exactly that.

His lips *finally* brushed the skin right beneath my ear, triggering an outbreak of shivers that ran down my body, not sparing a single inch of flesh. 'It's becoming really hard to make myself wait.' Another pass of his lips over the same patch of skin. 'You are very close to driving me out of my mind.'

A humourless chuckle left his lips then, the soft puff of air caressing and tickling my skin too. I sensed him come a step closer, and my heart raced.

'But I am a man of my word.'

My breath hitched in my throat when his lips came into contact with my neck once more, that time remaining there a heart-beat longer.

Aaron's fingers trailed up my arm, reaching the other side of my neck and cupping my face. Just how he had done earlier. 'Do you want me to step away?' His thumb grazed my jaw slowly.

My lips parted, and all I managed was a weak shake of my head.

An approving *hmm* left Aaron. That sound alone did crazy, dangerous things to my belly.

'You want my touch then.'

I did. Oh God, did I ever. But—

'Good.'

His fingers trickled down my throat, reaching the neckline of my sleeping T-shirt, liquefying every rational thought. But there was a warning in my head somewhere, something I should be remembering.

'Aaron,' I whispered.

The contact of his skin against mine was so gentle, so impossibly delicate, and yet it had the power to make me lose my mind. To ignite something in me. Just how he had proven ever since the fundraiser.

'Aaron,' I repeated.

His fingers halted, lifting off my skin right above my collarbone. I felt the loss of his touch immediately.

'What are we doing?' I asked, sounding desperate to my own ears. I released all the air in my lungs very slowly, grieving the way I had felt a heartbeat ago. But this was important. I had to say something to feel safer. To make sense of this. Otherwise, I'd sink under my own weight. I knew I would. 'Is this . . . still pretending?' I swallowed. I hated my own words, but I couldn't stop myself. 'Is this just for practice?'

A loud voice in my head yelled at me to shut up. Not to ruin the moment and to let myself take as much as Aaron was willing to give me. But the truth was that I was terrified. Deep in my bones, I was shaking. Beneath all the ways my body kept reacting to every touch and word and craving more and more all the ones to come, there festered fear.

I felt Aaron's sigh on my skin, and I was tempted to reach out and latch on to him before he stepped away. I had probably ruined everything.

But he didn't.

'Would that make you feel better? I'll pretend a little longer, if that's what you need.'

'Yes.' The word left my lips in a rush.

I knew I'd come to regret saying that, probably sooner than later. This was a dangerous game. But in that moment, the only thing that seemed to matter was the safe bubble I had created around us. The lifeline I had begged him to throw me, and I was holding on to for dear life. If I inspected Aaron's words too closely, I'd open my eyes, my brain would start functioning again, and our mouths would be busy talking.

His lips fell on my skin once more, resuming where they had stopped. His mouth skimmed along my jaw, and my heart seemed to come back alive in my chest, making me realize I hadn't really noticed how it had ceased to beat without his touch. 'I don't think I'd be able to deny you a single thing if you asked, Catalina.'

He followed that with one openmouthed kiss against the side of my neck, almost ripping a whimper out of me.

My eyelids must have fluttered because Aaron said, 'No. Don't open them yet.'

And I didn't. I couldn't. Aaron was in absolute control of my body now.

'Good girl. Keep them closed.' He brushed another openmouthed kiss as a reward. 'We'll play this game a little longer.'

My stomach plummeted to my feet in response.

'For practice purposes,' he said, and the hand that was cupping my head started trailing down, down, down over my clothes, stopping on my waist and leaving a burning path behind. It sent my head spinning. 'I can show you exactly what it would be like.'

I felt him fisting the fabric of my shirt, as if he was stopping himself from doing more. Then releasing it and returning his palm to my waist.

'If you were *really* mine, I'd do this all the time.' His long fingers draped around my hip and pushed me against him from the waist down. Hot – he felt so hot and hard, branding my skin, even with layers of fabric separating us.

'If you were mine, you'd crave this.' He then closed the rest of the distance that separated us very slowly. Bringing our bodies flush together with such softness and at such a painful pace that I praised and cursed him at the same time. 'You'd welcome this. You would want it.'

And wasn't I doing all those things?

Before I could delve into that, Aaron's large body shifted, and my back was against a hard surface. My hand travelled across it absently. The wardrobe. He was caging me against what felt like the wardrobe door, and I didn't know how we had ended up there. Not really. But he was pressing deliciously into me, sheltering me from the world around us. Like the human-sized shield he had shown me he could be for me. Rooting me to the ground and sending my senses flying all at once. So, I didn't care. Instead, my body craved more contact. It throbbed for more.

'If I were yours, I would not be capable of functioning without touching you.' His words made something in my chest constrict. 'I couldn't go a few minutes without doing this,' he added, squeezing my waist with his hand and slipping his thumb below my sleeping shirt, robbing me of the following breath. 'Or something like this.' Aaron stepped further into me, pressing his hips against mine.

A helpless whimper left me.

The runaway thumb that had snuck below the fabric of my shirt trailed a few inches up my side, rumpling my shirt on its way.

A very shaky exhale escaped my lips. I couldn't do much

more than that, hardly breathing, barely surviving until the next touch. Every nerve in my body felt like it was about to be lit on fire. My blood boiled, burning every vessel and organ in its path. Everything burned.

I thought a new whimper had escaped me because I was rewarded with another openmouthed kiss. This time on my temple. Then, Aaron's lips travelled down the side of my face, the air leaving them warm and enticing.

His mouth stopped at my eyelids, still shut, and he held his lips above them for a second. It wasn't a kiss; it was more of a featherlight touch. And, God, that soft brush of his lips alone was so sweet, so fucking tender that it made me want to weep.

He continued down, stopping at my nose and repeating the soft caress.

Then, he did it to my right cheek. My left cheek. My chin.

Aaron left soft kisses everywhere he stopped, turning me inside out.

Pure, unfiltered need pulsated through my body with every inch of skin his lips travelled over. And when they reached the corner of my mouth, I felt like I would detonate like a bomb if he didn't touch me there too. If he didn't brush his lips over mine and kiss me.

I felt the large and masculine body that pressed against me sigh. His lips hovering above mine.

Breaking my restraint, my hand lifted and landed on his upper arm, which I discovered was braced against the wardrobe surface, right next to my head. Barely able to take ahold of his flexed biceps, I wrapped my fingers as well as I could around the hot and tense skin. Everything strained and tightened under my touch. And I wondered if he was holding himself back, holding back from wrapping both arms around me and lifting me in the air. Perhaps pressing me harder into his body. Or doing more than just leaving featherlight kisses and soft brushes of his fingers.

Unsure if what he needed was my encouragement, I increased the pressure of my hold on his arm. My nails dug into his skin.

A deep and throaty sound left Aaron's mouth, landing right between my legs. Just where all the ever-growing need had gathered.

I latched on to his arm harder, my body arching into him unconsciously, barely able to contain myself any longer. I was very close to begging, and I would if I had to. In response, Aaron came a little closer. Pressed against me a little harder.

I could feel him throbbing against my belly.

'Lina.' My name left his lips like a soft prayer. Or a warning. I wasn't sure. 'I'm going to kiss you.'

His words fell on my lips, close, so close. So, I was left with no option but to increase the pressure of my fingers around his arm, so I wouldn't dissolve right there. To slip away and disappear before I could touch him. And I wanted to so badly. His neck, his lips, his jaw, the little wrinkle between his brows – everything. I wanted to slip my fingers through his raven hair and run them down his chest, all the way to his thick thighs.

I wanted Aaron to deliver his promise. I wanted him to kiss me.

Another brief touch of his lips, this time against mine. Soft, full, sweet, just like honey running down my mouth. I wanted – no, I needed – more.

'Please, Aar—'

A door slamming shut somewhere in the apartment startled the plea out of my lips. Aaron's mouth pulled back from mine before I even properly tasted him, my eyes falling back open.

I was welcomed by the image of a man on the brink of losing control. His gaze was hazy, clouded by the same need that was pumping through my bloodstream.

Aaron's forehead fell on mine. I watched his chest heave, hauling air in and out of his lungs with effort. Just like mine was doing. And we remained in silence for a long moment, surrounded by only the sound of our wild and unrestrained breathing.

'You called me Lina.' Out of everything that had just happened, that was what my foggy brain decided to go with. 'You never do. You only have once before.'

Still resting on my forehead, Aaron's head shook against mine. Very briefly. Then, a breathy laugh reached my ears. It made me smile.

But that part of my brain that was supposed to work out all the rational reasoning came back to life, wiping that smile off my face.

Holy shit. We almost kissed.

Aaron had warned me he'd kiss me, and then he almost had. The man whose arms and body were currently caging me against a wardrobe had tortured me with his fingertips, his mouth, and then he had almost kissed me. Right after he called me Lina. But—

'Oh my God,' I whispered. 'What the hell was that noise?'

Aaron lifted his head slightly, just enough for me to be able to watch how his eyes moved across my face, bouncing from every spot he had brushed his lips over to the next, as if he couldn't decide where to set camp. Eventually stopping at my lips. Some- thing that looked a lot like pain flashed across his expression. 'Your cousin, I hope.'

Charo.

Of course. That . . . made sense.

Aaron sobered up slowly, his expression eventually going back to normal. 'I'll go check,' he announced before ripping himself off me.

My body grieved the loss almost immediately, feeling cold and unbalanced without him.

Willing my legs to remain strong, I limited myself to following Aaron's march to the door, feeling numb and all over the place. He looked back at me right before he opened it.

'Catalina.' There it was again. Not Lina. *Catalina.* 'I'm glad I didn't kiss you.'

Something halted in my chest.

'Why?' The word was nothing more than a shaky whisper.

'Because when I finally take those lips in mine, it will be the furthest thing from pretending. I will not be showing you what it would be like if you were mine. I'll show you what it is. And I sure as hell won't be showing how good I could make you feel if you called me yours. You'll already know that I am.'

He paused, and I swore I could see the restraint in his posture. As if he was stopping himself from pouncing and returning us to our former position, right against the hard surface of the wardrobe door.

'When I finally kiss you, there won't be any doubt in your mind that it is real.'

CHAPTER TWENTY

The moment my eyes popped open to the glorious darkness that only a country where blinds were religiously installed could provide, I knew I wasn't in my bed.

For one, I was used to waking up to bright beams of sunlight flooding my studio apartment. Then, there was the surface beneath me. It felt different. Softer and bouncier than the one my body was accustomed to. Same went for the pillow where my head rested – too flat and low.

But what really screamed at me that this wasn't my bed – that I wasn't in my apartment in Bed-Stuy, Brooklyn – was the dead weight currently resting on my waist. It was heavy and warm and felt a lot like an oversized limb that surely couldn't belong to me.

The drumming occurring in almost every corner of my head was probably not helping me get any clarity on what was responsible for that vice around my body. Or why I wasn't in the comfort of my room, rolling on a mattress that had made it worth punching a hole in my bank account.

Blinking a few times as I brushed some of the sleepy locks of hair off my face, my eyes adjusted to the darkness.

My gaze searched for whatever was behind the weight on my midsection.

An arm. Just as I had suspected. It was dusted with dark hair and corded with muscle. So, it wasn't mine. My eyes followed that muscular and long limb all the way up until reaching the very masculine shoulder it was attached to. A shoulder that led to a strong neck that ended in a head that—

Mierda.

The owner of all those body parts I had been studying in the darkness shifted. I froze. That robust and heavy arm that was latched to my waist moved slightly, his hand partially slipping beneath my shirt. All five fingers splayed on my skin.

My breath got stuck somewhere between my throat and mouth.

Do not fucking move, Catalina, I ordered myself.

But it was hard when those fingers felt so hot against my skin, causing my whole body to tingle.

Only a few inches separated me from Aaron.

Aaron. Last night.

A series of F-bombs were dropped, blasting across my mind as blurry images flashed through my head.

No, no, no, no.

Those fingers brushed my skin again, and a deep and throaty noise left the man sleeping beside me.

A dream. All those images had to have been a dream because we couldn't have almost kissed. That was completely crazy. That was—

At the fastest pace known to man, all the events from last night solidified. They tumbled down my memory, flashing behind my eyes and making me recall every last one of them. Each and every one of those images, snippets – memories – replayed in my mind in painfully slow motion.

All the *sidra*. Aaron's fabricated story about how we had started dating. The way his eyes had been locked on me all through the night. Us dancing in the middle of a dark club with sticky floors, lost among the sea of bodies. My freak-out. Aaron sitting with me on the sidewalk, taking care of me, telling me about himself. Opening up and laying out a piece of himself for me. Him pressing me against the wardrobe. My body coming alive – being lit on fire – with all those featherlight brushes of his lips and fingers. *Lina. Aaron had called me Lina.* Right before he brushed his lips over mine.

We had almost kissed.

No. I had almost begged Aaron to kiss me, and I would have done more than just that.

'*When I finally kiss you, there won't be any doubt in your mind that it is real,*' He had said that before going to check if what had burst our bubble of madness was Charo.

And I had lain on the bed and passed out immediately.

Fuck, fuck. Mierda, joder.

I needed to get out of this bed. I needed time to think, to process. Away from Aaron. Before I did something stupid. Or reckless. Something like almost kissing him.

A low groan climbed up my throat, and I had no other choice but to muffle it with my hand. The sudden motion made the mattress bounce under me.

Shit.

Aaron stretched beside me.

Don't wake up, please. Please, universe. God. Anyone. I just need a couple of minutes to gather myself before I have to face him.

I felt Aaron's body settle back, his breathing remaining deep and constant.

Returning my hand back to my sides – very fucking slowly – I thanked the universe for listening to me this one time and promised I'd make up for it. I'd go to church with Abuela next time I came home, I swore.

I was being a complete chicken, but I wanted a few minutes to myself. Just so I could appease everything that kept darting through my mind. To make peace with it and move on like nothing had ever happened. Also, to hunt down a painkiller and kill the throbbing in my head. Coffee would be good too.

And the first step was getting the hell out of this bed – from under the arm I had desperately been gripping for dear life only a few hours ago – as fast and as quietly as I possibly could before Aaron's eyes opened and found me losing my shit.

Lifting Aaron's heavy limb as delicately and slowly as I could, I rolled to the side, right to the edge of the bed, and then I deposited his muscular body part back onto the comforter. Aaron moved, turning on his back and lifting that arm that had been on top of me so it rested behind his head.

That position caused his biceps to flex and look all big and delectable and—

Jesus Christ, Catalina.

Pulling my eyes off the man on the bed, I moved through the room on my tiptoes. I made my way out and closed the door behind me. My head fell against the wooden surface, and my eyes closed.

'Vaya, vaya. Mira quién ha amanecido,' a high-pitched voice welcomed me from outside the kitchen. *'Buenos días, prima.'*

The blood in my body froze.

I couldn't catch a freaking break.

My lips curled into a forced smile. *'Hola, Charo. Buenos días,'* I greeted her, straightening my back and trying to look the furthest from someone who had just snuck out of a room.

I walked into the kitchen, keeping my steps breezy and casual. Passing my cousin as she stood rooted to the white tiles, studying my every move, I proceeded to open cabinets and drawers, looking for the coffee beans so I could at least caffeinate my brain before Charo started the questioning. Or Aaron woke up and I had to face him.

'He dejado una cafetera preparada,' Charo chimed behind me.

She had prepared coffee for me. That could only mean one thing: she was up to something. *'Está ahí, mujer. En la encimera.'* Coffee was on the countertop.

With my back still to her, I muttered my thanks and proceeded to pour some black goodness into a mug.

Much to the displeasure of my hungover head – but not any surprise – she continued with her monologue before I could even take the first sip.

'*Hay suficiente para ti y para tu novio.*' There was enough coffee for me and my boyfriend, she told me. '*Imagino que no tardará en despertarse ¿no? Oye si quieres ir a llamarle para que no se enfríe el café . . .*' Charo went on.

If she was trying to get me to go and fetch Aaron so the coffee she had prepared wouldn't get cold, she had another thing coming. The coffee would spontaneously turn into ice cubes before I willingly went back inside that room.

'*Menuda sensación ha causado en la familia. Tu madre no podía parar de . . .*' And then she proceeded to tell me about *when* and *how* and *what* had been said about my – fake – boyfriend, Aaron, in the mere twenty-four hours he'd been in the country.

Which had been a lot, considering the short amount of time.

That was exactly why having Charo sharing accommodations with us was so dangerous. She had no social filters of any kind and no regard for privacy. I was genuinely shocked she wasn't thrusting herself into our room and plundering my fake boyfriend out of bed, so she could continue her perusal.

Charo's chatter kept filling the kitchen as I nodded my head absently. '*Y justo como le dije a tu madre, llegará un día en el que Lina tendrá que superar lo de Daniel.*' Just how I told your mom, one day, Lina will have to get over Daniel. '*Sino se va a quedar para vestir santos y . . .*'

Jesus, my cousin had just used that Spanish expression I hated so much. The one I had heard directed at me more than once, always muttered or whispered, or just like she had done, loud and clear. *Se va a quedar para vestir santos.* Which literally translated as something about dressing saints and meant that I'd stay single and dedicate my life to God for the rest of my life.

Feeling completely defenceless, standing all alone with my cousin, I couldn't decide if sleepy Aaron was a blessing or a curse anymore. Yesterday, when he had been with me, facing Charo, my sister, Daniel, and everybody else, it had been unexpectedly easier than it was now on my own.

I realized now that as much as I had brought him to Spain with that particular purpose, I had never truly expected that it would work. Or that we'd become a team. That he'd instill strength in me – even if I'd use it to lie to my family – or that he'd make me feel like I wasn't alone in this.

And the scariest, most terrifying part was that all that was starting to bleed through the lines that defined our deal. In a little over a day.

The proof was last night. We had almost kissed. We had done more than just that. More than practising or pretending.

Crazy. It was crazy, but it was also true. I was honest enough to admit that to myself.

But that didn't mean I was brave enough to acknowledge it out loud. I was still the coward who had walk-of-shamed her way out of that room like her ass was on fire before I was forced to have a conversation.

And I'd do that again.

Aaron would soon become my boss, and that would change everything. Having him here – in Spain, in my home country, attending my sister's wedding as my fake date – was already dangerous. It was reason enough for me to shake in my boots at the prospect of someone at work finding out. It didn't have anything to do with a weird company policy or with me having a pet peeve. I had already been involved with someone where a supervisory relationship between us had existed, where I had not been the one in the position of authority. And where had that led me? To being the only one having to deal with the dirty and poisonous tongues that hadn't thought twice before stigmatizing me and everything I had worked so hard for. Just for what? For a few laughs? For pointing a few fingers? For bringing me down, so they'd feel a little better?

History could repeat itself, and this time, I would be the one to blame. It would be me who had tripped over the same stone for a second time. This time, I'd be jeopardizing my career, too, not just the credibility of my work, my reputation as a woman, or my social life. And it would all be on *me*.

Taking another sip of coffee from my mug, I tried to shove all that aside.

Whatever I thought was going on between Aaron and me would have to ... not go. Anywhere.

Because it couldn't. It wouldn't. And it was all a lie anyway.

As if the very devil was being summoned by Charo, who kept talking about him, or by me, who kept thinking about him one way or the other, Aaron materialized in the kitchen. His eyes immediately found me, as if I were the only thing between these four walls.

My mug froze midair. My lips parted, and my gaze was hungry to take all of him in. But how could I not? The simple tee that covered his broad chest did nothing to hide a body I now knew had been carefully cultivated to perfection for years. Decades. Those loose pyjama pants I had seen hanging low on his hips last night still did so. Enticing me. Making me think of how he had pressed those hips into me with painfully delicious softness.

But it was the look on his face that started – no, rekindled – the fluttering sensation in the pit of my stomach. His features were seemingly snug with sleep, relaxed, and his hair was adorably ruffled. But his eyes ... well, there wasn't a trace of sleep there. They told a whole different story. One I had the strong suspicion was extremely similar to the one bubbling in mine.

And that only encouraged the flutter to take flight and spread to the rest of my body.

Averting my gaze before all this gawking and daydreaming damaged my brain, I forced my lungs to take in the oxygen my body seemed to need in that moment.

'*Ay!*' Charo's screech made me flinch. '*Mira quién está aquí!* Good morning, Aaron. We were just talking about you.'

Peeking at Aaron, I saw his eyes widen and then quickly return to its normal size.

'Good morning,' he said into the room, looking still startled. It was cute. No, it was actually shocking that he had not spotted Charo's bright red hair like a beacon in the distance. 'I hope everything you guys were saying was good.' He accompanied that with a teeny-tiny, lopsided smile.

'Of course, of course.' Charo waved a hand in the air. 'We have been waiting for you to wake up. I bet Lina was missing you.'

My back stiffened, and Aaron's head whirled slowly in my direction.

Dammit, Charo. My lips curled in a tight smile that I hid with my mug.

My cousin continued, 'There is fresh coffee. Would you like some? Do you take it black? Would you like some milk with it? Perhaps sugar too? Brown or white? Or maybe you don't like coffee. Lina hasn't said anything, so I assumed you would have some. Unless you don't, of course. I won't force you to drink it.'

Aaron blinked, looking a little lost.

'You should get yourself a cup,' I muttered.

My fake boyfriend cleared his throat and walked in the direction of the coffeepot. 'I . . . I think I'll serve myself a cup. Thank you, Charo.'

Charo's answer was a satisfied grin.

Aaron poured himself some coffee, and before the man even finished filling his mug, Charo was at it again.

'So, did you have fun yesterday, *parejita*?' My cousin sang that last word. *Parejita* – little couple.

I rolled my eyes.

'I wish I could have made it, but I'm not young and wild anymore. Not like you guys. I hope the bed in your room is still standing after seeing how the other one ended up. Although I guess if that had happened, I would have definitely noticed. The walls are *veeeery* thin.' She followed that with a wink.

In the periphery of my vision, I watched Aaron wince. Couldn't blame him. I winced too.

'Anyway,' my cousin continued, 'you guys got home really late last night. I heard the front door closing.'

'Yes, we did. I'm sorry about that, Charo.' My gaze followed Aaron as he walked decidedly across the few feet that separated us, finally settling on one of the three high stools placed around the narrow breakfast bar. Right beside where I had sat down myself.

'*Ay no*, don't worry about it,' I heard my cousin say as I kept my eyes on my fake boyfriend's movements. 'It did not bother me. I was actually happy to know you had made it back safely.'

Aaron scooted his stool closer to mine, and his scent hit me like a freaking moving truck, plunging me back to last night, when it had completely engulfed me. My eyelashes fluttered, and I had to avert my gaze.

'Oh, okay. Good. That's good,' I absently told my cousin, feeling my cheeks flush.

'And I wake up a few times during the night anyway. I'm a light sleeper.' Charo's voice kept fading in the background as the knowledge of having Aaron's body within reach sank in. 'So, if you ever hear weird noises at night, it's just me walking around the apartment.' She chuckled. 'With a little bit of luck, I won't accidentally walk in on you naked or something.'

Naked. Aaron *naked*. My mind seemed to short-circuit the moment it ventured into that mental image, pushing me off my stool as if my ass were on fire.

Space. Air. I needed . . . something. Anything.

Not being able to go very far, considering the dimensions of the functional kitchen, I opened a couple of cabinets, making sure my back was to Aaron until all that blood that had somehow risen to my face returned to its original place.

I fanned myself with one of the cabinet doors. *Good, good. Better.*

Needing an excuse for my very unclassy getaway from the stool, I snatched a package of chocolate chip cookies.

'So, tell me everything, Aaron,' I heard Charo say behind me as I ripped open the cardboard. 'What do you think of our little hometown? I am sure it's very different from New York. We don't have skyscrapers or any of that, but there are plenty of places to visit. Nature, beautiful beaches. The coast is really amazing. Lots of stuff to do.' She paused, and I extracted one of the cookies from the package. 'How many days will you guys stay, by the way? I heard that you were here only for the wedding. That's such a shame! You should book a holiday and just—'

The doorbell rang, interrupting Charo.

'Oh, I'll get that,' my cousin announced quickly and then slipped out of the kitchen.

My eyes narrowed.

While I was busy wondering if we were expecting anybody, it took me by surprise when an arm – which I was starting to get very well acquainted with at this rate – snaked around my waist and pulled me backwards.

My ass landed on something hard and hot, immediately moulding into the space.

Aaron's lap.

His breath caressed the shell of my ear. 'You didn't say good morning.'

My back straightened as I remembered my lame runaway moment. 'You almost made me drop my cookie, Mr Robot.' It was so weird, so strange, calling him that, like I had done so many times in the past. As if that belonged to a whole different life. To two different people.

Aaron chuckled, and it tickled my neck. 'I wouldn't dare. I know better than that.'

His arm tightened around me, and I had to restrain myself from wrapping my hands around it.

'What are you doing?' I whispered loudly.

Charo would come back in at any second.

'I was feeling lonely,' he admitted, lowering his voice and making my mind fly with everything he wasn't saying.

Stupid. I need to stop being stupid.

'And if I'm going to sit through this one-sided interrogation, the least you can do is keep me company. Plus, you owe me a conversation.'

'I was right there.' My voice came out strangled. 'And Charo is not here now.'

He hmmed, and that noise travelled straight to my lower belly. 'She will be back though. You know I like to be extra prepared.'

I did. I knew him pretty damn well, I realized.

And just like that, with that thought floating around my mind, Charo's head popped up in my field of vision. Her eyes widened, and then her face broke into a ridiculously large smile.

Jesus.

She clapped her hands. 'Oh, look at you two! *Ay Dios mío.* You are adorable.'

Aaron's chest grumbled with a laugh, and I felt it in my back.

'See?' he whispered in my ear.

No, I didn't see shit, frankly. It was hard to focus on anything, being swaddled in Aaron's lap.

My mouth opened, but all words died when a second head popped up in the kitchen.

Charo turned in the direction of that second head topped with the same bright shade of red. *'¿No ves, Mamá? Te lo dije.'*

'Tía Carmen?' I mumbled. *'¿Qué haces aquí?'* What was Charo's mother doing here?

The woman, who was an older and rounder version of my cousin, pointed a finger at me. *'Venir a saludarte, tonta.'*

She was here to say hi? I doubted it. She'd see me at the wedding tomorrow.

My eyes turned to Charo, who had guilt written all over her face. She busied herself with something on the counter.

Aaron moved underneath me, his legs flexing and his hand holding my waist securely, just as if—

Whoa.

He stood up. 'We haven't met before,' he told my aunt. Then, he stepped forward. Somehow keeping my body in his delicate but skilled hold. 'I don't want you running for the closest exit,' he whispered in my ear.

What the—

'Soy Aaron. Encantado,' he said louder for my aunt. While keeping me tucked to him.

So, he was going to carry me around in his arms until I talked to him. About last night. About our almost kiss. My head swivelled back, eyes narrowed.

'No, no, no,' Tía Carmen called, stopping Aaron's advances in her direction. 'You can sit back down, *cariño*. No need of formalities. We are all family.'

Aaron obeyed, placing us both back on the stool immediately. Charo, who had been hovering around the kitchen during the exchange with my aunt, placed a tray on the breakfast bar. It contained fruit, cereals, nuts, a plate with all different kinds of cheese and *embutido*, and a few slices of bread too.

My eyes widened as I wondered how and when had that arrived at the apartment.

'I got a few groceries yesterday,' my cousin explained.

Cocking a brow, I zeroed in on her. That meant planning. 'Have you tried some *jamón*, Aaron?' she asked, ignoring my glance.

'I have. It's delicious but—'

Tía Carmen leaned on the table. 'Do you like chorizo too? This one is really good.'

'Here,' my cousin said, not waiting for his answer and serving him a few slices of both Spanish delicacies on a small plate. She placed it in front of us. 'Try it. I always buy the best kind.'

My fake boyfriend thanked her, probably staring at the plate and wondering if they actually listened when people talked. Taking pity on him, I patted his forearm, which was still around my waist.

'*Y qué intenciones tiene este chico con nuestra Linita?*' Tía Carmen asked my cousin as she snatched a slice of bread off the tray. *What intentions does he have with our little Lina?*

My jaw fell to the floor.

Charo seemed to think about it for a moment. '*No lo sé, Mamá.*' Her eyes zeroed in on the man behind – or rather beneath – me. 'Aaron, what are your intentions with Lina? You are not just fooling around, are you? What do you think about marriage? Because Lina is about to turn thirty and—'

'Charo,' I interrupted her. '*Ya basta,*' I hissed. 'And I'm only twenty-eight. Jesus.'

Aaron chuckled behind me. 'Marriage is one of my favourite institutions.'

My jaw hit the floor.

'I've always wanted to get married.'

My breath hitched, my mouth still hanging open.

'Have a bunch of kids. A dog too.'

Swallowing hard, I tried my best to conceal my pure shock. I tried to take ahold of my mind, which had wandered away with dangerous rose-tainted images, born of Aaron's words.

Fake. He's only saying what every family wants to hear.

And then he really went for it. 'We love dogs, don't we, *bollito*?'

Managing to pick up my jaw from the floor, I answered with a weak, 'Yeah.' Then, I shook my head and somehow recovered. 'That's why we'll have a bunch of them. Instead of kids.'

His chuckle tickled my ear.

'But there's plenty of time to talk about that,' I gritted out with a fake smile.

'*Ay que bien!* Dogs, babies, true love. Just in time before you are a little too old.' Charo clapped, and I shot her a look. '*Mujer, no te pongas así.*' *Don't be like that*, she said. 'Did you try that *jamón*, Aaron? If you ever get married and move to Spain, you'll have all the *jamón* you'd ever want.'

Move to Spain? Jesus, what did she want? To make me lose my shit?

My cousin continued, 'You see, Lina had to leave to America all those years ago because of everything that happened and—'

'Charo,' I cut her off, my breathing growing heavy. '*Déjalo ya, por favor,*' I begged her to drop it.

The doorbell rang again. And I muttered a not-so-quiet curse under my breath.

'Oh! They are here!' my cousin announced.

What? Who?

Then, she proceeded to link her arm with her mother's, and they slipped out of the kitchen together.

Aaron's hand squeezed my arm gently, and I released all the air in my lungs.

I was on edge after that. And I was going to ignore – no,

forget – his comment about marriage and kids and dogs because it was completely irrelevant.

And I did, as soon as his fingers trailed down to my wrist. The touch – the caress – so featherlike, so brief, but so very powerful that it created a riot of shivers to spread across my whole body.

'Relax,' he said in my ear. His fingers started moving in circles over the skin of my wrist. The brush of his fingers was lazy, calming. 'That's it,' he whispered as his fingertips kept flicking over my skin.

My shoulders gradually relaxed until my back settled completely against his front.

Aaron's chin rested on the top of my head, and then he said, 'We've got this.'

I wanted to believe him, to believe that we could fake date our way through this improvised family reunion today and then tomorrow. But as I finally surrendered and let my body fall into his, it felt like way more than just that. I realized a part of me didn't want to believe in just that. Because it felt right to be in this kitchen, sitting on his lap, while he brushed his fingers over the sensitive skin of my wrist as we endured my family's inappropriate antics.

We felt like a *we*, Aaron and I.

And when it was my mother's head coming into view, followed by my *abuela*, my *tía*, and Charo, that realization solidified somewhere in the middle of my chest. Like a brick or a block of cement. Heavy, firm, and really hard to ignore. But it was when Aaron briefly peeled himself off me – just long enough to introduce himself to my *abuela* – that I felt the brick click into place, inserting itself like a Tetris piece in a nook that had been waiting to be filled. And by the time he returned his arm to my waist and my body to his lap, just after he looked down and smiled that smile just for me, I knew with certainty that I'd never be able to get that damn brick out of there.

It was there to stay.

CHAPTER TWENTY-ONE

Surprisingly, everything was going smoothly. So far, no awkward or embarrassing moments had made me regret all my life choices, and no one had dropped any inappropriate questions that made me want to open a hole in the ground and plunge myself in.

With a little luck, I would even be able to get through this one dinner unscathed. And I really thought I would.

I hoped this sense of contentment humming satisfactorily under my skin wasn't a by-product of the food I had devoured. Because that was what a Spanish feast could do to you. It could cloud your judgment.

We were all sitting at a round table on the terrace of a restaurant that faced the sea. The sun was setting on the horizon, about to reach the thin line where the ocean and the sky met, and the only sound filling the air around us besides the low chatter was the crashing of the waves against the rocks lining the coast.

To put it in a simple way, it was perfect.

The soft touch of a hand on my arm sent a handful of shivers rolling down my spine.

'Cold?' a deep voice I had come to anticipate in ways that made my breath hitch asked close to my ear.

Shaking my head, I faced him. Only a few inches separated us. Our lips.

'No, I'm fine.' I wasn't fine. I had learned that when Aaron came this close, I was everything but fine. 'Just full. I might have overdone it.'

'No place for dessert?'

My eyebrows bunched at the audacity. 'Don't be ridiculous, *osito*. I always have space for dessert. Always.'

Aaron's lips curled up, and his smile reached the corners of his eyes, transforming his whole face.

Wowie. I hadn't been prepared for it, if the butterflies in my stomach were any indication.

'Lina, Aaron, more wine?' my dad asked from the other side of the table.

My parents had insisted we order wine even if the wedding was tomorrow – where alcohol would certainly flow in rivers of *sidra*, wine, *cava*, and whatnot. Nobody had tried to complain. Not even Isabel or Gonzalo, whose faces displayed the repercussions of our almost all-nighter. But in the land of wine, one simply didn't go to dinner and not order a bottle.

'No, thanks. I think I'm going to save myself for tomorrow,' I answered, removing my glass from my dad's reach. The bottle had already been hovering midair.

Unlike me, Aaron was too slow. So, before he could muster his answer, my dad was already refilling his glass.

'You snooze, you lose,' I whispered, leaning in his direction.

That bright smile that had taken over his face returned, throwing me off my game in the blink of an eye. And then the arm that had been around the back of my seat stretched, and he playfully pinched my side.

I jumped in my seat, almost knocking a few glasses off the table.

Aaron's other hand reached for his wine, bringing it to his lips. 'Don't be cute,' he said over his glass, pinning me with a look that made me shift in my chair. Then, he dipped his head and lowered his voice. 'Next time, I'll do more than just pinch you.' His lips finally met the glass, taking a sip.

Keeping my eyes on his lips for a few intense seconds, I was sure something had just popped in the vicinity of my female reproductive parts.

Cheeks flushed, I swivelled my head, searching for any evidence that someone at the table had heard that. My *abuela* was still busy cleaning her plate off. Gonzalo and Isabel seemed about to pass out from exhaustion and most likely a food coma by the time we reached dessert. My parents chitchatted animatedly with a waiter I hadn't even realized was standing by our table. And Daniel – who had come alone because his and Gonzalo's parents were arriving early tomorrow – was looking down at his phone like it held the secrets of the universe.

That day weeks ago, when I had untruthfully declared that I was dating a man after being told that Daniel was engaged and happier than ever, I had done it in panic after picturing a scene almost identical to the one we'd found ourselves in. Except that the chair next to me would have been empty. Or occupied by someone else like my *abuela* or Daniel's fiancée, knowing my luck. Or hey, maybe it would have been that escort I had briefly considered hiring. But either way, it would have been someone who didn't make my heart race with nothing more than a look or my belly tumble with one of those smiles that I was beginning to covet just for myself.

So, as I looked in Daniel's direction, I realized a few things. First and foremost, my gut reaction to lie and thrust myself – and Aaron – into this ludicrous plan had been, perhaps, a little excessive. Then, there was the fact that despite being excessive, having Aaron with me had made everything easier in a way that I would never have fathomed. And last – and I struggled with wrapping my head around this one – there was a considerable part of me, one that I was trying really hard to ignore but failing to do so, that didn't regret any of it.

And that was extremely dumb of me. Because the man I found

myself flushing around – and not regretting having by my side – would soon become my boss.

'So, Aaron,' my mother said, returning me back to the present, 'Isabel explained how you two met and started dating.' Her eyes sparkled, and I bet it had to do more with the wine. 'That story you told them last night in the *sidrería*. It sounded so romantic, just like one of those movies we watch on *the Netflix*.'

Of course, my mother would veer the conversation in that direction.

'It's just Netflix, Mamá,' I muttered, playing with my hands on the table. 'And yeah. A proper office romance, just like in the movies, right?'

'Only this one is real,' Aaron said.

Real.

His words came rushing back into my mind. '*I talked her into believing that she needed me. Then, I showed her – proved to her – that she did.*'

My heart tumbled down my chest.

'So, how much do you two actually work together?' My mother's gaze was directed at Aaron, an inquisitive smile on her lips that told me she was dying to know everything there was to know.

'We both lead different teams, and we don't work on the same projects, but we see each other often.' He sent me a side-glance. 'And if we don't, I make sure we do. I try to catch her on her break, steal a glance or two in the hallways, pass by her office without having an excuse. Anything that will put me in her head for just a few moments a day.'

I dipped my head, staring at my empty plate. Was that true? Aaron had had a way of popping up out of thin air. But had that been intentional? Even if it was to get on my nerves. I was beginning to struggle with something as simple as telling apart what was real from what wasn't. Everything that left Aaron's mouth was based on reality – us working together, us knowing each other for almost two years. And then it had an element of deceit – us dating, being in love. But everything else, everything that somehow lay between those two sides – all those ornaments he hung off both truth and deceit – belonged to a gray area I did not know how to define.

'*Qué maravilloso.*' My mother beamed.

Then, she translated what Aaron had said for Abuela, and the old woman I owed my slightly frizzy hair to beamed too. Honestly, Abuela had been charmed by Aaron since the moment he had greeted her with two kisses and told her how proud she must be of her granddaughter. Which, in turn, had turned me into a beaming idiot too.

'You know,' my dad chipped in, 'not everyone is able to handle our Lina. She has the biggest heart in the family, but she can be a little . . .' He trailed off, one of his eyebrows rising on his forehead. '*Ay*, what's the word in English?' My dad paused, his lips puckered with frustration. 'She can be—'

'A total dork?' suggested Isabel, who had just – very conveniently – come back from the dead.

'¡*Oye!*' I exclaimed.

At the same time, my dad answered, 'No. Not that one.' He scratched the side of his head.

'Short?' offered Gonzalo. 'Clumsy?'

My head whipped in his direction.

Aaron hmmed. 'Ridiculously stubborn?'

Not bothering to turn toward him, I rammed my elbow into his side. He gently grabbed my arm and laced our fingers together, placing them on top of the table. I stared at our linked hands, all outrage immediately vanishing.

Then, Aaron dipped his head and told me in a low voice, 'I didn't want to be left out.'

I looked over at him and found yet another of those smiles that made me weak in the knees. Something fluttered low in my belly.

'*Gracias*, all of you,' I murmured.

My dad kept searching his mind for whatever word it was that he couldn't remember. 'It isn't any of those words. Just let me think.'

Daniel cleared his throat, finally taking part in the conversation. 'What if you tell us the word in Spanish, and we can translate it, Javier?' he suggested.

My mom nodded her head. '*Claro, usa el Google, Javier.*' Use the Google, Javier.

'Papá,' I told him with a sigh, 'just let it go—'

'Firecracker,' he blurted out. 'Our Lina is a little firecracker.' All right. That was actually not that bad.

'So, she can be too much to handle. Often.'

Oh. I deflated a little in my chair, my hand remaining in Aaron's.

'She's always chattering like she has too much to say and not enough time to do so. Or laughing like she doesn't care she'll wake up the half of the world that's sleeping. She can also be a little defi-ant, and God knows she is stubborn as they come. But that's all fire. Passion. That's what makes her our Lina. Our little *terremoto*.' Our little earthquake.

My dad's eyes started shining under the light of the few lamps that had switched on as we entered the night. Something in my chest constricted.

'And for a while there, it wasn't like that. All that lightness faded out, and seeing my daughter going through something like that wasn't easy. It broke our hearts. Then, she left, and even if we knew it was what she wanted and needed to do, our hearts broke a little further.'

Tears were rushing to my eyes by then, the pressure behind them increasing with every word from my father. With every memory he unearthed.

'But that's in the past. She's here now, and she's okay. Happy.' My mom reached out, taking my dad's hand in hers.

Not able to hold myself any longer, I stood up on shaky legs and walked around the table. When I reached my dad, I wrapped him in a hug and kissed his cheek. *'Te quiero, Papá.'* Then, I did the same with my mother. *'A ti también, tonta.'* All the while, I held my tears in as if my life depended on it. I wouldn't cry. I refused to. 'Now, stop it, okay? Both of you. Save something for tomorrow.'

When I returned to my seat, I watched my hand reaching for Aaron's. As if it no longer conceived not being held in his. Absorbed by my own gesture, my heart flopped in my chest when his hand met mine midway, linking our fingers and bringing them to his mouth to brush his lips over the back of my hand. It was all so fast that by the time it was over and our linked hands rested on top of the table, I wouldn't have known it had really happened if not for the scorching imprint of his lips on my skin.

My mother spoke next, returning my attention to her, 'It makes me so happy to have you home, *cariño.'* Then, her eyes landed on Aaron. 'To see you like this.' Her smile widened, the sadness vanishing.

A pang of guilt sliced my gut, followed by something sultry and dense. Something that tasted like regret and hope.

'For a moment there, I thought she wouldn't really bring you, Aaron. I even questioned if you were real.' She chuckled, and I swore my lungs stopped working for a heartbeat. Her gaze met mine, a light smile on her face. 'Don't look at me like that. You've never talked about anyone you were seeing or brought anyone home from New York the few times you came back. And it was all so . . . sudden.'

'Honestly, *hermanita,*' Isabel pitched in, sounding suspiciously interested, 'we thought you'd end up like one of those old ladies who dedicated their life to a bunch of cats. But instead of cats, it would have to be fish. Or like . . . geckos because you are allergic to cat fur.' She snickered. 'We constantly talked about it in family gatherings.'

'Thanks for the faith,' I muttered and then stuck my tongue out in my sister's direction. I couldn't believe they were saying that kind of stuff with someone they believed I was dating at the table. Or better yet, with someone they knew I had dated sitting right there. 'I'm lucky to have you.'

Aaron's fingers gripped mine a little tighter, and I felt mine returning the gesture.

'No, we did not talk about such things,' my mother firmly denied, shooting her other daughter a look. 'Stop teasing your sister, Isabel. You are getting married tomorrow.'

Isabel frowned. 'What does that have to do with any—'

Mamá sliced her hand through the air, dismissing my sibling.

I snickered, watching her cross her arms over her chest.

'We never thought you'd end up alone, Lina. But we were terrified you would be lonely.' She looked over at Aaron, her eyes softening. 'And knowing that you're not, that you have someone to lean on and to return home to, maybe someone to call home one day, makes me sleep a little better at night.'

The man beside me didn't hesitate when he spoke, 'I can promise you that much.' His voice reached my skin like a caress. Pushing my heart to bang against my chest walls, wanting out as much as I didn't want to hear whatever was to come. 'She'll always have me.' His thumb caressed the back of my hand. 'She doesn't know it yet, but she is stuck with me.'

I couldn't not look over at him. After that, I couldn't not want to search his handsome face. At this point, it shouldn't have surprised me all that much. Aaron held that kind of power over me. So, I did exactly that. I allowed myself to turn. His eyes had already been on me.

Does he feel that pull too? That urge to search my face for whatever answers he thinks he'll find?

Trying to get my heart under control, I peered into that ocean blue with trepidation. With anticipation too. And I found something utterly terrifying. Something that shouldn't – couldn't – have been there, considering that this was supposed to be a farce so therefore his statement was not true. But I struggled to deny what was in front of me, that those emotions were really there, radiating off his gaze. Raw honesty. Conviction. Faith. Reliance. A pledge. All of that looked at me from Aaron's eyes. Demanding to be acknowledged.

As if he was making *me* the promise and not my mother.

As if what he had just proclaimed wasn't part of our game in deception.

But I couldn't accept that. As much as my body shook with effort to restrain myself from wrapping my arms around his neck and begging him for answers or to tell me exactly where in the gray area we found ourselves, I wouldn't allow myself to play with the questions spinning in my head and knotting together all my heartstrings.

Because perhaps I didn't really want to hear any of the answers to questions like: Had we gone from coworkers to deal associates to friends? Were we friends who vowed to be there for each other now? Friends who almost kissed and shared soft brushes of their lips? Was that promise really true, like his eyes pleaded with me to believe? Or was that nothing more than an ornament? And if it was, then why would he say something like that? Had he no disregard for my poor heart? Didn't he see that I was no longer able to discern one thing from the other? But if it wasn't a simple embellishment of the truth – an act, a tool in this farce – then what in the world was he doing? What were *we* doing?

Not able to remain under everything that looked at me from Aaron's gaze anymore or to process all the questions and doubts cramming my head, I straightened my legs with a brisk motion, and my hand let go of his. The chair underneath me screeched across the floor.

'I need to use the ladies' room,' I rushed out, snagging my gaze off Aaron.

Then, I walked away as fast as I could without looking back. I did not turn. Not once.

Not even after I heard my sister say, 'So, now that she's gone, can we talk about me? I'm the bride, and I'm supposed to be the centre of attention. I'm feeling neglected.'

Had my head not been a mess, I would have laughed. Probably gone back and tugged at her hair for being a pompous, self-centered brat, but I was too busy running. Being a complete chickenshit again, which at this rate, I'd probably master by the time the weekend was over.

I went through the motions of washing my hands and splashing some water on my face while I thought about nothing and everything, feeling completely overwhelmed by my own stupidity.

That was probably why when I exited the bathroom, I didn't realize there had been someone on the way until I was collapsing against a male chest with an *oomph*.

'*Mierda,*' I muttered under my breath, going back a couple of steps. '*Lo siento mucho,*' I added right before noticing who was in front of me. 'Oh, Daniel.'

Brushing a few strands of hair off my face, I inwardly cringed.

My ex didn't show any sign of feeling as awkward as I did. 'Are you okay?' he asked me in Spanish.

Now that it was just us and Aaron wasn't around, I answered in Spanish too, 'Yeah, I'm fine. It was nothing. Just a little bump.' Clearing my throat, I dusted off imaginary specks of dirt off my pleated skirt. 'Sorry again. It was really my fault. I was a little distracted.'

'It's all good, Lina.' That dimple in his cheek made an appearance.

I stared at it, a little lost in thought. And to think that all those years ago, it was that dimple that had set everything into motion. Now, I couldn't even bring myself to feel the slightest hint of warmth when I looked at it.

'I think I shouldn't have come tonight,' Daniel confessed out of the blue, returning me to the present.

I nodded slowly, trying to come to terms with the odd sense of sympathy I suddenly felt toward him. He wasn't wrong. All throughout dinner, he had been nothing but a ghost. No one had really addressed him – something I could understand, considering our history – and he hadn't talked on his own. Putting myself in his shoes, I didn't think I would have accepted coming myself.

'No, coming was the right thing to do if you believed you had to be here.' I clasped my hands together, keeping them from fumbling. 'You did it for Gonzalo, and that's very brave of you.'

He laughed with bitterness. 'I don't think anyone at that table would agree with you. Except maybe Gonzalo, and he wouldn't use the word brave.' His hands slipped into the pockets of his slacks.

Again, he wasn't wrong about that either. My parents had always been polite even if distant, but just for Gonzalo's sake. For Isabel's sake too. They knew how important Daniel was to him and how, without him, they wouldn't have Gonzalo in their lives, and they loved him to pieces. But I still didn't have a doubt that they'd never forgive Daniel for breaking my heart all that time ago. For having a part in what I had gone through.

'Listen,' Daniel said before releasing a breath. 'I know it's probably too late for this, but I wanted to tell you that I'm sorry. I don't think I ever did.'

No, he had never apologized.

'But I never meant for everything that went down to happen. I never even imagined it was a possibility.'

Of course he hadn't, and hadn't that been part of the problem? He dragged me along, and when things started looking ugly, he fled the ship. Leaving me there to sink with it. And that had been exactly what I did; I had been pulled under the surface, and I'd had to fight my way up. Alone.

His apology was long overdue – perhaps it was even too late – but at least I was finally getting one. And that counted for something.

'It's water under the bridge,' I told him, and I meant it. Even though a little part of me would always remember that he had been a big player in something that left a scar I'd always carry around. 'Don't worry about what my dad said, by the way. He's a little emotional.' I waved my hand in front of us, stopping myself the moment I realized I didn't owe Daniel a single thing. I shouldn't have been trying to make him feel better. I cleared my throat. 'You know how weddings bring out the best and worst of us.'

I was the living proof of that, my fake boyfriend sitting at a table with my family, finally facing my newly engaged ex.

Although the problem with coming back home for Isabel's wedding – single, dateless – had never been about seeing Daniel. It was about facing everyone else while doing that. It was the anticipation, the idea, of having every single person who had seen me grow up, fall in love, get my heart broken, lose a little part of myself for a while, and then flee to a different country. It was about facing a man who had clearly put his life back together when I hadn't. That was what had set this whole thing into motion, exactly what had made me push the panic button.

And how stupid had that been? How dumb had it been to let something like that drive me to lie? To create and sell them this ridiculous and wholesome image of myself that I'd thought would make me complete and happy in their eyes?

I realized now, as I stood in front of the catalyst of this whole mess, that it had been very fucking stupid.

'I hope you mean that, Lina. This whole thing is better left in the past anyway.' Daniel looked at the ground for a moment and then nodded his head. 'Are you happy now? With your life? With him?' He tilted his head. 'You don't look completely happy.'

My throat dried, my eyes widening, as I tried to process his words.

'Of course I am,' I said, but it came out in a breathless way. Pure shock swirled in my body, mixing with stupid fear at being called out on my lie. 'I'm happy, Daniel,' I repeated, those two emotions turning into something else. Something that tasted a lot more bitter.

'Are you sure about that?' he asked calmly, in a confident and patronizing way that had me rearing my head back. 'He seems like a stand-up guy, this Aaron. Although he looks a little ... dry. Stuffy,' Daniel continued, and my eyes fluttered closed for a fraction of a second, a strong sense of protectiveness washing over me. 'But I guess he's good to you. He has been stuck to your side since the moment I met him.' He chuckled. 'Not my style, this guard-dog vibe, but I could understand the appeal.'

My lips parted as I found it hard to believe the words Daniel was saying.

'But are you really happy, Lina? I know you, and this is not the carefree Lina you are. You have been on edge in the short time you've been here, and I'll be honest, I can't help but be concerned.'

Concerned? I blinked. Then, I did it again. And again and again.

Had I been on edge? I could believe that. I had certainly felt that way more than once. But ... whether what he thought was true or not wasn't important. It was the fact that he believed he had any right to deny something I was telling him myself.

Oblivious to my growing outrage, Daniel kept going, 'It could be coming back home. That must be a lot of pressure for you. Or maybe it's that Isabel is getting married and you aren't.'

A breath got stuck in my throat.

'Or maybe it's him. I don't know, but—'

'Stop,' I hissed. Something lit up inside of me. Like a bonfire. I could even hear the flames crackling and sizzling. Burning away the remains of my patience. 'Don't you dare do that, Daniel.'

His brows wrinkled together, his expression one of confusion. 'Do what?'

'*Do what?*' I repeated, my voice going up an octave. Closing my eyes, I tried my best to get back my composure. 'Do not pretend that you care or that you even know me anymore. You have no right to judge or doubt my happiness.' The pace at which my breath entered and left my lungs increased, my anger not receding. 'So, stop throwing in my face whatever it is you think you know or see. You lost that right a long time ago.'

He shook his head, sighing loudly. 'I've always cared about you, Lina. And I always will. That's why I'm worried about you. Why I'm trying to have a conversation.'

'You've always cared about me? You'll *always* care?'

'Of course,' he puffed out. 'You are like a little sister to me. We are about to become family.'

Something deep inside of me turned to ice. The marrow in my bones freezing, rooting me to the spot.

'I'm like a little sister to you now?' His statement tasted like something tart in my mouth. 'You've got to be fucking kidding me, Daniel.'

His expression assembled into one that was meant to impose. To convey authority. I had been well acquainted with that face when I used to sit across from him in his classroom. 'Don't be like that, Lina.'

'Like what?'

He tsked, bathing me in condensation. 'Don't be a child. We are both adults now. You can talk and act like one.'

Now. He had said *now.* Opposed to what? To when we had dated?

'Had I been a child when we were together, Daniel? When you dated me? Made me feel special? Told me you loved me?' I watched his jaw set into a tight line. 'Is that all that I was to you when you dropped me like a hot potato after you so much as sniffed a little trouble coming your way? I guess that would explain everything. Why I'm only getting an apology now that you deem me worthy of one, having finally turned into an adult.'

I took a step back, hearing my heart drumming in my ears as I watched him remain very still.

'You know what? I'm over this.' Shaking my head, I laughed bitterly. 'I don't owe you a single thing. And you don't owe me anything either. You never cared about me, Daniel. Not enough at least. Otherwise, you wouldn't have let them eat me alive.' I swallowed, pushing all those memories away as much as they banged and screamed, demanding to be let out. 'I really wish you hadn't said all this. I really do. Because these last few minutes have wiped out the little respect I had for you.'

Watching him as he stood in front of me, barely moving, I took another step back.

His mouth fell open, but no words came out besides, 'Lina.'

'It's okay,' I told him. 'I don't expect anything from you. As I told you, it's water under the bridge now.'

His lips snapped closed, his shoulders falling in what I hoped was acceptance.

'But I can tell you this much: I *am* happy.'

And I was. Confused too, if I was being honest. Yes, my heart was mixed up and disoriented. Terrified on top of all that. But there was a force that seemed to tear the shell of fear that covered that poor and beat-up organ, seeping through the cracks and wanting to obliterate all those doubts if I let it. Promising safety and comfort.

But that wasn't a conversation I owed to Daniel. I did to someone else.

Someone I needed to make my way back to.

I was about to turn on my heel and do exactly that when someone who always managed to put a smile on my face turned around the corner.

'What have you been doing here for so long, *cariño*?' Abuela asked in Spanish, looking over at Daniel. 'Oh, I see now.' She shot him a sideways glance and ignored him altogether. When she looked back at me, her lips were tugging up, mischief written all over her face. 'That boyfriend of yours is sitting at that table, looking like an abandoned puppy.' She linked her arm with mine, and I felt a little lighter already. 'He ordered you dessert, you know? And he keeps staring at where you left, like he's holding himself from coming to get you.'

My belly flopped, a fluttering sensation taking over. 'He is?'

Abuela patted my arm. 'Of course he is, *boba.*' She clicked her tongue, pulling us back to the restaurant. 'He didn't even ask for two spoons, so he knows that getting you to share is fruitless.' She snickered, and I tried to ignore how the flutter was now spreading to my chest.

'He . . . he's pretty perfect,' I murmured, surprising myself.

'Yes,' she said without thinking much about it. 'That's why you shouldn't leave him sitting alone for so long. He's too beautiful for his own good.'

He was – for my own good too.

'You think he will save me a dance tomorrow?'

'I think he will.' I didn't have a doubt in my mind he would. 'Only if you ask nicely, Abuela.'

She giggled, and I knew without a doubt that I'd probably have to fight my own grandmother over my fake boyfriend's attention.

Then, the woman who had snuck chocolate after bedtime more than a million times guided us back to where the rest of the family was, chatting animatedly.

Right before reaching the table, she lowered her voice. 'They didn't make men like that back in my day. Abuelo was handsome but not like that. Although it wasn't his looks that won me over.' She winked. 'You know what I mean.'

'Abuela!' I loud-whispered.

She patted my arm. 'Don't play coy around me. I'm old. I know better. Now, go.'

A pair of blue eyes immediately found mine. They bounced to

Abuela and then somewhere behind me. Looking around, I noticed Daniel was a few steps behind us.

After parting ways with my grandmother, I let my gaze fall back on my fake date as I made my way to him. I could see the unease edged in Aaron's handsome face. His jaw was clenched, and his forehead was bunched. When his gaze met mine once more, his eyes held questions and that protectiveness I had felt a few minutes ago when Daniel had mentioned his name. It was clear as a cloudless summer day.

Aaron was worried. He was holding himself back from meeting me halfway and asking me what the hell had happened. He cared. He cared about me. And he'd shield me, hold me, or just stand by my side if I so much as opened my mouth to ask. I knew. Hell, he would even if I didn't ask.

Honest, genuine concern. Contrary to whatever Daniel had claimed. Letting myself fall delicately on my chair, I took a moment to plaster a calm smile on my face. A neutral expression. But my lips probably curled the wrong way, my features displaying everything still churning inside of me after my exchange with Daniel because when I turned and faced Aaron, his eyes flared more intensely.

I willed my lips to inch higher, and a muscle in his jaw twitched.

My sister started chattering about something – what exactly, I couldn't tell. My head was somewhere else.

My hands were in my lap when I felt Aaron's palm fall against them. For the second time tonight, he interlaced our hands. Our fingers weaved together, each and every one of them. But this time, he kept our linked hands right where they were – on the top of my thigh. As if he was trying to tell me that this way – with them below the table, hidden from everyone else – meant that this was just for us. Not a part of the charade.

He squeezed my hand with purpose, his fingers tightening around mine, his palm warm against my skin. *Just for us*, it seemed to reassure me. To promise me.

And like the biggest dummy in the universe, I found the greatest comfort in those five long fingers. In that warm palm. So, I brought our joined hands closer to my belly, and I squeezed right back.

~

There was something lodged right in between my ribs that felt a lot like a ticking bomb.

'I can hear the gears in your head spinning,' Aaron said as he crossed the room in that pair of pyjama pants, which was doing mad things to my belly again. Same went for the T-shirt. He was wearing the one he had slept in yesterday.

At least he was wearing one. I didn't think I could take shirtless Aaron right now.

'I'm okay,' I lied, my head throbbing with every replay of my conversation with Daniel. It had been on a loop since we left the restaurant. 'Just going through everything I need to get done before the big day tomorrow.'

Which was what I should have been busy doing.

Clad in my sleeping clothes too, I aligned the two pairs of heels – the ones I'd wear and the backup – on the floor. Right against the wall. Meticulously leaving the same space between them.

I stepped back, admiring my work. *Nope.*

Unconvinced, I knelt and rearranged them.

When I had something on my mind, I did one of two things. I compulsively ate or organized. And considering we had just had dinner and seeing the pile of neatly stacked clothes and perfectly in-line items displayed on top of the dresser, it seemed that this one time, it was the latter.

Out of the corner of my eye, I sensed Aaron plopping himself on the bed with an ease and finesse no one his size should have.

'There's smoke coming out of your ears.' He rested his back on the headboard, and the wood complained under his weight.

I reached for the shoes again, moving them an inch to the right. 'I don't think so,' I said in a clipped tone. Then, I moved the two pairs half an inch to the left. 'For that, I would need to be overthinking something. And I'm not doing that.'

'Oh, but you are,' he said from his position on the bed. 'Talk to me.'

I didn't bother answering him. Hearing his sigh, I kept my focus on my task.

Maybe if they face the wall—

'Catalina,' Aaron called.

And the way he had said it made me turn around and face him.

'Come here.' He patted the bed with his hand.

Brows bunched, I sent him a look.

'Sit with me for a little while, and then you can go back to torturing those shoes into perfection,' he told me with a sigh. 'Just for a few minutes.' Then, he placed his palm on the comforter again. When I didn't say anything or move, he added very softly, like it would break his heart if I didn't give him this one thing, 'Please.'

That *please*, that freaking please and the way he had said it, launched my legs forward.

Before I knew what I was doing, my ass was on the bed, right beside his hip. I knew what he wanted to talk about. That cocktail of emotions and memories and questions that had slowly been assembling in my head. The one I had brought back to the apartment, and that I knew if I so much as opened my mouth, it would burst and spill right out of me. But that meant completely confiding in Aaron. Telling him about a part of my past that I didn't find any joy in revisiting. Giving him a key that would help him understand – know – me better. And did I want to do that? Could I do it without wanting to tuck my head in his chest and look for comfort in him?

'I don't want to bore you with the melodramatics of my life,

Aaron,' I sighed, and I meant it. What I didn't tell him was that beneath all that, there was only fear. 'You don't need to worry—'

In one smooth motion, Aaron picked me up and placed me between his open legs. Another sigh left my parted lips, but this one had nothing to do with exhaustion or whatever was brewing in my head.

'Anything that bothers you matters to me, and I want to hear about it,' he said from his position behind me. 'Nothing about you is boring or doesn't interest me – ever. Understand?'

I felt myself nod and perhaps mutter a quiet, 'Yes,' too. My heart drummed too loudly in my ears to know.

Aaron continued, 'If you want to talk about whatever happened, then we'll do that.' His hands fell on my shoulders with a tenderness that disarmed me. Then, he brushed my hair to the side, and his fingers travelled to the back of my neck. 'And if you don't, then we'll talk about something else. But I want you to relax. Just for a few minutes.'

He paused, and his thumbs started massaging along the line of my spine. I had to hold back from whimpering like a stricken animal. Only I wasn't in pain.

'Sound like a plan?'

'Yes,' I answered, incapable of not melting into his touch.

There was a beat of silence, and Aaron's fingers trailed up the back of my neck, gently kneading the muscles there. Another sound rose in my throat, almost leaving my lips. But I held it in.

'What your dad said during dinner made me think of something my mom used to tell me when I was a little kid.' Aaron's fingertips kept working my skin, easing more than the tension in my shoulders. Turning me into softened butter as I listened to his deep voice taking me out of my head. Trusting me with yet another piece of himself. 'Back then, I didn't really understand or care about it. I didn't until I was older and she was diagnosed and the possibility of her leaving us became real. But she used to tell me how the moment I was born, she knew she had found her light in the dark. That one lighthouse that, no matter what, was always up. Lighting up the night and signalling her way home. And as a kid, I thought that was either corny or very dramatic.' A low and humourless chuckle left him.

My heart broke all over again for him, hurting and begging me to turn around and give him any comfort I could. But I stayed put. 'You must miss her so much.'

'I do, every day. When she passed and my nights got a little darker, I started to understand what she'd meant.'

That was a loss I hoped I wouldn't experience in a long time.

'But what your dad said – about you having this fire inside, that lightness and life, and how it dulled for a period of time ...' He paused, and I swore I heard him swallow. 'It just ...' He trailed off, as if he was scared of his next words. And Aaron never feared speaking his mind. Aaron was never scared. 'You are all that, Catalina. You are light. And passion. Your laughter alone can lift my mood and effortlessly turn my day around in a matter of seconds. Even when it's not aimed at me. You ... can light up entire rooms, Catalina. You hold that kind of power. And it's because of all the different things that make you who you are. Each and every one of them, even the ones that drive me crazy in ways you can't imagine. You should never forget that.'

My heart skipped a beat. Then another one. And then one more. Until no air was getting in or out and I could tell my heart had stopped beating completely. For the longest of moments, I remained suspended in time, thinking I'd never bounce back from this because my heart was not functioning anymore, but hey, if those were the parting words I had to leave this earth with, then I'd be happy.

And when my heart resumed, I wasn't relieved. I simply couldn't be when it started thrashing against the cavity of my chest with a wildness I had never experienced.

Some people claimed that the most beautiful thing anyone had ever done for them was writing them a poem, composing a song, or confessing their undying love in an epic gesture. But right then, as I was cocooned in Aaron's long legs, his fingers delicately massaging my neck simply because I'd looked tense, I realized I didn't need or want any of that. If I never got my epic declaration, I'd be fine. Because his words were, without a doubt in my mind, the most beautiful thing I would ever hear said about me. *To* me. And for me.

My body wanted to turn, screamed at my head to allow it. But I knew that if I did, whatever he saw on my face would change everything. Every single fucking thing between us.

I'd ... *dammit*. This man. He kept showing me how perfect he was. Kept unveiling all these beautiful parts of him that made me giddy and dizzy and hungry for more.

But I still felt like I was standing on the edge of a cliff, looking down at an ocean that whirled in the same deep blue that coloured his eyes. Would I dare to jump?

'I fell in love with Daniel in my second year in college,' I said without turning. Not daring to free-fall. Not completely. 'I was nineteen. He was my Physics professor. He was younger than any other member of the faculty, so he stood out. Was popular among the body of students – the female section of it particularly. At first, it was a dumb crush. I'd anticipate his lectures. I'd maybe put a little extra care into what I wore and sit in the first row. But I wasn't the only one. Pretty much every other girl – and a few of the guys – had been charmed by the dimple in his cheek and the confidence with which he strolled across the room. Even when his course was one of the hardest we'd ever had to study for.'

Aaron continued working the tension out of the muscles that corded along my neck and shoulders. He remained quiet, and it felt almost as if – except for his fingers – he had grown still too.

So, I continued, 'Imagine my surprise when I started noticing

that his gaze would rest on me for a moment, just a little longer than
on anybody else. Or that his dimple would come out a little more
often when it was me he was watching.' My eyes closed as Aaron's
hands drifted lower, travelling down my spine.

'Throughout that year, it all built up to a point where we would
sneak a few innocent touches in between classes or during tutoring
sessions. It was so ... exciting. Exhilarating almost. He made me
feel special, like I wasn't one more of the students pining for him.'
I heard my voice drifting lower, lost in the memory, so I tried to
bring my tone back up.

'Anyway, we didn't start dating until the moment I was through
with the two semesters his course lasted. Officially, publicly dating.
Not on campus or anything like that, but we'd go out like any other
couple. He introduced Gonzalo and Isabel, and they fell desperately
in love in the span of a heated look.'

A real smile tugged my lips up at the thought of the moment
Isabel and Gonzalo had locked eyes; it had seemed as if they had
been waiting for that to happen. As if each had unknowingly been
waiting for the other.

Aaron's legs shifted, cocooning me further into his lap. Or perhaps it was me who kept bending into him. I didn't know, but I
wouldn't complain or move away.

'And I was in love too. After one year of daydreaming about
something I couldn't have, hoping for it, I was blinded by the joy at
finally being able to have him. To call him mine.'

His fingers stopped briefly, as if they hesitated before their next
move. Then, they resumed and continued kneading at my shoulders.

'It lasted a few months. Then, I heard the first whisper, the first
ugly and poisonous rumour that blackened all that happiness. And
after that one, many more followed. Whispers turned into loud
gossip, which spread along the corridors on campus. There were
Facebook posts, too, and threads on Twitter as well. Never directed

at me, but about me. At least in the beginning.' I brought my knees to my chest and hugged them. *'The whore who slept around with her professors*, they said. *Of course she's graduating with honours. That's how she aced Physics when more than half the students fell through. She fucked him, and she'll fuck her way through college.'*

I heard Aaron's outward breath. Felt it on the back of my neck. His fingers tensing and halting very briefly.

'It was all so hurtful.' My voice sounded different – void and bitter. And it reminded me of a Lina I didn't want to remember. Or ever be again. 'The things that were said about me quickly turned into pointed fingers and into disgusting photos that someone had Photoshopped with my face. Into . . . really ugly stuff.'

Aaron's touch turned into mere brushes of his skin against mine, soothing me, moving me forward, telling me, *I'm here. I got you.*

'It was all turned into this despicable tale, where I was the cunning, dirty woman who seduced professors for grades. All the hard work and the long nights I had studied were brought down simply because . . . I don't know. To this day, I don't know the reason or the motivation. Jealousy? A laugh? But I know that if I had been one of my male classmates and Daniel had been a female professor, perhaps I wouldn't have gone through that. It would have been the professor. She would have been accused of being a cougar, and the student would have gotten a few high fives. Instead, I was almost harassed into dropping out. I didn't want to attend any lectures. I didn't want to leave the house. I was still living with my parents because I could drive to campus from their house, and I didn't even want to talk to them. I deleted my profiles on all of the social media sites. I closed myself off from every single person in my life, even my sister and even those few who had remained my friends.' I focused on the soothing circles Aaron was drawing on my skin, grounding and rooting me to him and to the present. 'It was all too much. I just felt . . . ashamed. Worthless. I felt like everything I had done was worth nothing. Consequently, when my grades and performance sank, my average went down the drain. And I didn't even care.'

A beat of silence that seemed to stretch too long made me realize Aaron hadn't spoken a word. I knew he wouldn't judge me, but I wondered what he thought. If the way he saw me had now changed.

'What did he do?' he finally said. His voice sounded rocky, rough. 'What did Daniel do about everything that was being done to you?'

'Well, things started looking a little bad for him. There was no rule that stopped him from dating a former student. But everything that was going down got to be too much for him.'

'For *him*?' he repeated, a new edge to his voice.

'Yeah. And so, he broke things off, told me it was too complicated and relationships shouldn't be that hard or messy.'

Aaron's fingers halted, not moving any longer. Simply hovering above my skin.

'He thought that we weren't supposed to make each other trip and fall and that the moment we did, then it didn't make sense to be together. And I . . . I think he was right. I guess he was.'

Aaron didn't say anything. Not a word left his lips, but I could tell there was something wrong with him. I could feel it in the way his breath had quickened, deepened. And the way his hands remained frozen above my shoulders.

'I often wonder how I managed to graduate, but I did. At some point after the breakup, I woke up. Showed up to the exams and passed. Then, I somehow put together an application for an international master's programme and left for the US.'

Aaron's palms resumed. Very gently, but I felt them move along my shoulders. Nothing like before, but at least he was touching me again. And I needed that, more than I cared to admit.

'I wasn't escaping him, you know? Everybody thought I was, but I wasn't. Daniel had bruised my heart, but I wasn't running away from that. It was everything else. Everybody looked at me differently. Like I had changed or something had changed in the way they saw me. As if I were this broken thing now. Dropped by Daniel, harassed, made fun of. Everybody whispered, *Oh, poor thing. How is she going to bounce back from this?* They treated me as damaged goods. They still do. Every time I came back home alone, they look at me with pity. Every time I said *I'm still single*, they nod and smile sadly.' Shaking my head, I released all the air in my lungs. 'I hate it, Aaron.' I could hear the emotion in my voice choking my words because I did hate it. 'That's why I came back as little as I did.'

But then I also hated how much I feared that a part of it was perhaps true. Why hadn't I been able to trust anybody with my heart otherwise?

'Everything that had happened hurt me, left a scar, but it didn't break me.' I swallowed the lump in my throat, wanting to believe my own words. 'It didn't.'

A sound, deep and husky and pained, came from behind me. Before I knew what was happening, Aaron's arms came around my shoulders, and I was engulfed by him. Wrapped into his chest. Warm and hard and safe and . . . a lot less alone. A lot more complete than I had been seconds before.

Aaron buried his head in the nook of my neck from behind, and I felt the urge to comfort him. So, I did.

'I'm not broken, Aaron,' I told him in a whisper, although perhaps it was for my own reassurance. 'I can't be.'

'You are not,' he said on my skin. Tightening his hold on me. Bringing me closer. 'And I know that even if something did break you – because that's life and no one is invincible – you'd still put the pieces back together and remain the brightest thing I'd ever seen.'

My hands went around that pair of arms wrapped around my shoulders, which pulled me into his chest, as if he were scared I'd go up in smoke if he didn't. And I hung on to him equally desperately. As if my next breath depended on it.

We remained that way for a long while. And slowly, very slowly, our bodies relaxed into each other. They melted together. I focused on Aaron's breath, on the earnestness of the moment, on his heartbeat against my back, his strength. On all the things that he'd kept handing to me so freely, like they were nothing. Like he was supposed to give them away and I was entitled to take them from him.

Neither of us said anything as time stretched, our holds gradually loosening as we lost the battle to sleep.

My eyelids eventually fluttered shut, but right before darkness engulfed me, I thought I heard Aaron whisper, 'You feel complete in my arms. You feel like my home.'

CHAPTER TWENTY-TWO

What an idiot I had been.

A big, dumb, foolish idiot.

Earlier that morning, when my alarm had gone off a little after dawn and I had slipped out of Aaron's warm embrace quietly – but not panic-ridden – I had immediately regretted agreeing to meet my sister hours before the wedding. So, once I got everything packed and was ready to go, right before sneaking out the door without waking him up – even though I had learned by then that he, too, slept like the dead – I leaned very silently and brushed a soft kiss against his jaw. Because I didn't want to go, not really, and I was a weak, weak woman when it came to him.

Just in case, I left Aaron a note, telling him that I'd see him in a few hours because I'd be getting ready with Isabel. Charo would be driving him to the wedding venue.

Be strong and don't succumb, I wrote down. Then, I signed it with, *With love, Lina.*

My choice of words had my heart skipping a beat, but I promised myself it wasn't a big deal and left it there.

Not more than an hour after leaving the apartment, I started to miss him – like properly brooding and sighing and wondering what he was doing – so I texted him.

Lina: Did you get my note?

To which, he replied no more than a couple of minutes later.

> Aaron: Yes, I'm hiding in the bathroom. Charo was
> trying to sneak a photo of me with her phone.
> Martíns are relentless creatures.

That had me snorting so hard that the make-up artist ended up brushing eye shadow all across my forehead. She tried to play it cool, but I could tell she was pissed.

But none of that was the reason why I was pretty sure I was a big, dumb, foolish idiot.

Somehow, somewhere between slipping into my velvety fawn heels and the graceful, airy burgundy gown I was wearing, my head had started spinning questions. Important ones. *Will I be able to find Aaron in the crowd?* And also: *Will he be okay? Will he get to the venue and find his seat?* And the star of the show: *Maybe I won't see him until after the ceremony. What if I can't find him?*

So, when I came to my place to the right of the bride, on a glorious summer day, surrounded by arrangements of peonies in all shades of baby pink and pearly white, in front of the people who had seen us grow and turn into the women we were today, my head turned.

My gaze effortlessly zeroed in on a pair of ocean-blue eyes. And all those questions immediately died away.

What a big, dumb, foolish idiot I had been to even question that my eyes wouldn't be drawn to Aaron Blackford in a matter of seconds. How in the world could they not?

He was dazzling, standing under the sun in a navy-blue suit. And when he smiled that wide and furtive grin that I was beginning to think was only for me, I swore he could have blinded me if I hadn't blinked. That smile – Aaron's smile, his handsome face, him completely and entirely – made my knees weak and my chest tight.

That was exactly why, once the ceremony ended and Gonzalo made a show out of eating Isabel's face right then and there for everybody attending to see, I turned around on shaky legs. The crowd proceeded to throw rice and confetti as the bride and groom made their way down the aisle, and by the time they were jumping inside a yellow Volkswagen Beetle to drive to where they'd have a pre-dinner photo shoot, everybody started shuffling to the restaurant area. A quiet silence was left behind, except for the sound of my heart, which was trying to stumble right out of my throat.

Aaron waited by the exit, standing with his hands in the pockets of his navy pants and his jacket partly opened. Right where the rows of creamy chairs ended. A few tiny pieces of confetti stuck in his hair.

His gaze stayed on me as I walked down that aisle, my legs feeling like I was walking on sand. Heavy and clumsy.

Only when I reached him did he take a step toward me; it was fast and rushed, as if he had been stopping himself from running to me and couldn't hold it in any longer.

I watched his throat work, his eyes swiping up and down and up again, eating up what was in front of them.

'You look like a dream.'

What a silly thing to tell me when he was the one who couldn't be real. The one I couldn't believe was here, making my chest full with things I didn't understand.

I shook my head, trying to pull myself together enough to answer. 'You look amazing, Aaron.'

His gaze searched my face for a brief moment, and whatever he found made him smile. Again, that grin. Only for me. What a lucky bitch I was.

Aaron offered his arm, and I struggled not to launch myself at him right then and there. 'May I have the honour?' he asked slowly.

A deep belly laugh left my lips. Slowly, I took it. 'Now, you are just pushing it.'

His palm fell on top of the one that was resting on the crook of his arm. 'What do you mean?'

'Only romance heroes say stuff like that. And we are talking about the ones in a Jane Austen novel. Not even your run-of-the-mill romance hero would butter up a woman that much,' I explained as we moved forward, in the direction of the adjoining restaurant, where everybody else was, probably a glass of wine – or two – already in hand.

'In my book, having the most beautiful woman on my arm classifies as an honour.'

I hoped the foundation the make-up artist had had to apply for a second time covered the way my cheeks flushed. 'If the bride so much as gets wind of what you are saying, you'll be in so much trouble.' I heard his chuckle, but he didn't retract his words. 'She'll kick you out of the wedding, and I will not be able to help you. You are too tall and big to sneak in, unnoticed.' *And too damn handsome too*, but I kept that part to myself.

Aaron chuckled again, the noise travelling down my spine and leaving a trail of shivers. I was finding it really hard to ignore how good his arm felt under my fingers or how right it was being tucked against his side.

It was only when we were a few feet away from the open area, where all the invitees were gathered, that Aaron spoke, 'It would be worth it, you know.'

My head turned, taking in his profile as he kept his gaze up front.

'For seeing you in that dress and having you enter any place on my arm, I'd endure pretty much anything.'

My lips parted, and had Aaron not been providing his support, I would have tumbled down to the floor, rolled the rest of the way, and probably stopped only when my back came against a chair or a table.

'Even your sister's rage.'

Then, a flash went off right in our faces, snapping me out of my trance.

Blinking away the bright white spots, I got a glimpse of a camera.

'Maravilloso!' a high-pitched voice I was well acquainted with screeched. 'What a beautiful couple you two make.'

My mouth snapped shut and then opened again. Not having my sight back completely, I kept blinking until a bright red mane started coming into focus. *Charo.*

'Oh, your babies are going to be the cutest things ever.'

I cursed under my breath and smiled tightly while Aaron seemed surprisingly unconcerned. The dumbest mental image took me by surprise. One of Aaron holding a chubby, blue-eyed baby in his large arms.

Stepping out of my cousin's trajectory and veering for the wine, I tried to recompose myself.

'And so it begins,' I muttered under my breath. The day I had feared and dreaded for months.

Only, in that precise moment, with Aaron's arm under my fingers and his smile aimed at me, I came to realize that what frightened me was nothing I had ever come to expect.

~

If I'd known that my sister had hired a kiss cam for the wedding reception, I would have claimed to be sick and hidden in the bathroom. Ironically, I wouldn't have had to lie all that much. My dinner kept climbing up my throat every single time the tune announcing the start of the most painful thirty seconds of my life reached my ears. During that time, which stretched into a hellish eternity, the camera scanned the crowd seated at the round tables scattered across the lush green garden of the restaurant before coming to a stop on a couple and displaying their image – framed by a heart – on a conveniently installed projector.

Every single time the camera so much as passed over my fake date and me, my heart ceased beating before resuming at breakneck speed.

Apparently, the possibility of having my first kiss with Aaron displayed on a big screen in front of my whole family was going to give me a heart attack.

And just as if my thoughts had somehow conjured it, the tritone tune announced the start of a new round of: *Will Lina die of nerves and anticipation tonight? Or will she lose her shit and commit camera murder?*

'Oh, what a fun idea this was, Isabel!' my mom hollered with excitement from across the table.

My sister seemed to pride herself on it even more, if that were possible. 'I know.' She smiled giddily. 'They'll even put all the film together, edit it, and send me a montage with all the kisses,' she explained over the relentless tune of doom.

One eye on the projector screen, I watched the camera hover on a table close by.

'I had to book an extra package for that, but it's totally worth it.'

The camera swiped over our table, displaying Aaron's and my faces on the screen.

My face blanched. My hand somehow jerked, dropping a fork. I dipped after it, too briskly, and almost knocked over a glass. Cursing under my breath, I picked up the fork from under the table, resurfacing just in time to see the camera moving along.

Close. That was so close.

Reaching for my wine, I actually considered sneaking out and putting an end to this. But that would be running. Being a coward. Again. Something I'd kept doing a lot of lately.

If the camera stops on you, you will kiss Aaron, I told myself as I downed the rest of my wine. *A peck on the lips. It doesn't need to be a movie kiss. Just a kiss.*

But my pep talk didn't help. It only made my chest tighter and my belly flutter.

Peeking at the man that I'd probably have to kiss in a handful of seconds, I was surprised to see a muscle in his jaw jumping. Studying him more closely, I realized Aaron looked . . . like New York Aaron again. Not like the relaxed and playful version I had shared these past days with. His gaze was set on the screen, and while his face gave nothing away – at least not to those who hadn't mastered the art of reading Aaron like I had – there was something about him that told me he wasn't as fine as he looked.

Once more, the camera glided over us, putting our faces on the screen for a tense second, and moved on.

My heart resumed.

Before I could feel any kind of relief, it came right back, as if it were performing a dance especially choreographed for me, teasing my heartbeat until sending it into cardiac arrest. Little droplets of sweat formed on the nape of my neck. Aaron remained quiet by my side, steadfast, his eyes drilled into the screen. So much so that concern started seeping in.

'Whoo!' the crowd hooted as the camera cruised across our table again, the speed decreasing gradually.

Looking at Aaron, it was hard to notice much else besides him. I was barely aware of how the others on our table had come alive, clapping and whistling to the tune of the goddamn kiss cam. My eyes zeroed on Aaron's lips, pressed firmly together. Anxiety and anticipation – yes, powerful and silky anticipation – built in the pit of my belly. My gaze took in the whole of him, stoically sitting by my side. Amid the chaos around us, I still managed to catch the movement of his knee. It was vibrating up and down. The motion barely lasted more than a couple of seconds. But I had seen it.

My gaze leaped back to his profile. *Is Aaron . . . nervous? About kissing me? It can't be.*

Not after the way he had almost done that right after teasing and plummeting me to a point where I would have begged for his lips.

Unaware of my eyes on him, his knee resumed its movement, the muscle on his jaw twitching again in sync.

Oh my God, he is.

Aaron was nervous. He was all jittery and high-strung, and it was because of me. Because chances were, he'd have to kiss me. *Me.*

Something took flight right between my ribs. I couldn't believe how a man so confident, so composed — one who had made my body come alive and sing with nothing more than the softest of touches — could be fretting over having to kiss me. The flutter in my chest stirred, making me itch to reach—

A loud cheer exploded around us, taking my attention off Aaron. People chanted, *'¡Que se besen! ¡Que se besen!'* Kiss! Kiss!

My eyes leaped around desperately, my heart rising to my mouth. Everybody was looking in our direction.

I'll do it. I'll kiss him.

As I zeroed in on the screen, something lurched deep within me in response to what I saw.

My dad reached for my mom's face and planted a kiss on her lips.

It wasn't relief. What had pierced my body was disappointment. Baffling, inexplicable disappointment at me not being the one framed by the silly string of hearts. Because my parents had been targeted by the kiss cam. Not us.

I felt Aaron move beside me. Turning in his direction, my gaze hopelessly fastened onto his lips again. His mouth. That speck of disappointment grew, obliterating everything else and turning into something thick and heavy that promised a rich taste on my tongue. One that made my heart speed up.

Want, I realized. What I felt was need. I wanted him, needed him to gather me in his arms and kiss me like he had promised.

'Because when I finally take those lips in mine, it will be the furthest thing from pretending.'

That was what he had said. And wasn't what I was feeling

inside – what threatened to spill out and turn my life around – the furthest thing from a lie? From pretending?

It *was*. Consequences be damned, but it was.

I was long past this deception scheme. And the ball of emotions that came with that realization collapsed down my chest, crumbling along the rest of my body and taking everything in its way with it. Real – what I was feeling had to be real.

'When I finally kiss you, there won't be any doubt in your mind that it is real.'

I wanted it to be real. Real, real, real.

Aaron must have felt the shift in me – naturally, as he was the one person on earth who seemed to read me like he owned the only copy of *The Handbook of Lina*. His gaze sharpened, roaming across my face as I watched in awe how his lips parted.

It was in that precise moment that I felt like something had finally clicked into place, unhinging everything I had been keeping on a short leash.

I couldn't know how or why. Didn't even have the slightest idea. And wasn't that part of the mystery of life? Part of what made it breathtakingly exciting? Unexpectedly beautiful? We couldn't control and tame emotions to our convenience.

And what I felt for Aaron had turned into a wild beast that I mercilessly fell prey to.

That was exactly why when Aaron quietly reached for my hand, took it in his, and stood up, I followed. Every single thing that had stopped me in these past few days was obliterated in the chaos that had built around us. We had to cross the space, sidestepping people who now danced animatedly, eluding relatives with red cheeks and ruffled hair who lunged in our direction, ignoring the music filling the outdoorsy space that called everybody to the improvised dance floor. But what did I care? Nothing mattered, except following this man wherever he took me.

Like a glass, I had been filling up, droplet after droplet. Slowly packing all these things he had given me – the softest, most provoking touches; precious smiles that were just for me; his strength; his faith in me – to the brim and heaping it with everything I had been feeling. I found myself on the verge of being toppled down. Of helplessly spilling and revealing everything I had worked so hard on bottling up.

We were somewhere outside still, perhaps on one of the sides of the patio of the restaurant. The music from the party reached my ears, muffled by the distance, and the only light illuminating this section of the garden came from a lonely lamp perched on the far edge of the building, leaving us almost in the dark.

Aaron came to a stop, finally turning around and facing me. His jaw was clenched again, the rest of his features screwed securely together so they gave nothing away.

But I knew. *I knew.*

My feet slid on the gravel beneath them, telling me this couldn't be a frequented path for guests if my heels didn't seem to get a grip for more than a few seconds.

Or perhaps it was just the way my body trembled that was making it so hard to keep my balance.

Aaron took a step forward, his body angling toward mine. Deliciously crowding me and forcing my back to come against the coarse surface of the wall.

'Hi,' I croaked, as if we were just seeing each other after a long time. And, God, why did it feel so much like we were? Like I was finally here. Finally coming *home.*

I watched Aaron's throat work, and then he took a deep breath before he spoke. 'Hey.' His palm came to rest on my jaw, cupping my face. 'Ask me what I'm thinking.'

My heart raced with the prospect of doing so as I anticipated his answer with a trepidation I had never known. But it was better than him asking me the same question.

'What are you thinking, Aaron?'

A hum rose in his throat, the sound deep and husky. It shot straight to my chest. 'I'm thinking that you want me to kiss you.'

My blood swirled at his words, turning thicker. *I do. I do.*

'And I'm also thinking that if I don't do it soon, I might lose my goddamn mind.'

The palm that was cupping my face fell, and a finger trailed down the skin of my arm.

I didn't speak. I didn't think I could.

His gaze travelled down my throat, leaving a path of shivers on my skin. 'But I was serious when I said that when I finally took your lips, you'd know what it meant.'

He stepped closer, the tips of his shoes grazing mine, our bodies almost touching. I braced my hands on his arms, not trusting myself anymore, seeing how much I was shaking. How I shivered.

'Do you know now, Catalina?' His nose brushed my temple, making my breath hitch. 'Do you know what this means?'

Aaron's mouth flicked along my cheekbone, making my back arch, my shoulders coming flush against the wall behind me. My lips parted, my answer stuck somewhere in my throat.

He released a shaky breath, his body tight with restraint. 'Answer me, *please.*'

His forehead came to rest against mine, and I watched his eyelashes hide that ocean I'd gladly drown in if he let me. Eyes closed, he inched closer, his lips almost coming against mine.

'Put me out of my misery, Catalina,' he gritted out, cupping the back of my head with trembling fingers.

My heart – my poor heart – lost it at the desperation in his voice. At the unfiltered need I heard.

'*Real,*' I finally breathed into his mouth. 'This is real,' I repeated, needing to hear the words, feel the truth on my skin. 'Kiss me, Aaron,' I told him breathlessly. 'Prove to me that it is.'

A growl – a deliriously low growl – left Aaron's throat. And before
I could even process how the sound had seeped deep, deep inside of
me, right into the marrow of my bones, Aaron's lips were on mine.

He kissed me – Aaron was kissing me – as if he had been starving
for an eternity. Just like a beast meant to devour me. His hard body
coming against mine, desperately seeking anything I'd give him.

Our lips opened, ravaging each other's mouths, while his large
palms roamed down my sides. Down, down, down they went,
stopping below my waist. My hands flew to his chest, and I relished
how hard it felt, how warm, how perfectly solid and just for *me*.

My heart drummed against the walls of my own chest, and a
sound climbed up my throat when I felt Aaron's heart do the same
against my fingertips.

The noise only fuelled Aaron to press into me with his hips. To
reward me with a wild sound of his own. His hands gripped my
waist, bringing me even closer to him, making me feel the heat of
his hardness on my belly and punching another moan out of me.

Aaron, Aaron, Aaron, my mind seemed to chant as my body went
on sensory overload.

His hands roamed over the fabric of my dress, coming around me,
dragging down my back, all while his tongue danced against mine.

Another press of his hips against mine made my body spin out of
control and sent more and more heat to pool between my thighs.

Aaron's lips left mine, revealing he was breathing as violently as
I was. Without wasting a moment, his mouth landed on the soft
spot between my jaw and neck. Looking up at the dark sky, I bared
my throat for him. Another whimper left me, carried away by the
breeze coming from the sea.

'That sound,' Aaron breathed into my skin. 'That sound is driving
me goddamn insane.'

Insanity – that was what this was. What was pumping in my veins.

He kissed a path up my throat, veering for my ear, leaving little nips that left my blood roaring. Thundering across my body. My hands toured up his wide chest, reaching the nape of his neck. My fingers tangled in his hair, pulling at it softly when he nibbled at the skin below my earlobe. When he grazed his teeth over it, I pulled a little harder.

'Hold on to me, baby.' In a swift move, Aaron picked me up from the floor, my legs going around him and my arms wrapping tighter around his neck.

Somewhere in the back of my head, I worried about the fabric of the dress, about it not being airy or thin enough so it'd let me feel him. *Aaron. All of him.*

Every doubt fled my mind as he pushed against me once more. My back came harder against the wall, and I could feel his length nestled between my legs.

Hot – he was so hot and hard.

'That's not enough. More,' I implored. I wanted more, more, more. I'd shred the dress to pieces if I had to.

As he rocked his hips in one firm motion that made me see the stars, his lips found mine again, muffling another of my moans.

'You are killing me, Catalina,' he said against my lips.

My hold on his neck tightened, trying to bring him even closer. *More.*

'I know,' he gritted out, and with another motion of his hips, he positioned himself right against my crease, almost tipping me over the edge. Aaron pressed himself against me, the heat of his hardness furiously seeping through the layers of clothing between us.

'More,' I begged again. I wasn't ashamed. I'd do it again. And again and again.

'So demanding.' A husky chuckle caressed my lips. 'If I snuck my hand under your dress,' Aaron rasped against my mouth, rocking against me and throbbing between my legs, 'how wet would I find you, baby?'

He wouldn't believe just how much. I didn't think I'd ever been this turned on, this aroused, this recklessly desperate for more.

Aaron grazed my lips with his, the touch barely enough to appease me. 'I'm not going to do that.' His voice was husky, bathed in the need I felt washing over my body. 'Not now.'

'Why?' I breathed out.

'Because I wouldn't be able to help myself,' he growled in my ear. He rocked his hips against me once more, pressing me harder against the coarse surface behind my back. 'And the first time I'm inside of you, it's not going to be a quick fuck against a wall.'

I whimpered at his words. At the loss of not having what he had just painted so clearly in my head. I'd give anything to have him bury himself deep inside me. Perhaps that way, I wouldn't feel this void in the centre of my chest.

His forehead came to rest on top of mine again. Every motion came to a painful stop. 'I'd die a happy man if I could make you come right here and now,' Aaron whispered, making me shiver. 'But anyone could walk by and see us, and that's a privilege I want for just myself.'

Sighing, I trailed my fingers through his hair and then around his neck until coming to cup his jaw. Slowly, I came to my senses. 'You are right.'

My lips puckered, pouting.

Blue eyes that shone like they had never done before crinkled with a smile. 'Look at that,' he said before kissing me firmly. Way too briefly for me to be anywhere satisfied. 'I will get foolish, crazy ideas if you start agreeing with me so easily.'

That got my pout to fall just a smidgen, and perhaps a small smile peeked out. And just as I was considering puckering my lips again, remembering how hot and bothered I still was, his head dipped again, and he kissed the remainder of that pout off my face.

'Let's go. Your family is probably wondering where we are.' He slowly dropped me to the floor. Then, he brushed his fingers over a few strands of hair that had come out of place, the back of his hand grazing my cheek before he stepped back. 'Perfect,' he said, looking me up and down.

And the word travelled straight to the middle of my chest.

He offered his hand, and I took it before it hovered in the air for a complete second. I was a needy woman, it seemed. And when it came to Aaron, I'd take from him as much as he was willing to give me. And then perhaps I'd beg for more.

CHAPTER TWENTY-THREE

Ignited. That was exactly how I felt.

It was what Aaron had done to me. He had lit me up. Unravelled something that, I realized now, had been humming beneath my skin for a long time.

Everything rioting deep inside of me hadn't been shaped out of just a few moments or an impossibly loud physical connection. What caused this uprising had already been there, buried. I had kept it submerged under the weight of *buts*, fears, and doubts. Pushed down by my own stubbornness too. But now that it had burst out, resurfacing and streaming out of me, mixed with need and want and something that was exhilarating and absolutely terrifying, I knew that I had reached a point of no return. I wouldn't be able to push it down, shove it aside, or ignore it any longer.

And I didn't think I wanted to.

Not after having a taste of what could be *mine*. And I wasn't talking just about Aaron's lips. For the first time since we had landed in Spain, every touch, look, smile, or word was *real*. After that kiss, every time Aaron grazed my arm with the back of his hand, it was because he *wanted* to. Every time he brushed a kiss on my shoulder, it was because he wasn't capable of helping himself. And every time he gathered me close and whispered something in my ear, it wasn't because my family was looking and we had a role to play. It was because he wanted me to hear how beautiful he thought I looked and how lucky he felt to have me in his arms.

We danced for hours, this time with nothing hanging over our heads, and I kissed that smile that was only for me. More than once. I simply couldn't help myself.

Tonight, I had decided I'd stay in our bubble and deal with what awaited us in New York when we got there. Tonight was ours.

Aaron closed the door of the room behind him, and I couldn't help but stare at him from my position at the end of the bed. We had just gotten to the apartment, and I had decided to give a rest to my wobbly legs and hurting feet while he fetched some water from the kitchen.

One of his arms was behind his back, making me tilt my head with curiosity. He smiled, and when he revealed what was in his hand, I almost screamed at him to stop going after my poor, weak heart. Because it wouldn't survive.

A doughnut, glazed and filled with chocolate cream. They had served them as a snack late in the night. And I had probably eaten more than I should have.

'Aaron Blackford,' I said, feeling as if something were being squashed in the vicinity of my heart. 'Did you smuggle doughnuts out of the wedding in your pocket?'

His smile turned into a grin. A bashfully, unassumingly handsome grin. And my poor chest squeezed some more. 'I knew you'd be hungry.'

'I am,' I admitted, my voice sounding all wrong. 'Thank you.' He strode across the room and placed the doughnut on a napkin on top of the dresser. I took the chance to tell my heart to chill the hell out before it was too late and we both went down.

Aaron turned, as if he knew I needed one more minute to gather myself. But instead of doing that, I gawked at his back. Watched how he shed himself of his suit jacket and delicately placed it on the only chair in the room. Dangerous thoughts started piling up in my head, traveling to the bottom of my stomach. When Aaron finally faced me, just as he was undoing the knot of his tie, those dangerous, reckless thoughts were probably displayed all over my face.

Our gazes connected, and an uncontrollable blush rose up my neck, reaching my cheeks. Ironic, how I had been devouring his lips hours ago, and now, a simple look turned me inside out.

Restless and flushed, I averted my gaze and leaned, reaching for my right foot. My fingers were clumsy as they worked at the strap of the beautiful yet painful high-heeled shoe. Exhaling with frustration, I fumbled with the thin band tied around my ankle for an embarrassing amount of time.

I sensed Aaron coming closer, right to where I was, sitting on the bed as I unsuccessfully tried to untie the clasps of my right heel. If he found my predicament funny or ridiculous, he didn't say. Instead, he knelt on the floor in front of me and placed his palm over my hands, bringing my attempts to a halt.

'Let me,' he said. 'Please.'

I did. I was beginning to understand that I'd let him do almost anything if he asked.

Aaron's strong fingers unclasped the fine straps and slowly slipped the shoe off. Killing me with a tenderness I would never – not in a lifetime – have enough of. His hand captured my foot, placing it on top of his thigh. Simply that gesture, the contact of my sole on his leg, had the power to undo me.

And it did. It cracked me wide open as Aaron's fingers slid to my ankle, kneading and easing the tension away as they went, robbing me of my breath.

Those hands. What those hands could do to me if the simplicity of what he was doing sent bolts of electricity up my legs, straight to that neglected point low in my belly.

The enemy that my own mind could sometimes be decided that this was a good moment to remind me that it had been a long time since I

had been intimate with someone. And Aaron . . . well, one just needed
to take a look at him to know that he probably had more experience
than me. Anybody would. I had barely dated after Daniel and—

'Relax.' A deep voice jerked me back to the moment. Aaron's fingers were still delicately rubbing my right ankle, softening the stiff
muscles. 'I don't expect a single thing from you tonight, Catalina.'
He looked up at me, our gazes meeting. There was only earnestness
in the blue of his eyes. 'Earlier, when I kissed you, I let myself get
carried away. Came on a little too strong, and I apologize.'

My lips parted, but nothing came out.

'You have to say something, baby. You are very quiet, and that's
starting to freak me out.'

Baby. That *baby* did things to me. I liked it. Far too much.

'You have nothing to apologize for.' I tried really hard to swallow
all those stupid insecurities. 'So, don't apologize, please.' I looked
into his eyes. 'You were perfect. You . . . really are.'

That last part left my lips as nothing more than a whisper. The
blue in Aaron's eyes simmered, darkened with determination. It
stayed that way for a moment that stretched and stretched until he
cleared his throat and resumed his work.

Turning to my other foot, he repeated the process, leaving the
left stiletto where the other one rested on the floor. He massaged my
left heel, his fingertips making their way up my ankle too. And only
after he finished kneading the muscles and tendons there, he spoke,
'All set. Let's get you out of that dress, and you'll be ready for bed.'

And that was what did it.

His unassuming words, the tenderness with which he had bared
my feet and the way he looked up at me from his position on the
floor, as if his only goal here was making sure I was cared for. All
of it broke something inside of me.

I swore I even heard the cracking sound, slicing the silence in
the room in two.

'No.'

His back straightened, his gaze rising until eye-level with me. 'Then, tell me.' His jaw hardened. 'Tell me what you want.'

Instead of voicing it, I reached out and placed my hand on the nape of his neck. I pulled, attempting to bring him closer. And Aaron let me, allowing me to show him where I needed him. Our faces were mere inches away. My memory of the taste of his lips was almost too powerful for me to resist him any longer.

Still on his knees, Aaron inched closer. Placing his torso between my thighs and his hands on each of my sides. Right next to my hips.

'What else?'

I could hear the need in his voice. I could almost taste it.

Unable to stop myself, my fingertips pulled at the strands of raven hair at his neck. *You*, I told him with that tug, incapable to articulate a word.

'I need to hear you say it,' he breathed into my lips. Not closing the gap, still not sealing it.

My other hand landed on his upper arm, and I noticed immediately how those toned muscles bunched beneath the fabric of his shirt, constrained. As if he was physically stopping himself from coming closer.

'Tell me what you want,' he repeated, his voice almost breaking.

'You,' I rasped out, a dam breaking. 'I want anything you're willing to give me.' I needed him to inch closer, to eat the space between us and make it disappear. To come on top of me until the outlines of our bodies blurred. 'It's you I want.'

Never in my life had I imagined breathless words like mine would be the key to something so powerful. A growl escaped Aaron's body, his eyes turning feral. Hunger like I had never witnessed – not even earlier, when we had kissed – burrowed itself in Aaron's features, giving way to a pained expression.

'I'll give you the world,' he said against my mouth. 'The moon. The fucking stars. Anything you ask, it's yours. *I'm yours.*'

And then my world exploded. Aaron's mouth was against mine, nothing soft about the branding contact. He parted my lips, his tongue plunging inside, while his hands slowly trailed up my back.

He pulled me to him, leaving my ass resting on the edge of the bed. My legs went around his waist, a little too high to make the contact I craved the most – that I knew would make me see those stars he had just promised me.

My head spun out of control, the feel of his strong body between my thighs overwhelming, intoxicating, provoking. I wanted to stay right here forever – with Aaron on his knees and my body wrapped around him. With his lips against mine. His hands in my hair.

No. I wanted more than that, but I needed all these clothes to go away first.

Aaron pulled me closer into his chest, making my body churn, looking for the friction I ached for.

Without breaking the kiss or his hold on my body, he stood up on strong legs, taking me up with him. Holding my legs around his waist, he positioned me exactly where I was coming out of my skin for him to be, sending a twirl of pleasure through every cell in my body at the maddening sensation of having his hardness nestled between my thighs. The warmth of his hands on my ass seeped through the clothing of my dress, the heat of his length throbbing against my centre. Hot, so hot that my skin burned.

In two strides, Aaron had me against the wall. He rocked against my centre, just once, and it ripped a pained whimper out of me.

'Tell me if you want me to stop,' he gritted out against my lips, his body stiff and rocklike beneath my hands. 'Tell me what's okay for me to do.'

Pushing his hips into me to hold me against the wall and bringing to my sight a starry sky of delirium, he dragged his hands up my sides. Stopping when he reached the swell of my breasts, his long fingers grazed the thin cloth covering them.

'Does this feel good, baby?' he rasped.

Nodding my head, I arched my back, pushing them against his hands. Hands that didn't waste a second in accepting my offering. Aaron kneaded my breasts leisurely, his thumb grazing over the fabric that covered my nipples. That urge of shredding my dress off my body returned with a vengeance. And I had to physically fight my hands from exposing my skin, so he'd touch me. Not the stupid gown. Me, me. Just me.

As if he had just read my mind, Aaron's hands flew to my shoulders. He took ahold of the straps of my dress, playing delicately with the fine material before asking, 'Can I bring these down?'

His watchfulness, his never-ending diligence at making sure I was comfortable, kept tearing at something inside my chest – something I was afraid that once brought down, wouldn't crystallize back as it had been ever again.

'Yes,' I told him. Hearing the urgency in my voice.

Catching me completely off guard, instead of bringing the straps down, Aaron's hands slid to my waist, dislodging me from his body. He deposited me on the floor, and my fingertips drifted from his neck to his chest at the difference in height.

Frowning at the loss, I looked up. Aaron's soft chuckle and radiant smile barely registered when those two large palms that rested on my hips turned me around. Briskly.

My hands fell flat on the wall.

His breath caressed the back of my neck, launching a riot of shivers to gallop down my body. Strong fingers reached for the zipper of my dress, just above the small of my back. He brought it down, my underwear peeking out, if I recalled correctly how low that zipper went.

I felt myself swallow, just as I heard a strangled sound leaving Aaron.

His fingers slowly trailed up my spine, a flock of tingles taking flight. When he reached the straps at my shoulders, he pulled them down. The dress slid down my body and pooled on the floor, leaving me in nothing but my panties. And, God, I had never been happier about wearing a dress with a built-in bra.

Looking over my shoulder at him, I found a troubled expression marring his handsome face. Unconsciously, my body tried to turn, but Aaron's arms came around me. One hand landed on my stomach while the other went to my hip. He pulled me into him, the heat of his whole body on my bare back, overrunning my senses.

His chin dipped, falling on my shoulder. 'Give me a minute,' he breathed into my ear.

After a few seconds of neither of us moving an inch, just taking it all in, I felt his lips on my neck.

'I'm trying to take this slow, Lina. I swear I am,' he continued, his hand drifting up my stomach. His thumb grazed the skin of my breast. 'But you are driving me right out of my mind.'

That fingertip brushed over my nipple, eliciting a deep moan out of me. Earning me one of his in return. The hand that rested on my hip slid down to my thigh, close to the edge of my panties. Just a few inches from the point where all this heat running through my body gathered.

'I'm dying to learn every inch of skin on your body.' He took my nipple between his index finger and thumb and pulled softly.

I whimpered, demolished. Devastated.

'To memorize you.' His voice danced with the same desperation rushing down my belly. 'Do you want that?'

'Yes.' My voice sounded brittle, just as much as my sanity if he denied me. 'I need you to touch me.'

Aaron grumbled, his chest rumbling with the sound. My hands flew back, landing on his shoulders and arching my body for his taking.

His arm pulled me closer, my backside flush against him.

He rocked his hips, and then his hand trailed up and down my thigh. 'Open up for me,' he demanded into my neck while pushing my legs open with his knee from behind, widening my stance so it granted him easier access. 'Let's finally see how wet you are.'

His fingers snuck under the edge of my panties, grazing the hair and skin there and making my legs wobble at the pleasure of the powerful contact. Aaron's hold on my hip tightened, pulling my back against his hard length, and I felt it pulsating against my skin, even through the fabric of his pants. Continuing his path, his fingers finally reached my wet folds, pressing for just an instant and then gliding down slowly.

My lips parted as a moan climbed out of my body. I hadn't been this wet or turned on in my entire life.

'Fuck.' Aaron's curse wasn't more than a rasp. 'Is this all for me?'

If I'd managed to whimper an affirmative reply, I couldn't know. I just guessed that whatever my answer had been, it satisfied Aaron. Because his fingers moved up and down my folds, coating everything in my pleasure, turning my blood into molten lava.

'If I slide my fingers inside your pussy, I'm going to lose control,' he told me in a deep and inky voice. A warning, a promise. 'Is that something you are ready for?' His thumb started circling my clit, almost bringing me to my knees.

My back arched. 'Aaron.'

His voice lowered even further. 'That's not an answer, baby.' His fingers increased their pace, making me light-headed. 'Do you want me to get you off and hold you until you fall asleep?' His other hand rose to my breast, teasing my nipple. 'Or do you want me to claim it with my cock?'

So commanding and yet so fucking thoughtful. Cherishing me, ravishing me. He was everything I needed. Everything my body craved and my heart had been missing.

For what I would soon learn was the last time tonight, I told him what he'd demanded to hear. The truth that I had kept under key deep inside. 'I'm ready, Aaron.' I brought my hand to his, which was partly covered by my panties. 'Take me. All of me.' I tightened my hold on him and pressed both our hands against my centre. 'Claim me.'

Aaron didn't lose any time. One of his fingers slid inside me in one swift motion, a moan forming in the depths of my chest at the blissful invasion.

God. It had been so long since nothing but my own fingers had been there.

'You are drenched, baby. All for me.' Aaron kept thrusting inside, adding a second finger and bringing bright little spots to the backs of my eyes. 'All of you, mine.'

Something started unravelling, cracking me wide open. Tilting my body toward the edge. 'Aaron. This . . . this is too much.'

Panting. I was panting as I lost control over my own body.

'It's not too much. This is what *real* feels like,' he murmured against my neck as his other hand grazed one of my breasts.

I was so close to toppling over. A million different sorts of sensations cascaded down my body, spreading from every point where Aaron was touching me. Tattooing my skin. The way he thrust his fingers inside of me. Or how he played with the tips of my breasts. The rocking of his hips against my backside, in sync with the plunging of his hand. It was all too much. Too much.

'That's it. I can feel your pussy gripping my fingers.' His words pushed me a little closer to the edge. Every single second of this blissful torture blinding me with more pleasure. 'Ride them, baby. Come on them.'

And I did. Oh God, I did. I tipped over the edge. My head went spinning; my limbs were robbed of all strength. And while I moaned and whimpered senseless words mixed with Aaron's name, his fingers kept driving inside of me. Dragging it out, walking me through it, until eventually slowing down and coming to a stop over my still-pulsating centre.

After what could have been a couple of seconds or a few minutes, Aaron extricated his fingers from me. Tipping my head to the side, I looked up because I wanted to see his face. His handsome face and ocean-blue eyes. I found him gazing down at me with a smile that was new. It was one that I had never seen. One mixed with hunger and need and something else. Something more powerful than all that.

As I eyed him, probably with a spent and blissful look on my face, I watched how he lifted the fingers that had been inside of me moments ago and introduced them inside his mouth. His eyes closed, and his face contorted into an expression I would never forget. An expression that would be branded in my mind for the rest of my goddamn life and that would haunt me in the wet dreams I'd start having now.

Aaron grunted, opening his eyes back and finding mine. 'I could come just with your taste. With you in my arms like this.'

So primal, so basic, so hot.

I couldn't begin to articulate an answer, to move. He must have seen that because one of his arms went below my legs and the other around my back. Picking me up from the floor, he carried me to the bed and placed me on top of the velvety linen.

Aaron stood to one side of the bed, his fingers flying at the buttons of his shirt.

One of them unclasped, his chest peeking out of the fabric. My hands itched to touch him. That was what tore through my absorption. I wouldn't let him get that away from me. I *wanted* the privilege of undressing him. Crawling across the bed as my gaze zeroed in on that next button, I made my way to him. Straightening on my knees when I reached him.

'I want to do this.' My hands replaced his, taking infinite pleasure in every little button that came undone under my fingers. One by one, I worked down his torso. Feeling how Aaron's chest swayed up and down, his breath coming in and out heavily. When I was done, I shed him of his shirt, discarding it on the floor.

If I had thought his chest was flawless the day I had seen it for the first time, now – with everything else, with every powerful emotion humming under my skin – it was simply heavenly. My palms landed on the taut skin, and I was catapulted straight into heaven.

My fingertips memorized every mount and valley, every inch of skin that seemed to have been sculpted in stone. Tight, smooth, glorious.

All of him for me.

Grazing my nails down his chest, I reached his stomach. Aaron shivered under my touch. Not satisfied, I slid my fingers further down, following the thin line of dark hair. Enthralled, my gaze devoured every one of my motions. God, there wasn't enough time in a lifetime for me to get tired of this sight. Of him under my hands.

Reaching the button of his pants, I looked up. Just in time to watch Aaron's jaw bunching, the blue in his eyes glazing. My fingertips brushed lower, feeling him thick and hot through the dark fabric of his suit. He grunted, pushing his hips up into my hands.

My knees wobbled under my weight, my head lighter as I grazed my palm over him.

Aaron's head dipped, his lips falling on my temple, brushing a kiss there. His hands came up and landed on top of mine. Fumbling with the button together, we undid it. Next was the zipper, and I . . .

Hesitated. Froze.

Even if I felt like I would implode if I didn't bring that zipper down, I hesitated. My fingers shook with the thought.

We are doing this. And fuck . . . this feels like more than sex. It feels like so much more.

'What's wrong, baby?' Aaron whispered against my temple.

Looking up, I searched his face. How could I tell him that all my bravado had somehow died? That my hands shook with need but that I realized I didn't really know what I was doing? What we were doing?

Aaron released a breath, his jaw setting with decision. Something clicked behind his eyes.

He took both my hands in his and placed them above his chest. 'My heart is beating a million miles an hour too. Do you feel that?'

I nodded my head, some of my fear dissipating.

Then, he brought my hands against his hard length. 'Do you feel this too, Lina? Do you feel how hard I am in my pants?' He punctuated both his questions by thrusting his hips into my palms.

I exhaled through my nose at the throbbing contact.

'Yes. It's all because of you. It's you who makes my cock this hard. And it's you who makes my heart want to break out of my chest with a brief touch or a simple look. But it's nothing to be scared of. We are in this together, remember?'

His words fuelled something inside of me, unearthing the need from beneath my sudden insecurities. My doubts. My fears.

I dipped my head, placing a kiss above his heart. 'We are.' Then, my hand moved over the fabric of his pants, palming his length. Very slowly.

Aaron groaned, and I felt his lips falling on my temple again. He placed an encouraging kiss there. 'Take me out.'

I obliged. I was at his mercy. I'd do anything if he asked. So, I unzipped his pants, zeroing in on the bulge contained in his boxers. Following his demand, I slid down both his pants and underwear. Just enough so his length sprang free. My fingers circled him, giving him one single stroke.

A strangled sound emerged from Aaron's body. 'Jesus, that feels so good.'

Stroking him once again, I relished in the feel of his cock between my fingers, smooth and hard, throbbing under my touch.

I wondered how it'd feel under my tongue. Following my hasty impulse, I leaned down, hearing Aaron's gasp at my sudden change in position. I placed my lips on his shaft, circling him then with my mouth, making contact with my tongue.

God. All the blood in my body pooled down in my centre, my need pulsating and piercing every one of my senses.

Taking hold of my hair, Aaron pulled delicately. 'Baby.' He tugged at my hair again. This time, his hips reared back, just enough to make me stop. 'I want this – I do – but I'm not going to come in your mouth tonight.'

Moving his hands to my shoulders, he pulled me up. In a deliriously swift move, he had me on my back. In another one, he got rid of his pants and boxers.

Aaron is naked.

Every single thing about him was solid and delectable. Big. Powerful. Perfect. *And all for me.*

My breath hitched at the thought.

Hungry blue eyes, which I would gladly get lost in, swiped up and down my body as I lay on the bed. Just as I wanted to learn by heart the lines delineating his flexed arms and chest, memorize that jutting thickness that had me licking my lips, commit to memory those powerful thighs that had always driven me crazy. I wanted to tattoo all of it in my mind. Keep it forever.

Aaron walked to his toiletry bag, which rested atop the small dresser in front of the bed, and grabbed a foil package.

Walking up to the bed, he let the condom fall on top of the covers, right beside me. I followed all his movements, enthralled, unable to move myself.

Looking down at me with burning intensity, Aaron brought his hand to his length and pumped his hardness. One hard pump.

'I don't know how I'm going to take this slow,' he rasped, giving his cock another rough and hard thrust with his fist.

'Then, don't,' I begged, eating up the image before me. Stopping myself from pouncing on him. 'Don't take it slow. I want all of you. All around me. Inside of me. Everywhere.'

Before my own words registered, Aaron was on top of me, his mouth devouring mine. Devouring me. His hips between my open legs, which I had wrapped around his waist. His pulsating thickness nestled against me.

'These need to come off. Now,' Aaron grated in my ear as his fingers fumbled with the flimsy fabric of my panties.

Next thing I knew, they were on the floor, and Aaron was settled between my thighs once more, nothing between us. Right where I needed him. Where he seemed to belong. He went on his knees, granting me the view of his large and hard body.

The pace of my breath increased. My blood swirled.

Reaching for the condom, he ripped open the foil and rolled it down his length, his eyes remaining on mine.

'You are the most beautiful thing I've ever seen, lying right there. All for me.' His gaze softened, reaching into my heart and pulling something out, leaving a little hole behind. One that I wasn't sure I'd ever be able to fill again.

Aaron bent down, his lips falling somewhere beside my hip, grazing the skin all the way to the junction of my thighs. He placed a kiss there. Then another one. And another one. He grunted and then dipped lower, as if he couldn't help himself, his tongue delving into my centre.

The contact was brief, but it sent my senses flying, a moan breaking out of me.

Pleasure erupted out of that point. Spreading out like electricity, snapping every nerve ending in my body.

Aaron's reaction was immediate, his whole body coming alive, bustling. His lips made their way up my body, leaving a trail of charring kisses. Brushing soft kisses along my jaw, neck, and shoulders.

And when his weight finally settled over me, I could only reach for his face with my hands. Bringing him to my mouth, I kissed him. Slowly but intently. Leaving both of us panting.

'Aaron,' I whispered between heavy breaths, 'is this real?' I couldn't believe it; it felt like a dream. Like I would wake up at any moment.

Aaron looked into my eyes, probably peeking into a place deep within me. One that I didn't have access to myself. But in return, he granted me that access himself. Everything we felt, all that had been buried and denied, surfaced. Bared. We were stripped of all pretences before the other. Exposed.

'This is as real as it gets. As anything will ever be.' He brushed a kiss against the corner of my lips.

His words, the raw openness in the blue of his gaze, the heat of his body, the way it wrapped around me . . . all of it made my heart burst. Made every cell in my body shake violently and blow up into a million fragments.

Aaron must have felt the same because our bodies emerged from the fog and went into a frenzy. His fingers and tongue outlined my body. Lips, neck, collarbone, breasts. Everything burned under Aaron's lips. His hips rocked against my core, pushing his length between my legs, the tip sliding down with every sway of his body until reaching my entrance.

When he lifted his mouth from my seared skin, his gaze returned to my eyes. Asking permission without words.

'Yes. Yes.' I accompanied my answer with a push of my hips into him. 'Please,' I breathed, pushing again. Feeling how his cock slid inside me just a sliver. Not enough.

Placing a kiss on my collarbone, Aaron finally pressed into me. One slow and deep thrust, filling me completely and sending my head, my body, my soul to a whole new galaxy.

'God,' I whimpered, blissfully full.

Aaron's grunt fell against my temple. 'Oh fuck, baby.' His hips rocked, retreating and sliding back in with more force now, eliciting a cry of pleasure from me. His mouth nuzzled my neck. 'That sound, Catalina.' He thrust in again. 'It's going to be my end.' Another one followed.

My hands flew to his hair, pulling it with my fingers, goading him to lose the remains of his restraint.

And he did. With another grunt, Aaron thrust into me harder, pushing my whole body up. I moaned, certain I'd drown in the waves of pleasure rocking my body.

'Grab on to the headboard,' Aaron growled, taking hold of my wrists and bringing them up himself.

I obeyed, closing my fists around the bars, hoping they'd resist our attack.

'I need this,' I whimpered. 'Need more.'

Aaron rocked into me as he braced himself on the headboard. His pace gave away all remnants of control. 'You need me,' he grunted, thrusting into me even faster.

My back arched in return.

He plunged into me hard. Then, he did it again. Harder. 'It's *me* you need.'

God, didn't he know – wasn't it painfully obvious – that I did?

Another brisk thrust. 'Say it.'

'Yes,' I moaned, my body losing all its strength under the waves of pleasure. 'You, Aaron. I need *you.*'

That last word broke the thin grasp of sanity he had seemed to be holding on to. And his thrusts lost all sense of rhythm. They came harder, faster, deeper. All of it at once. Aaron rocked into me with abandon. Our flesh clashed together while I remained holding on to the headboard and watched his body move above me. His cock slid in and out of me, the muscles of his abs flexing. His powerful shoulders bunched. All of it jamming me closer and closer to the edge.

'I want to feel you milking me, baby,' Aaron said before stealing my mouth. One of his hands flew to my breasts, closing over my rosy peak. 'Come for me,' he demanded in a husky voice. 'Come on my cock.'

His words, his feral rhythm, his body pinning mine – all of it made my eyelids flutter shut. My body burned. Blazed with every thrust.

A desperate plea escaped my lips. 'Aaron.'

'Look at me. I want you to look at me.'

He lifted my weight, placing me against his chest. He moved me, burrowing himself into me from below, lifting and pressing me into him. Wrapping my arms around his neck, I felt the high coming alive. I tugged at his hair. Hard.

Aaron pulled both my arms behind my back, securing my wrists with one hand. My back arched.

'Look at you, at my mercy.' He increased the rhythm of my hips, of the way he jerked me onto his cock. 'Just where I've wanted you all this time.'

One deep and hard thrust after, Aaron's jaw tightened at the same time his other hand reached between us, his fingers landing above the spot where we were connected. Circling, rubbing. And before I could do anything about it, I was sent flying. Right at the same time as I felt Aaron pulsating his release inside of me.

My name left him in an animalistic growl. Pure, unadulterated bliss shocked me as the motion of his hips continued, his thrusts growing slower, riding us both through the climax. His arms tightened around me, his face burrowed in my neck, the outline of our bodies a blur until his hips came to a stop.

We remained right there, suspended in time. The beating of our hearts against each other's skin and the soothing rhythm of his pulse under my touch.

Eventually, Aaron pulled out of me and laid us on our sides, his arms still wrapped around me. He nestled me against his chest, and I knew I was ruined for any other embrace. Nothing else could ever compare.

He brushed a kiss against my neck. Then one against my temple, leaving his lips there for a long moment. 'Was that too much?'

I turned my face into his chest and placed my lips above his heart. 'No, never.' And I meant it. 'I . . .' I trailed off, my voice turning into a whisper. 'I liked how you lost control. I liked it a lot.'

'Careful.' I felt his hand on my hair, his palm brushing down the tousled locks. 'If you get any more perfect, I'm going to believe you were made just for me.'

My lips curled up in a giddy smile with the thought, and I had to press my mouth into his chest, so I wouldn't say what was on my mind. *Keep me. It's the least you can do if I was.*

After a few minutes, Aaron shifted. My arms locked tighter around his neck. 'I need to take care of the condom, baby.'

He tried pushing away, but I refused to let him go. His chuckle came light and sunny and just like a blow to the chest. It distracted me enough for him to slip out.

I whimpered, disappointed and cold. I guessed I was a greedy woman when it came to cuddles.

Or perhaps it was when it came to him.

'I'll be back before you blink, promise.'

Luckily for him, he was. And the sight he treated me to as he strolled, flawlessly naked, across the room helped his case. Once back on the bed, he wrapped himself around me, tucking me to his side. He pulled the light comforter over us and hmmed with deep, sultry content.

Yep, I thought. *Same here.*

'See?' he said against my hair. 'Not even a full minute.'

I sighed into his chest. 'I'm needy, okay?' I admitted, unashamed. 'And I'm not talking just snuggles needy. I'm spider–monkey needy.'

I made my point, throwing my leg over his and my arm over his chest, tangling our bodies in a way that I guessed wasn't anywhere close to being cute.

Somehow, even with my face buried in his neck, I knew he was smiling. Then, his chest rumbled, confirming that he wasn't just doing that.

'Are you laughing at my misfortune?'

'I wouldn't dare. Just enjoying you being all greedy with me, spider monkey.' His palm trailed down my spine, stopping at my backside. He squeezed. 'But if you don't behave, we will never manage to get any sleep tonight. And as devastating as it is, I only had that condom.'

My grip on him loosened a little, 'Did you ... expect this to happen?' I asked, thinking of him slipping a condom in his luggage. A rush of anticipation rose beneath my skin.

'No,' he answered softly. His fingers making their way up my back. 'But I'm not going to lie to you; a big part of me hoped it would, and maybe that's why I left it in. It had been in there forever anyway, so I thought it wouldn't hurt.'

'I'm happy you did,' I told him truthfully, and his hand came to rest at the nape of my neck. His fingers slipped in, tangling with my hair. 'It's too bad you didn't think of throwing in more.'

The sound that came out of Aaron's throat gave me life. 'Oh yeah?'

Instead of answering what I hoped was a rhetorical question – because how could I not mourn the loss of more mind-blowing sex like that? – a different question popped up in my mind.

'Can I ask you something?' I ventured, leaning back so I could look at his face.

Aaron's head tilted back too, finding my eyes. 'You can ask me anything.'

'How in the world is your Spanish so good?'

His lips tugged up sheepishly.

'Seriously,' I continued, grilling him for an answer. 'I had no idea you spoke a word of Spanish. You never told me you were so good at it.' I watched his eyes sparkle at the compliment. I liked putting that there. Just as much as I liked making him smile. 'To think that you might have understood all the names I called you.'

He sighed, his cheeks turning a little pink. 'I really didn't.'

'What do you mean?'

'You said everything had to go absolutely perfectly.'

I searched his face for the meaning behind that. 'So, you just . . . what? Started a crash course before flying here?'

It had been a joke, but Aaron shrugged his shoulders.

Understanding sank in slowly. 'Oh my God, you did,' I said under my breath. *For me. He did that for me.*

'It's not like I had never learned Spanish before. I did, in school.' He reached for my hair again, playing absently with a strand, curling it around his index finger. 'And now, there's an app for anything. I learned enough to make a good impression. I still have a long way to go.'

Something must have been plastered all over my face – some-thing I hoped wasn't the adoration I felt for him in that precise moment – because Aaron's eyes seemed oddly interested in studying me.

Then, he brought me even closer to his chest, tucked me securely against him, and placed a kiss on my shoulder. I melted into that brush of his lips like butter left under the sun.

'I bet I'm still missing all the interesting vocabulary,' he added, sounding thoughtful. He brushed another kiss on my shoulder. 'The best words.'

'Oh.' My lips curled up, interested in the direction the conver-sation was taking. 'You want me to teach you all the dirty words?'

I looked up at him and wiggled my eyebrows. Aaron gave me a lopsided smile that would have made my panties drop to the floor had they been resting on my hips.

'Well, you are in luck; I'm a wonderful teacher.'

'And I'm a highly dedicated student.' He winked. And that god-damn wink disrupted the beating of my heart. 'Although I might get a little distracted every now and then.'

'I see.' I placed my index finger against his chest, watching Aaron's eyes dive down quickly before returning to my face. 'Maybe you need the right kind of motivation to keep your attention on the subject.'

I trailed that finger up, travelling across his pec and then up his neck, following the line of his jaw until reaching his lips. They parted with a shallow breath.

'This . . .' I pushed myself up and kissed his lips gently. 'This is a six-letter word in Spanish. *Labios. Tus labios.* Your lips.'

The only answer he gave me was taking my mouth in his again. As if the only way he'd learn the word was tasting it.

'And this,' I said before parting his lips and making the kiss deeper, our tongues dancing together, 'is another six-letter word. *Lengua* – tongue.'

'I think I really like that one.' Aaron's head dipped low, his new favourite word reaching my breast. 'And this? What do you call this?' he said, grazing his mouth over the peak.

A giggle that soon turned into a moan left my mouth before I was able to answer. 'That's a five-letter word. *Pezón.* Nipple.'

Aaron hmmed while his lips travelled up my chest, placing soft kisses on his way.

'So, we have worked on six- and five-letter words.' He placed more of those pecks on my skin. 'Just for the sake of sticking to your method, we should go over four-letter words. Would you teach me one?' Aaron's wish fell against my skin.

A four-letter word. It shouldn't have been complicated. There were probably thousands of four-letter words in my mother tongue. But my mind was a treacherous thing, and it betrayed me. Often.

And the only word I could think of was a very particular one. One that, despite not being too long, was powerful enough to change things. To change people's lives. To move mountains and start wars.

It was a big word that I had promised myself I wouldn't give anybody without being sure I meant it with every single molecule in my body. Without being sure I was safe.

My silence seemed to give Aaron the perfect opportunity to keep exploring my skin. His mouth causing my heart to pound against my chest.

'I don't know,' I murmured distractedly. Scared and turned on too.

More kisses were brushed against my skin, making me fight to catch my breath.

'It's okay,' he said like he really meant it. 'We can break the rules. That's the magic in being us, the ones making them.'

He took my mouth keenly, getting me out of my head for a blissful moment. And when we came up for air, his head dipped one more time, placing an openmouthed kiss above my heart. '*Corazón*,' he said softly, so softly that the word seeped into my blood, mixing with my own so it would never be able to leave. 'Heart. That's your heart. Seven letters.'

Looking into his eyes for a long moment, I swore I could see in them everything he wasn't voicing. *I'll make it mine.* And everything I wasn't brave enough to say. *Take it.*

When Aaron finally spoke, it sounded like a promise. 'I'll earn my four-letter word.'

And there wasn't a doubt in my mind that he would. But at what cost?

CHAPTER TWENTY-FOUR

The experience of waking up next to Aaron that following morning had absolutely nothing to do with the two other times I had opened my eyes to find him lying in the same bed.

For one, we were naked. Something I thought I could quickly get used to. Effortlessly.

Then, there was this teeny-tiny thing that separated this morning from the previous ones. A technicality really. And that was the beaming grin already on my face. It was stupidly wide, and I was afraid I might have slept with it. Ridiculous, I knew. But who had the time to be embarrassed when Aaron Blackford was right there, all big and naked and ready to be eaten?

Not me.

And not when something definitely not tiny was throbbing against my thigh.

Aaron grunted, shifting and pushing that pulsating part of his body into me.

Ah, hello, new favourite limb.

'Morning,' he rasped. His voice was thick with sleep, begging me to snuggle into him.

'Mmm,' I managed to answer.

It was terribly rude of me, but I was busy with more important stuff. Like learning every inch of his chest with my hands. Or the abs that topped his stomach. And that narrow trail of dark hair. Yes, I needed to get well acquainted with that too.

'Your parents are picking us up soon,' he told me almost breathlessly.

'Yep.' I was aware. 'But one hour is sixty minutes, and if we manage to pack our suitcases in five and shower in ... three? That leaves us with fifty-two whole minutes.' Time I was planning to spend learning more of Aaron's body. 'One can do many things with so many minutes. It's all about time management.'

My fingers continued their pathway down, down, down. Finally closing around his length. Aaron pushed his hips up into my palm.

'Baby.' The word sounded strangled. But I continued palming his hardness up and down. 'Do you want to kill me?'

He kept asking me that as if I had the answer. 'No?' I rasped, my focus completely gone. 'Yes?' His hips thrust into my hand again. 'What was the question?'

Aaron groaned, and his hand came to rest on the small of my back, pulling me to his side – hard – making me straddle his hip. Unconsciously, instinctively, I rocked against him, looking for release. Just like Aaron was doing into my hand.

At that moment, I was starting to consider the possibility of forgetting about my suitcase, my parents, our flights back, work, life, and basically anything outside this bed. Anything that wasn't Aaron. I simply didn't care enough.

And the next thing I knew, we were up in the air. Well, I was.

With my body in his arms, Aaron crossed the distance to the en-suite bathroom in a few long strides. He turned the shower on without placing me on the floor.

'I hate to be the bearer of bad news, but fifty-two minutes is not nearly enough time for what I want to do to you. So, we'll need to multitask,' he explained, placing me under the stream of hot water. His eyes roamed up and down my body, hunger obscuring the blue in them.

'Time management *and* multitasking,' I told him, watching him step inside the shower with me. 'You have an impressive résumé, Mr Blackford.'

His hands came to rest on my hips. The grip of his fingers demanding. Desperate. 'And I don't shy away from a challenge. Please add that in there too.' His body pressed mine against the cold, smooth tiles. 'I'll just have to make you come with my tongue while we shower.' My new favourite word peeked out, travelling along his lower lip.

Hot fucking damn.

'And maybe again while we pack. All of it under fifty-two minutes. But I'm pretty sure I'll manage.'

Oh boy. And did he *ever*.

~

Against all odds, we had made it on time.

Turned out that Aaron's soft skills were really that impressive.

My parents drove us to the airport with more than enough extra time to have breakfast in the terminal before boarding.

Once in the plane, Aaron's arm draped around my shoulders, and I snuggled right into his side. My head rested in the crook of his neck, his delicious scent engulfing me and causing a multitude of happy sighs to leave my lips. The feeling of this new sense of normalcy that had been born between us calmed me enough to knock me out, even before take-off.

It wasn't until we touched American ground that a familiar alarm went off in my head. *The conversation.* If I were smart, I would have used that large amount of time we had been confined in the same space to have one. We needed to draw lines, to define and box whatever this thing between us was. To ... decide what to do about it.

Because while I wouldn't normally feel that kind of pressure, Aaron wasn't just anybody. He wasn't a man I had started casually dating or one I had had a night of amazing, mind-blowing sex with. He was Aaron. *My Aaron.* My work colleague. Soon, my boss. And that screamed to take a different approach to *this*. Whatever he wanted it to be. Whatever we wanted to make it.

But for that, we needed to talk.

His hand came to rest at the small of my back, his thumb brushing a circle over my T-shirt. I looked up at him, finding his gaze already on me. Damn, those eyes of his were quickly becoming my favourite thing in the world. Even more so than triple-chocolate brownies.

We had just crossed the Arrivals gate, so we found ourselves in the middle of the terminal. On New York soil. Only a few feet from what awaited us outside the airport. Whatever that was.

'Lina,' he said softly.

Judging by the way he had uttered my name, the weight with which he had said it, I knew he was going to tell me something important. But that simple word – my name, not Catalina, but *Lina* – from his lips did things to me. To my chest, to my head.

'I love hearing that. My name.' My confession left my lips quietly, as if it were meant to be just a thought. 'You don't call me Lina nearly enough.'

Aaron looked into my eyes for a long moment, not speaking. Not acknowledging my fleeting comment. It wasn't until I thought he wasn't going to say anything at all – that we would walk out of that airport in silence and continue our merry separate ways – that he spoke, 'Come home with me. To my place.'

Caught off guard, I blinked. In stunned silence, I thought about how I would love nothing more than to spend more time with him. To get lost in him for a little longer before having to go back to real life. Before we had to talk, have that conversation that would con-solidate – or not – every single thing that had changed between us.

A conversation I feared more and more with every passing minute.

I wanted to take the leap. Badly. But my experience told me otherwise, warning me not to make the same mistake twice.

And I knew deep in my bones that recovering from that – from losing Aaron, or from possibly ruining years of hard work under dirty and unfair accusations, if history was to repeat itself – would not be easy. It would be the hardest thing I'd have to do in my life. I already knew.

As all that swirled in my head, I watched something that looked a lot like trepidation, fear, dance in Aaron's features.

'Come with me, Lina.'

My eyelids shut briefly.

'I'll feed you, make sure we stay awake so the jet lag doesn't last for the rest of the week. Tomorrow, early in the morning, we'll drive to your apartment, so you can grab whatever you need, and then we'll head to work.' He paused. 'Together.'

It sounded like a dream.

Just like him. He had to be if he thought he had to convince me to go with him anywhere. I wanted to, so badly. I'd follow him anywhere if he asked. But . . .

But . . . there was always a but, wasn't there?

'Aaron,' I breathed, 'I'm going to be very honest with you.' I owed him – and me and us – at least that. 'I'm . . . scared. Terrified. You are going to be promoted. To my division leader. And that's going to change things.'

I switched my gaze to his chest. There was too much in his eyes. They distracted me, stole away my sanity.

'We are not in Spain any longer. This is real life. And this' – I waved a hand between us – 'is going to complicate things.' Or perhaps it was the other way around – him being promoted to a position above me would complicate whatever this could be.

He snatched my hand and brought it to his chest. So warm and firm, so full of all the things I wanted but was terrified to reach for. 'We'll talk about it. Later, once we have cleaned up and I have you comfortable and relaxed.' His other hand came to my chin, tilting my head back so he could peer into my eyes. 'And tomorrow, we'll talk to HR. We will ask Sharon, if that gives you any peace of mind.'

Why? Why, world? Why did he have to be so thoughtful? So fucking perfect?

'But before doing that, you'll have to give us a chance.' It was his turn for a shaky breath to leave his lips. 'Do you trust me?'

My hand, which still rested over his chest, right above his heart, fisted the fabric of his shirt. Unable to do anything else but hold on to him. 'Take me home, Aaron Blackford.'

~

Staring at the screen of my phone, I deliberated for the hundredth time if I should reply to the message with the truth.

She's gonna flip. She's going to kick my ass so hard that she'll send me right back to Spain.

Lifting my gaze off the screen and looking at my reflection in the mirror – Aaron's bathroom mirror – I didn't like what I saw. It had nothing to do with the bags under my eyes or the messy knot that had been promoted to chaotic probably somewhere across the Atlantic Ocean. What bothered me wasn't something I could point out with a finger or fix with a shower, a few hours of sleep, and a brush.

Turning away, I leaned on the edge of the impressive and enticing bathtub. Large enough to accommodate two Aarons, just like everything else in his apartment. Spacious and luxurious in a very sober and tasteful way. It suited him so perfectly.

I peered down at my phone again to reread her message.

> Rosie: Are you back? How bad was it? Tell me
> everything in front of a coffee. Or two? Maybe three?
> How much is there to tell?

Just as I finally worked up the courage to answer, three dots started dancing on the screen.

> Rosie: I can come by your apartment, bring the
> caffeine to you. In one hour? Thirty minutes? Now?

I could picture my friend batting her eyelashes at me. Rosie had never drilled me so hard for a story.

> Lina: I'm not at my apartment.

> Rosie: Still at the airport? I can come by later. Just
> give me a time.

Taking a deep breath, I typed my answer.

> Lina: I don't think I'm going back to my place tonight.

Those three dots bounced back to life on the screen. She typed and typed and typed. For a stupidly large amount of time. I frowned at my phone, bracing myself.

> Rosie: I KNEW IT.

A strangled sound climbed up my throat. *That's all she was typing?*

> Rosie: SO? Spill it. Type it, so I can tell you that I saw
> it coming.

I chuckled under my breath. Had I been that blind?

Lina: . . .

Rosie: SAY IT. SAY IT OUT LOUD. Say. It.

Lina: Chill, Edward Cullen.

Rosie: Catalina, if you don't start talking, I'm going to get pissed. And I never do that. You still don't know what a pissed Rosie looks like.

Lina: Aaron's. I'm at Aaron's apartment.

Rosie: Of course you are. I want to know the rest.

Lina: The rest?

Rosie: A condensed version – for now.

Lina: We sort of kissed. Kinda slept together.

Rosie: SORT OF? KINDA? What does that even mean?

Lina: 😊 We did. Kissed. Had sex.

Rosie: AND?

And so, so much more, I was about to type. But my thumbs froze above the screen. Ugh. Then, they worked at breakneck speed.

Lina: . . . and I'm a mess. I'm scared and giddy.
Stupidly happy too. And he's so good to me. So
good that it feels like a dream I'm going to wake
up from with cold sweat sticking to my skin. And
you know how much I hate when that happens.
Remember when I dreamed that I was getting
raunchy with Joe Manganiello and the fire alarm in
my building went off right as he was unclasping his
belt buckle, and I was cranky for a whole month?

Lina: This feels a million worlds better than that
dream. Galaxies better.

It was, and I wasn't just talking about the way my body seemed
to come alive under his touch. Hell, that was the smallest part of
all of this.

Lina: I don't want to wake up, Rosie.

Rosie: Oh, sweetie.

I could almost feel the hug that would have followed that.

Lina: Anyway, I'll tell you everything about
it tomorrow.

This wasn't a conversation we should be having via text anyway.

Rosie: You'd better do that. Otherwise, I'll
kick your ass.

A knock came from the door.

'Baby?' said a deep voice from the other side. The word making my heart pound. 'I'm going to start thinking that you are hiding from me.'

God, I sucked so much.

Aaron continued, 'Come out, and let's go get something to eat. You pick.'

My jet-lagged stomach grumbled at the thought. 'Even fish tacos?'

'Especially fish tacos.'

Dammit. He was really going after my heart.

'Okay, one minute!' I called as I typed another message to Rosie.

Lina: Gotta go. We are picking up takeout.

Rosie: Okay. But tomorrow, you and I. We're talking.

Lina: *Sí, señorita.*

Rosie: And, Lina?

Rosie: It doesn't have to be a dream you need to wake up from.

With that thought – no, with that *hope*, because that was exactly what I felt as I read my friend's message, foolish hope – I left my luscious and tiled hiding spot and went hunting for Aaron.

I found him standing in his living room, looking out the industrial-style windows facing the waterfront.

Aaron's apartment was in Dumbo, an area of Brooklyn I wasn't all that familiar with but I was starting to love more and more. The place was incredible. Spacious and stark, elegant but simple.

Walking up to him, I peered out the massive windows myself. 'These views of the East River are breathtaking.'

'I'm very lucky to be able to afford all this,' he said, and he sounded thoughtful. More than he usually did.

Turning and angling my body in his direction, I laid my back on the windows and faced him. How could I tell him that this view – of him – was just as beautiful? One simply didn't say stuff like that. So, I limited myself to look and soak it all up.

Aaron stared into the distance, the sunlight coming through the glass of the windows and kissing his skin. His blue eyes glinting under the light.

But there was something on his mind. I could tell.

'Is everything all right?' I reached out and placed my hand on his arm.

Only then did he look at me. 'Come here.' In a swift motion, he had me tucked against his chest. He squeezed me, swaying us. 'Better. Now, everything is much better.'

I couldn't disagree with him. Anything that involved being in Aaron's arms was far better than anything that didn't. I let him tug a happy sigh out of me, and I revelled in the way he hmmed when I squeezed him right back.

When he finally released me, his gaze wandered out of the window again, but this time, it did so with a small smile on his face.

Baby steps.

My eyes somehow ended on an industrial-style console that perfectly complemented the vibe of the windows – and the rest of the place. The only items on its surface were a framed photo and what looked like a textbook.

Feeling curious about who was in that photo, I walked over to it and picked it up. A woman. A beautiful, blue-eyed woman with raven hair and a smile I immediately recognised. My heart warmed.

I felt his arm come around my shoulders, and then a kiss brushed against my hair.

Letting my body fall into him, I asked, 'What was your mom's name?'

'Dorothea.' I felt his voice rumbling in his chest, right against my back. 'She used to complain about it constantly. She made everybody call her Thea.'

'Tell me more about her, about your family.'

He released a breath, and it hit my hair with a puff. 'It was her grandmother's name. "A pretentious old lady's name," my mom would say. Her side of the family was very wealthy but always unfortunate when it came to their health. They called it a curse.' He paused, sounding a little lost in his memories. 'When I was a kid, my mom was the only living member left, so I never met my grandparents. And when my mom passed away, the last one of the Abbots became me. So, I inherited everything. That's how I can afford this place.'

'That makes sense,' I murmured. I considered myself lucky to work for a company like InTech. For having a good wage coming in every month. But this place belonged to a whole different kind of life. One where studio apartments could fit in bathrooms. 'So, you don't really need to work a nine-to-five job.'

'No, but I love what I do. Even if some might call me a workaholic cyborg.'

I snickered. 'Oops, I deserved that.'

I didn't think anyone at the office knew about this. Aaron had always been so ... private. But the fact that he didn't need to work and yet worked harder than the vast majority of us was commendable. It made me love him –

Whoa. I shook my head.

'I have always admired you, you know? As much as I've bugged you for being so pragmatic and hardheaded, I have always, always admired you.'

'I ...' He trailed off, sounding at a loss for a moment. 'Thank you, baby.'

I smiled as I put the frame back on top of the console. 'Your mom was beautiful. I can see where you got your looks from.'

Aaron chuckled softly. 'You think I'm beautiful?'

'Of course. You are more than just beautiful. Don't sound so shocked. You know you are.'

'I do, but I never thought you were all that attracted to me. Not for the first few months at least.'

I snorted. If he only knew. Then, I thought about how he had phrased it. 'What gave it away? What changed after that time that made you realize I was not made of steel, Mr Oblivious?'

His hold on me grew a little tighter, and then he exhaled. 'Remember that colloquium InTech hosted for high schoolers a few months after I started? We realized there weren't enough chairs when the kids started filing in. I saw you sneaking out, and somehow, I knew where you were going.'

I remembered that day. Jerkface Gerald had miscounted the number of attendees. 'Folding chairs.'

'Yes, you shot out of there to fetch the folding chairs we kept in storage.'

Aaron had appeared out of thin air that day, exactly how he always did. Then, he had given me shit about wanting to carry the chairs on my own, that it wasn't my job to do that.

'So, what gave it away? Was it how I almost smacked you with a chair for being an overbearing jackass?'

'It was how you shivered when I came behind you to help you with one that had been stuck to a shelf. You know, right before you pulled again and went toppling down to the floor.'

Oh. Oh yeah. I remembered that precise moment exactly.

I had felt his body behind me. His arms came around me without touching me, and I stared – and shivered and flushed and had gotten all worked up – at how they flexed under his dress shirt as he tried to disentangle that damn chair. It had been like a slap on the face, how hot and bothered that left me.

'That gave it away. I just knew that the red spreading through your neck and cheeks had nothing to do with you calling me a stubborn, heartless robot.'

'Did it . . .' I trailed off, unease growing in my stomach. 'Did it ever bother you, everything I called you? Everything I said when we butted heads?'

My heart raced, as I feared his answer.

'No,' he said simply. 'At that point, I took anything you were willing to give me, Catalina.'

Something staggered in my chest.

'The story I told your sister about how we met? I was only speaking the truth.'

My eyelids fluttered shut, and I thanked the heavens I was currently leaning on Aaron, that he was holding me against his chest, because I would have tumbled to the floor otherwise.

'By the time I realized how much of an idiot I had been by pushing you away, you already hated me.'

I tried to swallow the lump in my throat. 'I heard you talk to Jeff. Accidentally.' That knot wouldn't go away, squeezing my throat tight. 'You said you'd work with anybody else, anybody but me. And I felt as if you had just pushed me aside. Deemed me worthless as a professional because you didn't like me. Because I had crossed some line I hadn't known existed. I . . . how could I look at you and not think about it after that? I blacklisted you.'

'And I deserved it.' Aaron turned me around delicately, flushing our bodies together very slowly. He looked down at me. 'I meant what I said. When you brought that welcome gift to my office, something tore inside of me. You . . . distracted me. You stole my focus, Lina. Like nothing I had ever experienced before. So, I panicked. I refused to let that happen. When Jeff suggested I work closely with you, I convinced him that it would be a bad idea. I convinced myself of that too.

'But then I got to know you.' Aaron looked down at me intently, something weighing behind his eyes, pushing me – pushing us – closer and closer to an emotion that took more and more room in my chest with every second I spent looking into his eyes. 'I watched you work, laugh, be this bright and kind woman that you are. And the crack that had opened that first day widened. It only kept growing. Making me realize how much of a fool I had been. By the time I knew I didn't want to push you away anymore, that I couldn't do it, it was too late. So, I took whatever you had for me even if that was hatred, antagonism, your obvious dislike, anything if that gave me a few minutes with you every day. If that put me on your mind, even for a little while.'

'Aaron . . .' I trailed off, everything inside of my chest, my head, my memory stirring into a loud and raging thunderstorm. 'All this time.'

'I know.'

I watched his jaw twitch, his features hardening impossibly.

'You let me antagonize you. All this time, you sat there and let me do that.' My voice shook with emotion. With the loss of a time that we could have had. But it also shook with the lie that hid in my own words.

Had I really hated him at all? It didn't seem possible at this point. Hadn't I done the same and convinced myself of that because he had hurt me?

'Why?' The question left my lips in a whisper, for him but also for myself.

'Because it was all you were willing to give me. And I'd rather have you hating me than not have you at all.'

My body trembled; it shuddered under the weight of his words. With the truth underneath the ones rising to my lips.

Love. It had to be love – the uproar causing havoc in my chest. Realization grew in me as quickly as lightning hit the ground.

'I didn't hate you,' I breathed. 'As much as I wanted to, I don't think I ever did. I was just ... hurt. Perhaps because I had always wanted you to like me, and you made me believe you didn't.'

Something flashed across Aaron's face. The space between our mouths crackling with electricity and an emotion I had never, ever felt before.

'I want your heart, Catalina.' Both his hands rose to my shoulders, trailing up my neck and cupping my face. 'I want it for myself, just how I have given you mine.'

It's yours, you beautiful and blind man, I wanted to tell him. *Take it. I don't want it anymore*, I wanted to scream at him and anyone that would listen.

But I didn't. I didn't think one could be petrified by pure, sheer joy. It never seemed a possibility. Yet there I was, standing in front of him, just as he laid his heart in my hands, and all I could do was stare at him with a thousand unsaid words waiting on the tip of my tongue.

So, I showed him. My hands reached for his face, just as he had been doing, and I brought him to my lips. I told him with a kiss that I was his. Gave myself to him with those lips that didn't seem capable of articulating any words.

Aaron lifted me off the floor and took me in his arms with a tenderness, a reverence that left me breathless, just how I imagined him doing with my heart. My legs went around his hips as his lips parted mine, his tongue taking, governing mine.

With long strides, he crossed the open space in his loft, carrying me in his arms as neither of us stopped to breathe. He placed me on the countertop of the kitchen. Beneath the hem of my shorts, the cool granite caressed the backs of my thighs.

Aaron's mouth dragged down my neck, his teeth scraping my skin, finally catching on the neckline of my tank top and pulling it down until revealing my bra. He grunted, and I felt the noise reverberate against my skin.

Hands on my hips shoved me against him with roughness, leaving me right on the edge of the counter. God, he was unleashed. My man was ravenous as he pulled at my top, briskly tugging it down to my waist, and then popped open my shorts, almost bursting the zipper. He didn't care, didn't seem to realize he had come undone.

I did that. I cracked him open at the seams.

The same kind of urgency hummed under my skin, under my fingertips, as I pulled at his T-shirt. In a swift motion, it lay on the floor. The warm, sizzling skin of his bare chest came against mine, his hips nestling between my legs, as those strong arms fused me against him, merged me with him.

I whimpered, the rest of my sanity leaving me with the sound.

Wanting the rest of his clothes gone, I tugged at his jeans. Desperately. Just as I arched my back, looking for the friction I ached – no, died – for, Aaron pushed his hardness into me, pleasure shooting through my body, even with the barrier of our pants and underwear.

I felt him hot and thick as he rocked against my centre, and that alone made my eyelids flutter, my toes curl, and my world explode. He moved again, creating more friction between us, and I saw myself coming if he did that one more time.

'Again,' I told him, begged him.

Aaron's hands palmed my ass, thrusting me against him. Then pushing into me harder, ripping a chain of moans out of me. Hustling me closer to the edge.

'God, I haven't even touched you, baby,' he rasped into my mouth. Then, he took my lower lip between his teeth as he kept moving against me. 'Haven't even been inside you yet.'

His hands took control of my useless body, mercilessly rocking me against him, and my head fell back, a prayer on my lips.

'Come,' he grunted into my ear, our hips moving against each other's. Fucking each other with our jeans still on. 'Come, so I can fuck you better.'

That – *that* – toppled me over. No, it bulldozed into me. My mind left my body, leaving me behind as I burst into pure, boundless sensation. Not even Aaron's name left my lips, even if I wanted to scream it until my voice grew raw. I was spent, rendered empty. Weightless.

His arms went around my back, and in a heartbeat, I was standing on wobbly legs. My back came against his front, immediately feeling him hot and throbbing with need. The sensation – the knowledge of having the power to do that to him – bringing me back to life.

In another heartbeat, he brought my shorts and underwear down my legs, helping me step out and shoving them aside.

I felt the warmth of his chest on my back, and then his fingers closed around my wrists. 'Hands on the counter,' he demanded, guiding my palms to the surface. Then, he widened my stance with his knee, right as he brushed openmouthed kisses down my spine. His hands grabbed on to my hips, one of them trailing down my bare backside. 'I should take you to my bed.' He kneaded my ass, and then his palm traveled to my thigh. 'I should lay you there and fuck you deep and slow.'

Whimpering, I pushed into his hips. He grunted and then reared back. I heard him unzip his pants. Then, I felt his hard length against my ass. He moved up and down, and I could tell he had just pulled himself out of his jeans, hadn't even bothered to push them down or take them off.

Madness. It drove me fucking crazy.

'You know the times I have jerked off to the thought of you on your hands? On your elbows?' He passed his shaft along my ass, making me moan in need. 'Or bent over my knee after getting all mouthy with me?'

Another moan, this one soaked with agony. Just like I was at the image of bringing his words to life.

'Oh,' he whispered. Then, his voice lowered. 'Sounds like you'd love that as much as me.'

•

One of the drawers opened and closed, and then a foil was ripped open. 'This time, I'm prepared. Have a whole box right there. It has been there for months.'

'Aaron,' I begged him. I wanted him now, or I would combust into a cloud of dust. 'I need you.' I looked over my shoulder, eyes ablaze. And saw a feral expression on his face. 'Now.' It was my turn to grunt.

The back of his hand delicately caressed my jaw, and then his palm fell on my back. He pushed me onto the counter. 'Grab on to the edge,' he growled. 'I'm going to take you fast and hard, baby.'

With a deep thrust, he was seated inside of me. I whimpered, feeling wonderfully, heavenly full, and before I could ask for more, for all that he had promised, Aaron pushed out and thrust in again. We both moaned.

One of his hands came around me and landed on the counter, the other one fisting my hair. I'd dissolve. If I didn't come soon, I'd disappear under his weight, under the rippling pleasure pooling down my belly.

'More,' I managed to say.

And the rhythm of his thrusts increased, pushing me into the granite surface, his grunts falling into my neck.

Fingers gripped my hip. 'I can give you more.'

That hand lifted off my skin and fell back with a tight slap on my bare ass. A moan like no other moan to ever leave my lips emerged from my mouth.

'I can give you my all.' Another soft smack. Pushing me down, down, down.

'Yes,' I whimpered.

True to his word, he gave me everything. He thrust his cock into me uncontrollably, the sound of his hips against my ass encompassing our pants.

'Come with me.' His front fell on top of my back, deliciously caging me. Burying me with him. His fingers now rubbing my clit, accompanying his thrusts. 'I want to feel you coming on my cock as I go off.'

One more frantic, desperate thrust. That was all it took for both of us to detonate into bliss. Groans equally powerful left both our mouths, our names blessing each other's lips with them.

Aaron's hands came around my middle, holding on to me more than holding me to him. Then, he brought us upward, slipping out of me. I turned around in his arms and leaned my chin on his chest, and he brushed a kiss on my forehead. Another one on my lips. Then another one on my nose.

'You feel and taste like you are mine.'

I looked up, right into his eyes. 'I am.'

Just two words, two simple words that were used so often in casual conversation that they shouldn't have held much meaning. But they did. Those two ordinary words uttered in that precise moment mattered. I knew because Aaron's face lit up with them. Breaking into the most beautiful smile to date. Burning down the last of my defences. And as I stared into the blue of his eyes, I watched those walls of mine collapse as if I hadn't spent all this time building them up.

'I am,' I repeated, crushing the last remnants of the wreckage with my hands.

Aaron kissed me again, sealing those two words with his lips. Adding a few more of his own. 'I'm going to prove to you that you are.'

~

This time around, instead of having the tacos to go, we devoured them right on the spot. Post-sex hunger did these things to you.

'Seriously,' I said, inserting a finger in my mouth and savouring the sauce that had stuck to it. 'I'm just saying that if vampires are going to make a comeback, the least they can do is sparkle.' Finding Aaron's gaze on my mouth, I let my hand hover in the air and felt the light blush covering my cheeks. 'Are you listening, Blackford?'

His eyes bounced up and then down again. 'Yes, vampires. Sparkles.'

I wiped the rest of the sticky sauce off my hands with a napkin. 'I still can't believe you'd be a vampire over a werewolf, by the way.'

Something else I couldn't believe either? Aaron had had that conversation with me without batting an eyelash. Not only that, but he had seemed to know a fair bit about paranormal creatures. And I had questions.

Aaron retrieved the paper from my grip and threw it in a trash can that stood next to the food truck. 'They are immortal,' he said as if there were no other point to be made.

'But you are so ... werewolfish.'

True to my accusations, those blue eyes glinted with a hungry edge. 'Am I?'

'Yes. First off, you are big and hot and—'

'Oh, I'm already loving this.' One of his arms curled around me, tugging me to his side. 'Please continue.'

'Get your mind out of the gutter.' I grabbed his hand, lifting it in the air in front of us. 'See? These are like paws. And when I say hot, I mean, temperature-wise, like ...' I trailed off. Only thinking about phallic-shaped hot stuff. *Dios*, had all the sex killed off that many of my brain cells? 'Your skin feels hot to the touch, yeah. Like a ... a heated, weighted blanket.' I turned, watching him frown. 'I say it as a compliment. I mean it in an *I'd love to get under you and snuggle right now* way.'

That frown disappeared. 'I can live with that.' His head dipped, and he placed a kiss on the tip of my nose. 'What else?'

'You are loyal.'

He hmmed in agreement.

'Also private. You keep to yourself. And even if people think that you are cold and unfriendly, it's just that you have a stoic approach to most things. You watch everything so that you can anticipate every single thing that comes your way, which, honestly, is really impressive but very annoying too.' I peeked at him over my shoulder, finding him looking at me strangely. 'What?'

'Nothing.' He shook his head, getting rid of whatever it had been that was making him look all dazed. I watched him compose himself. 'You are forgetting something.'

My eyebrows rose. 'And what's that?'

'I bite,' he said before grazing his teeth over my shoulder. Then, he nibbled on the sensitive skin where my shoulder met my neck.

Giggling like a madwoman, I let my body burrow into his embrace. But just as I was doing so, someone caught my attention out of the corner of my eye. I couldn't be sure, but I thought it was someone from work. One of the guys on Gerald's team, if that glimpse of blond hair and slender shoulders was enough to recognise him by.

Apprehension sank deep in my belly, killing my fit of carefree giggles.

Aaron didn't seem to notice the shift in me, and if he did, he didn't say anything.

'Let's go home. I have a weighted-blanket reputation to uphold.'

～

True to his word, Aaron had curled his body around mine in that gigantic and dreamy sofa that was planted in the middle of his loft. It had probably been the mixture of exhaustion, jet lag, and warmth coming off his body, but as much as I had tried to fight it, I had passed out in under two minutes flat after returning to his apartment.

Looking down, I caught a glimpse of a big and hefty hand trailing up my stomach. We were lying on our sides, and judging by the silence around us, the TV was no longer on. Aaron had probably turned it off as soon as I drifted off.

Long fingers splayed along my front, reaching the underside of my breasts. Shifting under the sensation travelling down my body, I burrowed myself further into him.

A grunt sounded in my neck. 'It's dark outside.'

My gaze went to the massive windows that faced the waterfront, as if I had needed confirmation that night had fallen. 'We fell asleep,' I said, returning my eyes to those five fingers on my stomach, my toes already curling with anticipation. 'I thought you wanted us to fight jet lag together, mister.'

'I did, for a while.' Aaron chuckled, and I felt the sound in my back. My lips curved upwards as my mind pictured his beautiful face smiling. 'But you are so fucking soft, curled up against me.' His hand trailed up and then down, and then I was pulled against him. 'I couldn't help myself. You made me lose perspective.'

I turned in his embrace, rolling so I could face him. His hand fell on my lower back, the change of positions making my mouth almost come into contact with his neck. I looked up into his eyes.

'Excuse you. Are you putting this on me?'

'Never.' He tugged me closer again, our fronts flush together. My eyes fluttered closed, and a contented sigh left my lips.

'Would you take me to bed, Aaron Blackford?'

He never uttered his answer. Instead, he peeled himself off the sofa with me in his arms. Wrapping my legs around his waist, I giggled at his sudden enthusiasm. With long, quick strides, he carried me across his apartment, passing the marble kitchen island and then making his way down the wide and uncluttered hallway and straight into the master bedroom. His bedroom. A shot of something sultry curled its way along my body. I was about to sleep next to Aaron – in his bed, wrapped in his soft, lush linens, my head on the plush pillows where his head had rested many times.

And just when I was ready to be dropped onto that king-size mattress that looked like a dream, I was carried into the en-suite bathroom instead.

My eyes took in our reflection in the mirror, not expecting how much I would love what I saw. Me, hands clasped behind his neck. Me, in his arms. Me, cheeks flushed and a dazed expression on my face because it was him holding me. Me, happy.

Aaron attempted to place me on the black-and-white tiled floor.

'Nuh-uh.' I shook my head, holding on to his neck a little closer and keeping my legs around his waist. 'I like it up here.'

'Yeah?' His voice was coated with humour but also with something thick and glossy.

I tightened my grip on him.

'That much?'

'Yep,' I admitted into his neck. 'I think you can carry me everywhere from now on. Walking on my own is not going to cut it anymore.'

His palms rearranged me around him, shifting me to his side. He dropped a kiss on my temple. 'And I think I could get used to that very quickly.' He reached for my toiletry bag, opened it, and extracted my toothbrush. Handing it over to me with a small smile, he then repeated the process with his own toothbrush. 'Teeth first, then bed.'

With a nod, we did exactly that. We brushed our teeth as we looked at each other in the mirror, all the while with me hanging off his side like a clingy and needy spider monkey. Not that I cared. I'd do this every single night to come. Once we were done, he carried me to bed.

'Aaron,' I whispered after he tucked me under his light comforter. We were facing each other, my hands were below my cheek, and only our feet were touching. 'I'm glad you came with me to Spain.' I heard him release a shaky breath as my own words seeped in, although they didn't really do justice to how I actually felt. 'Not because our plan worked. I'm actually happy that you were there with me. I'm ... more than happy. I don't think I told you, so I wanted to let you know.'

His hand cupped my cheek, his thumb brushing my jaw and lips.

'Are you glad too, Aaron?' I asked him as I covered his palm with mine.

'I don't think I can put into words just how much.' He brought my hand to his mouth and skimmed his lips over the back of it. 'And it's not only because I somehow managed to get you exactly where you are.'

'Right into your bed?' I inched closer, my thighs now brushing his.

He tugged at my hand some more, encouraging me to move even closer. 'Yes. But right here with me too. Exactly where I have always wanted you.'

I hmmed, sparks of happiness flaring up in my chest. 'They loved you, you know?' I moved my head into the space between the underside of his jaw and his collarbone. 'I mean, I can't believe I'm going to say this, but it's kind of hard not to.'

I placed a kiss on his skin, wondering how I had not realized this myself a long time ago. How ... loyal and caring and soft he was beneath all that frowning and scowling. Although maybe I had. Maybe that would explain why I had been so hurt over him brushing me aside. Over him not wanting anything to do with me. Over him not letting me in. I shook my head. It didn't matter. Not now.

'My mom has never talked so highly about someone. Isabel told me she wouldn't shut up about you. *Aaron speaks Spanish so well. Aaron is so tall and handsome. Aaron has the bluest eyes I have ever seen. Have you seen Aaron smiling at our Lina like that? He came all the way from America to meet us.* And she wasn't the only one. I was scared Abuela would try to steal you away from me, I swear. She was so ...

enamored; it kind of got a little awkward at some point.' I laughed lightly at the memory. 'Do you think I'll have to fight my own grandmother over you?'

Expecting him to chuckle, I was shocked when a deep sigh left him instead.

I looked up at him, not able to discern much in the dark. 'Hey, what's wrong?'

'There's nothing wrong, baby.' His voice was coated with a kind of emotion I didn't quite understand.

I tugged at the fabric of his shirt, encouraging him to tell me.

He sighed again. 'It's just that ... I've never had that. Not ever. Your family is so ...'

'Messy? Loud? Kind of overstepping all the time?'

'They are but in the best kind of way.' He paused, his hand coming to the back of my head. Long fingers brushed my hair down. 'The closest I've ever come to that was when it was the three of us, and somehow, I forgot what it was like.'

My chest hurt at hearing that, and I came even closer to him, wishing I could take all that pain away from him. Wishing I could breathe a little warmth into him.

'Your family loves you, and that's a kind of bond you can't force. It's a kind of love one doesn't find anywhere else. It can be over-whelming, but that's only because it's always honest. And being part of that, even if only for a few days, meant ... the world. More than you could ever know.' His lips fell on my hair with a fierceness that hadn't been there before. 'I wasn't pretending, Catalina. Not for a minute. It was all real for me. That's why it meant so much.'

'Aaron,' I breathed, not really knowing what to say. How to explain the uprising inside of me.

'So, it's me, the one who's glad. The one who's fucking relieved you took me and not someone else with you. I'm the one who's thankful.'

I swallowed, trying my best to push back the unfiltered joy threatening to flood my system and rob me of my next breath. 'You don't ever have to thank me for something like that, Aaron. You never have to.'

His chin fell on top of my head, and I felt his breath on my hair. 'I do, baby. I do.'

CHAPTER TWENTY-FIVE

'Oh my God, you look like you just came out of a sex marathon.'

'Rosie,' I hissed, smacking her arm.

Her cheeks turned red, and both her hands jumped to her mouth.

We were on the coworking space floor of the building at lunchtime, so more than a few tables were occupied with groups of people enjoying their break. We had been lucky to snatch one that sat close to the floor-to-ceiling windows.

My friend looked around. 'Shit, I'm so sorry,' she whispered.

'It's okay.' I snickered. She looked so flustered; it was even cute. 'No need to apologize.'

'It's just that you look all glowy and ruffled.' She kept her voice low and quiet.

'You can stop whispering, Rosie.'

'Okay,' she whispered again. I rolled my eyes, and she cleared her throat. 'So, you guys are not keeping it a secret or anything, right?'

'I . . . guess we are trying to figure that out.' I shook my head. 'But there's a difference between not keeping it a secret and broadcasting to everybody that I just got laid.'

'You are right. Sorry.' Some of the pink returned to her cheeks. 'It's your hair, seriously. It looks . . .' Her hand spun in the air in an overexaggerated way.

'It's really windy today, okay?' I passed my hands down my

chestnut locks, trying to tame them. I lowered my voice. 'It's not like we are constantly going at it like animals.'

Although we sort of were. We had done exactly that earlier this morning. Just as soon as the alarm went off. Both of us equally voracious and greedy with each other the moment we had opened our eyes to a tangle of arms and legs.

Only thinking about his hands and—

'Oh my gosh,' Rosie loud-whispered.

I zeroed back in on her and found her green eyes widening.

'You are thinking of it right now, aren't you?'

I didn't bother to deny it; she knew me well enough to catch me on a lie.

'In the office?' she gasped. 'It's only noon.'

'No,' I gasped back, although a spark ignited something low in my belly at the thought of office sex. *Damn, am I sex-crazed?* 'Back at his place.' I shrugged my shoulders, unpacking the bagel we had grabbed on our way to work. It felt weird, thinking of Aaron and me as a *we* who picked up lunch and headed into work together. No, the flutter in my stomach didn't say *weird*. It said *different*. Light-headed, butterflies-in-my-tummy different.

She searched my face for a long moment, making me frown. Then, she broke into a sunny grin. 'Wow. You have it so bad.'

Maybe I do, I thought, biting into my bagel. 'So, what did I miss, Rosalyn?'

'Nuh-uh.' She popped open a metallic container, revealing a rice salad, topped with some greens. 'No time to talk about my boring life or work. Things are the same. Start talking right freaking now, friend.' She dug a fork into her food, a little too forcefully. 'I want all the details. And don't leave out the cheesy, swoonworthy ones.'

My mouth opened with a complaint.

'Again, no. Don't you even dare tell me there aren't a few movie-worthy moments because I'll unfriend you.'

Plopping my bagel on the table, I sighed dramatically.

'Spill the beans, Catalina Martín.'

'Damn, since when are you this bossy?' I asked her right before she pointed at me with her fork while she shot me a dagger or two with her eyes. 'Okay, okay.' I lifted my hands in the air, took a deep breath in, and then started reciting every single thing that had gone down between Aaron and me. Keeping the name of our soon-to-be boss out, just in case.

Once my friend was all caught up – and if her shit-eating grin was saying anything, she was more than satisfied with what she had heard – I snatched back my bagel and resumed my lunch.

'Fuck, Lina,' she said through her ear-to-ear smile.

I flinched. 'Rosalyn, did you just swear' – I blinked – 'while grinning like a Cheshire cat?'

'Fuck yes, I did, you goddamn idiot.'

Jaw hanging open, I watched her look around, lifting the few things we had lying on the table and putting them right back where they had been, an unconvinced expression on her face.

'What the hell are you doing?' My throat worked, trying to pass down my bagel.

'Looking for something I can throw at your head,' she answered nonchalantly. But that grin was still there.

Is this angry Rosie? It was unsettling.

'Maybe if I did, I'd knock some sense into your hard head. Although from what you are telling me, you are not only stubborn, but also pretty darn blind. So, really, I am at a loss here. I just want to smack you and see what happens.'

My mouth snapped shut. 'Smack me? That's where your loyalty lies, so-called friend?'

She levelled me with a look that immediately sobered me up. 'Lina.'

As I released a breath, my shoulders fell with defeat. 'I know, okay? I deserve some of that smacking.' I knew how fucking dumb I had been. How blind and stubborn. I knew she was right. But I was also starting to understand what I felt for Aaron and how big and scary it was. 'Rosie, I think . . . no. I know that I—'

'Oh no,' she cut my words off.

And at the same time, a head popped up in my field of vision. 'Hi, Rosie, Lina. How are you ladies doing?'

As of right now, not too well anymore, I wanted to tell him. 'Hello, Gerald,' I muttered instead.

Neither of us bothered to answer his question.

Not that he cared, apparently, because he stayed rooted in place. 'So, how was the vacay, Lina?'

The vacay. It hadn't even been a holiday – I had just taken three days off, for Christ's sake – but there was no point in correcting him.

Turning in my chair and facing him with what I hoped wasn't a grimace, I braced myself for a few tortuous minutes of small talk. 'Wonderful, thank you.'

He gave me a knowing nod, followed by a blatant smirk. I frowned.

'Big day tomorrow with Open Day, huh?' He leaned a hand on our table, the buttons of his shirt struggling under the strain.

Why did he have to stuff himself in clothing two sizes smaller? Someone should tell him. He didn't deserve the courtesy, but the world didn't deserve this kind of sight either.

'You have an outfit picked out and all? I know you girls take your time deciding.'

My teeth grated together with the sheer effort of not turning the table over and flipping him off. 'Yes,' I answered through my teeth. 'Now, if you don't mind, we were having lu—'

'Did you have trouble putting everything together?' Gerald asked, not caring about my brush-off.

I thought I'd heard Rosie mutter something that sounded a lot like *jerk* under her breath.

Damn, she's ragey today.

'A little. But it's all sorted now,' I told him with a neutral expression.

'I bet you managed to find some *help*.'

That last word – *help* – the way he had said it, accompanied by a twitch of his eyebrows, sounded as if it meant much more than it was supposed to.

I felt the blood rushing out of my face, a chilly sensation slowly advancing in its place. 'Yeah, I did.'

I hadn't thought to hide that Aaron had helped me; there wasn't a point, but of course, that had happened before Spain. Now, there was something between us. Something new and wonderful and so very fragile.

'Yes, I just bet,' Gerald commented casually. 'I guess it's as easy as batting your eyelashes and asking nicely, right?'

Cold – glacial, icy cold – started seeping in all across my body. I shuddered.

'Things are easy for girls who ask nicely.'

My spine stiffened. *Nicely.* 'Excuse me?'

Gerald laughed, waving his hand. 'Oh, I'm just chatting, honey.'

'Lina.' My voice was frosty, but how could it not be? The chill had penetrated, made its way into my bones. *Don't let him get to you,* I told myself, begged of myself. 'Not honey. My name is Lina.' I watched his eyes roll. And it bugged me. It fucking angered me like it had never before. 'I've always been very polite to you, Gerald.' My tone dripped with fury now, so much that I almost couldn't listen to the petrifying fear beneath it. Threatening to come out. 'So, I'm going to invite you to leave our table.' I didn't want to hear whatever he had to say. If I did, everything would quiver, shake so violently that it would break. 'I don't have time for you and your sexist crap.'

His cackle travelled across the whole room, and heads turned in our direction. 'Oh, *honey*.'

'Gerald, please leave.' Rosie stood up from her chair, but he gave no indication that he'd heard her.

No, a man who wore that face, the face of someone about to lash out, was not going to listen to anybody. 'Well, well, well.' Gerald's mouth curled in grim mockery. 'Look at that.' He raised his voice. 'Gets cosy with the boss and thinks she can go around telling people off. Calling me stupid names.'

My whole world came to a halt. It simply stopped spinning. All that icy anger melted to the floor. The fear roared like a beast let out of a cage after an eternity in captivity.

There was a sharp beeping in my ears. My vision blurred. Memories from a past I had thought was left behind came rushing back, smacking into me with the force of a truck.

Whore. Slut. You fucked your way through college. Sucked some dick to get those grades.

I had done it again, hadn't I? Stumbled upon the same fucking rock. Although this time, I hadn't just scraped my knees. This time, I had gone down with everything I had. And I didn't think standing back up, brushing it off, and moving on was some- thing I'd be able to do. Not this time.

My career. All these years I had worked my ass off in a field that wasn't exactly easy for a woman. Everything I had accomplished. All lit on fire by a vile man who had turned a beautiful thing –a treasure I had only just found – into gruesome mud and used it against me.

The warm grip of a hand against my arm. Delicate. Soft too. Familiar in a way that was contradictory because it felt like I hadn't had enough time to learn. To tattoo it on my skin, so I wouldn't forget.

'What's going on, Lina?' a deep voice that spoke directly into my heart came through the chaos in my head.

My gaze wandered around, finding pairs of eyes upon more pairs of eyes staring at us. Eating it all up like one looked at a train wreck. *How morbid. How very sad.*

'Catalina?' I heard Aaron say with growing urgency.

I finally zeroed in on him, a smile wanting to claw its way out of me but dying off before it could. 'Nothing,' I breathed out, shaking my head. Wishing to will him away from here. I didn't want Aaron anywhere near this. I didn't want Gerald's poison to touch him, to splatter onto him. 'Nothing's going on.'

Something in his face was screaming at me to touch him, to cup his jaw and comfort him with soft kisses. But I didn't do any of that. I simply watched how he turned toward my friend.

'Rosie,' Aaron said, sounding so . . . wrong. So unlike Aaron. 'Tell me what's going on.'

I looked at my friend, silently begging her not to say a word. He'd be enraged, and I knew Aaron well enough to be certain that he'd do something. *He'd do anything.*

But Rosie shook her head. 'Gerald knows.'

Aaron didn't need more than that to guess what had just happened because his profile hardened into granite.

'Not like you two tried to hide it.' Gerald laughed again, as if this were all a big joke to him. 'Paul saw you two yesterday, but hey, I get it. It's not a big deal, man.'

Everybody was watching, enraptured by the unfolding drama. And, God, I was so . . . weary and worn out. I wanted to rewind life and go back to any point before this.

'A word of advice? Don't shit where you eat, Blackford. Word gets out. Especially if you are sleeping around with employees. But good for you, and hey, not that I blame her either. I see the appeal in getting it on with the boss.'

Silence. Thick, loaded silence engulfed us.

Then, Aaron's voice sliced right through it. Sharp as a razor. 'Do you want to keep your job?'

Oh no. Aaron's words had been meant for Gerald, but they harpooned their way right into my chest.

'Aaron, no.' I stepped forward, my hand coming to his arm.

'Oh, my mistake, Blackford.' Gerald tapped his head with a finger. '*Future* boss, you are not there yet. So, I think the firing privileges are out of your reach for now.'

Aaron shook off my hand, stepping in Gerald's direction, into him. 'I asked you a question.' One more slow, heavy step, and he got in the other man's face. 'Do you want to keep your job, Gerald? Because I can end you. Your golf friends up there won't be able to do a single thing, and neither will your minions at HR.'

Gerald turned quiet, the mockery falling off his face.

The frustration at being so powerless, so helpless at how everything had unravelled so out of control, brought a familiar pressure to the backs of my eyes.

I hate this. I hate it with all my fucking soul. Why do people find pleasure in bringing down others? Why us? Why so soon?

Aaron's sneer, the way his body was so stiff and impossibly tense, told me that he was about to lose his restraint.

'Aaron, stop.' My voice faltered. I couldn't cry. I wouldn't do that. Not right here with half the people in the company staring.

But Aaron wasn't budging. He remained a marble statue, awaiting Gerald's answer, as if he had a whole lifetime to do so.

'Aaron, please.' I willed my voice to harden. But he was transfixed. Unmovable. 'You are making it all worse.'

Was that the truth? I couldn't be sure, but it was what had left my lips. It was what seemed to make it through and hit him like a physical blow, making him flinch.

I watched him turn slowly, and he – the man I had come to need and want in my life – faced me, hurt embedded in his eyes.

It broke my heart, putting it there, but what was the alternative?

I should have known better. I despised myself for putting us both in this situation when I knew firsthand what could happen. And it was happening.

Unable to take a single second more of it – of myself, the hurt in Aaron's eyes, *everything* – I turned and walked away. I saw myself leaving the room and striding across a long hallway. I kept going, taking turns and climbing down stairs without a clear sense of direction. I was on automatic, and cowering was my default.

'Catalina, stop running away.' Pure, unfiltered desperation governed Aaron's voice, and it sickened me.

I despised myself even more for putting on him yet another ugly thing.

'Talk to me.'

I kept walking, not wanting to turn and not knowing where we were in the building. An empty hallway somewhere.

'Catalina, would you stop fucking running? Please.'

My legs came to a sudden halt, my eyes closed. I heard – sensed because that was how it worked now; I could feel the warmth of his body, crave it – Aaron walk around me, and when I opened them back up, I was greeted by an angry, miserable man.

'Don't do this. You hear me?' His voice didn't crack or waver. 'Don't you even think of it. I won't let you quit.'

God, he knew me so fucking well. Better than I did myself because his words only solidified what had been bubbling inside of me in the last few minutes.

But I was furious, so mad at the world and at myself. 'Easy for you to say,' I snapped. Unfairly. But Gerald's poison was eating away at me. Blackening everything in its path. 'I'm the one whoring out anyway, right? You'll brush it off and move on.'

He blinked, his features contorting with outrage and pain. 'Easy for me to say? I'll brush it off?' he hissed. 'You think it was easy for me not to break his face on the spot? Maybe fuck up his mouth enough so he couldn't utter a word for a few weeks? Not to fucking end him for being a worthless pig?'

I believed Aaron would have done that. I knew he would have. And that . . . dissipated my anger, leaving anguish in its place. How could I ever have anything for him that wasn't adoration?

'I won't let you do any of that,' I whispered. 'He's not worth the trouble you'd get into.'

'But you are. You are worth all that trouble. You are worth walking through a fucking fire for. Don't you see that?' He exhaled roughly through his nose, his hand coming to my cheek, making me lean on his touch out of pure instinct. 'Whatever shit Daniel put in your head about you not being worth fighting for is wrong. Love is worth fighting for. And I am not him, Lina. This is not the past either.'

I shook my head, but his palm held on to my face harder.

'When there's a rock on the way and you fall, I tumble down with you. We fight our way up together.'

'It's not that easy, Aaron.' I wished it were. I wanted so bad for the world to be that goddamn easy. 'Those are just idealistic, beautiful words. At the end of the day, you can't protect me from everything, hold my hand, and fire whoever disrespects me.'

'Maybe I can't. But that doesn't mean I'm not going to try. When someone mistreats you and I have the power to do something about it, I'm going to speak up. I'm not going to wait on the sidelines and watch you take the hit of it on your own.' His chest heaved, moving up and down almost violently. 'Just how I know you would fight tooth and claw against anyone who tried to hurt me. We protect and heal each other. That's how this is supposed to be.'

'This is not only life we are talking about. This is my career. Yours too, Aaron.'

'It is, and I would never do anything to jeopardize it.'

'But what about everybody else? They might. Look at what

happened with Gerald.' I fought the sudden urge to lean on his chest and break down. 'What happens from now on? Every time I accomplish something, I will fear the possibility of someone pointing a finger and accusing me of sleeping my way to it.'

His jaw clenched, fury seeping into his features again. 'Things don't need to be that way. Gerald is not everyone else, Lina.'

I closed my eyes, not able to work around the lump in my throat.

Aaron continued, 'I'm not downplaying your fears, baby. I swear I'm not. But we can't give up at the first sign of adversity. We can't let everyone else matter more than we do. Not without giving us a fair shot.'

But what if we don't even get the chance of giving this a shot? I wanted to scream.

'I need you to trust in us, in me. Can you do that?'

'I trust you, Aaron.' I shook my head and stepped out of his reach. 'But this is just … too complicated. I don't think I can do it. Go through it again.' My heart would never recover if this didn't work. If Aaron fled the ship like Daniel had.

More hurt poured into the blue of his eyes. 'You don't then,' he whispered, his voice broken. 'If you mean that, then you don't trust me.'

Silence weighed down on us. Aaron's shoulders eventually falling.

'I love you, Lina.'

A crack sliced its way across my poor, beaten heart at how wrong those four words sounded. How void of happiness and full of sorrow they were when they shouldn't have been.

'How is it possible that it feels like you are breaking my heart, and I haven't even had you yet?'

My soul shattered. I broke in a hundred million pieces.

'I can't make you trust me like I need you to. With your whole fucking heart.' He searched my face, those blue eyes missing their usual light. Reflecting only hurt. 'I can't make you run into my arms instead of in the opposite direction. I just . . . can't make you love me enough to give us a chance.'

A hole opened in my chest, my knees almost giving out at the earth beneath my feet tilting the wrong way. Unbalanced.

We stared into each other's eyes for a long time, our hearts in each other's fists for all the wrong reasons. It all felt unreal. Like a cruel nightmare I'd wake up from any minute now.

But it never happened. At some point, I thought I heard his phone ringing, and I watched him ignore it until it rang again. And again. Then, I thought he pulled it out of his pocket and peered down at the screen. But I wasn't sure.

My head kept chanting, *Trust him, trust him, trust him*, making it hard for me to make sense of anything else but that.

I was trapped by my own mind. Sucked into a vacuum where I didn't grasp time or space. Although I did remember one thing. And that was Aaron's back moving away from me. His legs walking him down the empty hallway and him not looking back.

Not even once.

CHAPTER TWENTY-SIX

Rosie came home with me that night.

We curled under a blanket on my bed and rewatched *Moulin Rouge!* on my laptop. How tragic – to find love and see it slip through your fingers before your eyes. I always wondered what Ewan McGregor would have done had he known since the moment he met the love of his life that their story wouldn't last more than one hundred thirty minutes. Would he still take her hand in his and jump? Would he still hold on to every moment left even if only a few? Would he still lie down by her side, knowing that when she was gone, that space would never be filled again?

Rosie didn't even think before giving me her answer. 'Yes,' she whispered. 'When you find that kind of love, time stops mattering. Come what may, Lina, he would love her regardless of how long they had.'

Then, we both bawled our eyes out. Rosie because she could never hold it in when 'Come What May' kicked in, and me . . . well, mostly because I had welcomed the excuse.

So, I cried. I let those tears fall as I held my phone in my hand. Waiting for a call, a message, a sign that I knew I didn't deserve. But that was what dumb chickenshits like me did. They cowered, hid under a blanket, and cried to 'El Tango de Roxanne'.

Ugh. I didn't like myself one single bit.

But come what *fucking* may, I'd still have to live with myself for the rest of my life. Find solace in the little time I had shared with Aaron. Past tense. Because when he had asked me to run into his arms instead of in the opposite direction, I hadn't. When he had asked me to trust him—in us—wholly, I hadn't been capable of doing it, even when I thought I had. And that had pushed him to walk away.

I pushed him away. I was the only one responsible for that.

Fuck. I wanted him here. With me, mending the broken pieces of this mess together. I wanted him to tell me that he believed we could still be fixed. Glued back together and good as new.

But that was so selfish and so very naive of me. Stupidly so. Sometimes, as much as we wanted something, we weren't meant to have it. To keep it. Not when it complicated everything else. And this thing – love because that was exactly what it was – between us did. It complicated both our lives, the promises of both careers.

We were tripping each other, making each other fall, just how Daniel had said all that time ago.

We'd have grown to resent each other. Because that was what the poison born of malicious mouths did. It infected everything. And I knew just how much.

So, yeah, after *Moulin Rouge*-crying-gate, the following day obviously sucked. It was probably one of the worst, most miserable days I remembered, and I knew a fair bit about those. I dragged my feet the whole day, somehow managing to get through the eight to midnight Open Day for a bunch of faceless suits. Names and faces bounced right off me, and I presented topic after topic as if every word were being ripped out of me. If Jeff had been around to witness that lame attempt at being welcoming, accommodating, and approachable, he'd have fired me on the spot.

And I wouldn't have found it in me to care.

That was how ironic life could be sometimes.

When I entered the building on day two without Aaron – which

I realized was my new way to count down time – I waited for the whispers of my colleagues to reach my ears and their fingers to be pointed at me for no reason other than Gerald's public accusations. By the time the clock hit five p.m. – after I spent the day wishing I'd get a glimpse of Aaron and dreading it, all at the same time – nothing had happened. None of my colleagues had batted an eyelash at me. No disgusting rumours, no nasty accusations, nothing. Not a flash of Aaron either.

On day three without him, an odd kind of restlessness burrowed itself in me. I missed Aaron. I missed the possibility of what had been growing between us, and that started outweighing everything else. It didn't seem so important that the incident with Gerald had not led anyone to treat me any differently. I couldn't find it in me to be relieved. What did it matter when there was a hole in my chest?

I missed Aaron's face, the ocean blue in his eyes, his stubborn frown, the way his lips puckered when he was lost in thought, the wide line of his shoulders, how he effortlessly stood tall and big as life wherever he went, and his smile – that smile that was just for me. So much that I set camp in my office, left the door open, and waited for him to walk down the hallway at some point in the day. Or to hear his voice even if in the distance. That would have been enough to appease that need burning inside of me. But none of that happened.

On day four, I finally gave up and knocked on his office door, going unanswered. And when I asked Rosie if she had seen him around at all, she hugged me and said she hadn't. Neither had Héctor or the few other people I had somehow found an excuse to ask.

That was exactly why I was pacing from one corner of the hallway to the opposite one as I waited to be called into Sharon's office. Just like I had been doing at home last night. Or that morning in my office. Because he had disappeared. And I hated not knowing why, not seeing him, not having him around, not . . . having an excuse to call and ask him because I had pushed him away and the last thing he probably wanted to do was talk to me.

'Lina, darling,' Sharon called as her head peeked out of her office, jerking me back into the present. 'Please come in and take a seat.'

Following her inside, I let myself fall into one of the chairs. I watched the blonde woman sit down and lean over her desk with a secretive smile.

'Sorry about the wait. You know how some people think HR has the answers for everything.' She chuckled with bitterness. 'Even for things like New York City Council deciding to repave the part of the road right outside their window.'

Any other day, I would have laughed too. Perhaps make a joke about how only the fittest could survive the city that never slept and always closed some road to keep you awake at all times. But I simply couldn't muster the energy for that.

'I'm sure it makes up for a few awkward conversations.'

Sharon's eyes scanned my face, something like understanding dawning in her features. What exactly she found or understood, I had no idea.

'All right, let's cut to the chase.'

Good. I liked that. Just like I had always liked Sharon too.

'I've called you here in light of some serious allegations that have been made, which directly involve you.'

Something dropped to the bottom of my stomach, and I felt myself blanch.

'Oh . . . okay.' I cleared my throat. 'What do you want to know?'

She inhaled deeply before she spoke, as if she was readying herself for something.

'Lina,' she said, using a tone that I had heard from my own mother – comforting but also admonishing – 'we both are aware that Gerald knows the right kind of people, and frankly, I will never understand how someone so horrible manages to make so many good "acquaintances". ' Her fingers air-quoted that last word. 'But as much as he has remained untouchable so far, that doesn't mean that he can't be knocked down. For that, however, we must do something. We should at least try.'

I felt myself nod, still trying to process what Sharon was telling me. She was admitting to being on my side. Not only that, but also she wouldn't remain a silent bystander.

'If that's something you want to do, we can work together on an employee formal complaint. I can help you. You'd need to sign it and submit it to us, and after that, I'd try to push for a thorough investigation. I know many complaints are ignored, but more than a few people having your back will make a difference.'

More than a few people?

'What . . .' I trailed off, shaking my head. 'What people? I don't understand.'

She flicked her nails on the table, tilting her head. 'After the alter- cation in the coworking floor, a number of people came by my desk to inform me of what had happened. Half of them wanted to file the complaint themselves, but just like I told them, it has to be you.'

'I . . . I just . . .' My gaze fell on my hands, resting on my lap. I felt my heart expanding with gratitude. With something else too. Realization. 'So, they are on my side? They have spoken on my behalf and not Gerald's?'

'They are, Lina.' Sharon smiled. 'And they have. I know people like Gerald often go unpunished; it's how the world works some- times. But that doesn't mean we should stop trying to change that, does it? Doesn't mean that we stop fighting.'

Her words reminded me of those someone had said to me, begged me to believe, only a few days ago. Words that I had chosen to ignore.

'You can think about what I just told you. Okay? Take your time to decide what you want to do.'

'Yeah, I will.'

There was so much to think about. So much to process. To anybody else, this might have been nothing more than a bureaucratic process I should have thought of before, but to me? Learning that my colleagues – those who had witnessed everything – were actively taking my side, it meant something. Although it didn't change what I had done. How I had thrown away everything I could have had with Aaron. How I had denied him the one thing he had asked of me. My full trust. My faith in us. And over what? He would have given me that much, and I had just given up without a fight.

'And please,' Sharon said, 'if you could tell Aaron to come by as soon as he's back. I can't seem to get ahold of him.'

As soon as he's back?

'Oh, erm, I don't ... I just ...' My words tumbled out of me, mixing with the questions spinning in my head.

'It's all good, Lina. He was very clear about your relationship. Came here first thing this week to ask if there was any kind of company policy or contract clause that would perhaps complicate things.'

The heartbeat that had flattened, accompanying me during these days without him, came back to life, peeking out. He had come to HR to be sure that all fronts were covered. To reassure me. Because he'd known that I'd need exactly that. Because he had wanted me to feel safe.

Tears that hadn't been there before were in a rush to get to my eyes.

'Hey, it's okay, Lina. There aren't. There's no reason for you guys to worry. No stones in the way.'

No. The only one taking those possible obstacles on our way and turning them into impediments we couldn't get over was me.

'Okay,' I muttered, willing my eyes to hold tight a little longer. 'That's good.' Nothing was good. Not a single thing because I had ruined it anyway.

'All right, good.' Sharon's blonde head bobbed, her motherly eyes warming up. 'But please, do tell him to call me back, yes? I know these are hard times, but it's about his promotion.'

Hard times. Those two words echoed through my mind.

Sharon's earlier request bounced right back. *'Tell Aaron to come by as soon as he's back.'*

'Did ... did Aaron leave? Did something happen?'

Sharon's eyes widened, confusion mixing up with shock. 'You don't know?'

I shook my head, feeling my skin pale. 'No.'

Her head shook. 'Lina, this is not my place—'

'Please,' I begged, now desperate to know what was wrong. Need clawing at my skin. 'Please, Sharon. We had a fight, and I just ... messed up. It doesn't matter. But if there's something wrong, if something happened to him, I need to know. *Please.*'

She looked at me for a long moment.

'Darling,' she finally said, and that alone made all the alarms in my head go off, 'he had to fly home. His dad is ... he has cancer. He has been in a critical state for the last few weeks.'

CHAPTER TWENTY-SEVEN

There was this show I'd loved when I was a teenager. It was an American TV series we got on one of the Spanish national channels – naturally, dubbed. I absolutely loved it. High schoolers with big dreams and bigger egos – or hearts, depending on who you asked – angsty plot twists, and a level of drama someone at sixteen shouldn't have been experiencing, at least not in a small town somewhere in North Carolina. Or in the north of Spain for that matter. Which was perhaps why it all resonated so much with me.

There was this one episode in particular that had somehow stuck in a way others never did. It started with a voice-over narrator who asked something along the lines of, 'what's the minimum length of time with the power to change your life? A year? A day? A few minutes?'

The answer to that question had come to be that when you were young, one single hour could make a difference. It could change *everything*.

And I . . . wholeheartedly disagreed.

One didn't need to be young for their life to change in the span of an hour, a handful of minutes, or nothing more than a few seconds. Life changed constantly, wickedly fast and terribly slow, when one least expected it to or after a long time of chasing that change. Life could be turned around, inside out, backward and forward, or it could even transform into something else entirely. And it happened regardless of age, but most importantly, it didn't care for time.

Life-altering moments spanned from a few seconds to decades.

It was part of the magic of life. Of living.

In my twenty-eight years of life, I had experienced few but very different life-altering moments. Some had lasted seconds, no more than glimpses or moments in which a realization dawned. And others had lasted minutes, hours, even weeks. Either way, I could count those moments with both hands. Recite them from memory too. The first time I'd dipped my feet into the sea. The first math equation I'd solved. My first kiss. Falling in and out of love with Daniel. All the terrible months after. Boarding that plane to New York to start a new life. Watching my sister walk down the aisle with the biggest, happiest smile I had ever seen on her.

And then there was Aaron.

I thought I wouldn't be able to pick one single moment when it came to him. Because it was *him*, the one thing that made that span of time important. Life-altering.

Falling asleep in his arms. Watching his lips bend into that smile that I knew now had only been for me. Waking up to his voice, to the warmth of his skin against mine. Watching his face crumbling down. Him walking away. His absence.

All of them had left a dent in my heart. In me. All of them had changed me. Shaped me into someone who allowed herself to open up, to love, to needing and wanting to give herself not to anybody, but to *him*.

But as much as all those moments that had made me fall helplessly in love with him left a mark I'd never be able to erase, one that I didn't think would ever fade, it was the split second when I had *known* I needed to get myself on a plane to Seattle and find him, the one moment that felt ... transcendental. The realization that I had let him go too soon, too carelessly. So foolishly. The moment it had dawned on me that nothing else besides going to him mattered. That nothing should have stopped me from running into his arms. From being there for him when he needed someone the most.

But was it too late? Was the clock still ticking on my life-altering moment, so I could turn it around, or had I lost my chance?

My head spun with that question for six hours on the flight from New York to Seattle, continuously bouncing from blinding hope to the dread that could only come from anticipating loss. And when the plane touched ground, I still wasn't sure whether to feel hopeful I was closer to him or whether I should have employed that time to ready myself if Aaron told me that it was too late and asked me to walk away.

I thought about it some more as I waited for a taxi, drove to the first hospital on my list of medical centres with oncology specialists in Seattle, and asked in reception for Richard Blackford – a name I had dug out from the internet from what Aaron had told me about him and his past.

That question kept whirling in my mind as I turned around, got myself into a new taxi, and repeated the whole process with hospital number two. Then with hospital number three.

And right as my knees almost doubled with a mix of relief and trepidation at finally hearing the nurse at the counter of hospital number three ask if I was *family* or *friend*, that question that was stuck in my head was still screaming at me to be answered.

It still was now as I made my way to the waiting room on what would soon become the longest elevator ride of my life.

Did I throw it all away out of fear and stupidity? Am I too late?

So, when the polished and metallic doors finally opened, I stumbled out of the elevator like someone walking out of an interminable road trip. Limbs numb, skin sticky with dry sweat, and the sense of not knowing where you were. My gaze anxiously scanned the space along the hallway before me, all the way to the waiting room, where

I had been told he'd probably be – my Aaron, the man who I had to get to, to get back. And there, right there, sitting on a chair that barely accommodated his size, was my answer.

With his arms on his knees and his head hanging low between his shoulders, there was my life-altering moment.

And I realized as I stared into the distance – my heart feeling as weightless and hollow as ever when I saw him there, alone, without me – that as long as I had him, my life-altering moment would never be a measurement of time. It would never be as simple as marking a few points in the timeline of my life that I could identify as transcendent. It was him. Aaron. He was my moment. And for as long as I had him, my life would constantly be changing, be altered. I'd be challenged, cherished, loved. With him, I'd *live*.

And I'd fight for that. I'd fight for him like I hadn't when he asked me to. I wouldn't take no for an answer. He was stuck with me. Just like he had promised me in Spain, in front of the people I loved the most in this world. I'd prove that to him.

'Aaron,' I heard myself say. *Let me be your rock. The hand that holds yours. Your home.*

My voice was barely a whisper, too low and quiet to make it all the way to where he was. But somehow, it did. It reached him. Because Aaron's head snapped up. As he sat in that rigid plastic chair, his back straightened, and his gaze half-turned in my direction. I could see the disbelief in his profile, as if he thought he must have imagined me calling his name.

But I hadn't. I was right here. And if he let me, I could take care of him. I would caress his back while he sat in the dull and impersonal waiting room, brush his hair with soothing fingers, and make sure he ate and slept. I'd comfort him with hugs and be the shoulder he leaned his forehead on as he grieved the dad he might lose soon. The one who had missed so much, the one I knew Aaron felt like was already gone.

His gaze scanned the space that separated us with the sheer

determination I knew only he was capable of. And I'd never know why, but I waited. I held very still as he swiped around. And then, after what felt like an eternity and at the same time not enough time to prepare myself, blue eyes locked with mine. My heart toppled over itself, and I felt the commotion inside my chest.

I watched his legs straighten, bringing him up.

Then, his lips parted with my name. 'Lina.'

It wasn't the *Lina* instead of Catalina. It was the anguish in his voice – the need, the way his hair was ruffled, the bags resting under his eyes, the wrinkles in his clothes that screamed they hadn't been changed in a couple of days – that propelled me forward. My legs sprinted across that hallway that separated us like they had never run before. Towards him, right into his arms. Just how he had asked me to. And when I reached him, I launched myself at him. I locked my body around his.

It wasn't appropriate. It wasn't the time or the place, and he was carrying so much on his shoulders already. There was so much we needed to talk about, but it was right. I knew it in my bones as his arms closed around me.

He lifted me off the floor, squeezed me into his chest, held me in his arms.

I buried my face in his neck as I kept murmuring into him, 'I'm here. I'm here. I'm running toward you. I trust you. I love you,' hoping it wasn't too late.

And he kept repeating my name. 'Lina, baby. Lina, are you really here?' Hushed and broken, sounding like he still didn't believe it was me in his arms. That it was me who had finally come to him like I should have done days ago.

No. Like I should have done an eternity ago.

Aaron walked backwards, sitting back down as he held me in his arms. As I took him into mine. My body curled into his lap, and his palm cupped the nape of my neck.

'I'm so sorry, Aaron,' I breathed into the skin between his shoulder and the underside of his jaw. 'For everything. For your dad and for not being here, by your side, earlier. How is he? Have you seen him?'

I felt his throat swallow against my temple.

'He's . . .' Aaron shook his head. 'I have seen him, but he's been out of it all this time. I just . . .' He trailed off, sounding exhausted. Defeated. 'Are you really here, baby?' he repeated, holding me tighter. 'Or is this my imagination playing tricks on me? I haven't slept in . . . I don't know how many days. Two? Three?'

'I'm here. I'm right here.' I lifted my head and moved, so I could cup his face, take a good look at that face I had been so set on despising and now loved so much. 'And I'm going to take care of you.'

His eyes fluttered closed, and I heard a strangled sound coming from his throat.

'I love you, Aaron. You shouldn't be alone – ever. And I am the one meant to be with you. Here. Holding your hand.'

His eyes remained closed, his jaw pressed tightly.

'Let me do it. Let me prove to you that I trust you and that I can earn your trust back. That I am the one who's supposed to be by your side right now and as long as you'll let me.'

'You want to do that?'

'Yes,' I rushed out quickly. 'Yes, yes. Of course I want to,' I repeated. 'I need to,' I whispered, not trusting my voice. 'Let me be here for you. Take care of you.'

His eyes opened, our gazes connecting. After a long moment, a pained chuckle rose to his lips. 'You drive me so fucking crazy, Lina. I don't think you understand.'

One of his hands latched on to my wrist as I still cupped his face desperately. I was ready to fight. I was ready to beg if it was necessary.

'You came all the way here. You . . .' He trailed off, disbelief crumpling his face. 'How did you even find me?'

'I had to come to you.' My fingers trailed down the side of his neck, my palm settling against the warm skin. 'I remembered everything you'd told me. About Seattle, your dad being somewhat known here. So, I googled your last name, the university football team, the coaching staff. Then, I looked for a list of hospitals where he could have checked in. I knew you'd be here because you wouldn't leave his side if he was in critical condition, like Sharon had told me. And you haven't. You are here. It only took me a few tries. I would have turned the city upside down if I hadn't found you. I wouldn't have rested until I got to you.'

I finally allowed my lungs to take in a breath. And I found Aaron's eyes shining with something that made my chest ache in a warm and wonderful way.

'I did call you, but it went straight to voicemail, and then I just . . . didn't want to busy your head with anything else. And . . .' My voice lowered to a whisper. 'And I did not want to give you a chance to tell me not to come. I was terrified you wouldn't want me to. So, I didn't call again. I just came to you instead.'

A shudder rocked Aaron's body.

'You blow my goddamn mind, my rules, my world,' he breathed, those ocean-blue eyes capturing my gaze like they never had before. 'When I least expect it, I find you ready to dynamite your way right into my heart. As if you hadn't done that already.' The grip of his fingers on my wrist tightened, pulling me to him, and I could feel the soft air leaving his mouth, falling on my lips. 'As if you hadn't already dismantled me for anybody else. As if I wasn't at your mercy.'

Hope, warm and soft hope, fell over my shoulders. 'I have done all that?'

'You have, Lina.'

Aaron's forehead fell on mine, and I had no choice but to close my eyes. To take it all and control this whirlwind of emotion threatening to turn me inside out.

'With every smile, you have done exactly that.' I felt his lips brushing over mine briefly, sending a shiver down my spine. 'With every single time you have been infuriatingly stubborn and impossibly beautiful, all at once.' He placed a kiss on the corner of my eye. 'With every time you have shown the world how incredibly strong you are, even when you don't believe so yourself.' A kiss on the tip of my nose. 'With all the ways your mind amazes and disturbs me in ways I'll never understand and not ever tire of.' His lips landed on my cheekbone, flicking across the skin. 'With how every single time you laugh, I want to throw you over my shoulder and run somewhere I can covet that sound just for myself.' A kiss was brushed on my jaw, his lips then sweeping along until reaching my ear. 'And with every other unfathomable way you have made me completely yours.'

'*Yours*,' I repeated, my heart expanding in my chest. Lurching itself against my rib cage. Wanting out and into Aaron's. 'I'm yours too, Aaron. So completely yours. I have . . . fallen in love with you. I don't know how it happened, but it did. I love you.' I didn't recognize my own voice, not with the loud thumping in my ears. 'I was so stupid to let you walk away. So, so dumb. But I got lost in my head. I was so scared, Aaron. I didn't want to lose everything I had worked so hard for. To have people look at me like they had all those years ago. To lose you, too, when you realized that I was a complication.'

'You'd never be that.'

'I know that now, but I somehow convinced myself that letting you go was the best thing I could do to protect myself from that happening again.' I shook my head, pushing that dreadful emotion out of my chest. I'd tell Aaron about Sharon and the investigation into Gerald. But now wasn't the time.

'I'm sorry for not being here for you like I should have.'

He looked at me like he didn't want my apologies, but I didn't let him talk.

'I am.' My voice wavered. 'Knowing that your dad was sick and you were all the way here, alone. Taking it all without anyone to hold you. That he has been critical for weeks, and yet you came to Spain with me. That you . . .' I trailed off, my voice now shaking. 'That you would give me so fucking much without ever asking for anything in return. It destroyed me. But I'm here now,' I whispered, looking into his eyes.

'I'm here, and I'm not going anywhere, not because I believe that we can somehow be together now, but because I can't conceive of being anywhere else but beside you.' I swallowed hard, trying to rein in every emotion threatening to burst out. 'You know that, right?' I leaned in, my lips brushing over his. Very softly, almost tentatively. Waiting for his answer.

'I do now.' A low grunt came from his throat. His fingers tightened once more around my wrist. The arm around my waist brought me even deeper into his chest. 'I do, Lina. And I don't plan on letting you forget that.'

The hand that had been on my wrist trailed up my arm, his palm cupping my face. I leaned into his touch, feeling like I could live only on Aaron's caresses and kisses.

'I would have come back for you, you know? I told you I wouldn't let you quit on us. You still owed me that four-letter word.'

He had said that. And the realization made my stomach drop to my feet. How dumb I had been. Aaron hadn't given up on us; that had been only me. Only temporarily. While Aaron had been holding on to this. To us. All this time. Even when he needed someone by his side the most. And that . . . that made the heart in my chest burst into a hundred million pieces, only to reassemble into something different. Something that didn't belong to me anymore. It belonged to us.

'It's yours. Love and all the other four-letter words I could ever give you.' I placed a kiss on his mouth, not able to hold myself back any longer. I took my time with his lips, claiming them as mine. Claiming him.

A hum sounded deep in his throat. 'You are stuck with me, Catalina.'

Both arms cradled me closer in his lap, further into his chest. The side of my head rested against his drumming heart, his chin on the top of my hair, and peace – an overpowering kind of peace I had never heard of or experienced before – settled between my shoulders. And I knew then that we'd take anything on as long as we were together. We were a team. We'd light up each other's way, hold each other's hand, and push the other forward when we stumbled. Together. We'd do anything together.

Just like we would get through this. I'd get Aaron through this.

'Aaron?' I lifted my gaze and met his. 'I'm here for you now. I'm going to take care of you,' I told him simply.

He sighed; it was deep and slow, and it sounded like he carried the weight of the world on his shoulders.

'But just know that if I had known your dad was sick, I would have never let you come to Spain with me. Why didn't you tell me when you talked about him, Aaron? I know you don't owe me an explanation, but I want to know. I want to understand better.'

'Because everything … changed.' His throat worked, and his gaze took on a lost edge. 'He has been battling cancer for the last year. Ironic huh? First, Mom and now …' Aaron trailed off, needing a second to compose himself. 'Until a few days ago, I had planned on remaining away. Leave things the way they were between us. Even when I flew home a few weeks ago.'

'You did?'

'Yes, it was after my promotion was announced. That was what kept me from talking to you about our deal.'

I had not noticed Aaron taking days off back then, although work had been completely crazy, so I guessed I had been distracted. But it all made sense now.

'I would have talked to you eventually. I would have managed either way.'

'That doesn't matter now, baby,' I told him, meaning every word.

He sighed deeply. 'So, I came all the way to Seattle, but I couldn't bring myself to talk to him. To admit to myself, to show him that I still cared when he had pushed me away all those years ago. When he was the father I had already lost.'

My fingers drew circles on his chest, right above his heart. 'What changed then?'

'Everything did.' He exhaled, and it came out shaky and pained. 'I ... I somehow thought I had you, and then just as quickly, I didn't. And as much as I was set on not letting you quit on me, I saw it in your eyes. You had really given up on us. You believed in your decision.'

A shadow came over his face, and I instinctively leaned to place a kiss to the corner of his lips, dissipating that temporary darkness.

'The possibility that I could really lose you started solidifying in my head. And I just ...' He shook his head. 'God, it's not the same, I know. But I finally got it. I understood how hard it'd hit him, losing Mom. How lost he must have been at the reality of not having a way to get her back. How many reckless decisions he must have taken. It did not justify that he pushed me away, but I am to blame too. I had been so lost in my own head that I let him do that. And then I allowed both of us to keep it on for years.'

'Neither of you is at fault, Aaron. We are not programmed to lose those we love; there's no right or wrong way to grieve.' My hand trailed up his chest, my palm settling against his collarbone. 'We just try our best, even when, often, our best is not good enough. Blaming yourself now is not going to change the past; it's only going to take away energy that you should be spending in the present. And look where you are now; you are here. It's not too late.'

He brushed a kiss over my head. 'That day, when everything with

Gerald went down, I got a call from the hospital. They told me that things didn't look well for him. Apparently, my dad had asked for me. Several times. Demanded that I had to be contacted.' His voice trailed off, and I let my fingers play with the hair at the nape of his neck. Letting him know I was here. Listening. Having his back. 'It's like everything lined up, and suddenly, not only did I understand him in a way I hadn't before, but I also had this urge to see him. Not to apologize or to mend things between us, but to at least say goodbye. And I knew this was probably my last chance to do that.'

'Did you do that? Say goodbye?'

'The moment I got here, I went into his room with the intention to do that. Say goodbye, walk out, and just wait. But I . . . somehow ended up talking to him. Telling him everything I hadn't said in all these years we were apart. He wasn't conscious. I can't be sure if he was even listening, but I just went on. I couldn't stop. I talked and talked, Lina. Told him everything. I don't even know how long I was there. And I don't know if it was for nothing because maybe not a word was getting through to him, but I did it anyway.'

'You did good, *amor.*' I brushed my lips against the skin of his neck. 'You did so good.'

Aaron melted a little more into me, into my touch. 'They told me a few hours ago that he seems to be doing a bit better today. That he might get more time. They don't know if it's days, weeks, or months. But they are hopeful.' His chest deflated, the arms around me losing that desperate edge they'd had a while ago. 'I am hopeful too.'

A voice coming from somewhere on the other side of the waiting room reached us. Bursting the bubble we had been in. 'Mr Blackford?'

We both turned and looked over. A nurse stood a few feet away, his smile trained to be polite and calming.

'Yes,' Aaron said, his back straightening in the chair.

'He's finally awake. You can see him now.' The nurse slipped his hands in the pockets of his scrubs. 'Only a few minutes, okay? He needs to rest.'

Disentangling my body from his, I placed both feet on the floor and stood in front of Aaron, making space for him to walk to the nurse. He followed suit, his head still turned toward the entrance of the waiting room.

'Okay, yeah,' he said almost absently. But before he even stepped away, he looked at me. 'Come with me, please?'

My heart skipped a beat just then, the answer sounding loud and clear in my head. *I'd go anywhere with you if you so much as asked.* 'Yes, of course I will.'

I didn't wait for him to stretch out his hand and take mine. I did that myself. And I kept my hold tight and as reassuring as I possibly could as we followed the nurse to the room where Aaron's dad waited. We stepped in, and I did not know what to expect. Perhaps I should have readied myself on the way to the room, and the realization that I hadn't made a part of my bravado scatter away. This was the only living family Aaron had left, and I was about to meet him. And I . . . I suddenly tumbled a little under the importance of the moment. I wished it could have been under different circumstances, that there was more time, or that I was sure about what to say, how to handle this situation so everything went as well as it could.

But there wasn't time. This was what we had. What Aaron and his dad had. And even if a little scared or uneasy, I was humbled that Aaron wanted to share it with me.

'There's someone here to see you, Richard,' the nurse announced into the room and then looked over at us. His smile inched up. 'I'll be back in a few minutes, okay?'

Aaron took a step forward, and I remained a little behind him. Letting him have this moment to himself.

'Son,' the man perched on the bed said in a raspy voice.

I looked over at him and found the ghost of the features I knew so well. The hard jaw, the way both brows met, that intent and confidence about them. It was all there, although faded and worn.

'You are still here,' Aaron's dad said. And I could hear the surprise in his tone.

'Dad,' I heard Aaron answer, and the grip of his hand on mine tightened. 'Of course I'm still here. And there's someone I'd like you to meet.'

Blue eyes that looked in our direction from the bed trailed behind Aaron with curiosity.

'Hi, Mr Blackford.' I smiled at him, feeling Aaron's hand leave mine and fall on my shoulders. 'I'm Catalina, and I'm happy to finally meet you.'

Aaron's dad didn't return the smile, not completely. But his eyes told a different story. Just like I had seen his son do so many times. All under lock and key. 'Call me Richard, please.' His gaze searched my face, something akin to wonder slowly seeping in. 'Is this her, son?'

The question caught me by surprise, and so I glanced back at Aaron. I found him staring at his dad with a mirroring expression. Then, his profile softened.

'I wasn't sure you were listening,' he said almost absently. Then, his arm brought me closer to him, as if tucking me into him were nothing more than a reflex. 'Yes, this is her,' he answered louder, and my breath hitched in my chest. 'The woman I told you all about.'

Aaron looked down at me, his eyes shining under the fluorescent light of the room.

'Your Thea,' I heard Richard say, emotion coating his voice.

Thea. That had been his wife's name. Aaron's mom.

I peered in his direction, finding that smile he had hidden earlier. It was small and weak, but it was enough to make mine break free in return.

'Hold on to her, son. For as long as time lets you.'

'I will.' Aaron's words brushed the skin on my temple.

I looked up at him, finding those blue eyes smiling down at me with a devotion I had never experienced or imagined being on the receiving end of. With a warmth that I could feel right in the middle of my chest, pounding and expanding with every passing second I spent under his gaze, by his side. Aaron looked at me with a world of possibilities shining bright and dazzling in his eyes. A promise.

'This is the woman I plan on spending the rest of my life with. I'm not letting go of her anytime soon.'

EPILOGUE

One Year Later

'Catalina.' The deep voice that had lured me to sleep and ignited every cell in my body countless times in the last twelve months reached my ears.

My pen dropped from my mouth, smacking the glossy surface of the oak conference table.

'Catalina, I'm going to need an answer.'

My back straightened in my chair, my gaze meeting a pair of blue eyes as I cleared my throat. *Shit. I totally spaced out.* 'Yes, yes – ahem. An answer. Coming right up, Mr Blackford,' I rushed out. 'Just mentally recapping.'

I watched the corner of his lips tip up, his eyes simmering with an emotion I was more than familiar with. My heart skipped a beat. Because, apparently, I'd never *not* react to this man's smile. No matter how small it was.

'Rosie, if you could maybe assist Catalina as she mentally recaps,' he said, cocking a brow. 'We all have places to be, and I'd appreciate being through with this meeting in the next five minutes.'

'Of course,' my best friend and new team leader of our division agreed from my right. 'I'm sure Lina was being very thorough with the notes she was taking.'

'Yep, I was doing exactly that,' I confirmed, looking over at her and finding her cheeks flushed.

We both still sucked at lying.

I sent her a wobbly smile and mouthed, *Thanks.*

I heard Aaron's deep exhalation.

Impatient and sexy blue-eyed grump. He was lucky I was head over heels in love with him.

'Aaron was suggesting that perhaps now that Linda and Patricia are back from their maternity leaves, someone from your team could transfer to Héctor's,' Rosie explained, her fingers fumbling on top of her open planner. 'Just to temporarily cover the vacancy I left now that I'm leading Gerald's team after his ... departure.'

After the tedious and lengthy HR investigation Sharon had pushed for unearthed more than a few sexual misconduct instances, Gerald had been finally laid off. Aaron, our division leader and owner of my heart, hadn't hesitated, and the moment Gerald had walked out of InTech, Rosie's name had already been on the table for that position. Before we knew it, we had been celebrating her promotion.

'Do you think we can make that work, Catalina?' my future husband asked. Not that he had proposed, not yet.

As much as I had the suspicion he would soon, perhaps I'd be the one putting a ring on him before he ever did. I was impatient like that.

'One hundred percent,' I answered, scribbling a note on my pad. This time for real. 'I'll make sure to move around a few people and see who can support Héctor's team.'

The old man sighed. 'Thanks, Lina. No one will be able to fill Rosie's shoes, not really.' His shoulders bunched as he smiled sadly. 'But I knew for a while that I'd lose her soon anyway.' He shrugged, his smile turning brighter as he looked at my friend and his former team member. 'I'm so proud of you, Rosie.'

'Thank you,' Rosie said, emotion coating her words. She cleared her throat. 'Now, stop it. Crying on my first division meeting would be highly unprofessional.'

A notepad was snapped closed briskly. 'All right, I'll consider that done,' Mr Grumps concluded. I looked at him just in time to see him checking the clock behind me. 'Meeting wrapped up. Have—'

'But, Aaron,' Kabir called, his voice dancing with trepidation, 'what about—'

'Sorry, but I'm officially on vacation.' Aaron sliced his hand through the air.

Yep, we both were. Just half a day, but it had taken me some convincing, so I called that a success anyway.

'It will have to wait until Monday. Have a great weekend, everyone.' He pushed back the chair and stood up, gifting me with a view of his whole torso.

I sighed internally. Happily. All mine. All of that was just for me and for my taking, and what was even better, that strong and resilient heart beating inside his hard chest with loyalty, selflessness, and integrity was all mine too.

'Catalina?'

Snapping out of my temporary trance, I straightened, too, gathering all my things together. 'Coming, coming.'

I walked to where Aaron was waiting for me, right by the door.

He lowered his voice. 'You are awfully distracted today.'

A retort was ready to leave my lips, but the way he looked at me, with that brand of deep concern that melted my heart, killed it before it could ever come out.

'You are awfully distracting,' I said just for him.

His eyes glazed over, and I could see how he was stopping himself from pouncing on me. But we were at our workplace, and we were always meticulously professional. Not because we needed to be, as everyone knew and respected our relationship, but because we had made that choice.

So, I switched to a safer topic. 'I'm also a little nervous.'

'I know,' he admitted as we made our way down the hallway, carrying the packed laptop bags we had brought to the meeting. 'Our luggage is already in the car, so we'll make it to the airport just in time to pick them up.'

We entered the empty elevator, Aaron placing himself close beside me, our arms brushing softly.

'I checked earlier, and their flight will land as scheduled,' he said as the metallic doors closed.

'Thanks,' I breathed out, unconsciously inching closer to him. 'But I'm still a little anxious. It's their first time in the US, and everyone is coming. That's a lot of Martíns in an aircraft for everything to go smoothly. What if the flight was too much for Abuela? What if Papá forgot the medication for his tension? You know, I had to FaceTime him to explain to him how to set a reminder on his phone, so he would take it, but even that way, he probably snoozed it and forgot about that too. And I'm scared of what Mamá packed in her suitcase. Remember I told you that one time she wanted me to bring back a whole *pata de jamón* in my carry-on? That's a leg of a pig, Aaron. What if she is carrying some illegal produce, and customs thinks she's smuggling something into the—'

The elevator came to a brisk halt.

Then, Aaron's lips were on mine, the sudden kiss rendering me immediately speechless. Disarmed. Weightless. I melted into him, my legs turning to butter. I couldn't help it. Aaron would always have that effect on me; I knew it.

'Baby,' he breathed into my mouth. 'Stop overthinking.' He took my lips in his again, his arms coming around me. His body gently pushing my back against the cool surface behind me.

'Did you just stop the elevator, Mr Blackford?' My voice sounded breathless, not that I cared.

Aaron was fully aware of the power he held over me, and I wanted it that way. Neither of us wanted a single unsaid thing between us. There had been plenty of those in the past.

'Yes.' He brushed his lips along my jaw. 'And we have three minutes to get all those worries out of your head before the front desk is called.' His mouth trailed down my neck, warm palms falling on my waist.

My lips parted. 'Oh. Okay,' I murmured as he nibbled at the sensitive skin. My blood started swirling, certain parts of my body demanding attention. 'I like how that sounds.'

'I made sure your dad would take his pills with him when I talked to him on the phone before they left the house.' Aaron's hands trailed up, reaching the swell of my breasts. 'Cristina is only bringing a few cuts of cured meat,' he continued as his legs crowded mine. 'It wasn't easy, and I might have promised a few things I shouldn't have, but she compromised.'

A low chuckle left my mouth, but all humour died when his hips rocked briefly against mine.

'Abuela will be fine; she's tough as nails. Or don't you remember how I had to literally pluck her off that dance floor last Christmas?' He tugged at the lobe of my ear with his teeth. 'And Isabel's pregnancy doesn't put her at risk; Gonzalo called the airline to ask. Twice.'

I whimpered, relishing in the sensation of feeling Aaron all around me – his warmth, the strength of his body, his breath and voice falling on my skin – but also in how deep his words and actions ran. How much love and attention there was in them, in him.

'It's crazy how much my family adores you,' I told him, grasping both his arms with neglected need running through my body. 'You are like a Martín Whisperer. How did you manage to do that?'

'I thought that my success in convincing them about how serious I was about you after we confessed the truth about our deal was pure luck, but I might have a way with words when it comes to the Martíns,' he whispered like it was his biggest secret. 'With one particular Martín though, I want to believe I have a way with more than just that.'

My hands trailed up his strong arms, passing over his shoulders and finally clasping behind his neck. 'You do,' I murmured. 'I adore you too. Treasure you. Love you. Want you. Need you.' I pulled him closer.

'Who's being awfully distracting now?' he rasped.

I answered by grinding myself against his hard body, briefly but intently. A grunt fell from his lips.

'Look at you, teasing me like this. What an adoring and distracting woman I have in my hands.'

'How much longer do we have?' I arched my back, pressing our chests together.

He exhaled roughly. 'Not nearly enough for what I have in mind.' His palm fell on my behind, as if he couldn't stop himself. He squeezed me possessively, proving his point. His voice turned low. 'Later, I swear. As soon as I get you alone in our room.'

Aaron kissed me deeply then, silently promising all the things he'd do to me much later. Hours from now, when we finally reached the house we had rented in Montauk for the weekend and our family was settled comfortably inside.

'Okay.' Cupping his face in my palms, I brushed one last kiss against his lips. 'Have you talked to your dad?'

Aaron reluctantly peeled himself off me and pressed the yellow button on the panel. The elevator resumed its descent. 'Yes, earlier today,' he admitted almost guardedly. Just like every time he talked about Richard.

I knew Aaron hadn't let go of part of the guilt he carried

around, but father and son had come a long way. And they both knew Richard didn't have much time. This past year had already been a gift.

'He and Martha should be getting to the house in a few hours.'

Martha, his caregiver, was another gift sent straight from heaven. She was amazing to Richard and always kept us updated. We trusted her fully, and having her constant support and company not only reassured Aaron and me, but also soothed Richard.

'I'll check on them again while we wait for your family at the airport.'

The elevator doors opened in front of us, and we stepped out at the same time.

'Everything will be all right, *amor*,' I told him, breaking my rules and reaching for his hand in the middle of the lobby. 'Your dad will make it to Montauk safely, and he is going to love everyone. Just how everyone will love him.'

Breaking his own rules too, he brought my hand to his mouth, his lips brushing the backs of my fingers. 'I know, baby,' he whispered just for me. 'Everything will always be okay, no matter what. You know why?'

We stepped out of the building, right into one of New York's overwhelming summer days.

'Why?'

'Because it's you and me.' He smiled down at me then, meeting my gaze with the conviction his words held. Just as he held my heart in his hands. My love. My whole world. Confidently and completely. 'And no matter what comes our way, we have each other.' That Aaron smile, which was just for me and never failed to make my heart skip a beat, widened. 'We are in this together, for the long run.'

ABOUT THE AUTHOR

Elena is a Spanish writer, a self-confessed hopeless romantic and much Mr. B's dismay, a proud book hoarder. After years of devouring stories and posting – okay fine, yelling – about them on her Instagram @thebibliotheque, she has finally taken the leap and started creating some of her own.

While she'd never describe herself as adventurous, having a degree in chemical engineering and being the Monica of her group of friends, this definitely qualifies as the most exciting yet terrifying project she has ever taken on. She's probably biting her nails as you read this. Heck, she's probably full on freaking out.

But don't mind her, that's just a little of – hopefully healthy – stage fright.

Regardless, she cannot wait to finally share her dream with you. To perhaps gush over HEAs together, and who knows, maybe fall a little more in love with love. Because isn't that the point on all of this?

ACKNOWLEDGEMENTS

The only reason why you are currently holding *The Spanish Love Deception* in your hands is because a very special someone asked me the following question 'But Elena, why don't you publish it? You have to!' To be completely honest, I thought her completely insane (I still do, sometimes) but I guess having someone else's faith and encouragement can be enough to take a leap and reach out for your dreams. Ella, this book wouldn't have been possible without you. If I could get away with it, I'd write pages and pages about the reasons why you have become this crucial and huge piece of the puzzle that is my life. But you'd roll your eyes so hard, I'd have to take a flight and go visit you at the ER. So, I'll just say thank you. From the very bottom of my heart, thank you. For every word of encouragement, every piece of advice, for your guidance, for every single minute of those hour long VMs, for all the TMIs, for every single one of your 'shut up', and above all, for your precious friendship.

Cris y Ana ... tías, lo he hecho. Gracias por estar ahí para mí desde que éramos unas mocosas insoportables que se creían súper alternativas. Me habéis animado (y psicoanalizado, seamos claras) hasta que me he lanzado a seguir mis sueños. Por ello, siempre seréis parte de ellos. Vuestra amistad lo significa todo, ya lo sabéis.

Erin, I have a confession. The day I casually asked if you'd like to beta read this book for me, I played it cool but I was about a hair away from losing my shit. But oh my gosh, you accepted and just like you recently said, turns out we make a pretty great team. TSLD wouldn't be the same today if you hadn't beta read it (imagine how much everyone would have hated Gonzalo). Thank you, Erin. I really hope this was only our first.

Cristina, you have been so good to me. Your kindness and unconditional support meant the freaking world. I can't believe I used to go to you for romance recs and now, I am gushing over your absolutely beautiful and amazing review of TSLD. Thank you, hermosa. You have been a lifesaver and a total star, and your help has made all the difference. I swear, I'll write you the steamiest book with your Cavill-esque hero. It's a promise.

Mr B, I hope you got me flowers on release day. We live right across from a flower shop, so it's (literally) not that hard. I know I'm not the easiest when I'm stressed, and I've been a little on edge for the last few weeks. So that's the least you can do, don't you think? I'll bake you a cake. Please?

Jovana, my goodness, I can't begin to imagine the amount of work I gave you. This book wouldn't be the same without your magic. Thank you.

To every booktoker, bookstagrammer, booktuber and member of the book twitter fam that has cheered for me, messaged me, and given me all their trust and support. You guys rock my world and deserve all the flowers and cake. Oh my gosh, you guys. This wouldn't have been possible without you. Thank you.

You, the reader. Thank you for giving a chance. I know I'm a newbie, and this is just my first and imperfect attempt, but I hope with all my goddamn heart that you loved it. I hope you stick around, too. Because like Joey would say, without you, this is all a moo point.